The Originals

A novel of life, love, laughter, terror, and genteel mutiny during the Vietnam War

Don Truitt

AmErica House
Baltimore

ISBN: 1–59129–079–1
PUBLISHED BY AMERICA HOUSE BOOK PUBLISHERS
www.publishamerica.com
Baltimore

Printed in the United States of America

Dedication

Dedicated to those who didn't make it home, and those who made it home with wounds that time cannot heal. This humble project, The Originals, is filled with Tall Tales and Truth that you will best understand. God Bless you brothers and sisters, and God Bless America.

And special thanks to Loretta Burdette, who was responsible for smoothly coordinating a nerve wracking experience and much more.

Chapter One

Cam Ranh Bay
Republic of South Vietnam
2130 Hours, July 14, 1966
LOCATION: The deck of the USS Webster
CARGO: The 516th AG, United States Army, enroute to Vietnam

"Okay, who farted?"

No response.

"Whoever it was, it smells like you dyin' of somethin' bad–assed ugly. Oooeee! You must'a been feedin' your face with Care package shit from a momma that cain't cook! If yo' momma's cookin' that bad, ain't no wonder you joined the Army!"

Skins Williams had been in a foul mood since seeing his name on the guard duty detail roster the evening before.

"Muh'fuh' Lifers" Skins grumbled at the duty roster. His words were meant for the consumption of the other Originals who had gathered to read the various extra duty rosters that had been posted that afternoon. Skins didn't want no "muh'fuh" carrying around any "muh'fuh" idea he was a Lifer. His image as the most *un*–Lifer Original of all was more important to him than money itself, and Skins did enjoy flashing the green after the nightly poker games when he managed to kick ass with some Chi–Town seven card stud poker.

"Why they havin' guard duty on a ole rust bucket like this, floatin'aroun' out'n the middle the damned ocean, anyway? What duh'fuh' they thinkin' 'bout, man? Like as if some dumbass Vee–et Cong gonna start shootin'at us from fifty miles away? Man, it takes a muh'fuh' Lifer to come up with a muh'fuh' idea like that. And why they give us muh'fuh' M–14s to carry 'round on guard duty, and then don't give us any muh'fuh' ammo? What kind'a dumb–assed muh'fuh' idea is that?"

Despite all his bitching, Skins reported for guard duty at 1800 hours the next day, after evening chow, just as ordered, though he wasn't about to shine his boots and polish his brass, no matter what the regulations say. If the dumb–ass Viet Cong were dumb–assed enough to try to start shooting at the Webster, Skins Williams wasn't about to give them shiney stuff to aim at.

A gentle breeze whiffed past Skins, carrying with it the per-fume of a populated bit of coastal Vietnam.

"Oh, maa–an!" Skins whined from his guardpost on the port-side deck. "There it goes again. Man, it smells like somethin' died ever' time the wind come my way. Get me out'a this place, man! The Vee–et Cong trying to fry us with farts, man! Damn…CQ, where you at, man? Lewandowski, where you hidin' your sorry butt? Damn, come over here and smell what's happenin'. Muh'fuh' stink's peelin' the muh'fuh' paint right off the muh'fuh' deck. No shit, man. Sheee–it, I'm dyin' over here, Lew. I need a medic. Someone tell my momma I love her when I die. I cain't take much more'a this, man!"

Skins wasn't alone with his foul mood. The past several days had been a bummer for all the Originals on–board the Webster as it ventured ever nearer the port of Cam Ranh.

Skins Williams was the first of the Originals to get busted from PFC back down to E–1 Buck Private three weeks earlier, the day after he got his promotion to PFC E–3. Six more Originals were destined to lose their PFC stripes during the slow journey from the Port of Oakland to Vietnam, but only Skins could claim bragging rights to being the first. Which made him *Duh Man*! As icing on the cake, he had accomplished the feat with such class, such style, that the even the brothers back home in the South of Chi–Town would have to admit he was *Duh Man*.

Skins earned his reputation during a stint on KP, when he told Mess Sergeant Lugo what he could do with a hundred–pound bag of potatoes that needed peeling. It had been a moment of triumph that shocked even his fellow Originals, made even more memorable by the stuttering fury of fat Sergeant Lugo, whose Puerto Rican/Bronx accent suddenly became as as thick as his mashed potatoes. It was easily the finest moment Skins had experienced since the draft board in Chicago tapped him on the shoulder, saying 'Uncle Sam Needs You, man!' Though the golden moment had cost him his PFC stripes, Skins was able to walk away with his head held high when he exited the butt–chewing session with Lt. Masters. Never would anyone dare call Skins Williams a Lifer. His reputation as an Original had been firmly established. The Army may have drafted his black ass for two years, but his soul forever would remain that of a freedom–loving civilian.

PFC Charlie Edwards was about to add his own two–cents–worth. Edwards also had a rebellious streak, but he had been less self–destructive in the selection of targets for his draftee angst. Even so, he had gotten in enough shots against the Lifers to establish his credentials as an Original.

Both troops were just beginning to warm up to the subject of farts. Six weeks at sea can curdle even the best of minds.

"Someone call a muh'fuh' medic," Skins shouted again, hoping to ignite the flames of rebellion. "The Vee–et Cong is usin' gas on us!"

Charlie's high–pitched laughter cackled from afar. "That's gotta be the nastiest fart I ever smelled! Something straight from the black hole of Calcutta!"

Edwards had learned about the black hole of Calcutta from a porno novel he read during his second semester of academic probation at the University of Iowa. Which, not coincidentally, turned out to be his final semester of 4–A Student draft deferment, thus ending two glorious years of partying at the ATO house. Charlie wasn't particularly worried about the draft when he received the notice to report for the physical. He figured he had an ace in the hole…a childhood heart murmur that was reputed to be a rock solid guarantee for a 4–F medical deferment. And that might well have been the case during normal times, but the times weren't normal in early 1966, with the Vietnam War just beginning to Rock'n'Roll its way into the history books.

What Charlie hadn't been counting on was the open–minded flexibility a draft board and the Army Docs can show during a time of great national need. So it was that Charlie found himself passing the draft physical with room to spare. Two weeks later, he received his draft notice and on January 18, 1966 he found himself turning his head and coughing for an Army Doc with cold hands and a bored expression.

"Is that black hole that woman you always be jivin' about?"

Skins asked from his guardpost. "That POONtang you was gonna marry?"

A moment of silence followed, during which Charlie Edwards cursed himself for raising the subject of holes, black or otherwise. His small town Iowa childhood hadn't prepared him for the give and take of barracks grabass, also known as shuck and jive. Only once or twice had he been able to come up with a good *give* for the many *takes* he'd absorbed since Uncle Sam drafted his young, hairy white ass. And then his only victories had been against the few white guys who were even more inexperienced than himself. His record with blacks from the big city was particularly dismal, and Skins Williams was considered to be among the best of the brothers at coming up with solid one–liners that can severely wound or even decimate the opposition.

Charlie shouted, "Up yours, Skins!" but knew his comeback was suicidal even as he said it.

"You wish," Skins shouted back. "You muh' fuh' Iowa pig farmers like the boys, don't'cha? Man, your wimmen cain't be all that ugly. Or is they?"

"Damn," Charlie muttered under his breath. At such moments, he wished his parents had raised him in Chicago, or Philly or even Cincinnati, where he could have learned a little shuck and jive to provide some balance for Dr. Seuss during his early formative years. Edwards had no idea what to say next, particularly when everything he did say was likely to be used against him, so he absorbed the punishment and kept his trap shut.

His quandary wasn't to last for long. The Charge of Quarters—Specialist Four Alfred G. Lewandowski—had already heard more than enough grabass to last all night.

"At EASE out there!" Lewandowski shouted. "They can hear you all the way to Hanoi. You're supposed to be quiet when you're on guard duty."

As the Charge of Quarters responsible for the guard detail, Lewandowski would be the first to be standing front–and–center in front of Lt. Masters if any of the guards screwed–up. It would be his tit in the wringer, not theirs, and he had no doubt that Masters, the company executive officer, would be turning the wringer crank as hard as he could.

Lewandowski was easily the most miserable Original on board the Webster that night; a genuine island of self–pity, a martyr to the leadership qualities he had gained on the gridiron, beginning with Pop Warner Football back when he was a 125–pound ten–year–old just learning how to stuff–it to scrambling 65–pound quarterbacks.

"This guard duty stuff is serious shit," Lewandowski added in a tone meant to inspire the kind of sympathy, understanding, and cooperation that he wasn't likely to get from his fellow Originals. At least not since he was promoted to Specialist Four. "We gotta hold down the racket, you guys."

"At EASE, yo'sef," Skins shouted back. "You makin' more racket than all the rest of us put together."

Charlie Edwards joined the rebellion, glad to be off the hook with Skins. "Yeah, At Ease, Lewandowski." He paused a moment to add emphasis to the obligatory insult that would follow.

"Lifer," Charlie added in a clear monotone.

Distant Originals could be heard chuckling from their assorted guard posts.

Another moment passed before Lewandowski answered Edwards in a low, rumbling voice. "God's gonna get you for that, Charlie Edwards. He's gonna make you Re–up for six years and buy a brand new car."

The chuckles rose again, though not from the vicinity of Charlie Edwards, whose guard post was again wrapped in woeful silence.

The frequency and intensity of the grabass had been on the rise since shortly before noon chow, when Lt. Masters announced that the Webster would be arriving in the Port of Cam Ranh somewhere around 2400 hours that night.

The ambient tension mushroomed immediately. Nobody really knew what to expect from the next twelve months; not even Captain Ortega, who had been through a combat Infantry tour in Vietnam, and Warrant Officer 4 Mobley, who had seen combat in both WWII and Korea. Once in Vietnam, entire units and individual troops could be shuffled around from place to place like chess pieces on a board composed of triple–canopy jungle and rice paddies. Immediately, some of the troops retreated inward to deal with the tension, but most responded with extra rations of grab–ass, desperate to conjure enough humor and courage to laugh at the monsters that were banging away within the dark corridors of their morbid imaginations. The grabass was a male thing, a survival mechanism that comes into play when high levels of testosterone are mixed with high levels of anxiety.

Time hadn't yet allotted much opportunity to create a noble history for the 516th Adjutant General Personnel Services Company. Williams, Edwards, and Lewandowski were among the first of the raw basic training graduates to be assigned to the freshly formed 516th AG in Fort Benjamin Harrison, Indiana. It was there, while they were undergoing Advanced Individual Training, that they began referring to themselves as Originals, thus distinguishing themselves from the NCOs and Officers who filled out the ranks of the spanking new unit. It was a term that seemed to fit perfectly. Not only were they the original troops to be assigned to the 516th AG, virtually all of them had been drafted, and none at that time held rank above that of a PFC.

The accolade 'Original' had been sealed in concrete by the time the Originals learned they would be sent to Vietnam as a unit once they completed AIT. Soon, the term Original had evolved into a proud boast of elite status, with the members of the small club sharing a brand of Esprite de Corps that was as strong as it was unusual. While other units had their fist fights and barracks brawls, no such thing happened in the 516th AG, where it was an unspoken rule that Originals did not fight other Originals. Bound together as a unit, they recognized only one foe, and that was the United States Army, which even ranked above their various local draft boards.

The Originals were particularly unified when dealing with the Lifers who ruled their lives. Until recently, anyone holding rank above PFC E–3 was automatically considered a Lifer. From their viewpoint at the bottom of the chain of command, life in the US Army was a lot like living on the first floor of a three–story out-house, with the NCOs taking up residence on the second floor, and the Royal Family Officers commanding the penthouse seats on the third floor. Being stuck on the first floor, they knew exactly what to expect from anything that came Down From Above, which was the natural flow of all matters within the Army Way of Doing Things.

"Hey, Lew," Skins shouted to Lewandowski. "Edwards was telling us about his main squeeze back in Iowa. He said she's got this black hole of Calcutta thang that can drive the brothers wild, man. And I do mean wiiillld."

"Aw, I ain't gonna climb on that one, Skins," Lewandowski answered. "Charlie's taken enough flak from us on that."

Edwards had indeed taken a lot of flak since he received a Dear John letter from his fiancée, Beth Cooper, who was pledged to the Tappa Sister sorority back in Iowa City. Charlie further compounded that run of bad luck by sharing his sorrows with Lewandowski over cans of warm beer in the forward hold of the Webster. Beth's letter was a full ten–pages long, beginning with her confession that she had fallen in love with one of Charlie's Alpha Tau Omega fraternity brothers. Actually, the letter was rather artfully composed with only rare spelling errors, although it could be criticized for containing too many pilfered homilies and mixed metaphors.

Dear Charlie: If you really love something, you allow it to fly free and wish it well, just as I have set you free. And now you must do the same with me, so I can walk life's pathways without remorse. We both must be set free to fly wherever we wish. And I do wish you well, Dear Charlie. And I pray that you, too, will find a love who makes you as happy as I am with Chris.

It was a letter that spoke volumes about the students who dreamed of enrolling in the University of Iowa Writers Workshop. They might not have had anything worthwhile to say, but they knew how to say it very well.

"She can go free alright," Charlie mumbled after setting free a bubble of warm beer. "Straight to the free clinic for penicillin shots. Chris Harvey's had the clap so many times that they don't even make him fill out the forms anymore. They just jab him in the butt and turn him loose."

Lewandowski—who wasn't considered a Lifer at the time be-cause he shared Charlie's PFC rank—figured it was one of the funniest sad tales he had ever heard since entering the humorless, olive drab world of the United States Army. And because he had been raised to believe in sharing, he decided to share Charlie's romantic lament with the other Originals.

But that was a long time ago. Two weeks to be exact. It was no longer much fun to pile on Charlie Edwards.

The chuckles of the guards died down rather quickly. Lewandowski had made his point...maybe good ole Charlie had taken enough flak about his ex–fiancée. Besides, there was no telling when Lt. Masters, Captain Ortega or Numbnuts Bolton might decide to wander up on deck, and it had to be a bad omen to face a Court Martial upon arrival in Vietnam. Lord knows what that might lead to.

Lewandowski found himself ruminating once again on the odd nature of his promotion, an event that was so weird it could have been a featured on The Twilight Zone. Lewandowski wasn't the only Original to receive the unexpected promotion, but he had been the most unlikely recipient. All told, a dozen PFC's had been promoted to Specialist Four that day, and none of it made any sense to the Originals from their vantage point on the first floor of the outhouse. They didn't know that the 516th AG was in short supply of junior NCOs; anyone holding a rank of E–4 or E–5. Masters and Ortega had plenty of Staff Sergeants E–6 and Sergeants First Class E–7, and Lord knows they had plenty of PFC E–3s, but there were absolutely no E–4s or E–5s. So they had to create some ASAP.

Lewandowski's turn came when he reported Front and Center to the tiny cubicle Lt. Masters shared with Captain Ortega. He was at the head of a lineup of eleven other PFCs who had been tagged for promotion. At first, he couldn't believe his ears when Masters told him he had been promoted to Specialist Four. It wasn't the kind of news that was to be taken with a glad heart.

Lewandowski was perfectly content at that time to remain a PFC. His first reaction was an attempt to beg his way out of it, figuring—quite rationally, from his perspective on the first floor of the outhouse—that a promotion to E–4 would come fully equipped with a long list of responsibilities that looked a lot like things a Lifer would enjoy doing.

"But Sir, I'm sure there's troops in the 516th that're a lot more qualified than I am. Take Charlie Edwards, for instance, Sir. He's a real serious sort, whereas I'm sort of a joker. Sir. Always clowning around, Sir. And just to be perfectly honest, Sir, I'm not *really* a very good soldier."

Lewandowski was standing at a rigid position of Attention—Front and Center—with great rivers of sweat pouring from every gland in his thick skin.

But First Lieutenant Masters was in no mood to coddle Lewandowksi with a fair and open hearing. His mind was made up and there would be no changing it for reasons good or bad.

'This ain't the Boy Scouts, soldier. This is the United States Army. You can give your soul to God, but your ass belongs to me.'

Masters had developed a theory about Lewandowski that needed testing. He figured Lewandowski would continue being a disciplinary problem as long as he thought he had little or nothing to lose, but he could be controlled with an unexpected promotion and threats of dire consequences if he failed to perform. Besides, he had the raw makings of a real leader.

"Well, Sir. I'm just trying to look out for the best interests of the United States Army. Sir. I mean, I really am, Sir."

Masters answered Lewandowski's protests with an unperturbed gentleness that could send shivers down the spine. "Are you telling me you would rather be assigned to permanent KP than get promoted to Specialist Four?"

Lewandowski wanted to wipe his brow, but he was standing at Attention and couldn't remove his hands from his sides. He tried blinking his eyes to clear them of the burning sweat, but that only made it worse. He was trying to think, but the pressure was turning his mind into overcooked Malt'o'Meal.

"No, Sir," Lewandowski finally managed to answer, hoping he hadn't misunderstood the question. What was the question, anyway?

Masters smiled and raised his right hand to render a dismissive salute. "Good thinking, Specialist Lewandowski. I expect those stripes to be sewn on your sleeves by reveille formation tomorrow morning. You are dismissed."

It was a moment of history that Lewandowski wanted to forget, but couldn't. So he derailed the memory by concentrating on Cam Ranh harbor as they steamed toward four massive piers jutting deep into the black waters of the South China Sea. His attention was quickly drawn to the many lights on the distant docks, and the way they created an eerie imitation of daylight. Under the bright lights, he saw a distant world peopled by tiny ant–men scrambling about unloading tanks, helicopters, artillery pieces, and anything else that was needed to Make War, Not Love.

Troops began straggling up from below decks as the Webster edged ever deeper into the huge deepwater bay. Two tugboats pulled alongside to escort the Webster to her assigned berth.

A not–so–golden–oldie Top 40 tune arose from the depths of Lewandowski's erratic memory banks. The plaintive lyrics seemed so appropriate to this moment, time, place, and set of circumstances. He hummed a tentative few bars before venturing to sing the few lyrics he could recall in a whispery falsetto. "Please, Mr. Custer…I don't wanna go. Hey, Mr. Custer, I don't wanna go. There's a redskin waitin' out there, just a'fixin' to take my hair. Dum–de–dum–de–de–dum…Please, Mr. Custer…I don't wanna go."

The atmosphere was as hot and humid as a steambath in hell—and getting hotter by the minute—as the Webster slowly penetrated deeper into the stinking, sweating womb of Cam Ranh Bay. It was the kind of climate that could make a body break out in a sweat when drying off after a cold shower.

The curious were meandering up to the main deck in greater numbers now. The officers claimed the best vantage point at the bow, with the NCOs staking their claim to the forward port bow, forcing the Originals to crowd into the remaining real estate along the portside railing, with more than a few mumbling "F.T.A." as they jockeyed for space. *F.T.A.* was an acronym originally found on a 1950's recruiting poster that promised "F.T.A…Fun Travel and Adventure…Join the new Action Army." But the 'F' in F.T.A. was to take on unintended meaning as new generations of dratftees and first–term enlistees discovered the joys of life on the first floor of the outhouse. Thereafter, American GI's everywhere could express their affection for the US Army by muttering "F.T.A.", and they would be understood from the DMZ in Vietnam, to the perpetually frozen tundra of Tule, Greenland.

Voices in low conversational drones could be heard all over the deck of the Webster, occasionally punctuated by dull distant thumps that sounded much like approaching thunder, though the sky was devoid of clouds that night. The low, dark, mountains surrounding Cam Ranh Bay would suddenly blossom with brief flashes of light. Some of the bursts of light stayed bright for more than a few seconds, with the dull explosive thump arriving at the Webster well afterward.

Lewandowski ambled over to join his fellow Originals at the port side railing.

"Cam Ranh sucks," Charlie Edwards grumbled. "I wanna go home."

Lewandowski rested his big right hand on Charlie's shoulder. "Aw, stop yer griping, Charlie. You love the Army and you know it. You were born to wear combat boots. It runs in yer family."

Charlie shrugged off the heavy hand. "You're the one wearing Lifer stripes, not me," he countered. He could understand Lewandowski passing along his lamentations about Beth Cooper more than he could fathom Lewandowski—of all people—wearing Speck Four stripes.

After his promotion, Lewandowski protested far and wide that it wasn't his fault that he had been promted, but his trail of logic was overgrown by a lush bloom of self–interest.

"Hey, it wasn't my idea. Masters gave me no choice. It was either take the stripes, or spend the next year on KP. That's the only reason I did it. I swear."

It was generally agreed that Lewandowski's promotion was particularly inexcusable because he had always been the first to make fun of the Lifers, being particularly hard on Sergeant First Class Numbnuts Bolton, the acting–jack First Sergeant of the 516th AG. Lewandowski had always been a leader in bucking the system, resisting the Army Way. Every raw recruit learned the same mantra in Basic Training… "There's a Right Way, a Wrong Way and the Army Way. Do it the Army Way." Similarly, when learning drill routines in Basic Training, there was always a recruit who turned left when a Right Face had been ordered. And the Drill Instructor was almost guaranteed to shout something like... "Your *military* right, soldier! When I say *Right Face!* I mean your *military* right, not your *civilian* right!"

Charlie Edwards continued his assault on Lewandowski. "Admit it, Lew. You've found the home you've always wanted. You sing yourself to sleep every night with The Ballad of the Green Berets. You know the lyrics by heart. You're a Lifer, Lewandowski. And not just as a twenty–year man; you're in for the full thirty years. When you die, they'll plant you in an olive drab coffin."

A loud volley of appreciative whoops and hollers erupted from the nearby Originals, it being the best comeback ever heard from Charlie Edwards.

One of Charlie's future ex–wives would claim in court documents that he always seemed to know what to say to hurt her feelings. She figured it came with the territory of his being a licensed marriage counselor, with a doctorate in psychology. She had no idea that Charlie had honed his ability to cut to the emotional quick while serving his country in the United States Army.

"Ha! That ain't even funny," Lewandowski shot back, knowing he had lost points to Charlie's brilliant return volley. "They can take these stripes and shove'em, for all I care."

Which inspired Edwards to produce yet another brilliant return volley. "Okay then, why don't you tell Masters and Ortega right now? They're standing at the bow. You can even shout it to them from here. Go on, Lew. Tell'em what they can do with those stripes you're wearing."

The moment was painfully embarrassing for Lewandowski, ranking right up there with his semi–nude experience at the Army induction center. Charlie Edwards had stumbled upon the terrible Truth...that Alfred G. Lewandowski secretly coveted his Specialist Four patches, which carried the benefits of more pay for less work. As a Speck Four, he was only one promotion away from the rank of E–5 and his own seat on the second floor of the great three–story outhouse. Though Lewandowski had protested the promotion at first, he had become quite accustomed to it by the second day. He had even come to imagine himself deserving of higher rank.

Skins Williams had wandered back from his guard post to join the other Originals. Like the others on guard duty, he was wearing his steel pot, ammo belt and flak vest. His unloaded M–14 was slung over his right shoulder by the weapon's strap, the bayonet still in its sheath, hanging from his webbed belt.

"Hey, stop picking on my main man, Lewandowski," Skins said as he joined the group rag. "I believe him, man, even if nobody else does. He didn't kiss no ass to get promoted. No, sir, not Lewandowski. Muh'fuh' Lew hates the Army. Ever'body knows that. He's just countin' the days 'til he gets out. Uh huh, oh yeah. We knows aaaaalllll about it."

More chuckles and whoops rose from the ranks.

Lewandowski glowered at Skins as a dark rumbling sound rose from deep inside his XXL chest.

Frenchie Beaumont, a Cajun from the bayous of Louisiana, wanted a shot at Lewandowski. Frenchie was on guard duty, too, but figured what was good for Williams, Edwards and Lewandowski was good for him, too. Besides, how could any GI in his right mind ever seriously think the USS Webster was in danger of coming under attack within Cam Ranh harbor?

"Hey, Skins, that's no way to be talking to the Charge of Quarters, man. You keep givin' him a hard time, ole Lew's gonna write you up on his CQ report. You be doin' time in the stockade for *in*subordination, soldier."

Lewandowski particularly enjoyed taking shots at Frenchie, reminding him that his family tree had only one branch due to a long history of Southern Fried in–breeding. In return, Frenchie frequently reminded Lewandowksi that anyone from California has got to be a fag or a Lesbo. It was the kind of good natured give–and–take that could make Army life a living hell for boys who had been raised in polite households, where there was no name calling, no shouting, and nobody interrupting when others spoke.

More chuckles rose from the crowd. Had the ragging been taking place in the coliseum of ancient Rome, the spectators would have been pointing their thumbs to the ground. Ragging on Lewandowski had become a popular sport since his promotion. It was a sad come down for Lewandowski, a young man who had been thoroughly enjoying life just six months earlier, when he was enrolled at

USC. That was before his 1.88 grade point average was noticed by his draft board. As a 265–pound defensive lineman on the USC Trojans, Lewandowski had thought his skills on the gridiron would protect him from evil, but it wasn't to be so. Nor did the Army Docs pay any mind to the gimpy knee he pointed out to them at the induction station. He was told to go home and get his private affairs in order. Uncle Sam needed him.

Skins was about to lob another verbal round at Lewandowski, when he was interrupted by a sudden barrage of sights and sounds so unexpected, and alarming, that it would send adrenaline gushing all over the main deck of the USS Webster.

A flight of six F–4 Phantom fighter–bombers had risen from the airbase on a flight path that would take them directly over the Webster, gaining airspeed before shooting upward to a pre–determined rendezvous high above Cam Ranh Bay. The roaring, screeching overflight of six Phantoms on afterburner was enough to scare the snot out of nearly everyone on–board the Webster.

"What the hell was that?" screamed Edwards after the last Phantom screeched overhead.

"Are they nuts or what?" Frenchie shouted from the deck. He couldn't hug mother earth, but he, along with many others, had been making wild, passionate love to the deck of the Webster. "Why the hell they comin' so close?"

"Man, those were Phantoms," another Original shouted.

"What the hell is a Phantom?" someone wanted to know.

"MEAN motor scooters," another answered.

"Muh'fuh', man. That's cold, comin' at us that way," Skins complained as he stood, playing it cool now that he knew he was safe. *Never let The Man see you lose your cool.*

"Man, I was hopin' we'd make it to dry land before we went to war," someone joked. Nervous ripples of laughter rose around him.

Lewandowski pointed at the night sky. "Just look at those babies go! They got the pedal to the metal."

Only a few of the Originals had noticed the NCOs and Officers rising from the deck, though Captain Ortega and Mr. Mobley had remained standing. The two seasoned combat veterans exchanged knowing smiles and let it go at that. They wouldn't rag on the ones who hit the deck. Officers are gentlemen. They don't shuck and jive, and they don't grabass. And they don't say F.T.A.

We don't smoke, and we don't chew, and we don't go with the girls who do.

"Maybe we ought'a be bustin' our M–14s out'a the weapons racks, or somethin'," Hillbilly Williams suggested from among the huddled Originals. He had been promoted to Speck Four along with Lewandowski, but wasn't nearly as much fun to rag on. "It don't seem right to be standin' here damn near buck nekked. Man, we're just sittin' ducks out here in the middle of this big pond."

"It ain't near big enough for me," Frenchie added.

"No shit, Shylock," added a nearby drop–out English Lit major. About half the Originals were college drop–outs or flunk–outs, as with Lewandowski and Edwards, with more than a score possessing college degrees of some kind. The other half had little or no college, but had scored within the top ten percent on the General/Technical test that was administered to all recruits and draftees. Those draftees who answered that they preferred outdoor activities and camping in the psychological tests generally ended up being assigned to the infantry, no matter how high they scored on the GT tests. All in all, the Originals were an exceptionally bright collection of draftees who were not inclined to enjoy outdoor activities and camping.

"Where's Numbnuts when you need him," Lewandowski quipped, using the opportunity to turn the wrath of his brother Originals away from himself to a fresh target.

Numbnuts Bolton was just then brushing off his fatigues after kissing the deck.

Bolton had been a homesteader at Fort Ord, California, which meant he had been at one post since joining the Army in 1947. His prior life had been rather idyllic, his days filled with filled with sun, surf, and regular duty hours. That was until he received orders to report to the 516th AG in Fort Benjamin Harrison, Indiana for an unaccompanied tour, which meant he had to leave momma and the kids at home. It should have been a strong hint that Uncle Sam needed him in Southeast Asia. Nonetheless, it came as something of a shock when Captain Ortega said the 518th was forming a unit to go to Vietnam. If he'd had his twenty years in, Bolton would have put in his retirement papers on the spot, but he was stuck with only eighteen years and three months of active duty. He then saw a bad situation turn worse when he realized he would be ramrodding a unit filled with smartassed college boys like Edwards, ex–jocks like Lewandowski, and social misfits like Frenchie Beaumont and Skins Williams. It was almost enough to make him chuck it all and sell life insurance for a living, and he might well have done that if his wife hadn't given him direct orders to get in his twenty years.

"You better calm the men down a little," Ortega suggested to Bolton. Ortega almost never raised his voice or shouted. And it was rumored you had better bend over and kiss your ass good–bye when it happened, because Ortega was ready to ream tail.

"Yessir," Bolton said, and raised his arms along with his voice. "At *Ease* out there. Quiet down! At **Ease!**"

The yammering quickly subsided, then disappeared altogether.

"There's nothin' to worry about," Bolton announced. "Those were our boys. The commies don't have any airforce this far south. Only ground troops."

His speech was interrupted by Lewandowski, who was shouting, pointing skyward. "Hey, take at look that!"

Whenever possible, Lewandowski tried to steal the show from Numbnuts, knowing full well that he was driving the man insane.

A chorus of *oohs* and *ahs* rose from the Webster as the Phantoms began peeling off one by one to streak downward on a perpendicular path that seemed suicidal, but turned out to be a finely tuned tactic. At about 2,000 feet in altitude, the F–4s released canisters of napalm with their noses pointed straight down at mother earth. Then they came out of the dive and shot upward, leaving the canisters to fulfill their trajectory, finally ending in great blossoms of yellow–red liquid fire, carnations from Uncle Sam. A sizable patch of mountainside real estate suddenly became an extraordinarily beautiful cauldron of fire. First, there were two blossoms, then four, six, eight, ten, and finally, twelve.

"I'm glad they're on our side," Frenchie said, his voice low, uncharacteristically solemn and respectful.

"Damn," Edwards added with a similar tone. "I wonder how

many people just got cooked out there."

"Better them than us," Williams said. And they all knew it was true.

The grabass mood was long gone. There would be no more shuck and jive for the time being.

Bolton's voice broke the silence that followed. "We got a long day ahead of us tomorrow."

The Phantoms made another run at the target, this time releasing anti–personnel ordinance that produced only brief flashes of light

"Some of y'all will be acting NCOs tomorrow," Bolton continued, directing his next comments particularly to Lewandowski. "That means we expect you to start *acting* like NCOs. If you don't, I'm gonna own those stripes you're wearing. And I'm told we got a nice stockade in Cam Ranh for those of you who think you don't have to follow the orders of an NCO, whether he's an acting–jack or has stripes half way down his arm. Just follow orders, and you'll stay out'a trouble. It's gonna be assholes'n'elbows from now on, and we ain't gonna put up with any insubordination. You better take that to the bank, cuz I ain't gonna say it twice!"

Lewandowski had been promoted over Bolton's objections. Bolton hadn't been made privy to the thinking of Lt. Masters, who planned to mold Lewandowski into a first class supply sergeant and construction crew leader. Lewandowski was the man who would make Masters' dreams for the new company area—already dubbed tent city—become a reality.

It would have been a major understatement to say Bolton didn't recognize the raw leadership qualities that Masters saw in Lewandowski, beginning with his booming defensive linesman voice. But there was more to Lewandowski than his voice. There was his physical presence, and the predictable terror that Lewandowski exhibited in Masters' presence. Masters was convinced that he could channel Lewandowski's fear of coaches and Army officers into a force more powerful that that of ten typical drafteees. Great things could be accomplished within the next twelve months. Where Bolton saw only trouble in Lewandowski, Masters saw great untapped potential.

"Reveille is at 0400 hours," Bolton continued, then raised his voice two decibels to be heard over the cursing and groaning. "Chow is at 0430 hours! Then its gonna be all work and no play until we have the personnel center and tent city standing tall and ready for inspection!"

"Lewandowski, you'll be taking a detail to the supply depot to sign out for our vehicles. The other acting jacks will be squad leaders as we get our gear off the Webster and move it inland to the site for the new personnel center."

The Webster shuddered slightly as the tugs began maneuvering her toward her berth.

"We gotta have everything moved before the end of the duty day tomorrow, even if it means we work all day and all night," Bolton continued.

This time there were no moans, no curses. The troops were conserving their energy for the long day that lay ahead. There was no use fighting the Army Way of doing things. You either went along with it, or you did hard time in a stockade.

"You're about to become part of the biggest operation you've ever seen," Bolton promised. "Cam Ranh is nothing now compared to what it will be a year, or even six months from now. The only thing that's gonna stop it is if the commies call it quits and go back to where they came from. If they had a lick of sense, they'd drop out'a the game now, before they lose all they got. They ain't seen nothin' yet. Before this is over, they'll be sorry they ever pissed off Uncle Sam."

His words were greeted with more than a few cheers. Everybody wants to be on the winning team...particularly in matters of war, where losing is often accompanied by death. Bolton's impromptu speech struck a positive note with just about everyone, even Lewandowski. Logic was on his side. America was just too strong to be stopped in a war like this, with the communists transporting everything they needed piece by piece down the Ho Chi Minh Trail. The war was as much as won already. It was just a matter of time.

Bolton turned to Captain Ortega. "Do you or Lt. Masters want to say anything to the men, Sir?"

Ortega shook his head; Masters did the same.

Bolton did an About Face.

"Alright! Everything's copacetic! You have your orders! I don't wanna hear any pissing and moaning at 0400 hours! You still got plenty of time to get a decent night's sleep! Cum–puh–neeeee! Diiiis–MISSED!"

Chapter Two

With the arrival of dawn, the men of 516th AG had their first clear view of the Cam Ranh Bay miltary installation and the surrounding low mountains. Cam Ranh proper was a sprawling array of Army and Air Force sameness; an olive drab urban sprawl perched on an undulating sea of beige sand dunes and flatlands, only rarely broken by small islands of desert scrub brush. The massive air base was situated in the midst of a vast array of Army supply depots, many of them covering hundreds of acres. If an item existed and was even remotely connected with any aspect of modern warfare, it was likely to be found in Cam Ranh.

However varied the catalogue of supplies found within the port of Cam Ranh, it was an unlikely source for items *le toilette* beyond that of your basic M–29 white toilet seat, and rolls of standard–issue 400–grit toilet paper. In short, Cam Ranh Bay had no sewage system, no running water, and certainly no flush toilets. The nearest flush–style conveniences were a half–day's jeep ride away in the seaside resort of Nha Trang, where the best hotels came equipped with toilets of the French squat–and–bombs–away design. In Cam Ranh Bay, as throughout much of South Vietnam, the Army Way of Doing Things included overflowing pisstubes and daily shit burning details.

The nearest civilian enclave was Cam Rahn village, formerly a somnolent fishing village, now a booming sin city nestled along a narrow strip of sand skirting the northwest portion of the bay. The daily ebb and flow of the tides provided the only feeble imitation of a sewer system for Cam Ranh village, with the warm bay water manufacturing the gagging perfume that greeted one and all.

The real estate allocation for the 516th AG tent city was perched along a ridge of sand dunes overlooking the site for the personnel center, which was located within easy shouting distance of the many temptations of the flesh offered by Cam Rahn Village.

Everything had to be done yesterday, so the duty days for the troops in the 516th began and ended in darkness. Every GI retains the right to piss and moan about the dire straits of his life, so serious bitching and griping began immediately with the first wake–up call and continued without hesitation through lights–out after dark. The backbreaking nature of the schedule was just beginning to set in during their second day in–country, when even the NCOs were beginning to gripe.

The most unhappy camper of all was Alfred G. Lewandowski , who could see his ominous premonitions coming to life before his bloodshot eyes. Life wasn't going to be easy for Lew Lewandowski. Lt. Masters was becoming more demanding every day, and the dozen malcontents assigned to his tent city construction crew were doing their level best to live down to their sullied reputations as incorrigible rejects. They'd even taken to calling themselves The Dirty Dozen, after the movie of the same name. Far from being shamed by their stripeless sleeves, they saw themselves as the elite of the Originals—freedom fighters—civilians in uniform who refused to be fully militarized; idealists who had dedicated their lives to throwing monkey wrenches into the gears that drove the U.S. Army military machine.

Even so, Lewandowski had to hand it to Captain Ortega; it was a wise move to separate the Dirty Dozen away from the construction of the personnel center, where the less rebellious Originals were hard at work. The Dirty Dozen might not have withstood the constant barrage of temptations being fired inland from the cyclo girls who gathered behind the nearby village perimeter fence every morning shortly before the gate opened at 0800 hours. Most of the girls were wearing sneak–a–peek miniskirts and Jackie Kennedy bouffant beehive wigs, though some chose to wear skin tight toreador pants, knockoffs from Hollywood movies and black market fashion magazines.

Though the girls of the vill may have disagreed on clothing styles, all were awash in great waves cheap perfume so potent that even the wretched gagging stench of the bay was no match for their form of chemical warfare.

The girls of the vill would have made great sideshow barkers.

"Hey, GI! You wanna make love? Only 500 'P'!"

"I t'ink you beau ceau dep! You be my boyfrien', okay? No suweat, GI! No have VD!"

"Hey, GI! You come to vill, you ask for Mai, okay? Bring frien' for you. We have party togedder!"

"I t'ink I love you! We do boom–boom togedder!"

Captain Ortega decided it was time to have a heart to heart talk with his troops when they began assuming At Ease positions whenever particularly attractive girls joined the congregation gathered behind the fence.

The Captain was typically calm and collected when he addressed the reveille formation in the dark moments just before the dawn of their fifth day in–country.

"No passes to the Vill will be issued until the personnel center and tent city are up and copacetic. Keep that in mind the next time you're tempted to goof off, or when you see a buddy gold bricking,"

The sun was just beginning to peek over the horizon behind Ortega's back, blessing the South China Sea with a shimmering multi–hued glimmer that went unappreciated by all in attendance.

"We're in this together, and we all gotta carry our load," Ortega reminded one and all.

Late the evening before, enough corrugated steel to build four eighty–foot Quonset huts had been delivered to the site for the personnel center by Lewandowski and the Dirty Dozen, who had been humping butt without letup despite their bad attitudes. Day in, day out, without pause except for quick meals, Lewandowski and his troops had been driving to and from the various supply centers for loads of tools, lumber, corrugated steel, Olive Drab paint, bedding supplies, tents, field kitchen equipment and supplies, and anything else that was needed.

Tent city and the personnel center were on the receiving end for twenty–six troop tents, 230 canvas cots, 230 wall lockers and foot lockers, one M–60 machinegun with 800 rounds of linked ammo, eight .45 ACP sidearms, one M–79 grenade launcher with one forty–round case of grenades, 1000 rolls of toilet paper, sixteen toilet seats, 100 square yards of window screen, 460 sheets, 230 pillow cases, 230 pillows, 230 mess and field gear kits, 1,000 Olive Drab bottles of insect repellent, twenty–five 1,000 capsule bottles of orange malaria pills that were guaranteed to loosen any impacted bowel within 24–hours of ingestion, a complete field mess operation including a walk–in freezer, and a diesel generator to provide 230–volt electricity.

The 62nd Combat Engineers furnished a spare Lieutenant and three Sergeants to serve as advisors in the construction of the personnel center, but Lt. Masters was in charge of the design and construction of tent city. Lewandowski figured he had the toughest job in the 516th AG, working directly for Masters, who was never satisfied with anything Lewandowski did.

"We'll pour the floor slabs for the personnel center today and tomorrow," Ortega continued during the reveille formation. He was one for sharing mission goals with his troops, having learned through experience that a little shared knowledge could save lives in the field and go a long way toward eliminating morale problems at base camp. He didn't necessarily command by The Book, but he was always in command.

"After the concrete cures, we'll start assembling the Quonset huts. There'll be a lot of machinery moving around during assembly, so keep your head out'a your ass. I don't want anyone getting hurt. Just follow orders and stay out of the way unless you've got a specific job to do. I don't wanna be writing any letters to your folks, telling them how you got killed building a Quonset hut."

Ortega paused to gaze at the formation with a grim expression. When he spoke, it was with a particularly clipped, cold cadence.

"Next subject: If any of you are thinking of paying a visit to the cyclo girls in the Vill, you better Listen Up. You WILL be considered AWOL when you are caught….and I can guarantee that you WILL get caught."

He paused to make sure he had everyone's attention.

"Going AWOL in a combat zone is a particuarly serious offense. WHEN you get caught, you WILL be court–martialled and the sentence WILL be a Minimum of six months hard labor in the Long Binh jail. After your six months in Camp LBJ are completed, you WILL be glad for the chance to be an Eleven Bravo Infantryman in a Field unit that needs replacements because of combat losses. This is NOT a threat…it is a PROMISE. I WILL court martial anyone caught AWOL in the vill."

Ortega had their attention.

"You WILL pay with your life for a piece of tail that's likely give you the clap, or some other disease that the medics can't even define, let alone find a cure for. I'm giving you a break by warning you before you get busted by the MPs patrolling the Vill. Consider yourself warned. Stay away from the Vill until you've been issued a pass. Until then, keep your dick in your drawers and stay out of trouble."

Ortega scanned the formation a final time. "Are there any questions?"

The Originals reacted individually rather than as a unit. Some mumbled "No, Sir" while others shook their heads or cleared their throats, with none Standing Tall to be heard loud and clear. Altogether, it was a very feeble response, even for two–year draftees. The Originals knew the Captain wasn't harassing them. He was showing them—in his own military way—that he cared enough to throw the book at them if they went AWOL in the vill.

Bolton stepped forward to glare at the formation. "UH–TEN–SHUN!" he shouted.

The Originals immediately discarded their lethargy, snapping to the position of Attention. Bolton was showing signs of being genuinely pissed, and genuinely pissed could result in hours, if not days of harassment.

The officers stood by, observing without comment. Bolton was the company Top Kick and he would be supported, just as he was supporting Ortega. The pride of the Chain of Command was on the line. Bolton would look bad if he gave the troops any slack. He wouldn't last long as a Top Kick if he wasn't prepared to kick some butt.

"ONE...MORE...TIME!" Bolton shouted, pronouncing each word as if it were a bullwhip, the veins popping out on his neck, with strawberry red blotches appearing on his face.

"CUM–PUH–NEE, PUH–RADE REST!!"

Every man–jack in the formation slid his left foot eighteen inches further to the left while simultaneously clasping his hands behind his back, with his neck braced ramrod straight and eyes focused forward, with no hint of a smile. Slow or sloppy movement, or worse yet—a smile—was sure to bring down a world of hurt on the head of the offender.

There were no smiles, not even among the Dirty Dozen. Everyone knew Bolton was ready and willing to continue the Manual of Arms training until they did it properly as a unit. All would pass, or all would fail. Fighting the inevitable was a loser's game. The Originals figured it was their own fault, anyway. They should have Stood Tall and sounded off By The Numbers when Ortega asked if they had any questions, even if everyone knew Ortega wasn't really fishing for queries from the confused and misguided.

Every GI learned in Basic Training that he shouldn't raise his hand or speak up when asked, "Are there any questions?" It was easily the most loaded phrase that existed within the Army vernacular. In The Army Way of doing things, it was assumed that the subject at hand had been explained quite well by the officer or NCO in charge of the formation. Therefore, anyone with a question must have been skylarking or playing grabass when he should have been paying attention.

Bolton nodded at the crisp response to Parade Rest before clasping his hands behind his back to stroll along the front rank. He looked each troop up and down, holding them at the position of Parade Rest until he was sure he had made his point, then he slowly returned to the midpoint of the formation.

"NOW, LET'S HEAR AN ANSWER TO THE CAPTAIN'S QUESTION," Bolton shouted. "SOUND OFF LOUD AND CLEAR! BY THE NUMBERS! THE CAPTAIN WANTS TO KNOW IF YOU HAVE ANY QUESTIONS!"

"NO, SIR!!" the entire formation roared; no exceptions.

"ONE...MORE...TIME!! DO YOU UNDERSTAND WHAT WILL HAPPEN IF YOU GO AWOL WITH THE WHORES IN THE VILL?"

"YES, SERGEANT!!!"

"DO YOU UNDERSTAND THAT CAMP LBJ IS A HELL-HOLE?"

"YES, SERGEANT!!!"

Bolton nodded, glaring at the formation a final time before doing a crisp About Face to salute the Captain.

"There are no questions from the men, Sir."

Ortega nodded and returned Bolton's salute. "You may dismiss the troops for morning chow, Sergeant. The work detail formation will be at the regular time."

Meaning the Originals had wasted their time, not his.

Most of the girls gathered at the village fence weren't long removed from puberty, and usually there was at least one who was within a long day's march of menopause. There seemed to be something for everyone in the vill. And there it was, so close, yet so infuriatingly far away.

"Man, it just ain't fair," Frenchie complained after choking down a breakfast of World War Two C–ration hotdogs mixed with dehydrated eggs that smelled like a whiff of eau de vill. Like nearly everyone else, Frenchie obliterated the taste of the rank mixture with great gollups of Louisiana hot sauce and gulps of hot coffee from a canteen cup, taking care not to swallow the free–floating coffee grounds. Mess Sergeant Lugo called it his Breakfast of Champions.

Frenchie was the most vocal member of the Dirty Dozen, with Skins Williams coming in a close second.

"Every day, GI's are going into the Vill and coming out with big smiles on their faces," Frenchie continued sourly. "Meanwhile, we're stuck out here, beatin' the dog…workin' our fingers to the bone. Then we gotta put up with Manual of Arms crap from Numbnuts. I'd go AWOL, but I got no place to go. We're trapped like rats," he added, and looked around to see what impact his griping was having on the other members of the Dirty Dozen.

The tent city construction detail was lounging on the far side of the sand dune that guarded the south side of what would be tent city. Each morning Lewandowski allowed the detail—and himself—a few minutes to prepare mentally for the duty day. Lewandowski had assumed a prone position in the sand, with his legs comfortably crossed at the ankles, his fatigue cap nestled over his eyes to protect his baby blues from the rude glare of the early morning sun, his butt comfortably scrunched into the cool early–morning sand.

"Lemme give you a little bit of advice," Lewandowski said while enjoying his butt cradle. "The Army's like a football game, Frenchie, only it goes on for two years instead of four quarters. Both are just games. It's just that one takes longer than the other."

Charlie Edwards shifted position, trying without success to block Lewandowski's homespun wisdom from his mind. Lewandowski was trying to play Natural Born Leader again, conning the Dirty Dozen into thinking they ought to thank their lucky stars to have such a wise and compassionate crew chief.

Drawing upon his nine C–plus units of psychology at the University of Iowa, Charlie Edwards had reached the conclusion that Lewandowski's personality disorders were the result of being denied the breast as an infant.

Frenchie turned to Skins with a confused expression. "So this is all just a game, huh? Well, somebody gotta tell ole LBJ in the Whitehouse, because he thinks this is for real."

Skins translated for Frenchie. "What you talking about, Lewandowski? Or you be talkin' jus' to hear yo'sef talkin'?"

Lewandowski sighed, pumping whatever drama could be manufactured into an otherwise very dull moment. He sat up, bracing his elbows in the sand.

"This is how it works," Lewandowski continued. "Ortega and Masters want us to bust our butts so we get used to the pace. Then they can expect it out of us all year long. It's the oldest trick in the business. I've seen coaches do it a hundred times, going back to the days when I was in Pop Warner league. How do you think Knute Rockne made the Fighting Irish actually wanna fight? How do you think Vince Lombardi turned the Green Bay Packers from losers into winners?"

Frenchie turned to Skins. "Canoot who?"

Skins shrugged: 'I don't know; and I don't care.'

Lewandowski continued patiently. "Rockne was a football coach. Like Bear Bryant, but he was a Yankee."

Frenchie sniffed distainfully. "No wonder nobody knows who he is."

Skins nodded that he also understood, though he had no idea what Lewandowski was talking about. "Okay, but explain to me how we're winning this muh'fuh' game when Ortega and Masters got us humping butt sixteen hours a day. I think we're losing big–time, if you ask me."

"You call this humping butt?" Lewandowski demanded. "Skins, we ain't even broke a sweat."

Frenchie was insulted. "Hey, talk for yourself, man. I'm sweatin'."

"You're sweating because it's getting' hot," Lewandowski reminded him, his patience wearing a bit around the edges "Don't you know the difference between work sweat and hot sweat? No wonder the South lost the civil war."

"Hey, man. I told you before, that wasn't no *civil* war," Frenchie shot back. "There weren't nothin' civil about it. Besides, at least I ain't from California, the land of the fairy godfathers."

Frenchie chuckled at his joke and glanced around for moral support, finding none. He had gone to the same well too many times with the California fairy godfather insult.

"Oh, jeeese," Lewandowski groaned. "That is such a dumb thing to say. Your family tree must grow straight up, with no branches on it at all."

No laughter for that one, either. Half the Dirty Dozen had no idea what Lewandowski meant, while the other half no longer found it funny.

Charlie interrupted, offering to become the voice of reason in the midst of lunacy. "Frenchie, what Lew's saying is that we don't want to create high expectations."

Frenchie looked at Skins with a disgusted expression, then turned back to Edwards. "Hey, man, if you're really so damn smart, how come you got drafted and sent to Vietnam along with the rest of us dummies?"

"Thank you for the effort, Charlie," Lewandowski said. He figured it was time to bury the hatchet with Edwards. Masters had made it clear that Lewandowski and Edwards would be sharing bunk space in the supply tent when it was up and running. Someone had to be there at all times to make sure the weapon's racks were unlocked during the night alerts that would occur during the course of the next year.

"Sure, we'll get passes to the Vill a week or two earlier if we bust our butts, but it'll backfire in the long run," Lewandowski continued. "The Lifers will expect that kind of effort all the time.

That's what I mean by it being just a game, like football. We gotta pace ourselves, we gotta be thinking one step ahead of the Lifers all the time. If we don't, we'll lose the game. Won't we, Charlie?"

Edwards shrugged, then nodded grudgingly. "Lewandowski's actually making sense this time, guys. This is all just basic Psyche 101 stuff. Whatever we do now, we'll be expected to do the rest of the year."

"Yup," Lewandowski said before Charlie could change his mind. "Even Charlie says I'm right. It's all psychological. Like at reveille…we should'a stepped right up and said 'No, Sir!' when the Cap'n asked if we had any questions. It would'a saved a lot of trouble if we'd played our cards right."

"Y'mean we should'a kissed his ass," Frenchie added sarcastically.

Lewandowski paused before answering. "No, not at all," he said with exaggerated calm, thereby letting Frenchie know he was getting a bit too mouthy. Lewandowski deeply resented being accused, even obliquely, of kissing ass. He considered himself at least one step above that sort of behavior. "We just gotta play the game smarter than the Lifers, that's all."

"Take Masters, for instance," Lewandowski continued, using the opportunity to face down the monster that was dwelling in his personal closet of horrors. "He's got big plans in mind for tent city, but he needs us to make it happen. Without us, he's just shootin' blanks…pissin' into the wind."

Lewandowski's memory banks were reaching back to his high school days when he learned to never admit to himself that an opposing player had him psyched out. His favorite coach had a simple method for turning fear into a tool: If an opposing player scares the crap out of you, growl at him, show your teeth, make fun of his sister…make him think you're crazy enough to eat his liver raw for breakfast. Lewandowski realized he couldn't quite do all that with Masters, but he *could* start pretending he wasn't afraid of the big bad wolf.

"What'cha mean?" Frenchie asked, becoming genuinely interested.

Lewandowski recalled the conversation he'd had with Lt.

Masters the night before, while they were standing on the crest of the highest sand dune overlooking what would soon be tent city. The dunes below were covered with sleeping forms, some scratching at sand fleas because they didn't bother to douse themselves with insect repellent, while others were being carried to dreamland on their rubberized ponchos. None of the officers were sleeping on the sand dunes. The Royal Family was instead gathered in the Bachelor Officers Quarters several miles inland, where Masters would be going after he finished briefing Lewandowski on what he wanted accomplished during the next duty day.

"I want seven troop tents up by tomorrow night," Masters announced with no prelude. Like Ortega, he preferred not to raise his voice. Experience and a book of quotable quotes had taught him to speak softly but carry a big stick.

Lewandowski tensed. As usual, he had no game plan to deal with Masters, no defensive strategy to fall back on. Though he couldn't see Masters well in the darkness, he could feel the harsh glare of the beady little eyes.

"Sir," Lewandowski said, interrupting with great care, fearing he might anger the beast, wondering if he should surrender now and plead for mercy. "The Dirty Dozen weren't assigned to this detail because they're good workers…Sir."

Lewandowski felt like a man tossed overboard in a heavy gale, unable to swim but treading water as fast as possible, knowing the end was inevitable no matter how hard or long he struggled.

Even as he succumbed to panic, another part of his brain was saying that raising seven tents in one duty day was really a piece of cake. *I'll just tell the Dirty Dozen that Masters wants ten tents.*

Lewandowski had learned the art of negotiating labor agreements from his father, a Teamster's Union shop foreman in Studio City, California.

But Masters wasn't yet finished. "I also want my orderly tent up by noon chow tomorrow. And the supply tent. And two tents butted together to make one large mess tent. I don't want any more meals being served in the open after noon chow tomorrow. Later on, we'll make it a real mess tent, with four tents butted together and a woodframe kitchen and a separate dining room for the NCOs and

Officers. I want a room divider of some kind, too. Maybe with a planter box…and flowers…something along that line. Nothing real fancy, just nice. Very nice."

Lewandowski was scrambling to recalculate his output for the next day. The seven tents had become eleven, with the tasks multiplying like loaves and fishes. He might even have to kick butt at some point to get it handled, which—in turn—could lead to copious rations of harassment being heaped upon his shoulders by the Dirty Dozen.

Lewandowski moved to open negotiations. "That's eleven tents, Sir. We only did three today."

As with his father before him, Lewandowski was using padded labor statistics. True, the Dirty Dozen had raised only three tents in roughly eight hours that day. But, five of those hours had been invested in On the Job Training for the first tent, with two hours for the second tent, and only one hour for the third tent, which could have been raised in thirty minutes if a genuine kick–butt double–time pace were necessary.

"I don't care how you do it, just get it done," Masters said.

It was the kind of response that Lewandowski was learning to expect from Masters.

"Yes, Sir," Lewandowski answered, allowing himself a small sigh that was meant to suggest enough pain had been inflicted.

Masters smiled in the darkness. "Oh, I'm not done yet. By the end of the duty day tomorrow, I want a five–hole shithouse with a roof standing where we are right now. Your duty day won't be over until it is up and ready to rock and roll. You'll build one tomorrow and one the day after. See Sgt. Bolton about getting someone to cut–up some of those old 55–gallon fuel drums we got yesterday. That'll give us two shitcans out of every drum."

Lewandowski issued no more lamentful sighs for fear Masters might create even more work projects for the next day. He felt not unlike his father did on weekends, when momma Lewandowski presented him with a list of Honey Do's.

Masters continued. "I want four five–hole shitters in all. One for the officers, one for the NCOs and two for the enlisted men. After that, I want four urinal stations, each with four pisstubes, with one two–tube officers urinal within walking distance of the orderly tent. Bury old barrels in the sand for the piss tubes, with holes drilled in the sides and bottoms for drainage, and window screens over the top to hold down the splatter. All this has to be copecetic before Sunday, so we're ready for an inspection by the Brigade sanitation officer. No more slit trenches. They're for field units, not base camps like Cam Ranh."

"Divide the Dirty Dozen into two work details," Masters continued. "Edwards can head up one detail, under your supervision, and you can honcho the other. Let it be known that you're in charge. That's why you're wearing the stripes."

"I've got a shower hut design in mind...the same design we've got at the BOQs. It'll be big enough to hold a dozen water barrels on the roof, each with a shower spigot. Once its up, the 52nd Engineers can put us on their daily water delivery route. I want the shower hut completed by next Wednesday. I reckon the men won't argue with having a shower hut. They've likely had enough of bathing from their steel pots."

"Once we have all the troop tents up, the mess tent in operation, the shithouses and the pisstubes, you'll start expanding the mess tent," Masters assured him, "Turning it into something to be proud of."

Lewandowski thought he saw an opening. "Oh, heck, Sir, I don't think the guys care all that much about having a fancy mess tent. You don't have to go to all that much bother, Sir."

A long moment of silence followed. When Masters spoke, his voice was dangerously calm. "The men of the 516th AG are not guys, Specialist Lewandowski. They are soldiers. They can be called troops or grunts or GIs, but they are not guys. Guys belong to the YMCA, Lewandowski. Soldiers, on the other hand, wouldn't be caught dead in a 'Y'."

"Yes, Sir."

"I'm not doing this to make the *guys* happy, Lewandowski. This is not a summer camp, and I am not a camp counselor. I'm doing this because I want tent city to stand tall when we are inspected. Do you have any questions?"

"No, Sir,"

"When the mess tent is finished, I want boardwalks connecting every tent in tent city. After that, I want plywood floors for all the tents. And when all that's complete, we'll finally be inspection–ready."

Lewandowski could see the months ahead filled with the horror of non–stop inspections.

Masters paused, waiting for Lewandowski to acknowledge receipt of his grandiose plans for tent city.

Lewandowski took a deep breath of the aromatic Cam Ranh air, "Yes, Sir."

There was no use fighting the inevitable.

A series of explosions erupted along a section of the mountains, not far from the southwestern edge of the Cam Rahn perimeter. Several of the troops bolted into sitting positions, but the remainder paid little or no attention. Most everyone was adjusting to the sounds of life in Cam Ranh, including the man–made thunder that frequently erupted along the perimeter, particularly at night.

Masters continued when the perimeter was quiet again. "Oh, I almost forgot: I want a company movie screen and projection booth erected over there at the top of the dune, with the screen at the base of the dune, beside the shower hut. The screen can be made of sheets of plywood painted white. Take a look at other units while you're driving around. The basic design is pretty simple, but it has to be strong enough to take the wind that can pop–up during monsoon season. That should just about wrap up everything for tent city."

Lewandowski's own fantasies for tent city required much less work, with nothing special being done for the NCOs and nothing at all for the Officers, who should be encouraged by all possible means to spend their time elsewhere.

"That'll be all for now," Masters said. "You've got enough to keep you busy for awhile."

Lewandowski couldn't agree more. "Yes, Sir." He raised his right hand to salute, hoping Masters would take the hint and disappear.

But Masters didn't return the salute. He wasn't quite ready to let Lewandowski off the hook. "I hope it won't be necessary for me to check on your crew every few minutes to make sure the work is being done...."

"No, of course not, Sir," Lewandowski answered, doing only slight damage to the truth. As it was, he had absolutely no idea how he would get even half the projects completed in the timeframe outlined by Masters.

"Good," Masters said, nodding crisply. "Like I said before, I don't care how you get all this done. Just do it. Are you reading me loud and clear?"

"Yes, Sir," Lewandowski said, knowing he could expect no mercy short of heaven or a return to civilian life. "I read you loud and clear."

Masters nodded. "It's time we called it a day. You have a lot to do tomorrow."

Lewandowski summerized the lessons learned from the prior evening for the Dirty Dozen. "Masters has it all worked out. He's got everything scheduled day by day. He knows exactly what he wants done, how he wants it done, and when he wants us to do it."

Frenchie grinned. "Hey, what's he gonna do, send us to Vietnam if we don't meet his schedule?"

"Naw, he's got meaner stuff he could do to us," Lewandowski warned. "I don't think he'd blink an eye if he sent us to some suicide platoon on the DMZ. That man's as cold as ice."

"Muh'fuh', you think he'd really do that?" Skins asked.

"In a heartbeat," Lewandowski answered.

Skins somehow lost track of his skeptical smile. "Muh'fuh', that's cold."

"As cold as ice," Lewandowski repeated, knowing he was their only source of information on the inscrutable ways of William R. Masters, the cold–hearted executive officer of the 516th AG who had them all by the short curlies.

Which gave Lewandowski the upper hand with the Dirty Dozen. If he was going to keep his own tail out of trouble, he had to convince them that it was in their best interest to work long, hard hours with only minimum rations of bitching about Masters. And never, ever should they bitch at, or harass their kind, wise leader, Alfred G. Lewandowski, who was one helluva a good guy of heroic proportions and a downright noble protector of the downtrodden masses.

Lewandowski continued. "We can't tackle Masters head on. We gotta convince him that we're going along with the plan, just like he laid it out…that we're really busting our butts to make it happen. It'll make it harder for him to get on our case when things don't get done as fast as he wants."

"How we gonna look like we're humpin' when we ain't?" Frenchie asked suspiciously. "It sounds like we gotta *really* be humpin' butt if we're gonna *look* like we're humpin' butt."

Lewandowski rose from his butt cradle, brushing off his fatigue pants. "I gotta think about it…come up with a plan of my own."

"Wake me when you're done," Frenchie said, and laid back to grab a few Z's.

Lewandowski shook his head. "Negative, GI. We got work to do, and it ain't gonna go away by sleeping on it."

"Hey, I donno, man. Let's talk about it, chew the fat, make a plan," Frenchie suggested.

"Yeah, right," Lewandowski growled. "Up and at'em. We gotta work up some sweat."

Frenchie rolled over and forced himself to stand. "Man, Lew, you're beginning to sound like a real Lifer."

"Uhhuh, right," Lewandowski agreed sourly. "Yeah, I'm the Lifer that's gonna keep your butt out of the Hundred and First Airborne. Get your butt in gear, Frenchie. I won't let you or anyone else get my young butt in a world of hurt. If you don't like it, tough luck, but that's the way its gonna be."

"Alright, alright," Frenchie grumbled. "Don't get heavy about it, man. I was just horsin' around."

Lewandowski continued as the Dirty Dozen rose from the sand, ready for a day of hard labor. "Charlie's gonna head up one crew and I'm gonna head up the other. We gotta make some progress around here or we're gonna be up to our ears in alligators before we know it. Count off by twos. Start countin', Frenchie."

"Two," Frenchie said sourly.

"One," Lew growled back at him. "Skins, you're two. Keep it movin', people. By the numbers now, let's go. One–two, one–two, one–two. Charlie, you take the Twos to start on the shithouses, and I'll take the Ones for the troop tents."

Chapter Three

The personnel center rose from the dusty sand of Cam Ranh Bay like an ugly, olive drab phoenix. Ditto for tent city, which had developed a personality of its own during its growth spurt. To complete their mission, the Originals and NCOs of the 516th AG transformed themselves into carpenters, cement masons, electricians, painters and practitioners of a dozen other necessary skills. They pounded nails, they erected walls, they built boardwalks, and they dug holes to bury the barrels that made the phrase "going to the can" more than just an endearingly quaint expression.

Historians might one day say the construction of the 516th AG personnel center was accomplished by troops unselfishly dedicated to a cause that was larger than any one man. And they would have been right, but for the wrong reasons. The Originals did work their butts off, but the motivation had much more to do with lust than military objectives.

With the shithouses completed, shit burning was added to the daily extra–duty lists that were posted outside the orderly tent. The term 'shit burning' made the detail sound like a horrible experience to endure. But the Originals soon discovered that the shit burners were accorded far more freedom, accompanied by far less harassment from the NCOs, who often used extra duty details as an opportunity to chew butt. However, the Lifers avoided the shit burning detail like the plague, thus freeing the shit burners to discipline themselves while enjoying otherwise unheard of freedom of choice, lazily wandering from shit house to shit house, where they would drag out the brimming cans and soak the contents with enough diesel fuel to feed a deuce–and–a–half troop transport truck for a week. Lastly, the shitburning detail would set the offensive muck ablaze and move upwind, where they would take short naps and shoot the bull until the contents were crisp enough for burial. All total, there were only about three hours of real work in the whole day, with no NCOs or officers within sight.

In the usual deference to Rank Has Its Privileges (R.H.I.P.), the piss tubes and shitters at the personnel center were segregated into separate facilities for the Officers, the NCO's and the run–of–the–mill enlisted men. It was the kind of social slight that the Originals had come to expect from the Army, but they couldn't allow the insult to pass without comment. So they decorated their own piss tubes and shitters with wooden signs that expressed their anonymous outrage. The piss tube with the least offensive sign constituted a memorial of sorts:

DEDICATED TO THE MEMORY OF
CHARLES R. CUTLER
FIRST SHORT TIMER OF THE 516th AG
LEST WE FORGET THOSE WHO PISSED BEFORE US

The message inside a nearby shithouse was more barbed:

FLUSH TWICE
THE PENTAGON IS A LONG WAY FROM HERE

Cutler was the first short timer of the 516th AG by virtue of a bit of very bad luck that evolved into very good luck. The Cutler odyssey began when he contracted spinal meningitis while in Basic Training in Fort Leonard Wood, Missouri, also known as Fort Lost In The Woods. He spent the next eight months recuperating in the hospital, plus another three months at home. He might have died, but he didn't, so his fellow Originals viewed his experience with envy rather than pity, figuring eight months in a hospital, and three months recuperating at home was a pretty good way to pay one's obligation to Uncle Sam. And Cutler did nothing to dispel the myths surrounding his bout with spinal meningitis. He rather enjoyed his status as a short timer and didn't want to muddy the water with medical technicalities.

Cutler was considered fair game for the ETS—Estimated Term of Service—game when he first arrived at the 516th AG, back in Fort Ben Harrison. The ETS game requires at least two players willing to compare their ETS dates. The GI with the least amount of time to do before his ETS was the automatic winner, as in: *'I'll be a Private Fucking Civilian on the streets while you're still wearing fatigues.'*

When Cutler first arrived in the 516th, it was assumed he would have an ETS date after the other Originals, which made everyone else "Short" by comparison. But the Originals soon learned that playing the ETS game with Cutler was something like playing Russian roulette with a fully loaded revolver. Cutler always came out on top when ETS dates were compared.

Lewandowski wasn't one to harbor his resentment with a glad heart. Shortly after the 516th arrived in Cam Ranh, he laid a curse on Cutler's head. "I hope you get the clap from a whore in the vill and your records get flagged a week before you DEROS."

In Vietnam, every GI had his DEROS date tatooed on his brain with indelible ink. His DEROS, or Date Estimated for Return from OverSeas—his final day in Vietnam—was like the beckoning distant warm, comforting light that has so often been experinced by those who undergo near–death experiences.

"Short," Cutler would always answer, particularly when he was being challenged by Lewandowski, thus forcing his would be tormenter to fall back on a fussilade of impotent insults.

"You'll Re–up. You love this life."

"Lifer," Cutler would always shoot back in a return volley. "NCO."

"Malingerer, goof–off, momma's boy."

"Two, twelve, 67," Cutler would say with a sublime smile that only he had a right to possess, thus throwing his DEROS date in the face of any fool willing to exhange barbs.

It was just the sort of comeback that could make Lewandow-ski's blood boil, but Cutler seemed to have no fear of ex–defensive linemen from USC.

"What's your ETS, Lew? May, June? What year did you say that was? Sixty–eight? Sixty–nine? Seventy?"

"Shuddup."

The personnel center was nearing completion when Lewan-dowski received a telephone call on the field phone in the supply tent, where he had been holding court with Charlie and The Dirty Dozen in attendance. Lewandowski had called a midmorning break—"Take five, people."—in the supply tent, which soon was littered with bodies, flopped here and there on piles of soiled bed linen, or wherever else they could use to crash and burn.

The field phone again buzzed for attention.

"Get it, Charlie," Lewandowski said over the incessant roar of two enormous electric fans he'd scrounged at the Supply Depot the week before.

The supply tent remained an unfinished work of art. Several dozen olive–drab metal storage bins remained in their packing cases, along with the makings of the countertop Masters wanted built. Lewandowski was waiting for Masters to order him to finish the supply tent, knowing the Dirty Dozen would call him a gung ho Lifer if he moved too soon.

"516th AG supply tent," Charlie answered. "Specialist Edwards speaking, Sir."

Masters insisted that proper military telephone ettiquette be used when answering the field phone, which was connected only to the orderly tent. It would be several more days before the support command connected tent city to the Cam Ranh Bay telephone system.

"It's me," Woody said on the other end of the line. It was always Woody. Lieutenants don't place their own calls; they have their company clerks do it.

Woody never allowed a day to pass without letting someone know how much he hated his job, though he never used Masters as a sounding board.

"Put Lew on."

"It's Woody," Charlie said, holding out the receiver for Lewandowski.

"Yeah," Lewandowski said into the mouthpiece, not bothering with the proper telephone protocol. Woody was an Original, not a "Sir."

"Lt. Masters requests your presence Front and Center," Woody said tonelessly, repeating the message exactly as directed by Masters.

"Now?" Lewandowski asked.

"You're already AWOL," Woody answered.

"Oh," Lewandowski grunted. "He's in one of *those* moods again, huh?"

"Ain't he always?" Woody confirmed.

"Okay, tell him I'm on my way."

Lewandowski handed the receiver back to Charlie as he rose from his own sweat–soaked pile of bed linen. "Break's over," he announced to the others.

"Muh'fuh'," Skins whined, opening his first salvo of complaints within a heartbeat. "I was just getting comfortable, man. It's muh'fuh' hot out there."

"Yeah," Frenchie agreed. "I think I'm comin' down with heat stroke. I'm feelin' all sick to my stomach. You can't make a man work when he's got heat stroke. It's in the regulations."

"Tell it to the Inspector General," Lewandowski growled. "I want you guys outside humpin' butt where Masters can see you. Look at it this way, we got two more days of this crap, then we get a day off with passes to the vill. If that don't keep your head straight and your dick hard, nothin' will."

Frenchie had a suggestion. "Man, you ought'a tell Masters to kiss your ass."

"Yeah, right," Lewandowski agreed sourly. "And find myself spending the next six months in Camp L.B.J. Why don't I just put a gun to my head and pull the trigger?"

Frenchie shrugged. 'Why not?'

"Up and at'em," Lewandowski ordered. "Masters probably wants to bitch about the tents that ain't got floors yet."

Only eight of the troop tents and the enlarged mess tent had been fitted for the plywood floors that Masters wanted, but Lewandowski didn't feel any burning desire to speed up the pace. Everyone knew what to expect when all the floors were in place. Masters would start conducting daily walk–through inspections, using stateside rules for neatness. As it was, tent city wasn't such a bad place to live. The Originals griped about the tents at first, but they soon realized they had it a heck of a lot better than the troops who were living in the stateside–regulation, two–story barracks found further inland, where daily walk–through, and weekly stand–by inspections were SOP.

The Dirty Dozen filed out of the supply tent, grumbling "F.T.A., All The Way" as Charlie led them to a partially completed floor panel on the far side of tent city, within full view of the orderly tent, so Masters could bear witness to their dedication and hard work.

Lewandowski began trudging through the sand to the orderly tent, his thoughts turning morbid as he pondered yet another Front and Center session with Masters. *'He expects me to do the impossible. Heck, I ought'a get a medal for getting any work out of guys like Skins and Frenchie. But does he see it that way? No, not Masters. He never lets up, he never gives me any slack. It'd be different if I'd wanted the job in the first place...which I didn't."*

Lewandowski paused to gaze at the enlarged mess tent, with clapboard sidewalls on the bottom half and screened windows on the top half. The roof remained a wide expanse of canvas, but would eventually be topped by corrugated steel, thus making the mess tent monsoon–proof. The kitchen was fueled by propane gas stoves, with two generator–powered walk–in freezers obtained through normal channels, and a third walk–in that was donated by an NCO in the supply depot who was eager to work a deal in return for an early DEROS. It was Lewandowski's first foray into the dark side of the art of Supply Sergeantry, under the guidance of Lt. Masters.

A third of the mess tent dining area was separated into a separate dining cove for the NCO's and officers. Under the direction of Masters, a waist–high planter box was constructed to separate the unwashed masses from the overlords of the kingdom.

'We hadda hump butt to get the messtent standing tall,' Lewandowski sulked, *'but did Masters say Thank You or Nice Job? No, of course not. He just reminded me that we were behind schedule on the shower hut.'*

Lewandowski moved his attentiond to the new shower hut, which was perched on the side of a sand dune just above the first row of troop tents. The sparkling white hut measured twelve by twelve, with a dozen 55–gallon water barrels perched on the roof, each with its own spigot and shower head. Every afternoon a tanker truck from the 302nd Combat Engineers stopped by to refill the drums with frigid non–potable water. Those who thought the mid–day heat of Cam Ranh would warm the water were wrong. The evening showers were a chilling ritual of splash–scrub–rinse, all done at doubletime, which turned out to be such an effective method of water conservation that the hut never ran out of H2°.

'He could have said good job when we finished the shower hut, but that would have been too nice of him…too civilian.'

Lewandowski had arrived at the conclusion there was no way to please Masters. He wouldn't have been surprised to learn the Dirty Dozen said much the same about him, but he would have defended his own management methods by saying he could name a thousand good reasons for demanding more than they wanted to give. With reason number one being that they made him work much too hard at making them work. Lewandowski figured he could goof off with the best of them, but at least once every day the Dirty Dozen made him feel like he might really be a gung ho Lifer. And they were the biggest bunch of crybabies he'd ever known. They could flat wear him out with their constant bickering and complaining.

Occasionally he wished he could be one of the Dirty Dozen, with no stripes, no responsibilities. At such times he was convinced his life would suddenly become much more pleasant if he could somehow wrangle becoming the thirteenth member of the Dirty Dozen.

Lewandowski paused before entering the orderly tent, making sure the Dirty Dozen were making a good show of actually working on the floor panel. That done, he removed his fatigue cap and opened the breeze flap before wading through the sand to the grey metal desk that belonged to Greg Woods, the senior company clerk.

Woody had been a Journalism major at Ohio State before getting yanked into the Army. Like many other Originals, his GT test scores easily qualified him for Officer Candidate School, while his psychological profile made him totally unqualified. His psychological profile scores also indicated that he hated camping. His exceptionally high vocabulary test scores landed him in personnel school before getting a permanent assignment to the 516th, where Masters made him the company clerk because he was the best typist in the entire pool of Originals, at 65 words per minute. Masters didn't give a hoot about Woody's vocabulary. The official language of the US Army utilized only certain words, none of which were creative.

When Lewandowski entered, Woody was perusing a manual of regulations he had to reference for yet another report that was to be submitted to Brigade. Charlie Edwards once analyzed Woody as a passive aggressive phobic–neurotic–compulsive personality disorder. Nobody knew what the analysis meant in real words, but Woody didn't care. He told Charlie he would beat the crap out of him if he ever said anything like that again. And there was something about Woody's dry, monotone that made it more than the typically hollow barracks threat. Charlie never mentioned Woody's personality disorder again.

Hanley, the Morning Report clerk, was at his desk frowning at a yet another multi–copy Morning Report form he had rolled into his Remington manual typewriter. Like most other morning report clerks, Hanley was filled with loathing for his job, which required near–perfect typing skills. Even one small typo on certain lines would render the entire document useless, forcing Hanley to start anew. He was almost always several hours late submitting the Morning Report to the personnel center because he tended to crack under the pressure. He rarely caught his mistakes before placing the typed documents on Masters' desk, where the Lieutenant would use a ballpoint pin to circle the typing errors before handing the forms back to Hanley, never saying a word, instead allowing his brazen circles to do his talking for him, occasionally leaving Hanley on the brink of tears.

Hanley was slowly going insane.

"Lew's here, Sir," Woody yelled over the roar of the big fans that were re–circulating the humid, odor–laden Cam Ranh atmosphere. His announcement should have been unnecessary—Masters could see perfectly well for himself that Lewandowski had entered the orderly tent—but Masters insisted that everyone follow protocol, demanding everyone recognize his office was separated from the front office by an invisible wall. So it was that Masters didn't 'see' Lewandowski's arrival.

Lewandowski was sweating buckets by this time, as was always the case when he was called to the orderly tent for a Front and Center with Masters. He never knew what might befall him in such encounters. Lewandowski's fertile imagination warned him that he might exit under armed guard, or he might find himself suddenly assigned to the Demilitarized Zone, where he would honcho the building of low profile shithouses. Charlie Edwards said his copious sweating was a Pavlovian response. Charlie also said it was an incurable condition.

Masters was sitting at his desk reading the most recent issue of PLAYBOY, which arrived just that morning. "Tell Specialist Lewandowski to report to me at once," he ordered while setting aside the Playboy.

Lewandowski slogged through the sand toward the invisible door in the midst of the invisible wall, all the time pondering his incurable Pavlovian sweat and how Masters always made him feel big and a slow–witted during moments like this.

Woody glanced up from his manual of regulations to pass along the order. "Report Front and Center, Lew."

Lewandowski took a deep breath and announced his presence. "Specialist Lewandowski reporting as ordered, Sir."

Masters glanced up. "Permission to report."

Lewandowski entered through the invisible door and positioned himself precisely Front and Center at Masters' desk. There he rendered a salute, which he was forced to hold until Masters went through the motions of inspecting his sweat–soaked jungle fatigues from top to bottom, ending with his jungle boots, which hadn't been shined since they had been issued three weeks earlier.

Masters returned Lewandowski's salute with the casual ease one shows when dealing with subordinates. "At Ease," he ordered, and watched without expression as Lewandowski assumed a modified position of Parade Rest.

Lewandowski was on guard. *'Why's he got it in for me? What did I ever do to him?'*

"Lewandowski…."

"Yessir."

"You seem to be nervous," Masters said in a kindly fashion, not unlike a female black widow spider luring a new boyfriend into her web. "Is there something you know that I don't know, but I should know?"

Lewandowski puzzled the question. "No, Sir. I don't know nothing you don't know, Sir."

Masters smiled pleasantly. "Good. Now, why don't I have a

floor in my orderly tent?"

"Sir?" Lewandowski asked, now totally confused.

Masters rephrased his question. "Are you trying to tell me I come after everyone else, that I must wait in line to get *my* floor for *my* orderly tent?"

Lewandowski sharpened his senses. Masters sounded dangerously unoffended.

"Would you like me to repeat the question?" Masters asked.

Lewandowski nodded. "Yes, Sir."

"Why don't I have a floor for my orderly tent?"

Masters leaned back in his chair to await the answer.

Lewandowski's brain tissues desperately seized unto a random thought that offered him a possible way out. When in doubt, kiss ass.

"Well, Sir, I know how you put the welfare of your troops first, so we've been working on the troop tents up till now."

Masters grimaced.

Wrong answer, wrong answer!

"But the last couple days I've been thinking," Lewandowski continued. "Golly, that really is unfair to you."

Masters smiled sweetly, "Unfair to you..."

"Sir," Lewandowski quickly added. "Unfair to you, Sir."

Masters nodded. The beast was satisfied.

Feeling new confidence, Lewandowski continued. "I've been meaning to ask, Sir, when would it be convenient for us to come in and make a floor for your orderly tent?"

"That's good," Masters said with a nod of approval. "Very good. Your attitude shows real initiative, Lewandowski."

"Yes, Sir," Lewandowski agreed, accepting the compliment with a widening grin. He was thinking how easy it was to totally bullshit Masters, and that he should do it more often.

"And were you thinking of building a room divider when you laid the floor?" Masters asked.

"Yes, Sir," Lewandowski lied, bursting with renewed confidence. "We'll do the whole nine yards all at once, Sir."

"And when were you planning to do all this?" Masters asked.

Lewandowski frowned, demonstrating deep thought and deeper concern as he contemplated the question. "Well, Sir, it's my guess—

based on my experience—that the whole thing will take a good three days of real hard work to get it handled."

Masters leaned forward to consult his desktop calendar. He didn't roll his chair forward because floor castors weren't designed to be used in sand.

"Let me see, today is Thursday...the Captain will be issuing passes for the Vill on Sunday. Are you telling me you intend to be working on my floor when the other troops are getting the day off?"

Red Alert! Red Alert!

Lewandowski backpedaled carefully. "Wellll, not exactly, Sir. You see, I was thinking we could start on the orderly tent next Monday, after I give Charlie and the Dirty Dozen the day off. They've been working awful hard, Sir, and...well, they need a break," he added with a confidential tone, one professional speaking to another.

"Hmmm," Masters pondered. "I was thinking you would start on it tomorrow. Are you trying to tell me that my little project doesn't fit into your current schedule?"

Lewandowski wiped his brow. "No, not at all," he said with a spastic shrug. "I'll work around any schedule you want."

Do not anger the beast!

"Sir," Masters said.

"Sir," Lewandowski added.

"I want my new floor and room divider in place by Sunday morning," Masters said, then paused to await Lewandowski's response.

"We can do that," Lewandowski admitted reluctantly, ready to kick himself for being so agreeable. "It'll mean heavy humping for two days straight, but I think we can do it."

Masters flashed a brief, humorless smile. "I *know* you can do it."

Lewandowski had to make one more effort to modify the mission timeframe. He began by slapping his forehead. "Darn, Sir, I forgot. I'll have to requisition more building materials from the Supply Depot. We don't have enough to get the job done. Boy, that'll add on some time, Sir. Darn, I wish I'd thought of that earlier."

"I'm sure you can get it handled," Masters said, flashing an evil smile before glancing at his self–winding Seiko watch, which cost only $9.95 at the importy–duty free main Post Exchange. "Oh, my, look at the time. You'd better be on your way to the supply depot, Lewandowski. I'm sure you'll want to start on the project first thing tomorrow morning."

"Yes, Sir."

Lewandowski jogged through the sand from the orderly tent to the Dirty Dozen and Charlie, who had been working hard at not working hard.

"Charlie! Everybody! Into the deuce–and–a–half, quick! We gotta scrounge lumber at the supply depot, on the double!"

Skins tossed his hammer aside with a loud "Muh'fuh'! I could use a change of scenery."

Lewandowski turned on him, taking out his frustrations on the nearest target. "Oh, YEAH? Well, listen up, soldier! We're gonna be humpin' butt the next two days. And if you don't goddammed like it, you can shove it!"

"Oh, yeah?" Skins countered weakly, unprepared for the anger, but not yet ready to back down. "Who says?"

"ME…I say we'll be humpin' butt," Lewandowski growled back at him, daring Skins or anyone else to take him on. "Got any problems with that?"

Skins raised his hands in surrender. "No, man. Jes' askin'. A man can ask, can't he?"

"I'll make it quick," Lewandowski said to them all. "If Masters don't have a floor and room divider in his orderly tent by Saturday night, we don't get Sunday off. And that means we don't get laid in the vill."

Nothing more need be said. Skins was in the lead as the Dirty Dozen scrambled for the supply tent deuce–and–a–half truck.

Masters observed from the back flap of the orderly tent as the big diesel troop transport roared out of tent city with the Dirty Dozen in back, Lewandowski behind the wheel, with Charlie Edwards riding shotgun in the front seat. He was thinking Lewandowski would make a truly fine Supply Sergeant one day, a genuine military asset, an NCO who could get things done when he set his mind to it. Who knows, Lewandowski might even be officer material. Stranger things have happened. Masters wasn't exactly gung ho himself during the first year or so in This Man's Army.

Masters had been much like Lewandowski when he was a first–term enlisted man...a bit rebellious, yet anxious to please his own Executive Officer. It had taken nearly two years before Masters realized the Army wasn't such a bad life afterall. Once he came to that conclusion, he started using the Army Way to his advantage rather than fighting it.

Masters pondered what miracles might happen. Never could it be said that he wasn't a dreamer. It would be quite a feather in his cap if he could get Lewandowski to Re–up and apply for OCS. Perhaps it could even be finagled for Lewandowski to be his Executive Officer when Masters was CO of his own unit.

Having pondered the improbable, Masters returned to his desk for another inspection of Miss August, allowing his imagination to wander over her air–brushed perfection. She reminded him of a girl he once dated in Columbus, Georgia...a very generous girl who had a soft spot for men in uniform, banana daiquiris, and red Corvette Stingrays.

An inspiration suddenly occurred to him: "Woody!" Masters shouted, forcing his eyes to stray from Miss August.

"Yes, Sir," Woody answered lifelessly.

"Remind me to appoint Lewandowski the company Re–Enlistment NCO tomorrow morning."

A moment of silence followed.

Woody perked up, a smile appeared on his face and in his voice. "Lewandowski, Sir?"

Hanley was chuckling, having forgotten the morning report form.

"Yes...Lewandowski," Masters confirmed.

"Yes, Sir," Woody said. "I'll start typing the orders right now, Sir. Would you like me to post an announcement on the company bulletin board?"

"Yes, that's a good idea," Masters agreed.

"Lemme do the announcement," Hanley whispered from his desk.

Woody nodded...he could be magnanimous with such an opportunity; he could share the joy of the moment.

"Uh, Sir, perhaps you would like to tell Hanley what you wanna say in the announcement while I type the orders."

"Yes, that's a good idea, Woody."

Masters dictated a brief unit–wide memo to the effect that Lewandowski would thereafter be the Re–enlistment NCO for the 516th AG.

It might work out just fine, Masters again assured himself. Stranger things have happened. If nothing else, it would keep Lewandowski just a tad off balance, which was exactly where Masters wanted him to be.

Chapter Four

"Is the new muh'fuh' Re–Enlistment NCO present or accounted for?"

The astoundingly rude question had been shouted by an Original standing near the end of a long line of Originals, all of whom had been waiting impatiently for the MPs to swing open the gate to Cam Rahn village.

Only one Original wasn't laughing at the snide reference to the Re–enlistment NCO. All others were thoroughly enjoying the moment, but Lewandowski could find nothing humorous in such tawdry attempts at character assassination. It was only through courageous self–control that he was able to maintain a calm facade. Inside, he was a great blubbering volcano of hurt feelings that threatened to explode and rain down retribution on all those who dared snicker at his predicament.

Lewandowski didn't have to search the line of faces behind him to know who had asked the loaded question. Yea and behold, it was the unkindest cut of all. Skins Williams was kicking him when he was down, taking pot shots at the man who had saved his young hide from six months in Camp LBJ. Which, by the way, was a sentence that Skins righteously deserved, followed by a year of Eleven Bravo grunting through the jungles and rice paddies. *That's the thanks I get for making him hump butt the past two days so's he could get a day off.'*

Though hurt by the barb, Lewandowski's demeanor remained heroically stoic. *'They're only harassing me cuz every damn one of'em knows I'd be the last one to Re–up. They're all sick, just plain sick. That's what war does to the weak minded.'*

Lewandowski had been suffering unrelenting indignities since his appointment as company Re–Enlistiment NCO was pinned to the orderly room bulletin board. It had been terrible to endure the verbal mayhem, but the harassment wasn't his greatest concern. He was beginning to wonder if perhaps Masters might be onto something. *'Am I doomed to Re–Up some dark day when I've lost my senses?'*

"Man, what's taking so long?"

That question was posed by the enquiring mind of Billy Ed—Hillbilly—Burns, a Speck Four from Jackson, Mississippi who received his draft notice the same day he was handed his Masters degree in Physical Anthropology. To his fellow Southerners he was Billy Ed, or just plain Bubba, but the Yankees zeroed in on his accent and his two first names to give him the handle of Hillbilly.

"Hey," Burns shouted to the MPs standing just inside the gate to the vill. "Cain't you guys tell time? It's eight o'clock, already, so open the goddamned gate."

"That's hillbilly time," Lewandowski called out from his place in the line. "My Yankee watch says it ain't eight o'clock yet."

"Yore Yankee watch is as wuthless as the Yankee that's wearin' it," Hillbilly shouted back. "I'm surprised you still know how to use a civilian watch, Lewandowski. I figgered a Re–Up–NCO–Lifer like you has gotta check with the Pentagon before he knows what time it is. SHORT!"

The retort brought whoops of laughter from the other Originals…Yankees and Southerners alike.

"That's tellin' him, Hillbilly," one of the Southerners yelled. "Yer too short to be takin' lip off a Re–up NCO."

"SHORT?" Lewandowski bellowed in retaliation. "Hell, Hillbilly's gonna be my first convert. He's gonna re–up and buy a brand new car when he gets Speck Five! All you Southern shitkickers are alike! You'd sell your souls for a new car and a steady job. You're a Lifer, Hillbilly! You got no future in the real world!"

"Tell it like it is, muh'fuh," Skins agreed. The only white Southerner he could condone was Frenchie Beaumont.

"Wooo!" a rebel Original whooped. "You gonna take that shit, Billy Ed? You gonna let a Lifer Re–Up NCO talk to you that way?"

"Lewandowski done fried his brain snortin' analgesic from jockstraps," Hillbilly shouted back. "You're the one who's found a home in the Army, Lewandowski. Masters' made the right man the Re–Up NCO. Hell, you're OCS material, man. Twenty and out, R.A. All The Way, Airborne–Airborne–Airborne!"

The grab–ass had been hot and heavy since shortly after the Originals began gathering at the gate at 0730 hours. Nobody was taking the jibes seriously…no fights were likely to break out with a day of freedom on the line and a squad of MP's standing just inside the gate. Only a deranged fool would jeopardize a day in the Vill with a temper tantrum.

A platoon of young female entrepreneurs was gathered on the Vill side of the fence, greeting the early customers, flirting with the troops, haggling over the menu of services and prices. Anticipation was rising, time was passing, the gates would be opening at any moment.

If there were going to be a fight, it was likely to break out between the Originals and the in–country vets who were also sharing space in the line. The old dogs of war were outfitted in faded jungle fatigues, and scuffed boots that might as well have been emblazoned with the words short timer. While the Originals came equipped with new jungle fatigues, and jungle boots that advertised their status as green pea fresh from stateside duty. Barely a minute would pass without some young yet grizzled in–country veteran muttering the word "Short" toward the nearest Original.

The encounters with the in–country vets had started early on, when Woody decided to get smart with the MP's as they arrived at the gate to start their duty day. Like MP's everywhere, they were textbook examples of military correctness from their polished helmets to the spitshined toes of their cordova leather jump boots. They could have made General Westmoreland look like a short–timer.

"Lifers," Woody mumbled under his breath, but loud enough for the MP's to get a good beacon on who said it.

The atmosphere abruptly turned arctic cold as the MPs slowly turned to face the long line of Originals. The MP squad leader, a buck sergeant who looked no more than nineteen years old, gave birth to a big smile and nudged the nearest MP in the ribs.

"Man, look at those fatigues. They're all green peas."

The Corporal grinned at the Originals. "Short."

The other MPs made use of the opportunity to add more fuel to the fire. "I DEROS out'a here in fifteen days," one of them bragged.

Yet another continued the return fire. "I ETS with a three month early–out when I hit Fort Lewis two months from now."

"Aw, geeze, thanks for making us all look like a bunch of

jerks," Hanley the morning report clerk grumbled at Woody's back. "We really needed that."

The harassment worsened when the dedicated Vill Rats began to straggle in wearing faded uniforms or strange arrays of civie clothes, styles and colors. Civilian clothes were allowed in the vill as long as the civies weren't too disgraceful, or they weren't mixed with military uniform. But there were no regulations against bad taste...which became the loophole the Vill Rats depended upon to keep them out of harm's way. A dedicated Vill Rat would combine striped Bermuda shorts with a polka dot shirt, green with blue, pink with red, with some wearing neckties over T–shirts. Gaudy silk smoking jackets were particularly in style, often topped by Aussie bush hats worn at cocky angles, advertising a very un–military Esprite de Corps. The end result being a personalized uniform, worn with great pride after long days of olive drab uniformity.

By comparison, the Originals felt very Regular Army (RA) in their new jungle fatigues, caps, and boots.

One of the Vill Rats fell to his knees in the sand and lifted his head skyward to say a prayer. "Oh, Lord, thank you for sending my replacement. Which one is he Lord? Just send a sign, show me which one he is so I can start packing my hold baggage."

Eventually the gates were opened, allowing the Originals to enter, flashing their passes as they passed the MPs. Several of their number were early casualties to nearby cyclo girls, but most found themselves being drawn deeper into the fragrant bowels of the Vill through a meandering network of narrow sand paths, bordered on both sides by hastily erected dens of iniquity.

Lewandowski found himself leading a pack of ten Originals.

"Good Lord, it stinks in here," Charlie complained at Lewandowski's side.

"We need beer, lots of beer," Lewandowski declared confidently, doing his level best not to breathe through his nose. "It won't be so bad once we get a buzz going."

Tantalizing whiffs of cheap perfume mixed with sickly sweet incense were drifting from the doorways of the surrounding bars. Scantily clad girls beckoned seductively, calling out outlandish promises, exposing body parts, challenging the manhood of those who bypassed their particular bar or steambath. Loud stereo systems thumped to the varying beats of rock and roll, country and soul music. The competition for the MPC dollar was fierce and highly specialized in Cam Ranh village.

The Originals learned early on that Green Back dollars were verboten in the Vill. GIs caught passing Green Backs were running the risk of getting busted for dealing on the black market. The currency du jour was MPC—Military Personnel Currency—also known as "funny money" due to the bright colors on the small bills. The second most popular currency was Vietnamese dong, also called Piasters or 'P'.

"Hey, GI. You doan like me, huh? You be cherry boy, I t'ink."

"You got American dollah, I do for you numbah won."

"Make numbah one love, you see. Doan go 'way, you break my heart, I t'ink."

"Hey, GI, you be my boyfrien'?"

…You be my honey."

…You make love to me?"

…Doan have VD, no suweat, GI."

Some of the sirens did have scruples, rules of the road on what they would or would not do to make an honest buck. Lewandowski and his recon platoon were trudging by the doorway of a small bar when a GI was suddenly 86'd by a girl half his size.

"Hey, you go to hell, I t'ink!" she shouted. "Maybe you be cyclo boy, huh? Maybe you doan like girls, huh?"

"You can kiss my ass," the GI shouted back. "You think I'm dingydow or something? I wouldn't poke you with my First Sergeant's dick. It's blow–job or nothin'!"

"Den it notting, GI!" she shouted back at him. "I doan do bow jobs. You wan' bow job, you go see Kim Le!"

Lewandowski continued leading his squad deeper into Cam Ranh village.

"I know where I'm going," he assured them when several tag–alongs threatened to go AWOL in nearby bars. "The best bars are down on the beach. This is clap heaven around here. That GI was right. You'll be down at the dispensary getting your shots within a week if you go skinny dipping in the low rent district."

"Howcum you know so much about it?" Skins asked. Skins had joined Lewandowski's entourage, having decided he would forgive Lewandowski for making him work so hard the past two days.

"A Supply Sergeant at the Depot told me all about it," Lewandowski explained.

"A muh'fuh' Lifer," Skins muttered, summing up his opinion of the reliability of the information source.

"A Lifer who thinks I'm gonna get him an early DEROS," Lewandowski corrected. He halted, motioning the squad into a Top Secret huddle. "We're sitting on a goldmine with this personnel center thing, guys. Lifers listen up when I tell them I'm with the 516th. They know—or they think they know—what we can do for them."

"Like what?" a clerk from the personnel center asked.

"Like getting them an early DEROS," Lewandowski said. "And extra R&R's to places like Honolulu and Bangkok, and bad marks on their records that suddenly disappear. All sorts of things. In return, we get what they have to offer...like cases of USDA Choice steaks and chicken and acres and acres of trucks and jeeps that need a good home."

"Yeah, and we could get an all–expense–paid one–way trip to Camp LBJ," Frenchie warned.

"No," Lewandowski said. "No–no–no–no–no! That's the beauty of it, guys. We run the personnel center, not the Lifers. We know the personnel regs a lot better than they'll ever know them. We work with the regs day in and day out, but all they do is sit at their desks and pretend to know what they're doing. If we know the regs that good, then we can find the loopholes in the regs, right? Think about it. We probably won't even be doing anything illegal. We'll just be using the brains God gave us to find the loopholes in the regulations the Army gave us. Hey, that's as American as apple pie and motherhood," he concluded righteously.

Skins looked confused. "Yeah, but how we gonna get all those muh'fuh' jeeps and trucks back home with us when we DEROS?"

Lewandowski slapped his forehead. "We don't take it *home* with us, Shithead. We use it here, in Cam Ranh, to make our lives a little more comfortable. That's the American Way, Skins. Taking jeeps and trucks home is called stealing. That's UnAmerican."

Skins shrugged. Comfortable in Cam Ranh was nice, but it would be even nicer if he could somehow manage to get a jeep back to the streets of Chi Town. His reputation would be made for life if he could pull that one off.

"Think about it," Lewandowski continued. "Spread the word. We control the personnel center...not the Lifers. We gotta get organized. We're smarter than the Lifers, and we gotta start using those regulations to make life easier. Y'know what I mean?"

The "we" Lewandowski was thinking of began and ended with the Originals working in the personnel center. He would be the deal–maker, the conduit through which all good things would flow.

Charlie changed the subject. "I don't care about jeeps and early DEROSes. I just wanna get laid."

"Yeah, man," Frenchie chimed in, using a particularly thick Cajun accent he used whenever he was getting upset. "Why you keepin' us walkin', Lewandowski? We got plenty of Marie–couche–toi–la for all of us. Why you being such a chinois about this?"

"That better not be an insult," Lewandowski growled.

"Quelle Chierie!" Frenchie answered.

"What's that mean?"

"I was just saying I want a beer, that's all, man."

"It better be all. Someday I'm gonna buy a Cajun dictionary," Lewandowski grumbled.

"Connerie," Frenchie grumbled back at him.

Lewandowski let it pass. It was time to do a little serious shop-ping, anyway. He wanted one of those fancy smoking jackets for himself. He paused a short distance from a vending stall, one of many that were manned by old men or women with teeth and gums stained a diseased blood red from chewing betelnut. Most of the products offered at the stalls were the usual war zone tourist trash. Tacky black velvet paintings of absurdly proportioned naked women were particularly popular, or equally absurd black velvet battle scenes emblazoned with unit insignia. Aussie bush hats were a big seller, along with lingerie for the wives and girlfriends back home, Chinese condoms, warm cans of black market PX soft drinks, cheap transistor radios, PX potato chips, cheese puffs, Spam and Japanese watches. It was a wonder that the Cam Ranh PXs had any inventory to sell after the black market had taken its cut of the merchandize entering the port of Cam Ranh.

Smoking jackets were always on prominent display, usually hanging from ropes draped along the top of the booths, or dangling from hooks and nails in artful disorder. A large portion of the silk smoking jackets displayed the same boldly embroidered message for all the world to behold.

YEA, THO I WALK THROUGH THE VALLEY
OF THE SHADOW OF DEATH
I SHALL FEAR NO EVIL
FOR I AM THE MEANEST
SONOFABITCH IN THE VALLEY

It was a message that could be found on everything from wall hangings to Zippo lighters. Certifiably stupid GIs could even have the message tattooed on their bodies with unsterilized needles.

"We need to get some of those jackets so's we look a little less RA around this place," Lewandowski suggested to the others. "The way it is, we're sticking out like sore thumbs."

"I vote we go for beer first," Charlie suggested.

Lewandowski continued his sales pitch. "Now, wait a second. You know as well as me that we're not about to do any shopping once we get into a bar. And look at it this way, we'll be able to haggle a better deal if we all pitch in together and make an offer they can't refuse. I'll bet we can even save enough money to get laid for free. Now, how's that sound? Volume pricing, and we get our tubes cleaned. It can't get any better than that, and it won't take five minutes to get it handled. Look at that old guy over there. He ain't got customer one."

Everybody looked at the old man Lewandowski was nodding toward. He had no customers and not many more teeth, with the remaining few teeth stained by betelnut. He was a living skeleton, unkempt and soiled from toe to topknot, with an unfiltered cigarette dangling from his stained lips. He looked simply awful, a corpse that refused to accept its own demise; a man who was in desperate need of a volume sale.

"Well, what'cha think?" Lewandowski asked.

When none disagreed, Lewandowski seized the initiative. "Okay, I'll haggle him down as low as I can on one for me, then I'll make him a Take–It–Or–Leave–It offer for all of us. We all buy, or we all walk."

All eyes were on Lewandowski as he approached the old man with practiced nonchalance.

The old man, who was squatting on a blue oil drum plainly marked "PROPERTY OF THE UNITED STATES AIR FORCE," removed a small silver smoking pipe from his shirt pocket, along with a Zippo lighter that proclaimed he was the meanest sonofabitch in the valley. He lit the pipe and puffed three times before returning the Zippo and the pipe to his pocket, seemingly unaware of Lewandowski's approach.

Lewandowski began thumbing through the smoking jackets hanging from a clothesline running around the top of the stall, inspecting several before landing on one that came within six inches of closing over his belly. It was iridescent purple, with black lapels quilted by white thread. A Huey helicopter gunship was embroidered on the back, with the helicopter shooting down a flying dragon with a wispy beard that made it look a lot like old Ho Chi Minh. The words below the battle scene said that the owner of the jacket feared no evil because he was the meanest sonofabitch in the valley.

Lewandowski glanced at the old man from the corner of his eye.

The old man ignored Lewandowski.

"How much money?" Lewandowski asked.

The old man glanced at the jacket. "Two tousan', five hun'red 'p'," he answered unflinchingly. One MPC dollar would buy 118 'P', so the jacket was a little over twenty dollars in funny money.

The old man's voice wasn't carrying to the others, so Lewandowski shouted the price for their benefit. "Two thousand, five hundred 'p'?"

The old man glanced briefly at the big loudmouth GI and the distant group of GI's, his face expressionless.

Lewandowski winked at his investors group and bellowed: "I'll give you One thousand 'p'."

The old man removed the pipe from his pocket again and re–lit the contents, taking two more quick puffs before returning the pipe to his pocket. Lewandowski crinkled his nose when the wisps of smoke drifted by. The aroma was thick and sweet, unlike any tobacco he had smelled before.

"Two tousan' four hun'red 'p'," the old man answered quietly.

Lewandowski grinned. He had the old man on the run now. "One tousan' one hun'red 'p'," he countered, thinking he might wrangle a better deal if he used Cam Ranh–style English. He continued to wear the smoking jacket, thinking of it as his own now that the haggling was seriously under way.

Lewandowski and Skins were arguing back and forth as they waded through the littered sand boulevard that bordered the water-front high–rent district of the vill.

"Hey, we got a good buy, so quit your bitchin'," Lewandowski said. "We paid half what he wanted for these jackets. He started at twenty–five, but we got'em for twelve–fifty."

"Yeah, great buy, man," Skins said sourly. "Mine's too muh'fuh' big and yours is too muh'fuh' small."

The beach bars were to their left, perched over the lapping waters of the South China Sea on wooden poles that looked far too fragile for the loads they were being asked to bear. To their right were more of the smaller, tackier tourist traps meant for GIs without discrimiating tastes. The beach bars were somewhat larger than the inland bars, with several extending more than a hundred feet into the lapping waters of the fragrant bay. Their signs advertised familiar names, such as the Dallas Club, the San Francisco Club, the Maverick, the California Club, the Chicago Club, the New Yorker; with the names of a few commonly known Vietnamese cities thrown in to give some balance to the infusion of Americana.

"Where else you gonna spend your money over here?" Lewandowski asked, still arguing over the jackets with Skins.

"I can think of lots of ways to spend my muh'fuh' money over here," Skins said defensively.

Charlie Edwards and Frenchie were wading through the sand a short distance ahead. Both were wearing Meanest Sonofabitch smoking jackets, but the similarities ended there. Charlie's jacket had white cuffs and lapels, with royal blue piping around the edge. Frenchie's had a scarlet and blue floral pattern, with black velvet lapels bordered by white piping.

Charlie had his eye on a beach bar just ahead, drawn by a sign that advertised it as the Saigon Club. Charlie was the type who preferred to experience the intrigue of Southeast Asia, though he suspected the Saigon Club was likely to be little different from the New York Club or the California Club.

He shouted back to the others. "I'm hot as hell and dry as a bone. It's time for some shade and a brewski."

The others followed him up wooden steps leading onto a veranda porch opening into the the Saigon Club. At the top of the stairs, under the roofed porch, they were greeted by a slender girl who shouted something into the club in the sing song pattern of Vietnamese. Seconds later, the Originals were being led inside by an equal number of hostesses wearing big smiles and the briefest of mini–skirts.

The slender girl took Lewandowski's arm as she guided her guests to an unoccupied section of the bar, where small tables and plastic chairs were quickly moved together to create ample room for all of the Originals. She again spoke to the other girls, several of whom seemed to be new at the profession...On The Job Trainees. The Originals were made comfortable in the plastic chairs before Lewandowski's hostess got down to business.

"You want beer now?" she asked.

"Sure," the Originals agreed.

"Make sure it's good'n'cold," Lewandowski added.

"You buy drink for girls, too?" she asked.

"Sure, why not?"

The girls headed for the small service bar in the back of the club, where they conducted business with an old woman who, in turn, gave directions to the bartender, another bargirl who was currently without a customer.

"Man, this is the life," Charlie said as he absorbed the ambiance, figuring he had made a good selection for his fellow Originals. The club had wide front windows offering an unfettered view of the inland clubs and the littered magnificence of beach boulevard. More windows were stationed along both sides, offering views of neighboring beachfront bars. The front area could easily seat sixty or seventy without overcrowding. A Buddhist shrine, surrounded by photographs of pretty young women, occupied the left, rear corner of the front room, not far from a doorway in the rear wall. The doorway opened onto a hallway lined by curtained entrances, with about six feet of wallspace allotted to each curtained room. Further back, an open porch extended the club another thirty feet over the waters of the bay.

An old woman filled the orders at the service bar. Only four other GIs were in the Saigon Club at the time, two at one table, with the other two at a more distant table. All the GIs had girls sitting on their laps, with sweating cans of PX Schlitz beer perched on the small tables situated in front of them. A quality PX stereo system provided the music, with the volume turned up to a semi–irritating level, playing WHITE RABBIT by the Jefferson Airplane. Two of the distant hostesses seemed to be enjoying themselves as they flirted with their customers, but the two girls further away looked as bored and vacant as their two GI customers, one of which had a short timer swagger stick sitting on the table in front of him.

The girls returned with the beer for the Originals and a variety of drinks for themselves.

Lewandowski's hostess continued to be the woman in charge. "You pay girls now," she directed her guests.

"What's the damage?" Lewandowski asked, reaching for his hip pocket, figuring he would spring for the first round.

"One hun'red 'p' for beer for you, six hun'red 'p' for Saigon Tea for girl," she explained.

Lewandowski's mouth dropped open. "Whoa. That's more than five bucks for your drink."

She shrugged unapologetically and held held out her hand for payment. "Sorry 'bout that, GI. Ever'body gotta live, y'know."

Lewandowski got out his wallet. He wouldn't be springing for any rounds at those prices. "It's highway robbery, if you ask me." he grumbled under his breath as he dished out MPC notes. "I'm paying a buck for a can of beer that'd cost me a half a buck back home in the world, plus another five bucks for tea, fer godsakes."

The girls collected the money and delivered it to the old woman at the service bar. A moment later they returned, full of flirtatious giggles as they took their places on the laps of the Originals.

"My name is Sally," the girl on Lewandowski's lap announced, and then began introducing the others. There were two Suzies, one Anh, two Kims and several who had Vietnamese names. None of the girls could be described as beautiful, but they were pretty and available.

"Now you tell us your names, okay," Sally said to the Originals.

The girls snuggled a bit closer when they had names to work with, now having passed the Getting–To–Know–You stage.

"You new to Vietnam, huh?" Sally asked Lewandowski.

"Don't remind us," Lewandowski groaned.

Sally laughed. "You doan like Vietnam, huh?"

Her laugh was pleasant enough to draw a smile from Lewandowski, who was still simmering about the prices being charged. "Aw, it's not so bad, I guess. Not as good as America, but not so bad either."

"Not so bad in Cam Ranh, I t'ink, " Sally corrected. "VC doan come here. Too many GI. Not so good outside Cam Ranh. Beau ceau people die alla time. Numbah ten, I t'ink."

Lewandowski nodded. "Maybe so," he said.

Lewandowski examined Sally more closely, deciding she was prettier than most other girls he'd seen that day. He figured she must be eighteen, nineteen years old; certainly not much more than that. He patted her on the hip and she giggled invitingly. Slyly, he edged the hem of her dress up enough to reveal black lace bikini panties. A long moment later, when he had gotten an eyeful, she clucked her tongue disapprovingly and pulled the hem down again while snuggling closer, brushing his cheek with her lips.

Sally whispered into Lewandowski's ear, inspiring a broad, lecherous grin.

"Alright, that's what I wanna hear," Lewandowski said with his grin growing wider.

The other girls seemed to be following Sally's lead. They too snuggled closer while whispering sweet business propositions to their guests. Romantic preliminaries had to take a back seat to the realities of productivity requirements.

Lewandowski whispered in Sally's ear and she answered by spanking his cheek affectionately. "No, I doan t'ink you can do that," she giggled, then gave his cheek another quick kiss. The snuggling and whispering continued until Sally took the initiative by rising from Lewandowski's lap, taking his hand in hers.

"Come, we go make love," she said with a sweetly lewd wink.

"We got some business to attend to," Lewandowski announced to the other Originals, sporting a grin so wide he could have swallowed the state of Rhode Island. "We'll see you when we get back. Don't send out search parties," he added with a wink that wasn't intended to be coy.

"He won't be gone long," Charlie predicted sourly, not impressed by Lewandowski's theatre.

Sally led Lewandowski to a cubicle midway along the right side of the rear hallway, where she pushed aside a flimsy curtain, ushering her client into her home and place of business.

Lewandowski paused at the doorway to issue a challenge to his fellow Originals before following Sally. "Are you guys just gonna sit there, or what? You ain't got hair one if you don't ride the slippery slough before we head back to tent city."

The gauntlet had been cast and within moments all but one of the Originals allowed themselves to be led into the back rooms. All except Charlie Edwards, who clumsily communicated that he needed to visit his cousin John before doing anything. Moments later he found himself standing in a closet–sized cubicle in the rear of the club, looking down through a hole in the floorboards at the lapping waters of Cam Ranh Bay. There he taried a reasonable length of time before returning to the front room, along the way overhearing a variety of sound effects as he passed the curtained rooms. He wasn't altogether comfortable with getting laid in such a public fashion, but his reputation was on the line. So he allowed his hostess to lead him to her own small room, where he exchanged 500 'p' for a half'n'half.

Over the next several minutes, the Originals slowly returned to the bar area, where they exchanged the predictable critiques. *'Hey, I really needed that. Got my tubes cleaned. Man, I feel ten pounds lighter.'*

Skins Williams was playing it cooler than cool, saying nary a word as he slouched comfortably into a chair beside Frenchie. He was just about to break his silence with an understated reference to his performance a few minutes earlier when he sniffed once...then twice. Finally, he nudged Frenchie in the elbow.

"Muh'fuh', smell that, man."

Frenchie sniffed and shrugged. "Yeah? So?"

"Man, that's reefer," Skins whispered urgently. "Someone's smokin' weed, man. It's gotta be comin' from one'a the back rooms."

Frenchie shrugged. "I didn't smell nothin'."

"Yeah, well I can sure 'muh'fuh' smell it," Skins assured him.

Frenchie sniffed again. "Man, I can't smell nothin' over the stink."

Skins glanced around the bar, noting the absence of the two bored GIs, along with their equally bored girlfriends. "I think I got it figured out, man. Jes sit tight. I gotta play this cool."

A moment later, the GI's and their hostesses returned to the bar area from the back rooms. The girls continued to the service bar as the GIs resuming their seats.

Skins rose from his chair, telling his girl to wait for him, that he'd be right back.

"Watch out for Sid," Frenchie warned, meaning to keep an eye peeled for the undercover MP's that specialized in the kind of crime that Skins was hoping to commit. "If they bust your ass, it'll be Camp LBJ."

"I'll be cool 'bout it,"Skins assured him, then began walking casually toward the distant table, arriving just as the girls returned with fresh cans of beer. The GI's glanced up with heavy–lidded curiosity. One of the girls had a small belly bulge indicating she was drinking, eating and smoking for two.

"Okay if a brother join you?" Skins asked.

The GI with the short timer stick looked Skins up and down a long moment before shrugging. The other GI seemed not to care either way, so Skins pulled up a chair and sat down. His opening was vague enough to allow denial, should the two GI's be Sid agents.

"I was hoping you could give me some advice," Skins said, keeping his voice low.

"Advice?" the short timer asked. His accent was heavy with south Bronx. "What'cho mean by advice?"

"Like, maybe, where could I go to score some good weed?" Skins spoke in a near whisper, his eyes darting around the room to see if anyone might be eavesdropping.

The GI's exchanged brief glances.

"Nope, never touch the stuff," the short timer answered.

Skins nodded. The answer was to be expected.

"What unit you with?" the other asked.

"The 516th AG," Skins answered.

"Never heard of it."

"We're new in–country," Skins explained, his enunciation more clear and crisp than it would be around the Originals, being not yet sure of himself. "We'll be running the new personnel center, starting tomorrow."

The two inspected his uniform with a brief glance, noting the fresh green color.

"I'm not a Sid," Skins offered. "I'm just a brother looking for a little score, that's all. I could show you my I.D. card, if you want."

The short timer shook his head. "Like I told you before, man. I don't know nothin' about scorin' dope. I'm too short to be messing with that shit."

Skins rose from his chair. "Hey, I'm sorry for the hassle, man. I can dig what you're saying."

"No problem. I wish I could help you, man, but I can't."

Skins returned to Frenchie. "Well, at least I know they're not Sid. They wouldn't give me the time of day."

"I'll bet Sally knows where we can score," Frenchie suggested. "She seems to be the honcho around here."

"I don't know, man," Skins said. "That old woman at the bar is handling all the money. I bet she's the honcho."

"Check with Sally when she gets back," Frenchie advised.

A moment later, Lewandowski and Sally rejoined the others.

"I feel a whoooole lot better now," Lewandowski assured all while Sally went to the old woman for another round of beer and Saigon Tea. "That was the best five bucks I ever spent."

Skins changed the subject. "Hey, Lew…you mind if I talk to your old lady for a minute in private?"

Lewandowski shrugged. "Ask her, not me. We ain't engaged."

Skins approached Sally at the service bar, pulling her aside to talk in low tones. A moment later he reached for his wallet and pressed a five–dollar MPC note into the palm of her hand. Skins returned to his seat as Sally disappeared down the hallway.

"What was that all about?" Lewandowski asked.

"You'll see," Skins promised, being cool, a man who was in control of the situation.

"Where's my beer?" Lewandowski reminded him. "You could'a brought it back with ya, y'know."

"Hey, muh' fuh', that's yer old lady's job, not mine," Skins answered. "Just hol' yor muh'fuh' horses, man. She be back, she be back."

Sally returned a moment later and sat the drinks on the table—"Saigon tea for me, beer for you,"—before leaning over to press something into the left hip pocket of Skins' jungle fatigue shirt.

"Well, are you happy now?" Lewandowski asked Skins as Sally resumed her place on his lap.

Skins winked at Sally. "All set." Another thought occurred to him. "Hey, uh, how much should somethin' like this cost?" He asked Sally, pressing smooth the collar of his smoking jacket, looking both swave and deboner.

"Yeah, tell him what the real world is like," Lewandowski chimed in.

Sally shrugged. "Maybe five hun'red 'p'. How much you pay?"

Skins gave Lewandowski a dirty look. "Twelve muh'fuh' dollars and fifty cents MPC," he muttered with a final glaring shot at Lewandowski.

Sally clucked her tongue disapprovingly. "Sorry 'bout that, GI. You pay too much money for same."

Lewandowski came to his own defense. "Yeah, but look at the quality of these jackets. We didn't buy the cheap stuff. This is real silk, not some crummy imitation."

Sally smiled and took a small sip of her diluted drink. "Alla same," she said. "Very cheap. Look okay for now—numbah one—but very soon it be numbah ten; no good. You listen to Sally, next time you doan pay so much."

"Next time I do my own muh'fuh' hagglin'," Skins grumbled.

Sally moved on to the next item of business. "You have house-girl yet?" she asked Lewandowski.

"Housegirl?" he repeated. "No have housegirl. What you mean housegirl?"

"Housegirl that wash clothes for you, make beds, keep ever'ting clean and nice for you. That kinda housegirl. Do you have same? Alla GI in Cam Ranh have housegirl. And Vietnamee KP, too. Men who clean messhall for you."

"No have housegirl," Lewandowski repeated sourly. "No have KP, either. Maybe alla GI in Cam Ranh have housegirl, but they don't have Lt. Masters running the show."

"I can get same for you," Sally said brightly. "Doan cost you very much. Maybe two t'ousand 'p' for one month, and she do ever'ting for you."

"Everything?" Lewandowski asked with a wicked grin.

Sally patted his cheek. "Not what you are t'inking now. You come see Sally for dat. You doan wan' housegirl to make love to you, dingydow. Make too much trouble for you. Pretty soon ever'body be mad at each other, act dingydow, get in figh'. I know. I see happen before. You want housegirl do only clean for you."

Charlie had returned just in time to hear Sally's sales pitch. "Talk to Masters about it, Lew. Tell him it'll be a morale booster for the troops."

"Yeah," Frenchie agreed. "Ask him how he can expect you to get us to Re–up if we don't have housegirls and KP's. You're the Re–up NCO, man. Its your job to tell him stuff like that."

Charlie the psychologist had more to say. "You can do it, Lew.

Masters likes you. Why else would he make you Supply Sergeant, give you Speck Four and make you the Re–up NCO?"

Charlie grinned, relishing the ironies.

"Yeah, right," Lewandowski growled dryly. "The guy loves me. With friends like that...."

"Yeah, man," Frenchie interrupted. "He'll do it, if you play your cards right. Like you said before, we're smarter than the Lifers. You been to college, Lew. Play with his mind a little. Make him think it's his idea."

Lewandowski's expression became vacant, indicating he was deep in thought. "Yeah, maybe you're right, Frenchie. He'll nix it for sure if it's my idea, but he'll order me to do it if he thinks it's his idea. That's the way his mind works. It makes sense to me now; I've been playing him all wrong. I've been reacting to his moves when I should have been faking him out, making him react to *my* moves. Oh, man, it's a whole new ballgame now. Masters is predictable. He's like an offensive lineman who blinks just before the ball is hiked."

Lewandowski smiled as confidence flowed into cranial spaces that held only despair moments before. "I gotta put some thought into this. I can't be telegraphing my moves. I've gotta keep him off balance, make him think I'll pull to the left when I pull to the right. It seems so simple now."

"Look at him, gentlemen," Charlie advised the others. "Genius at work."

"Yeah, man," Skins agreed, though the football analogies were meaningless to him. His knowledge came from the streets, not the gridiron.

"Things are gonna change around tent city," Lewandowski predicted, holding up his beefy hand to be slapped by the others. A high school football cheer was echoing in his mind, harking him back to a past moment of glory.

LEWANDOWSKI, HE'S OUR MAN.
IF LEW CAN'T DO IT, NO ONE CAN.

The Originals began straggling back to tent city just minutes before 1800 hours, when the gates to the vill were closed for the night. Sergeant Lugo and the dozen or so unlucky KP's for the day had cold cuts and bread waiting in the mess tent, a low–maintenance meal that was much appreciated. After chow, Lewandowski and Edwards climbed up the sand dune to the movie projection booth, ready to show a flick when the sun went down. The whitewashed eight–by–sixteen–foot plywood movie screen continued to be enough of a novelty to draw large crowds regardless of the movie being shown. Tonight it would be THE GREEN BERETS, staring John Wayne. It was the second time in a week that Special Services had issued THE GREEN BERETS. The Lifers tended to take the plot seriously, but the Originals heckled the actors mercilessly, shouting "Lifer" and "FTA" so often that it was difficult to follow the dialogue.

After the flick, Skins waited for Lewandowski and Charlie to rewind the film before joining them at the projection booth.

"Hey, man. Why don't we take a little walk up the hill and see what's happening out in the boonies?"

"I already know what's happening," Lewandowski said. "People are getting blown away in living color, and it's starting to get depressing, Skins. I think I'll take a pass tonight. Maybe I'll do a little reading in the supply tent."

Skins held out one closed hand to Lewandowski. "I got something special for us, man. Something you'll like." He dropped a fat hand–rolled cigarette into Lewandowski's palm, saying nothing more.

Lewandowski hadn't ever smoked marijuana, but he knew enough to figure out what was in the hand rolled cigarette.

"You know what it is, don't'cha?" Skins asked.

Lewandowski nodded. "Yup."

"Wanna try some?"

"Sure, why not? What's it gonna do, kill me?"

"No, man," Skins said. "It won't kill you. It'll just put things in proper perspective for awhile. The little stuff won't matter so much."

"Me, too?" Charlie asked.

"Sure, man," Skins nodded. "Frenchie's coming, too. There should be plenty for all of us."

The four of them climbed to the crest of the dune and headed for a remote patch of waist–high grass. They weren't alone on the hilltop. Groups of Originals were scattered about, with small points of light being passed from man to man.

When they were settled into a small circle, Skins lit the joint and took a deep drag before passing it on to Lewandowski, who took another deep hit before passing it to Charlie, who took his turn and passed it to Frenchie. The joint went around three times before it was burned to a nub too small to be handled with bare fingers. Skins carefully shredded the nub and scattered the remnants into the soft breeze. Nineteen more joints remained in the baggy Sally had slipped into his pocket. Unlike others who weren't as streetwise as Skins, he would keep the baggy away from his bunk and foot locker. It would be hidden in the sand nowhere near the tent he shared with eleven other Originals.

Charlie watched as napalm blossoms formed in the dark, distant hills. When he spoke, his voice sounded remote and hazy. "I never figured it would be so pretty. The war, I mean. It doesn't seem right somehow for it to be that pretty."

Lewandowski nodded, sharing the sentiment. His head felt heavy. He wished he could just roll over, fall asleep on the sand and wake up back in Studio City. "I'm glad I'm not out there," he said quietly. "I don't know if I could handle it. Maybe I'd shoot myself in the foot or something. Maybe I'd go for a Section Eight. I know I sure as hell wouldn't wanna get blown away for a place like this."

"You'd do just what those guys are doing right now," Frenchie predicted. "You'd be taking it a day at a time."

"Maybe," Lewandowski said. "I'd like to think I could handle it alright, but maybe I wouldn't. Maybe they got something inside them that I don't have. I almost wish we'd get hit here in Cam Ranh so I'd find out what I'd do."

"Don't talk muh'fuh'trash," Skins warned. "It could happen, man, if you keep talkin' like that. Keep the Vee–ET Cong out there. I don't care if I never see 'em up close."

"They've no place to run," Charlie said as he imagined himself being one of the troops who were depending on napalm strikes to keep them alive. "They're surrounded until they DEROS. It makes me wonder…what makes one guy a hero while most of us take the easy way out. Is is something we got inside us, or is it a matter of time and place and circumstance?"

"Damn, there he goes with twenty–dollar words again," Skins said.

"Sheesh," Frenchie complained. "Leave it up to Edwards to come up with a question like that. You had too much college, man. You've pickled your brains with bullshit."

"This is the *real* question," Skins said. "You wanna trade places with those dudes, or you wanna stay right here in Cam Rahn? Anything else is just mu'fuh' shuck and jive, man. Forget all that stuff about time and place and circumstance, whatever the hell that means. If you really wanna know what you'd do under fire, you'd put in a 1049 requesting duty as a rifleman with the 101st or the 1st Cav. Otherwise, stop talkin' trash. Like I said before, you keep talkin' muh'fuh' trash, and it just might happen."

"Yeah, don't drive yourself crazy thinking about it," Frenchie added.

Lewandowski rolled over to dig his elbows into the sand and spotted another hotspot across the bay. His eyelids felt heavy. "The Army sucks," he concluded.

"FTA," Skins and Charlie agreed.

Frenchie was beginning to wonder about the precarious position they were in. The possibilities for discovery on the dune crest were mushrooming in his drug addled cranium. What if a Lifer had seen them smoke the joint…or maybe an Original who would turn snitch to save his butt from Camp LBJ? He glanced over both shoulders to see what could be seen, and saw nothing, which made him all the more suspicious because he had expected to see joints being passed around in the other groups. His fears were multiplying. What if a company of MP's suddenly attacked their hilltop position? What if Skins is actually a Sid agent?

Like the songs says, *'Paranoia strikes deep. Into the heart it will creep. It begins when you're always afraid. Step out'a line, the man come and take you away.'*

Lewandowski nodded off, curling into a fetal position.

After a few minutes, Charlie stood to make an announcement.

"Lew's right. This is depressing. I'm gonna get some shut eye in the supply tent."

Charlie disappeared into the darkness.

Frenchie wondered if Charlie would return leading a marauding platoon of Sid agents.

Most of the Originals were already in their tents. Some would be trying to sleep despite the glaring light bulbs dangling from the tent poles, while others would be reading or writing letters home or occupying a chair in one of the ongoing poker games. Radios would be tuned to the Armed Forces Radio Network; stereos would be playing conflicting styles of music, annoying those who weren't fans of the style that dominated that particular moment in time and space.

The Charge of Quarters would start making his rounds soon, switching off the lights, telling everyone to hit the sack. "Orders from Cap'n Ortega," he would explain. "He wants everyone bright–eyed and bushy–tailed when we open the personnel center for business tomorrow."

The war would take on a more personal face when the Originals began processing the personnel records for the troops in and around Cam Ranh. There would be the mundane transactions for the replacements, and the DEROS paperwork for those who would be heading back to The World. But there would also be KIA and WIA paperwork transactions too, for those who were killed or wounded in action. At first it wouldn't be so bothersome, but after a time, the clerks who handled the personnel records for companies with high casualty rates would find themselves glancing at the ID photographs when they transferred a 201 file to a field hospital or graves registration. It would become almost an obligatory ritual for some of the clerks. After all, the guy deserved to be noticed, didn't he? Surely it wouldn't be right to just ship his file off to graves registration without even taking the time to see what he looked like. I'd want someone to do that for me. Wouldn't you?

Before long, the nightly visits to the dunes would offer unwanted clues about which records clerks would be particularly busy the next day.

Frenchie stood, "I'm goin' to my bunk," and departed.

Skins pondered Lewandowski's fate as Frenchie disappeared

into the darkness. "Maaan, what am I gonna do with you? Muh'fuh', wake up, Lew. Wake up, man."

He shook Lewandowski's shoulder. "C'mon, man. Wake up."

But Lewandowski remained dead to the world.

"Wake up, man. You can't sleep out here."

No response.

Skins considered his options before forcing himself to make his way back to his tent, which had evolved into a mecca for the more serious poker players. There he rummaged around in his footlocker until locating the small red travel clock his mother gave him before he went to Basic Training, unaware that the last thing a recruit needed was an alarm clock.

One of the poker players looked up when Skins started heading back outside again. "Where you goin', man? It's almost lights out."

"Lew's crashed on the hill, man. I'm gonna give him this so he don't sleep through reveille tomorrow morning."

"Do what'choo want, man. It ain't none'a my business."

"That's muh'fuh' right, it ain't."

Back on the hilltop he placed the alarm clock near Lewandowski's head and was about to head downhill when a breath of cooling breeze drifted by.

"Man, that felt good," he told himself, recalling the stale, smoke-filled heat back at the tent. "Maybe you got the right idea, man," and began kicking the sand into a comfortable bed for himself.

"It's just like camping out," Skins assured himself before lying down with the alarm clock between himself and Lewandowski.

The lights in tent city were being turned off as the CQ moved from tent to tent. "Lights out. We got a long day ahead of us tomorrow. Lights out."

Puff The Magic Dragon was making strafing runs along the perimeter, his mini-guns roaring, raining down solid streamers of orange-red fire on a Viet Cong position. This Puff wasn't a gentle rascal who loved to play with a little boy named Jackie. He was a C-130 that could place 20mm cannon rounds precisely on whatever target was below.

Skins nodded off to the comforting roar of Puff's mini-guns.

In war, one man's worst enemy was likely to be another man's best friend.

Chapter Five

Masters was nodding appreciatively, displaying a preciously rare good mood. He was standing beside Lewandowski on the crest of the sand dune overlooking the movie screen. Below them lay the olive drab magnificence of tent city. Lewandowski and his crew had done well.

"It looks good," Masters said. "Very good. Outstanding job, Lewandowski."

Lewandowski was beaming with pride. Tent city had matured into something much more than the typical sterile company area. It had a homey ambiance all its own, becoming so comfortable that it was almost civilian. Even from a distance, tent city had a lived-in personalized side to its military orderliness. Fallible men lived in tent city, not by-the-book sterile military automatons stripped of human emotions.

The troop tents were arranged into two rows of tent tents each, with the supply tent situated at the far end of the rearmost row. Each tent had room for twelve troops, with one standard issue canvas cot, wall locker and foot locker for each of each man, with ten or twelve troops assigned to every tent. Inside every troop tent, there could be found a diminutive PX refrigerator filled to capacity with PX beer and soft drinks.

The central boardwalk between the two rows was rigidly Regular Army uniform, with no personalized decorations, but all that changed where the tent flaps faced outward toward the two perimeter boardwalks. There the military uniformity gave way to the creative minds of the Originals. Even the NCOs had personalized the two tents they occupied. Several of the tents had screened porches, with picket fences and patios being commonplace, providing cozy little porches where the troops could lounge away the evening hours on aluminum lawn chairs purchased at the Cam Rahn PX. Every tent had been christened with a name that was proudly displayed in hand lettered signs hanging above the tent flaps. There was a Chi Town, a Big Apple, a California Dreamin', a Memphis East, a short timer City, and—of course—there was a Cam Ranh Hilton. The interiors of the tents had been decorated with a variety of tourist trash from the Vill, so each had a style and character all its own. Tent city was more than a company area; it was a home.

Lewandowski was wondering if perhaps this might be the right time to raise the subject of housegirls. Masters had approved the hiring of two aging Vietnamese men—Poppasan and Stoned Poppasan—as permanent KPs, but the subject of housegirls had yet to be breached.

"Yup, tent city is looking good," Lewandowski agreed, cautiously approaching the housegirl objective at an oblique angle.

"Yup, Sir," Masters corrected automatically.

"Yes, Sir," Lewandowski answered with uncharacteristic enthusiasm. "It's just too darned bad the troops are such complainers. To hear them talk, tent city ain't such a great place to be."

An undeniably pregnant pause followed.

"Oh…really?" Masters asked testily.

"Aw, Sir, you know how these guys are," Lewandowski said consolingly. "If you give'em an inch, they want a foot. Forget I said anything. It's so chickenshit I shouldn't even be bringing it up."

Masters wasn't smiling now. His good mood had vaporized, destroyed by a thick cloud of innuendo. "That's your job, Lewandowski. If there's a morale problem, I want to know about it, even if you think it is chickenshit."

"Yes, Sir. But I think you'll agree with me when you hear what it is, though."

"That's up to me to decide," Masters corrected, clipping his consonants the way he had been taught in Infantry OCS at Fort Benning, Georgia, also known as Fort Benning School For Boys. At Benning School For Boys he also learned a commanding officer should never shout 'Ten–hut!' when placing a formation at the position of Attention. A Tin Hut is a wall locker, and any officer candidate who made the mistake of shouting 'Ten Hut!' would find himself calling out commands to a wall locker, or a tree all night long…or until the tree or wall locker responded to the commands, whichever came first. As in, 'Tree, About Face! Tree, Forward March! Tree, Present Arms!'

"Yes, Sir. You're absolutely right," Lewandowski agreed,

sounding properly contrite, having been put in his proper place by his courageous commanding officer. "I should've told you about this sooner."

"Stop stalling," Masters ordered. "Just tell me what the problem is."

Lewandowski sighed. "Well, Sir, I guess some of the guys have been talking to troops in other units that have housegirls who keep everything nice and clean....and inspection–ready, Sir. Now they think they're getting the shaft because we don't have any. They do have a point though, in that we've been having problems with the Cam Ranh laundry. We don't always get back what we send in. But if we had housegirls, the laundry would be done right here. Nothing would get lost or stolen."

"Housegirls," Masters mused. "Officer's billets have housegirls, Lewandowski. Not Enlisted Men's quarters. This is the Army, not a resort hotel."

"Yes, Sir. That's just about what I told'em. Like I said, Sir, it would sound really chickenshit when you heard it."

Masters inspected Lewandowski for a long moment, wondering why his reluctant Supply Sergeant would ever be taking the side of the United States Army. It wasn't just the subject at hand, Lewandowski had been annoyingly cooperative in just about everything the past few days. He wasn't coming up with the long list of excuses he usually had at hand. He had been responding to orders with a "Yes, Sir" and get right on it. The old Lewandowski was becoming no more than a fond memory. The old Lewandowski was fun to order around...the new Lewandowski was boring.

"You say the other units have these housegirls?" Masters asked.

"Yes, Sir. That's what the troops are saying."

The old Lewandowski would have said 'guys', not troops, and Masters would have had the fun of correcting him. He was still having trouble with his 'Sirs', but even his lapses in military etiquette were happening less frequently.

"Maybe it isn't such a chickenshit complaint then," Masters mused, finding pleasure in finding fault with Lewandowski's reasoning.

"Sir?" Lewandowski asked, sounding confused.

Masters smiled. He enjoyed confusing Lewandowski. "I believe in treating my troops fairly. And I believe in uniformity. If the troops in other units have housegirls, then I want my troops to have housegirls, too. Particularly if it's creating a morale problem that could spill over into efficiency problems at the personnel center. Normally I'd laugh at the idea, but I'll check into it...make some phone calls. If what you say is true about the other units, I'll give it my approval."

"That's very generous of you, Sir," Lewandowski said, standing a bit straighter as he made the compliment.

Masters accepted the accolade without comment, recalling the motto of Fort Benning School For Boys: Follow Me. An officer should always lead by example.

But he did see one cloud on the horizon. "How do we find the housegirls, IF I give my approval? But I suppose I could ask around about that, too."

"Well, Sir, the guys tell me there's a bargirl in the vill who can make the arrangements. The housegirls charge each guy two thousand 'p' a month to take care of everything, including sweeping the floors, washing the uniforms, making the bunks. They do the whole nine yards, Sir."

Masters was back on guard. Lewandowski's response was too quick, too well informed, to be spontaneous. Plus, he once again referred to the troops as 'guys'. The old Lewandowski was still alive and well, camoflaged by only a thin veneer of military propriety. It was a thought that Masters found comforting. The months ahead would be infinitely more interesting if Lewandowski remained a challenge.

"Why don't you check on that for me," Masters suggested. "If it's true, I'll have you make the arrangements."

"Yes, Sir. I'd be glad to take care of it," Lewandowski offered respectfully.

Masters nodded, knowing he had been outflanked on the housegirl issue, though it wasn't a particularly upsetting thought. Indeed, Lewandowski's success offered him a golden opportunity to practice a classic flanking maneuver. A wise infantry commander never allows the field of battle to remain static. He answers maneuver with classic counter–flanking maneuver, always working to gain the ultimate advantage. He might even allow his opponent a temporary victory, hoping it would make him so overconfident that he was vulnerable to a counter attack.

Masters smiled pleasantly. "Do you remember the planter box I had you build in the mess tent?"

It was an offhand, innocent question; nothing to worry about.

Lewandowski was brimming with confidence. "Yes, Sir."

"Are there any flowers growing in the planter box?" Masters asked.

"Flowers?" Lewandowski asked. "Um, well, no, Sir. We don't have any flowers. Actually, I don't think we got much in the way of flowers around Cam Ranh, Sir."

Masters kicked at a tuft of the coarse grass that grew in stubborn patches scattered around the crest of the dune. No respectable flower could ever consider Cam Ranh its home.

"Yes, I can see what you mean," Masters said. "But even so, I've always wanted flowers for my planter boxes, Lewandowski. Native flowers…flowers with lots of color. Flowers I would be proud to have on display during a Brigade inspection."

"Yes, Sir, that would be nice," Lewandowski agreed pleasantly. "It's just too darned bad we don't have any around here, Sir. I reckon they need real dirt to grow in…not sand. We'd have to leave Cam Ranh to find flowers like that."

"I know," Masters said, and then paused for Lewandowski to catch the drift of the conversation.

A moment later, Lewandowski's smile evaporated and his mouth dropped open. "Sir, are you suggesting…."

"I'm not suggesting anything," Masters broke in. "I'm just saying I want real flowers—pretty flowers—in my planter boxes."

"But, Sir…."

Masters interrupted. "I want flowers, Lewandowski. You want housegirls and you'll get housegirls. Now I want flowers. Are you telling me I can't have any flowers?"

Masters paused, forcing Lewandowski to speak. But Lewandowski was wary; his lifer alert system was detecting a direct assault.

"Both are morale issues," Masters continued when the silence was begging to be broken. "I have to keep the troops happy and the troops have to keep me happy. It's what the scientists call a symbiotic relationship. Others would say it is just one hand washing the other."

Lewandowski's eyes narrowed. "We get housegirls if you get flowers. Is that what you're saying, Sir?"

"Correct," Masters answered.

"Sir...they shoot real bullets out there," Lewandowski pleaded.

Masters nodded. "I know, but they do most of the shooting at night. The days are usually rather quiet. Convoys are entering and leaving Cam Ranh all day long without a shot being fired. You should have no trouble at all, as long as you stay on Highway One and get back before dark. I have a friend who drives between Cam Ranh and Nha Trang twice a week, and he's never been shot at. Not even once."

"All it takes is once," Lewandowski muttered.

"Sir," Masters added.

"Sir," Lewandowski repeated, still recovering from the shock of the proposition.

Masters nodded. "That's better."

"Flowers for housegirls," Lewandowski mused. The idea was sounding less mad than it had a moment before. It might not be a bad idea to venture beyond the dull confines of Cam Ranh Bay, to get out and see what can be seen in the big world beyond the perimeter gates. Who knows, maybe get a good war story for the grandkids could come out of it.

Masters said nothing more. It wasn't the kind of mission that he could actually order his troops to undertake. The brass in Brigade might not think kindly of such a order.

Lewandowski took a deep breath and nodded. His mind was made up. "Alright, Sir. We'll get flowers for your planter boxes. I'll take out the Dirty Dozen and Charlie in the deuce tomorrow morning."

"And I'll have Woody type up something authorizing you to arrange for the housegirls," Masters reciprocated. "The papers will be signed and waiting for you when you return tomorrow afternoon."

'If we return,' Lewandowski pondered glumly.

Masters took the opportunity to admire tent city one more time before passing along a small tad of catostrophic news.

"Its too bad we'll be tearing all this down in a few months," Masters said.

Lewandowski jerked his head around to see if Masters was smiling, thinking it might be some kind of a sick joke, but the flat expression on the Lieutenant's face told him it was no joke. Homely, homey little tent city would be history in just a few short months.

"Why would we tear it down, Sir? We just got it built. It doesn't make sense to tear it down again."

Masters gave Lewandowski a disapproving look. Only officers were authorized to challenge the good sense of the United States Army, and then only with those officers who shared the same convictions and wouldn't destroy careers by ratting to a higher command.

Lewandowski scanned tent city as though saying farewell to a dear friend. Outside the distant mess tent, the two civilian KPs—Poppasan and Stoned Poppasan—were busily scrubbing pots and pans in steaming, soapy water that had been warmed to simmering temperatures by a pair of immersible diesel–fueled water heaters.

Lewandowski was beginning to feel the onset of great waves of self–pity. Just moments before he had been riding on cloud nine. Then within a heartbeat he found himself facing a suicide Search and Transplant mission to capture Viet Cong flowers, followed by the tragic news that wonderful, personalized little tent city had been given a death sentence. What more could go wrong?

"It's Orders From Above," Masters explained. "Brigade wants the 516th in regulation barracks, just like the units further inland."

"But, Sir, what about the personnel center?" Lewandowski asked. "Doesn't it make more sense to have us living right next door to where we work?"

"A much larger, more efficient personnel center will be built next door to the new barracks," Masters answered. "They've thought of everything, Lewandowski. We'll build a much larger messhall with a tin roof so we won't have to worry about the weather. The orderly room and the supply room will be in Quonsets, with more room and better ventilation. You name it, we'll have it. We'll even have a water tower for showers and the messhall. And with a little horse trading at the supply depot, you'll be able to get a water heater for the showers, so the troops can have hot showers."

Lewandowski already knew more than enough about the regulation uniformity of the two–story wooden barracks found further inland. Every barracks looked like its neighbor, every company looked exactly like the company next door. Everything looked spit–shined, Regular Army; a world in which everyone Re–upped for six–years and looked forward to the next inspection.

"Sir, I'm sure the men would be willing to do whatever is necessary to stay in tent city," Lewandowski offered, reaching out for any faint glimmer of hope that might be on the horizon. Perhaps this time logic could prevail, rather than the Army Way. Perhaps a deal could be made so the Originals could remain in tent city.

Masters shook his head. "Like I said, it's Orders From Above."

Lewandowski made an offer anyway. "We could give up the movie screen, Sir."

Masters shook his head again. "They want the men to watch the movies, Lewandowski. The movies are good for morale."

"The KPs," Lewandowski offered quickly.

"Captain Ortega likes the idea of having civilian KP's," Masters said. "Like you said when you brought up the idea, the two of them free up at least four GIs for regular duty. The KPs will stay."

"There has to be some way we can stop this, Sir. The guys really like tent city. They'll hate living in barracks."

Masters looked at Lewandowski with raised eyebrows. The US Army wasn't moved by such arguments.

"It'll destroy their morale," Lewandowski added quickly.

"They'll adjust," Masters said, letting Lewandowski know from the tone of his voice that the discussion was not only closed, but shouldn't have been opened in the first place. The 516th wasn't a summer camp. It was the United States Army.

And it was time to move on the next item on the agenda.

Masters opened with another compliment. "You've done a great job building tent city, Lewandowski. You've turned the Dirty

Dozen around, making them productive soldiers."

The time was ripe to drop the other shoe. "I expect you to maintain the same high standards when you build the new company area and personnel center."

Lewandowski groaned as Masters continued. "You're to report to the 62nd Combat Engineers next Monday for a six–day crash course in construction. The new project will require skills that weren't necessary when tent city was being built, and I expect you to come out of the class fully prepared to build the best company area in the Cam Ranh Bay support command. Ditto for the new personnel center. I won't accept anything less than the best. You can do it, and I expect you to do it."

The groan rose again from deep within Lewandowski's chest. He was breathless with sorrow, having just had the wind knocked out of him by a congratulatory slap on the back.

"You and Edwards can familiarize yourselves with the building site this afternoon," Masters continued, ignoring Lewandowski's emotional distress. "I want you to hit the ground running when you graduate from the school."

Lewandowski took a deep breath, inhaling the courage he needed to say what needed saying. "Sir, I uh, I…I just can't do it, Sir. I just can't be a part of tearing down tent city. The men put so much into building it, Sir. I mean…this really is home to us, Sir."

"You have no choice, Lewandowski. You WILL follow orders."

Lewandowski assumed a position of Attention. "Sir, I resign my rank for the good of my fellow soldiers."

Masters wasn't at all moved by the display of self–sacrifice. It wasn't the Army way of doing things. "You can't resign your rank, Lewandowski. You can get busted, but you can't resign."

His next comment was meant to dowse any subversive fires that might be smoldering in Lewandowski's devious mind.

"And I assure you, it would not be a good idea to create conditions that would lead to your loss of rank. It wouldn't end there," Masters added ominously, knowing that Lewandowski's imagination would create punishments far more dire than anything he truly intended.

Lewandowski groaned again, a heavy sound that might have been well received if he were in a Boy Scout camp or a commune filled with hippies who shared hugs with each other.

"I take that to mean you understand your new assignment," Masters said with no hint of compassion. Actually, he rather liked tent city, himself, though 'like' was a word for civilians who voted for presidential candidates because they were handsome, or smooth talkers who told them what they wanted to hear. If he had his druthers, Masters would have the 516th remain in tent city, particularly after his mess tent room divider was filled to overflowing with colorful flowers. But that wasn't possible. So, march forward to the next objective. Besides, the room divider idea could be transferred to the new messhall.

"Yessir," Lewandowski answered, confirming that he understood his assignment.

"Very well, then," Masters said. "Carry on with your duties. I'll be in the orderly tent if you need me."

Lewandowski raised his right hand to salute…"Yessir"…and watched as Masters descended from the dunetop, wondering if the man might been abused as a child.

Later that afternoon Lewandowski and Charlie Edwards clambered down from the cab of the rattling deuce–and–a–half and gazed with aching hearts upon the future home of the 516th AG.

The new company and personnel center area was in the outermost reaches of the militarily–correct suburbs, where civilization came to an abrupt halt. To their backs were the final rows of elongated two–story wooden barracks that were the norm for Cam Ranh, with all the structural elements aligned in precise formations. Even the olive drab sandbags placed on the whitewashed roofs had been perfectly aligned.

"This place gives me the creeps," Charly said with an unconscious shiver. "Who could be so sick as to design something like this on purpose?"

It was a rhetorical question that needed no answer. Charly opposed the school of psychological thought that insisted man was a genetically programmed creature, wholly predictable, a pawn of instinctive habits rooted deep in prehistoric experience. He would have made a lousy officer in the United States Army, where the theories of command structure were dependent upon the troops being thoroughly predictable creatures.

Lewandowski was so moved by the tragic implications of the moment that he felt the rare urge to try his hand at amateur philosophy.

"They're all around us, Charlie," Lewandowski announced sadly while doing a slow 360 of the area.

Lewandowski hadn't been much of a renaissance man during his past life. If out of desperation he were forced to be a philosopher, it would be done with a limited supply of knowledge. But inspirational characters were right up his alley, particularly if they were jocks. The most sophisticated character contained within his repertoire of non–jock heroes was the tragic Tom Joad, who lived and died within the pages of The Grapes of Wrath. Lewandowski met Tom Joad while perusing the Cliff Notes version of Grapes during a bonehead Freshman English course at USC. He had been particularly inspired by the "I'll be there" declarations Tom made to his mother before he went off and got himself killed by a band of roving rednecks. Lewandowski was so inspired that he made Tom Joad the focus of his "My Favorite Character" essay, for which he received a C–minus because of spelling errors.

Lewandowski's favorite movie was the *Lou Gehrig Story*, starring Gary Cooper, followed by, *The Knute Rockne Story* as a close second, with *The Babe Ruth Story* taking a distant third, primarily because William Bendix looked so damned silly wearing a putty nose.

Lewandowski was so inspired by the tragedy of losing tent city that he would now apply the Tom Joad Principle to life in the New Action Army.

"They're all around us, Charlie. They're in the water we drink, the food we eat, the clothes we wear, the bunks we sleep in. They're in the MPC we get paid, the shots we take when we get the clap from the whores in the Vill…the shitty movies we see at night. They're everywhere, Charlie. They're all around us."

Charlie was wondering if Lewandowski had finally gone over

the edge. "Who is all around us, Lew? Are you hearing voices?"

"The Lifers," Lewandowski growled. "Don't be an idiot. You asked who could have such a sick mind and I just told you. The Lifers. Do I have to draw you a picture, or what? Who else but a Lifer or a prison warden would design something like that?"

Lewandowski nodded his head distainfully toward the suburban sprawl, unable to gaze upon the dreadful uniformity for more than a moment. He preferred to look beyond the future home of the 516th AG, toward the barren windswept sea of sand that continued in low undulations until halted by clumps of sparse vegetation that eventually evolved into the dense jungles and mountains of central South Vietnam. The land looked so free out there, so unmilitary, it made him all the more saddened by the thought of losing tent city.

Charly also gazed out at the wildlands beyond, but with a growing sense of horror. "Hey, where's the perimeter?" Charly asked, suddenly alarmed. "What'll be standing between us and the Viet Cong? Good grief...we're sitting ducks if an attack comes from the West."

"The perimeter's about five miles that way," Lewandowski explained, nodding Westward. "Masters showed me the map when he was telling me how to get here. Cam Ranh's a big place, Charlie. We're not even in the middle of it yet."

"Good grief. Half the VC in Vietnam could be hiding out there and we wouldn't know it," Charlie insisted, becoming even more incensed by Lewandowski's calm. "What if they hit us some night with a surprise attack? We'd never be able to stop'em! Jeeze, just think...we've never even fired our M–14s! We don't even know if they work!"

"Now, Charlie," Lewandowski said, trying to calm Charlie's fears even as his own terrors were beginning to stand up and be heard. "That's a lot of open ground for the VC to cross...and we got the airbase...and they'd have to get through the perimeter in the first place. And besides...our guns'll work. They wouldn't give us guns that won't work...would they?"

Charly answered with a sour expression. "Of course they would. This is the Army. They're dumb enough to do damn near anything."

Maybe Charlie was right, Lewandowsi pondered. The scattered clumps of brush provided great cover for snipers, and sappers carrying machineguns, rocket launchers, and satchel charges. And it would be just like the Lifers to ignore the obvious because it wasn't covered by The Book, just like they did in Pearl Harbor. Thousands of drugged and illiterate Viet Cong could be hiding out there right now, ready to rise up and kick some American butt when it was least expected.

Lewandowski was ready for action. Extreme emergencies called for extreme measures.

"C'mon, Charlie. Let's get our tails down to the personnel center. We gotta let the Board of Directors know what's up."

Lewandowski maneuvered the big, lumbering, clacking diesel deuce–and–a–half into the personnel center parking lot, following the same unconventional route he had been using since day one. Instead of parking in the area set aside for commoners and then walking to his destination, Lewandowski preferred to wrestle the deuce over the sand dunes in compound–low, all–wheel–drive, with the nonchalant dexterity of a man who wouldn't be paying for whatever drive train damage resulted. Lewandowski figured he wasn't just another visitor, he was an Original, and he deserved VIP parking privileges right along with the 516th officers and visiting brass. And he had been known to brag that he hadn't met a sand dune he couldn't conquer with his big, ugly deuce.

Lewandowski finally arrived at his destination, a secluded patch of shaded sand resting under a palm tree that stood between the command hut and a neighboring Quonset.

"Tell Hillbilly and Jackson to meet me here," Lewandowski said as he and Charlie dismounted. "I'll get Peters and Donnatelli. Watch out for Conners. Hillbilly says he's been on the rag lately."

"Nothin' new about that," Charlie commented as he headed for the command hut.

The shadowy outline of Captain Ortega could be seen through the screens covering his office windows in the command hut, just a few yards from Lewandowski's personal parking place. He was sitting at his desk, signing papers from the In basket before moving them to the Out basket. He rarely bothered to read the reports, forms and cover letters because he simply didn't have the time for it. Four new unsigned documents would have arrived for every one he actually read. He would have been waist–deep in overdue documents if he had tried to read them all, so he trusted his support staff to do the tedious reviews and editing before the documents arrived at his desk.

Ortega didn't lift his eyes from the paperwork when Lewandowski arrived. He knew who it was. Only Lewandowski would go to that much effort to avoid walking from the parking lot.

Lewandowski headed for the first of the Quonsets as Charlie entered the command hut, removing his cap as he passed through the doorway. Charlie usually would have kept his fatigue cap on just to annoy Numbnuts and Warrant Officer Conners, who sat at desks on either side of the doorway leading into Ortega's office. But today Charlie wanted to blend into his surroundings. Numbnuts and Conners really didn't have that much to do, so they were always on the lookout for Orignals wearing headgear inside. They, much like Captain Ortega, figured the forms pausing at their desk had been checked and re–checked, edited and re–edited long before reaching their in–baskets.

Like the other buildings in the personnel center, the command hut was filled with the constant roar of the 30–inch floor fans Lewandowski had scrounged a week earlier at the Supply Depot. He had received the fans in exchange for early R&Rs and whatever other favors the 516th AG was capable of dispensing to their friends throughout Cam Ranh. No documents existed to trace the transactions, following the methods used by creative supply sergeants in wars past, beginning with the supply sergeant who scrounged boots and overcoats for the troops at Valley Forge.

The Board of Directors was created by the Originals to facilitate decision–making while reducing the number of names on the need–to–know list. For instance, if the personnel center was in dire need of hard to find items, such as 30–inch electric floor fans, the five–member Board of Directors would call a meeting rather than go about the messy business of involving dozens of Originals. Such matters couldn't be handled in a willy nilly fashion, with Originals freelancing whenever and however they wished. There were Army regulations to be considered. One of the five Originals elected to the board was Louie Donnatelli, who summed it up best when he said uncontrolled freelancing would devalue the products being offered and create public relations problems with unhappy customers, which then might lead to C.I.D. investigations, followed by trips to Camp LBJ. Louie had an MBA from NYU and could sound absolutely brilliant when he was in a mood to do so. If favors were to be exchanged to better the lives of the Originals, which everyone agreed was a patriotic business objective, there had to be a screening committee, and thus evolved the Board of Directors.

Conners and Bolton kept their eyes focused on Charlie Edwards as he approached the desk of Ed "Hillbilly" Burns, one of four Originals who acted as document filters in the command hut. Ed and his cohorts didn't have time to actually read the documents they passed on to Conners and Numbnuts, but they did their best to catch the errors that survived the previous filters.

The Lifers of the 516th AG were new at the business of running a personnel center, being infantrymen for most of their careers. Only Warrant Officer 2 Mobley possessed the training and experience necessary to mount a challenge to a decision made by an Original. Mobley had accumulated enough time in the Army to know just about everything about everything.

Charlie stepped in front of Hillbilly's desk, placing his back to Conners and Bolton as he relayed his short message. "Something big is up," he said quickly. "We're meeting out back by the supply truck."

"Now?"

Charlie nodded to the affirmative.

Hillbilly made a sour face as Charlie left the command hut, on his way to the neighboring Quonset to pass the word to SP4 George W. Jackson.

Hillbilly continued working a moment before casually reaching for his fatigue cap, followed by an equally casual exit from the command hut.

Numbnuts Bolton was watching and raised his eyebrows, catching the attention of WO1 Conners, who had been watching as well. It was as plain as the noses on their faces...the Originals were up to something underhanded.

Charlie walked into the neighboring Quonset, where only Originals worked at the eighteen olive drab desks that were hidden by a forest of 54 olive drab four–drawer file cabinets and still more roaring floor fans. Charlie paused at Jackson's desk.

SP4 George W. Jackson was a graduate of Temple University, where he majored in Business Administration with a minor in Economics. He also played a little football and did a little wrestling, so he was no one to mess around with.

"What's up?" Jackson asked when Charlie arrived.

"Big meeting, out back, by the deuce," Charlie explained.

"Can't this wait until we're off duty? I'm up to my elbows in paperwork, man."

"It's an emergency."

"What kind of emergency?" Jackson asked while scanning a document for glaring errors. He didn't have time to actually read the document page by page, word for word. That sort of thing was being done at a lower level.

"Tent city's in trouble," Charlie answered over the roar of the electric fans. He immediately had the full attention of all within earshot.

Charlie particularly enjoyed starting rumors. He figured he might write a doctoral thesis about starting rumors one day, and the 516th AG was his petrie dish. His training in psychology had made him particularly adept at starting rumors.

"What kind of trouble?" Jackson asked suspiciously.

"Big trouble," Charlie explained vaguely, knowing the gaps in the facts would be creatively filled by those who would carry the rumor far and wide.

Jackson gauged Edwards with wary eyes, refusing to be had by a cherub–faced honky from Iowa. As a brother with a reputation to maintain, he might never be able to live down something as shame-ful as that. Reluctantly, he laid aside the document and reached for his cap.

"This better be good," Jackson warned as he followed Charlie out to the glaring sunlight.

The other clerks reached for their telephones, eager to spread the horrible news: tent city was doomed.

Lewandowski entered the second of four Quonset huts in search for PFC Theodore Peters. Peters hadn't yet sewn on his new PFC stripes. He had lost them twice already and figured sewing them on was bad luck. Lewandowski asked around and learned Peters was filing reports in the documents section, the final resting place for the file copies of the thousands of documents that were processed through the personnel center.

Peters rather liked his job. Nobody paid much attention to him as he went from file cabinet to file cabinet with handfuls of documents. Sometimes he was able to accomplish doing no productive work at all for an entire day. On such days he was particularly tempted to head out to the dunes for a little shut–eye, a habit that had cost him his stripes on two previous occasions.

"Yo, Peters," Lewandowski announced as he entered the dark recesses of the file Quonset. Peters wasn't visible among the precise rows of four–drawer Olive Drab metal files, so he raised his voice. "YO, Peters!"

"That you, Lew?" a sleepy voice answered.

"No, it's General Westmoreland! Where you at, man?"

Peters rose from his hiding place with a small oscillating fan in one hand, rubbing his eyes with the other hand. "Hey, Lew. What is, brother?"

"We got a meeting out by my truck," Lewandowski said. "Be there or be square."

"Dig it, man. I'm on my way."

Lewandowski then exited for the fourth Quonset in search for Louie Donnatelli—formerly of Brooklyn—who was now the section leader for twelve clerks responsible for the personnel records for twelve field units protecting the perimeter of Cam Ranh. Louie had completed two sections of his CPA exam—making him a CP—when Uncle Sam tapped his shoulder. Louie barely passed the pre–Induction eye exam, and should have been rejected for a variety of medical issues, but here he was.

Louie wasn't one to shout FTA or directly buck the system. It just wasn't within his personality makeup. He was more of a bureaucratic guerrilla fighter.

"Hey, Louie," Lewandowski announced. "We got a meeting about to start outside by my deuce."

"Why now? Why not after duty hours?"

Louie was instinctively protective of time–and–task efficiency.

"It's an emergency. I'll explain it to everyone all at once."

Louie rose from his chair, leaving open the 201 file he had been auditing for errors. It was a thick, puffy personnel file belonging to a Command Sergeant Major, containing every significant document relating to his career assignments and re–assignments, promotions, demotions, awards and medals, training and job skills accumulated since 1942. Louie had been going through the file page by page, making sure everything was perfect. Like Jackson, he took his job seriously, even if he hated the job. He figured he owed it to the guys out in the field to at least make sure their records were kept straight arrow.

Louie sighed. "Let's get this over with." The Hurry Up And Wait ways of the Army were particularly infuriating to him.

Lewandowski followed at his own slow pace. He had the mind of a defensive lineman who knew he had to pace himself if he were to continue to be effective in the fourth quarter. Besides, he was the chairman of the board. The meeting couldn't start until he was there.

Lewandowski joined the others at the deuce. Crouching behind the cab, he covered the problem without a great deal of dramatic overstatement. He wished he had a Gipper story to tell them, but he was unable to present any possible solutions to the dilemma at hand. He couldn't even blame Masters for this problem. "Orders from above" came from an opponent that couldn't be seen....the bureaucratic chain of command at the brigade headquarters complex.

"The good news is, we'll be getting the housegirls," Lewandowski concluded. "The bad news is, they'll be working for us in stateside RA barracks, if we don't figure a way out'a this."

"We're screwed," Jackson said. "The Man's made up his mind. He wants us living like we were in a stateside assignment with all the wall locker, footlocker inspections he can lay on us. The Man ain't happy if he can't harass us."

Jackson defined The Man as the system rather than an individual. The Man brought his ancestors to America as slaves...The Man delayed his career in business for two years with the draft...The Man would be moving them out of tent city.

Lewandowski stood to ease the strain on his battered knees. He needed time to think. Everything was happening too fast.

"We're concentrating on the wrong problem," Louie said calmly. "The problem isn't...."

Distant movement caught Lewandowski's eye. "Oh, boy," he interrupted. "There's Conners poking his head out of the command hut, looking for trouble."

"He's probably countin' the minutes I'm gone on piss breaks," Hillbilly suggested only half jokingly.

"Let's shove on over to the shithouse," Lewandowski said. "Yesterday was malaria pill day. If he bitches, we can say we got the runs. Let him prove we don't."

They took different paths back to the enlisted men's shitter. A moment later, the Board of Directors was convened in the screened shitter, with their pants down around their ankles.

"The problem lies in stopping or slowing the construction of the new barracks and personnel center," Louie summarized from his allotted hole, brushing away a fly as he continued his analysis. "We can't change the decision to move us to the barracks, but we might be able to delay the construction long enough to finish our tours in tent city."

"How we gonna do that?" Peters asked.

"I'm not an engineer," Louie said, "but I do know accounting. Time overruns and equipment and material shortages can be relied upon on to happen under even the best of conditions. It's just the nature of the construction business. And then there are the mistakes that can double the time it takes to finish a project. We'll have a better idea what we're dealing with time–wise after Lewandowski finishes his training. It might be that all we need are a few convenient screw–ups to stay in tent city."

"I don't wanna get hung over this," Lewandowski said. "It'll be my ass on the line, not yours."

Louie had an answer ready. "Lew, if I were Masters, I'd be expecting you to screw up something."

"Oh, thanks for the vote of confidence," Lewandowski grumbled.

"It's nothing against you personally," Louie said calmly. "It's the nature of your training and experience, which doesn't include any of the skills you'll need to complete a major project like this. It takes more than six days to turn a jock into the manager of a major construction project like this. I'm not criticizing you, Lew...I'm giving you an out. Not to mention the fact that you'll be hampered by the Dirty Dozen. I don't see how the Lifers could ever build a case against you."

A truck horn sounded. They had left Charlie at the deuce with instructions to honk if he saw Connors or Numbnuts heading toward the shitter. A moment later, Numbnuts strode into view.

"The shitter patrol is on its way," Hillbilly joked.

"That man's got no pride," Peters added as Numbnuts strode toward them purposefully.

The horn honked again, two short beeps, to announce the imminent arrival of a second personality in the 516th AG chain of command, WO1 "Chuck" Conners, also known as The Rifleman, who was following several strides behind Numbnuts.

Lewandowski laughed. "Jeeze, they're both coming to check us out."

"Let's finish this discussion tonight," Louie suggested. He didn't like to be involved with direct confrontations. He felt much more at ease working behind the scenes, like a comptroller.

"Aw, hell, Louie," Lewandowski answered. "Think what a great story this'll be to tell your kids and grandkids."

"Yeah, man," Peters agreed. "You can tell'em how you fought off two crazy Lifers while you was takin' a dump."

"Get serious, you guys," Louie complained. "He'll be here in a second. We'll meet tonight, and again after Lew gets out of school. By then we'll have a better idea what we're dealing with and can make plans. Now we don't know enough to accomplish anything."

Lewandowski agreed just seconds before Numbnuts arrived. "Okay, you got it, Louie."

"What the hell's going on here?" Numbnuts demanded. "A tea party or a union meeting?"

"No, Sarge," Lewandowski said. "This ain't no tea party, and we ain't aware of no unions in the Army. Why do you ask?"

Conners was a bit out of breath from his brisk walk. "Alright, every damn one'a you guys owe me some extra–duty time for this."

Jackson replied calmly. "I don't think I'll be doing any extra–duty time for taking a shit during duty hours, Mister Conners. Not unless you can find where that's covered by the regulations."

Jackson's response nearly pushed Numbnuts Bolton over the edge. "You won't, huh!?"

"None of us will," Hillbilly added with an infuriating serenity. "We ain't broken no rules, Sarge. We're just doing what comes naturally after taking our malaria pills at chow last night. We all got the trots."

Being such a fanatic for accuracy, Louie felt compelled to set the record straight. "Uh, Sir?" he said, raising his hand for permission to speak.

"Yes, Donnatelli?" Connors said. He treated Donnatelli with more respect than the other Originals, being covertly awed by the precision of Donnatelli's thinking.

"Are you ready to tell us what is happening out here?" Numbnuts asked.

"No, Sergeant," Donnatelli answered respectfully. "I was just going to say there are no unit directives, USARV Regulations, Army Regulations or Department of Defense Regulations that cover this, Sir. You are accusing us of breaking rules and regulations that don't exist. I believe AR 720–14, Section Four, and the Uniform Code of Military Justice cover this situation quite explicitly when they state it is the duty of the Officer In Charge to establish rules and regulations that are in compliance with United States Army policy."

"Is that right?" Connors demanded impotently, his face glowing more from embarrassment than anger. He wasn't accustomed to having the regulations and the UCMJ used against him.

"God, that was beautiful, Louie," Peters said as he reached for the nearest roll of 400–grit toilet tissue.

"We'll let you off this time," Conners warned as the Originals finished their business and stood to lift their olive drab fatigue pants over their olive drab boxer shorts, thoroughly ignoring Connors and

Bolton as they buttoned their olive–drab flies.

"You got a Warrant Officer talking to you, troops," Bolton growled. "Pay attention…show respect when he talks."

Lewandowski led the exit from the shithouse. Once outside, he turned to Bolton. "Face it, Sarge. You struck out on this one."

Bolton looked ready to explode.

"I heard that," Conners said triumphantly as Lewandowski led the others back to the personnel center.

Hillbilly chuckled when they were out of earshot from Conners and Bolton. "Hey, Lew, that was alright. Face it, Sarge, you struck out on this one."

"I disagree," Donnatelli said from the rear of the procession. "There's no need to be antagonistic. The situation is bad enough as it is. There was no need to create new problems."

"Aw, he had it coming," Lewandowski argued over his shoulder.

Donnatelli wouldn't retreat. "When it comes to the bottom line, Ortega and Masters will support the Lifers over you. They have no choice. We won't be able to protect you if they decide to solve an insubordination problem by transferring you to a field unit."

"Okay, okay. I'll be start being nice to shitheads like Numbnuts and Conners," Lewandowski promised.

"That would be very wise," Louie said. "And it would be very unlike you, Lewandowski. I wish I could believe what you said."

"I'll try," Lewandowski promised. "Okay?"

"Do that," Louie advised. "We need you in charge of the construction detail if we're going to save tent city."

Chapter Six

F–Day had arrived.

Lewandowski would be leading the fearless Search and Transplant team deep into the boonies beyond the safety of the Cam Ranh perimeter. Objective: Flowers for the mess tent room divider.

Lewandowski began the fateful day by gathering the Dirty Dozen for a short refresher course on the care and use of the 7.62mm M–14 semi–automatic combat rifle. He began by assembling the Dirty Dozen behind the supply tent with their M–14's, bayonets, ammo belts, full canteens, flak vests, steel pots and a full complement of bad attitudes, as evidenced by the variety of slouching positions assumed by the formation.

Lewandowski and Edwards were standing Front and Center. Lewandowski held his M–14 aloft for all to see.

"Okay, gents, listen up." He had devoted a full thirty minutes of the prior evening to a review of the M–14 portion of his Soldier's Handbook.

"This is yer basic M–14 elephant gun. It shoots a big bullet, so watch out who yer pointin' the muzzle at when we're out there huntin' down flowers today. Let's try not to kill each other, okay?"

Frenchie was in no mood to be messed with. "Oh, man, how long we gotta put up with this crap?"

The other members of the Dirty Dozen were equally uninspired by Lewandowski's introduction. The murmur of discontent was threatening to get out of control.

"At Ease," Lewandowski ordered.

"We ain't got no ammo," Frenchie complained back at him.

"That's right," Lewandowski said. "And you won't be gettin' any ammo until we're ready to roll. And we won't be ready to roll until we get this part over with. So you might as well quit yer bitchin' and let me say what I gotta say."

Lewandowski glared at Frenchie, daring him to utter just one more word.

"Kiss my ass," Frenchie mumbled, but not loud enough to draw a reaction from Lewandowski.

"Okay, none'a'these guns have been zeroed in," Lewandowski began anew.

This time he was interrupted by Skins Williams.

"Hey, man," Skins said. "Get it right, will you? These ain't muh'fuh guns...these're muh'fuh weapons. Remember what they taught us back in Basic? This is my weapon, and this is my gun." He grabbed his crotch to show he knew where his gun was holstered. "This is for fightin' and this is for fun. Man, how you gonna lead us into battle if you don't know the dif'rence between a weapon and a gun?"

Chuckles rose from the ranks. Even Edwards couldn't hold it back.

"As I was saying!" Lewandowski roared. "DON'T expect to hit what you're aiming at, unless it's real close in. In fact, I'm giving you an order right now: Don't open fire at nuthin' until I give the order."

"Yeah, right," Frenchie said with a humorless snort, his voice dripping with sarcasm. "Like, I'm *really* gonna ask your permission to shoot at some sonofabitch that's tryin' to kill my ass. You're talkin' dingydow, GI. I'm cuttin' loose with everything I got, even if I don't hit nuthin'. I want those VC bastards to be as scared as I am."

All heads were bobbing up and down within the Dirty Dozen, along with Charlie.

"I wanna see the Inspector General, man," Skins Williams demanded. "There ain't no way I'm gonna get my ass shot off just so some Lifer Lieutenant can put flowers in the mess tent."

Lewandowski hadn't yet bothered to tell them it was a "volunteer" mission. He simply told them Masters wanted flowers and left the rest up to their imagination. He knew he'd being going out in the boonies all by his lonesome if they knew no actual orders had been issued. Like most military decisionmakers, he figured there were some things the troops simply didn't need to know in order to successfully complete their assigned mission.

"You can see the IG when we get back," Lewandowski answered with acidic sweetness, then lowered his voice to an ominous growl. "But you might as well start packing your duffel bag for reassignment to a suicide squad in the 101st Airborne, if you bring the IG into this."

"What'cho mean?" Skins demanded. "I got the right to see the muh'fuh' IG any time I want to. They can't do nuttin' to me for that."

"You won't be getting transferred for going to the IG," Lewandowski continued with a very strange, leering smile. "They can do it for a hundred other reasons. Like for being such a pain in the ass around here that you can't be trusted to do the job you were trained to do at the personnel center. That's why you'll be packing your duffle bag, Skins. Officially, it won't have nothin' to do with going to the IG...but unofficially we'll all know why it happened."

"Man, that muh'fuh' sucks," Skins grumbled, though he knew Lewandowski was speaking the righteous truth.

Lewandowski addressed them all. "You'll find yourselves assigned to a field unit so fast that you won't know what's happening. And what're you gonna do when you get there? Tell them that you don't wanna be a grunt? Hell, they're taking casualties every day. They need warm bodies to fill in the ranks. Do you think an IG in a field unit would listen to you? Hell, no. It'll be rice paddies and jungle, or six months bad time in Camp LBJ followed by more rice paddies and jungle. Only the next time they won't be so nice to ya."

"Man, you sound like muh'fuh' Numbnuts," Skins grumbled.

"Call me a Lifer if you want," Lewandowski said self–righteously, "But it don't change the facts. I'm giving you the straight skinny on what'll happen if you start making too many waves around here. They got us by the balls until we DEROS. Sure, we could all be down at the IG's office right now, but we'll only find ourselves being transferred from the frying pan right smack into the fire. Look at it this way, guys. If we do this one little thing for Masters, it'll make him happy. He might even give us some slack for awhile, once he's got his flowers."

"Fat chance," Skins grumbled. "He'll just come up with some other dumbshit idea."

Skins turned to his comrades in arms. "I tell ya, we muh'fuh' gotta stick together on this," he pleaded. "The IG would listen if we all went in there at once. We gotta hang together. Like brothers."

But the masses were mute. They were thinking about sudden

transfers to field units and rice paddies and jungles and hidden enemies that wanted them to die. So much for the brother's theory of unity. Even Frenchie was looking everywhere but at Skins.

Skins turned away in disgust.

"Hey," Lewandowski said consolingly. "All we gotta do is dig up a few flowers. No big deal. We could even fix it so we scared the shit out of Masters when we come back."

"*If* we come back," Frenchie added with a dry laugh.

Ignoring the comment, Lewandowski's face was beginning to glow with the warmth of creative thinking. "We could shoot up the deuce a little and tell Masters we got ambushed. It'll scare the life out of him. That's the kind of story the IG would listen to. We could tell him we got ambushed and only made it out by the skin of our teeth, fighting Viet Cong every inch of the way. Hell, you could even write to your congressman."

Lewandowski had their attention now. The idea of turning the tables on Masters was very appealing.

"Maybe we could shoot one of you in the foot to make it look even more real," Lewandowski added brightly. "Why stop with shooting up the deuce when we could come back with some real blood? Masters would shit a brick."

"Man, you're sicker than Masters," Skins said.

Lewandowski nodded in agreement and lifted his M–14 to Port Arms, ready to return to his apocalyptic refresher course.

"Okay, this is yer basic M–14. Be sure you shove yer bolt forward with the heel of your hand when you lock and load. If the bolt ain't set, you'll just hear a click when you pull the trigger. Keep yer eyes peeled, but don't start shootin' unless you know yer target. We don't wanna be shootin' innocent civilians. That's a good way to get yer tail in a helluva jam. Remember that part about the bolt. I don't wanna be hearing any clicks if we gotta use these babies."

"How'cum we ain't got M–16's like they got in the field units?" Frenchie demanded. "If these guns are any good, they'd be carrying M–14's, not M–16's."

"Yeah, man," Skins agreed, ready to take to the streets on any issue. "How'cum we muh'fuh' ain't got M–16's?"

"How do you expect me to know the answer to a question like

that?" Lewandowski asked. "What am I...a General? Do you see any stars on my shoulder? All I know is, we got elephant guns instead'a M–16's. Try to think positive about this, okay? Our guns are bigger than M–16s...they shoot farther, they...."

"They don't hit what they're being aimed at," Frenchie interjected before Lewandowski could finish his thought.

"Hey, it's not ours to question why," Lewandowski said.

Skins shook his head in disgust. "God, what a Lifer."

Lewandowski had experienced about as much abuse as he could take. It was time to move Charlie onto the firing range as an upright target.

"Now, Specialist Four Charles Edwards here is gonna go over the defensive tactics we'll use in the boonies."

Chuckles rose from the ranks of the Dirty Dozen. Charlie had gotten his Speck Four stripes on the same company orders that made PFC's of the Dirty Dozen. He spent the evening before sewing the new stripes on his fatigues, enduring the harassment of the many Originals who made a point of stopping by the supply tent to give him a hard time as he fumbled with needle and thread.

"Okay, listen up," Charlie began, sounding thoroughly unsure of himself.

Frenchie chuckled. "Listen up, he says. It didn't take long for the stripes to go to his head. He sounds like Numbnuts. Maybe that's what we ought'a call him. Little Numbnuts."

"Charlie's gonna Re–up now that he's got Speck Four," Lewandowski announced with a lewd wink.

"Re–up, my ass," Charlie shot back. "Alright, you guys," he said with new vigor. "Listen up. This is serious stuff. We gotta have a plan out there. We can't just do whatever we feel like doing. We gotta be a team. We gotta have tactics."

Ignoring the catcalls from the Dirty Dozen, Charlie took them through his tactical plan step by step. He too had spent considerable time studying his Soldier's Handbook the night before. It required a great deal of patience and self–control, but he eventually made sure everyone had at least some idea of what they were expected to do if and when they found flowers out in the boonies.

Next, Lewandowski distributed the ammo clips—enough for

120 rounds each—and ordered the Dirty Dozen to mount–up in the supply deuce. The next stop would be the northern perimeter gate.

The big deuce idled to a stop, adding itself to the line of vehicles waiting to get through the MP checkpoint at the perimeter gate. Charlie was driving. Usually Lewandowski did the driving, but today he told Charlie to get behind the wheel. Lewandowski insisted on riding shotgun, his M–14 propped between his knees, ready for action.

"Why should I drive?" Charlie demanded when they were mounting–up in tent city. He wanted to have his hands on his own M–14 instead of wrestling the big steering wheel of the deuce.

"Cuz I'm a better shot, that's why," Lewandowski grunted, sounding more grumpy than scared, though he was much more scared than grumpy.

"You can't order me around any more," Charlie said with uncharacteristic fire. "You don't outrank me now. We're both Speck Fours."

"Yeah, but I got date of rank on you," Lewandowski reminded him.

"Up yours with your date of rank," Charlie answered.

"Okay, then I'll beat you up," Lewandowski said.

"And I'll pay you back when you're sleeping," Charlie countered, looking like he meant it.

Lewandowski stared at Charlie, pondering how quickly rank can go to a guy's head. Charlie used to be such a nice guy. Now he wants to argue over every little thing.

"Aw, c'mon, Charlie. We gotta get this show on the road or we're gonna be stuck out there after dark and get ambushed, all because you don't wanna drive the deuce."

"Hurry up, already," Frenchie ordered from the cargo bed. "It's hot as hell under this tarp. Let's get rolling and get some air moving."

"Okay…I'll make a deal," Lewandowski said. "It's worth a six–pack to me if I get to ride shotgun."

"A six–pack and say please, as in 'this isn't an order…it's a request'," Charlie counter–offered.

Lewandowski held out his hand. "It's a deal. Please do the driving, Charlie. It would make me so happy if you did."

Charlie shook hands. "It will be a pleasure."

"Asshole."

"Prick."

They finally made it to the perimeter gate shortly after 1000 hours. By then the Dirty Dozen had rolled the heavy, dusty tarp to the front of the support braces, improving both the air circulation and their field of view. Several of them were lounging on the six cases of C–rations Lewandowski tossed onto the cargo bed before leaving, just in case they were ambushed by Viet Cong who might be as willing to wheel'n' deal as were the GIs in the Supply Depot. *You let me live, I give you ham and beans.*

An MP was walking along the line of vehicles waiting to be allowed through the gate.

"All weapons MUST be cleared in Cam Ranh," he shouted as he neared the 516th deuce. "ALL personnel with locked and loaded weapons WILL clear those weapons NOW! I repeat....NO weapons will be locked and loaded until you leave Cam Ranh! Listen up! All weapons MUST be cleared ASAP!"

The MP was glancing at weapons to make sure they were cleared as he strolled down the line of vehicles, finally arriving at the 516th deuce. A quick glance was enough to tell him it was a truck-load of support command personnel, most likely leaving the relative safety of Cam Ranh for the first time.

"You boys planning to start your own war with all those weapons?" he asked with a wise–ass grin.

"Eat shit and die, dog breath," Frenchie said.

The MP glared at Frenchie. "What'd you say?"

"I said I don't wanna die, man. What'choo think I said?"

The MP glared at them all now, seeking a chink in the group armor, but seeing none.

The line of vehicles inched forward as the MP moved further down the line. The deuce followed, lurching forward with the grace of a clattering three–legged elephant before again screeching to a halt.

The worry lines began to double among the Search and Transplant "volunteers" when only four vehicles remained between them and the boonies beyond the perimeter.

They found themselves gazing transfixed at the battered terrain beyond the gate, then back at the perimeter network. The innermost wall of the perimeter consisted of sandbags and concrete, with machinegun slits backed by mortars and light artillery. The outside surface of the wall was pockmarked by scars from prior attacks. A barren no–man's land prevailed beyond the wall, filled by a succession of barbed wire and razor wire obstacles made even more deadly by landmines, tripwires and Claymore mines. The no man's land was extended by defoliated jungle for at least two hundred yards beyond the barbed wire entrapments, increasing the free–fire zone to some 300 meters. Beyond the defoliated earth lay the tangled green of the jungle, where the brand of warfare waged by the Viet Cong and NVA was most effective.

Frenchie crossed himself when he looked at what lay beyond the gate. "Sweet Jesus," he murmured, perhaps feeling a bit guilty for the wisecrack he'd made to the MP, who might well be asked one day to forfeit his life protecting the perimeter that protected the 516th AG.

Two squads of infantrymen were in the no man's land, heading back to the perimeter after pulling patrol duty in the jungle. Their weapons were locked and loaded, ready for use. Despite the nearness of the perimeter, nothing could be taken for granted. Murphy's Law of Warfare being what it was, a guy was most likely to get zapped when he was getting short or when he was approaching the safety of his own perimeter.

Signs pockmarked by bullet holes were posted at the gate as a reminder to travelers.

**WARNING
YOU ARE ENTERING
A MINED AREA
DO NOT LEAVE THE ROAD
FOR THE NEXT 300 METERS**

WARNING
MAINTAIN SPEED OF NO LESS THAN
40 MPH BEYOND THE PERIMETER
DO NOT HALT, KEEP MOVING

WARNING
STAY ALERT, STAY ALIVE
LOCK AND LOAD BEYOND THE PERIMETER
MAKE SURE YOUR SAFETY IS ON

The other voyagers were locking and loading their weapons while passing through the gate, as did the Originals, who were now as serious as two heart attacks. The grabass was history. They positioned themselves low in the cab and the cargo bed, hoping the thin sheets of sidewall steel would protect them from random sniper rounds.

Charlie put the pedal to the metal, intending to catch up with the forward vehicles, thus gaining strength through numbers. But it was no use. The drivers of the distant vehicles had their own pedals to the metal.

Skins pointed to their right when they had traveled about a mile. "Hey, look over there," he said to Frenchy. "Is that a church steeple I'm lookin' at?"

Those who ventured a quick glance saw an unmistakable church steeple poking through the roadside foliage, topped by a Christian cross. A moment later, the deuce roared past a narrow road branching off from the highway, leading to a barely visible church. Several nuns with large winged hats were leading a column of children on a leisurely stroll toward the highway. The kids came in all colors.

"Man, what's a muh'fuh'church doing out here?" Skins asked.

"It must be one tough parish," Frenchie observed, squeezing some humor out of the dark circumstances. He rose to his knees on the bouncing cargo bed and shouted through the back window of the cab. "Yo, Lewandowski! How far we gotta go, man?"

Lewandowski looked down at the map on his knees. "The jun-

gle opens up in about three, four more klicks. After that, we go
through a village. Then it's open country until we reach the 17th
Aviation group. If we ain't found any flowers by then, we dig up
whatever we find and call 'em flowers. If Masters don't like it, he can
go get his own flowers."

Lewandowski pointed to a large formation of precisely aligned
trees straddling both sides of the highway up ahead. "That's the
Michelin rubber plantation we see gettin' hit all the time! Keep your
eyes peeled! It's supposed to be loaded with VC."

Within seconds the Dirty Dozen were aligning themselves in
prone (hide–my–head–and–hope–I–don't–get–shot–in–the
–butt) positions behind the walls of the cargo bed. Fortunately,
Lewandowski had decided against bringing along hand grenades, so
they didn't have to be concerned about release pins being acciden-
tally dislodged. Nor did he bring along any claymore mines, though
he had considered bringing along the lone M–60 machinegun
assigned to the 516th.

The rubber plantation suddenly evolved into flatlands just before the highway entered a village straddling both sides of the road.
The big deuce roared through the village, flashing past thatch huts,
garden plots and open spaces filled with chickens, children and
potbellied pigs. There were no young adult males, and only a few
very young boys were in sight. The male adults left in the village
were old enough to rate wispy beards. The women wore conical
straw hats and loose fitting black pajamas. Most of them ignored the
deuce as they went about their work, with the older children caring
for the younger children. The few who paid any mind to the deuce
had vaguely hostile expressions.

"Man, this is worse'n driving through Mississippi with a white
woman," Skins joked.

Frenchie was lost in his own negative universe and didn't answer.

Diked rice paddies were spread over a wide plain beyond the
village. A few younger men and boys could be seen wading knee–
deep through the murky water, but most of the field workers were
women and older children.

Lewandowski was using his binoculars. "I see some flowers up ahead, alongside the road. Lot'sa flowers, boys! I see the enemy, and he is ours!"

Moments later, Charlie downshifted the deuce and angled for the roadside, finally bringing the truck to a screeching halt on a narrow strip of black earth separating the asphalt highway from a shallow ditch.

The 17th Aviation Group was within sight a short distance ahead, concentrated within three concentric perimeter rings. At least a dozen "Huey" helicopter gunships and Medivac "slicks" were landing and rising, while more were being tended by ground crews. The central structures were built with only a foot or two of sandbag wall and roof exposed to incoming rounds. Distant gunships were testing their weapons systems over a freefire zone, creating a deafening roar of miniguns, rockets and grenade lauchers.

"Alright, everybody out!" Lewandowski shouted as he jumped down from the cab of the deuce, landing with his M–14 locked and loaded. Two deuces roared by, honking their horns, waving and shouting garbled words that sounded a lot like "Dumb Shits!" along with a variety of other S.O.P. GI insults.

"Form up the guard detail!" Lewandowski shouted. "Now, now, now! Move it, move it, move it!"

"Transplant crew, get those trenching tools and buckets down from the deuce! I want every flower dug up and in those buckets before I can count to fifty. Move it, move it! This is not a Test! I WANNA SEE ASSHOLES AND ELBOWS!!!"

The six crew members assigned to the guard detail ran to their predetermined stations as Lewandowski climbed up to the cargo bed, commanding the high ground so he could spot enemy activity with the field binoculars. Four members of the guard detail positioned themselves behind the wheels and fenders at the four corners of the deuce, their M–14's locked and loaded, ready to engage the enemy. Two extra guards crawled under the midpoint of the deuce to assume prone firing positions covering both sides of the road.

The six members of the transplant detail—including Skins and Charlie Edwards—dashed into the ditch with their buckets and trenching tools, their M–14's strapped to their backs. Several lost their headgear in their frantic search for anything that even vaguely resembled flowers. Once spotted, the flowers—all of which looked suspiciously like weeds—were quickly unearthed and transferred to the half dozen empty five–gallon paint buckets Lewandowski scrounged from the supply depot.

Lewandowski propped his elbows on the cab to steady the binoculars while giving the area a good 360. He could see no Viet Cong, but he was able to identify a particularly interesting structure situated near the gate of the 17th Aviation Group. After one more 360 scan, he returned the binoculars to the two–story structure.

"My, my, my…what have we here?" Lewandowski asked himself. Even as he spoke, two GI's emerged from the front door of the distant abode, escorted by two girls in tight miniskirts. A jeep was parked alongside the porch, plus two three–quarter–ton trucks. The two deuces that just passed them were pulling into the parking lot.

"Man, what a gold mine. Right out here in the middle of nowhere," Lewandowski murmured to himself. "No competition for at least fifteen miles. That's what I call a prime location."

Frenchie started to shout in a loud falsetto. "Lewandowski! Lewandowski! Take a look over there at those dinks in the rice paddy." He was hiding behind the right rear tandem wheels of the deuce, guarding the quadrant he had been assigned by Charlie Edwards.

Everybody froze in place, drawn by the terror in his voice. Suddenly, the transplant detail hit the dirt they had been transplanting to the buckets. At least two other quadrants were going unguarded, now that Frenchie's quadrant was the focus of attention.

"They're pointing at us!" Frenchie screeched. "WHY are they pointing?! Use your glasses, man! Maybe they're directing fire! Sweet Mother of Jesus, let's get the hell out'a here! To hell with Masters and his flowers! I don't wanna die for a bunch of crummy flowers!"

Lewandowski inspected the distant field workers with his binoculars. "Hmmm. It looks like they're laughing."

"LAUGHING?" Frenchie screeched, adding an insane cackle of his own. "THEY'RE LAUGHING?!"

"Yup, I can see'em clear as a bell. They're pointing right at us…and they're laughing."

"LAUGHING?" Frenchie screeched again, unable to grasp the concept. "WHY LAUGHING?"

Lewandowski lowered his binoculars and shrugged. "Hmmmm. I don't know. That is strange."

"STRANGE?" Skins shouted from where he was hugging mother earth. "IS THAT MUH'FUH' ALL YOU CAN SAY...THAT IT'S STRANGE? CAN'T YOU COME UP WITH SOMETHING BETTER THAN THAT? GOOD GOD ALMIGHTY ...MAYBE THEY PLANTED LANDMINES AROUND HERE, MAN! THAT'S IT! THEY'RE LAUGHING CUZ THEY KNOW WE'RE GONNA GET BLOWN TO HELL!"

"Don't say hell," Charlie pleaded from his hiding place in the ditch. "Anything but hell. Don't say hell."

"Good point, Skins," Lewandowski acknowledged as he noted the nearly full five–gallon cans. "I think we got enough flowers now, anyway. Come on back to the truck, guys. And try to step where you stepped before, okay? Skins might be onto something with that landmine idea of his."

"Man, I can't believe I'm doing this," Skins muttered as he slowly rose to a crouched position; not exactly frozen with fear, but certainly well frosted. He reached for his bucket of dirt and some-what mangled flowering weeds. "Dear Mrs. Williams, your son was killed while digging for flowers."

"Please don't say that," Charlie pleaded as he tried to retrace his steps back to the deuce, having little luck matching his return steps to the patches of crushed grass he left behind.

After long harrowing moments, the transplanters reached the relative safety of the highway.

"Let's get out'a here," Frenchie pleaded.

Lewandowski had overcome his fear of sharpshooters. At the moment, he was being influenced by a different primal urge. "Hold it. Everyone At Ease. We got business to discuss."

"What's with you, man?" Skins demanded. "We gotta get out of here."

Lewandowski looked down at Frenchie from his vantage point on the truck bed. "Come on up here. I got somethin' to show you. It'll just take a sec."

Lewandowski hefted Frenchie up with one arm and presented him with the binoculars. "Look over there and tell the guys what you see."

"Man, I don't see nothin'," Frenchie said. "Let's go home, man."

"Scan to your right," Lewandowski directed.

A moment later, Frenchie was smiling. "OOO–EEEE!"

"What'cha see?" Lewandowski asked.

"A whorehouse," Frenchie chuckled.

"Look again," Lewandowski said. "Do any of those GI's look worried?"

Frenchie laughed again. "No, Cherie, dey ain' sweatin' nuttin'."

"I would say that is a secured base of operations, wouldn't you, Frenchie?"

"Damn straight," Frenchie agreed.

Lewandowski proposed his plan. "I think we ought'a do a little social reconnoitering before we head back to tent city."

"Aw, I don't know," Charlie cautioned. "A minute ago I thought I was gonna die. Now you're talking about getting laid. I don't even know if I could get it up."

"Aw heck. We got plenty of daylight ahead of us," Lewandowski argued. "And we're probably safer there than we are in the Saigon Club. We got the time and it's my treat…my way of saying thanks for a job well done."

"You're buying?" Frenchie asked suspiciously.

"My treat, your money," Lewandowski corrected. "Hey, what other squad leader can you name who would come up with a fun idea like this?"

"Your fun ideas are gonna get us all killed someday," Skins grumbled. "Okay, count me in."

"Get those buckets up here and mount up," Lewandowski ordered. "He who hesitates is lost."

All objectives of the Search and Transplant mission, both floral and social, were completed by 1500 hours, which left the crew with time on their hands when they started back to Cam Ranh. It wouldn't have been fitting to end a dangerous mission with a early arrival, so Lewandowski was open to suggestions on ways to fill their time until they could heroically pass through the gate just before sunset. Everyone agreed it would do Masters good if they didn't arrive in tent city until after dark.

"Why don't we check out that church we saw," Skins suggested.

"Sounds like a plan to me," Lewandowski agreed.

A half hour later, Charlie turned onto the narrow driveway leading to the church, easing the heavy deuce over a patchwork of cracked asphalt. He idled the deuce deeper into the rising forest until they rounded a gentle bend that abruptly opened onto the churchyard, which was filled with dozens of children at play. Several nuns were supervising the children. Behind the children was an old, weather–worn church. The church was flanked on either side by elongated one–story stucco buildings. At one time, the mission must have been beautiful, but years of neglect were showing. The stucco walls were weathered to a dull gray stained with large patches of green fungus; the red tile roofs had been patched and re–patched, repairing what should have been replaced. Everything seemed to be in dire need of repair or maintenance.

A large, well–tended vegetable garden with an accompanying rice paddy was located in a clearing behind the church. Several dilapidated outbuildings were sitting off to the side of the garden, including a small barn that looked ready to collapse of its own weight.

Several nuns were gathering the children, herding them away from the deuce toward the front doors of the church. It was an orderly retreat, with several of the smaller children bursting into tears for losing their playtime.

"Oh Jeeze, that's all we need," Lewandowski groaned. "We're scaring the hell out'a them. Is there enough room to turn around? We gotta get out of here doubletime. The shit'll hit the fan if word gets back to Masters and Ortega that we were terrorizing a bunch of nuns and little kids."

"We don't have room to turn around here," Charlie said. "I'll have to go all the way in to get the space I need to hang a one–eighty."

Lewandowski groaned. "Okay, if we gotta, we gotta, but do it real slow so they don't get the wrong idea. Jeeze, there's half–breed kids all over the place. It's gotta be an orphanage. I can hear it now. Masters will go apeshit when he hears about this."

The church door closed behind the last of the children.

"Well, should I go in and turn around, or what?" Charlie asked.

"Good grief, I donno," Lewandowski moaned. "Maybe we ought'a try backing out."

The church doors opened again and a caucasian nun dressed entirely in white stepped outside, pausing on the front steps with a stern expression.

"Thank God," Lewandowski said. "At least there's someone we can talk to. Stop right here, Charlie, and I'll set her straight."

Lewandowski started to climb from the cab with his M–14, but Charlie grabbed for it. "Leave that here," Charlie advised. "It'll look better."

"Yeah, you're right," Lewandowski agreed. He spoke to the Dirty Dozen through the rear window. "You guys keep your eyes peeled at those trees on the perimeter. I'm gonna talk to that nun and ease her mind a little before we dee dee mow out'a here."

Lewandowski clambered down from the cab and began walking toward the church, taking slow steps, making no rash moves. "I'm really sorry about this, ma'am," he explained as he approached the nun in white. "We shouldn't be here and we know it. We were just curious about the church we saw. We sure don't wanna scare nobody. 'Specially the little ones…the kids."

The nun raised one eyebrow, forcing Lewandowski to stop dead in his tracks, allowing her at least fifty feet of buffer space. He removed his helmet and clasped it to his chest with both hands, praying silently that he wasn't setting himself up as an easy target for a VC sniper hiding in the surrounding jungle.

"I'm sorry, ma'am, I really am," Lewandowski repeated, pleading for good old fashioned Christian forgiveness. "I'm afraid we gotta come in all the way to have enough room to turn around.

Once we do that, I promise we'll be on our way and you won't ever see us again."

The nun said nothing while holding the moral high ground. The GI's might have the weapons, but she was in charge.

"Excuse me, ma'am," Lewandowski said very respectfull, and turned to speak to the Dirty Dozen. "You better lower your weapons. We're probably scaring her."

He turned back to the nun. "Can you speak English, ma'am? If you don't, one of us speaks Cajun, and that's supposed to be a lot like French. We don't mean you any harm, ma'am. We're just a bunch of dumb GI's poking our noses where we're not wanted."

The nun smiled slightly. "I can speak English, Sergeant."

Her French accent was thick but understandable. "Did you not know that Nhan Ai is Off Limits?"

Lewandowski shook his head, filled with contrition. "No, ma'am, I can honestly say we didn't know that."

She allowed herself to smile, relieving the tension. "We are not accustomed to receiving visitors here, Sergeant. There was a sign beside the highway saying we are off limits, but it must have fallen down. Perhaps it was God's Will. It was not our idea to have such a sign. We don't mind when soldiers visit the orphanage. We rather enjoy such visits, if you mean us no harm."

"Oh, we don't mean you any harm, ma'am," Lewandowski said reassuringly. "We're sorry about scaring you like we did. It's all my fault, ma'am," he added, feeling safe to take responsibility now that it looked like things might work out just fine in the end...no harm done; no sweat, GI.

The door to the church opened part way, allowing one of the Vietnamese nuns to speak to the NIC (Nun In Charge), using French rather than Vietnamese. Tiny, curious faces peeked out at Lewandowski before being gently ushered back inside.

Skins nudged Frenchie and whispered. "What she say?"

Frenchie shrugged. "Cajun's different, but I think she asked if the Mother Superior was okay."

"Mother Superior?" Skins asked. He had attended the A.M.E. church as a child, but he'd seen enough Catholic movies to know that a Mother Superior was a ranking position.

The Mother Superior replied in French.

"What'd she say?" Skins whispered again.

"She told her not to worry, that we're more scared than they are."

"Hey...." Skins objected, though not strongly.

"Would it be all right if we drove in further so's we can get turned around, ma'am?" Lewandowski asked.

Lewandowski was raised a nominal Methodist and had no idea he was talking to a Mother Superior. It was his military horse sense that told him she must have some rank, or she wouldn't be the only nun wearing a white habit. He calculated she must be the equivalent of at least a light Colonel, if not a full Bird Colonel.

"Certainly you may do so, Sergeant," she agreed. "But perhaps you would like to spend a few moments with us before you go. The children so rarely get to see American soldiers, and you seem like such nice men. It would be good for them to meet you and your friends. I am Mother Marie–Teresa. Welcome to Nhan Ai."

Skins sighed. "Man, I love it when chicks talk French."

"Man, you're a pervert," Frenchie shot back, adding several oaths in particularly spicey back–bayou Cajun.

Lewandowski didn't know what to say, so he turned to the others for advice. "What'cha think, guys? If you got the mind to do it, we got the time."

"The place is off limits," Charlie reminded him.

"Like she said, the sign must'a fallen down," Lewandowski rationalized. "How were we supposed to know it was off limits?"

"We're supposed to stay on the road," Charlie reminded him. "Just being here is a violation of regulations." Charlie preferred to keep his Speck Four stripes on his sleeve after all the sewing he'd done the night before.

"Oh, like we stayed on the road back there when we were at the place of business we visited earlier," Lewandowski whispered back. "I didn't hear you objecting then. At least here we can say we're on a humanitarian mission."

"Humanitarian mission?" Charlie asked skeptically. "How do you figure?"

"Hey, we can drop off the C–rations I brought along. If we get caught we can say we came in to give it to the kids. I'd say that's pretty darned humanitarian of us."

"You will be safe here," Mother Marie–Teresa assured them all. "The Viet Cong are not operating in this vicinity now."

"Really?" Lewandowski asked. "How'd you know that, ma'am?"

"We have friends who keep us informed of such things," she explained. "It would be very good for the children if you were to join us for tea and pastries. Should anyone ask, I would say you are here at our invitation."

Lewandowski turned to his partners in crime. "Okay, let's do it."

The Dirty Dozen dismounted and leaned their weapons against the wheel wells…Life just ain't no fun unless you're willing to take a few chances. Charlie followed, reluctantly going along with the rule of the majority.

The Mother Superior spoke to the nun guarding the church door, using Vietnamese this time. A moment later the doors swung open, allowing an oversized platoon of children to file outside, escorted by a watchful cadre of nuns and older children.

"We will serve the refreshments out here so you can stand guard," Mother Marie–Teresa suggested. She spoke in Vietnamese again, sending several nuns and older children to an outbuilding before explaining to her guests. "I have told them to prepare green tea and some of our favorite delicacies that are very sweet, very good."

More nuns exited the church, carrying infants. Several of the uniformed teenage girls helping the nuns were attractive in a virginal fashion that was altogether different from the girls who worked the bars and steambaths of the Vill. It was a side of Vietnamese femininity that the Originals hadn't seen before. Adaptations had to be made: Nary a single obscenity would be used while they remained at Nhan Ai. It was an honor thing. Any of their number who was rude and crude in front of the nuns and the kids would have found himself in deep trouble.

However, some speculative conversation was allowable, if conducted privately.

"Man, no wonder they keep'em hidden," Skins whispered to Frenchie after a particularly attractive girl passed by. His tone was respectful without being saintly.

"Yeah, man," Frenchie agreed. "But I'll bet the nuns don't let'em out'a their sight. Catholic school is Catholic school, no matter where you go."

"Look at that little black sister holding the baby," Skins said. "She could walk the streets of Chicago and I wouldn't know she had any Vietnamese in her. I wonder if she speaks English."

Frenchie scanned the faces of the children milling around the nuns. "Some of'em look American, but you gotta look hard to see the American in others. The older ones, they must be French. We ain't been over here that long."

"Yeah, but there's a lot more of the little ones," Skins said as he scanned the faces. "Man, I keep thinkin' about that chick in the Saigon Club...the one that's knocked up."

Frenchie nodded "I wonder what kinda life her kid'll have."

"Yeah," Skins agreed, thinking particularly of the black kids.

Mother Marie–Teresa spoke to the Originals. "Please, gentlemen, sit down wherever you like while the food and tea are prepared. I wish I could offer you better, but we know you must stay outside and keep watch."

Lewandowski made a funny face at one of the toddlers. The child giggled and hid behind the skirts of a nun, just like kids back in The World.

Charlie introduced himself to Mother Marie–Teresa and opened with polite conversation. "This is a nice place you have here. You're doing good work, ma'am."

She smiled, accepting the compliment graciously. "It is our mission to undo some of the damage that comes from the sins of man."

Charly nodded uncomfortably.

The food began to arrive. "Please forgive me for being so proud of our food in Vietnam," Mother Marie–Teresa said as the tea and pastries were shared among the Originals. "The cuisine is a combination of the best from Asia and the best from France, bringing together delicate flavors that you will not find elsewhere.

Please make yourselves as comfortable as you can, and enjoy."

"What you have seen is not the real Vietnam," Mother Marie–Teresa explained to a group of Originals sitting around her on the grass, while other Originals played with children under the watchful eyes of attending nuns. The Mother Superior and several sisters were sitting on folding chairs, each holding an infant or toddler, completely at ease with the task of being mothers to so many children.

"The Vietnamese have very strict rules of moral conduct," she continued. "Marriage is for a lifetime. Chastity and family loyalty are the most important attributes a bride can bring to a groom. If there is no proof of virginity on the marriage sheets the next morning, the groom's mother can say the marriage is invalid."

Frenchie nodded, understanding the rigid code.

"Family responsibility and respect for one's ancestors is everything in Vietnam," she continued. "Some call it ancestor worship, but it is not worship as much as it is a deep sense of respect and obligation to one's family and ancestors. The obligation is so deep that a woman retains her family name when she marries, remaining forever responsible to her father and her ancestors."

"That is why it is so sad for these children. You see, they have no fathers to give them identity…a place in society. Without that, they can never be a whole person. Some Vietnamese can be cruel about it. They sometimes call them Children of Dust."

She paused for others to speak, but no one interrupted.

"What you have seen is a corruption of Vietnamese culture after more than a century of colonization and warfare. No society can withstand such pressures without sacrificing something, and much of what has been sacrificed in Vietnam concerns culture and morality. Most of the young women who work in the bars are doing so not because they love what they do, but because they must make money for their families to survive. By our standards, you are very rich…you can afford to spend your money foolishly in the bars, making babies you don't even know about. But your money has been very upsetting to our lives. Everything now costs so much more than it should. Our lives have been turned upside down. Did you know, a girl working in a bar can make more than a general in the Vietnamese Army? It has made everything very distorted."

"Your dollars are more damaging to your cause than the communists are," she cautioned. "The money is corrupting everyone so much that, very soon, the people will have nothing worth fighting for."

"It is a sad time for the Catholics," she continued later. "The communists have treated the church very badly over the years. If they win this war, I will probably go to prison or be sent back to France. I do not know what will happen to my Vietnamese sisters, or the priests and our parishioners, but I think they will not be treated kindly. It is what happened in North Vietnam when the communists came to power, and it is likely to happen here if they come to power. Life under the communists will be very difficult, and it will be twice as sad because we will all know we allowed it to happen."

"We're in too deep to get out now," Charlie said.

"Perhaps," she agreed. "It is a very confusing situation for many Europeans who live in Vietnam. We find ourselves caught in the middle. We want the Americans to leave, but we don't want the communists to win.

She bounced the child on her lap, silencing a tiny wail. "These are the most innocent victims of all. If I could, I would take them all to a place where they can feel good about themselves, even if they have no fathers. But I cannot do that. I must stay here to care for the new ones that are being brought to us."

"Why do the mothers leave their kids with you?" Skins asked.

"Many do not," she corrected. "Many of the mothers raise the children on their own. But it is very difficult to raise children in places like Cam Ranh. It is so bad there...so corrupt. Some of the mothers take the children home to be raised by their parents, but that is not an easy thing, either. The embarrassment can be difficult for a family to bear. It is assumed the mother is a prostitute if she gives birth to an Amerasian."

"What will happen to them when they're too old to stay here?" Lewandowski asked.

She shrugged, a very French gesture. "We never consider them too old. They have a home here forever, if they want. As for those who choose to leave, I do not know what their lives will be like. We try to educate them so they can work, but life will always be difficult because they don't have families to help them."

"I always figured the girls in the bars used the pill," Skins said.

"Birth control?" the Mother asked with an ironic half–smile. "This is not America…the girls cannot visit the pharmacy and order birth control pills. I have a question for you…why don't you use condoms?"

Skins shook his head, embarassed by the question. "Hey, I'm not gonna get into that."

"The girls have told me their boyfriends will go to other girls if they insist a condom be used. Such is life. The soldiers don't get pregnant, so they don't care. They can get venereal diseases, but they don't seem to care about that, either. You are soldiers, so you know more about those things than I do. Why don't the soldiers care about such things?"

Skins cleared his throat, growing more uncomfortable with the subject. Nuns shouldn't be talking about such things.

Lewandowski glanced at his watch. "We better get a move on," he suggested

Mother Marie Teresa rose with the Originals, offering each a vigorous handshake. "Please forgive me for being such a complainer. Sometimes I say too much. I don't want to make you angry or embarrass you. I want you to visit us again. The children need to see good men who are American soldiers. You can help them believe their own fathers were good, kind men. And that is a very important thing in Vietnam. Please come back to Nhan Ai whenever you can. You will always be welcome."

"No problem, ma'am. We'll be back," Lewandowski promised. "Is there anything we can do to help you? Maybe things we can get for you from the supply depot. We got some food rations we can drop off today, if that'll help."

She laughed. "We need everything. But most of all, we need you to visit the children. I have never seen them happier. You have made them love you."

"Grab your weapons, and mount up," Lewandowski said to the others. "We gotta get moving."

Poppasan and Stoned Poppasan were just concluding their long day of KP duties when the deuce rolled into tent city, coming to a rattling halt on the tarmac beside the mess tent.

"Eff–Tee–Yay, Puck De Armay," Poppasan called out to the Search and Transplant detail as they unloaded the buckets of dirt and flowers. The poppasans couldn't speak a word of English when they were hired as KP's, but the Originals were glad to give lessons in short timer English.

"FTA, poppasan," the crew called back.

Stoned Poppasan was sitting on a table top, smoking his small pewter pipe with the usual faraway look in his eyes. Between the two of them, they couldn't have weighed much more than one medium–sized GI, but they never complained and they were always on time, as regular as clockwork.

"Okay, let's get these flowers to Sgt. Lugo and head to the supply tent," Lewandowski said. "I've worked up a thirst for cold beer."

"What'cha make of those kids we saw?" Skins asked as he hoisted down a bucket of withered weeds.

"Well, it's a shame, but what can we do about it?" Lewandowski answered. "The girls in the Vill ain't gonna change any more than the GI's they do business with."

"What about wearing a rubber?" Skins asked. "What she said got me to thinking."

"Tell me somethin'," Lewandowski said as he accepted a bucket from Skins. "Have any of the bar girls ever asked you to wear a rubber when you made the deal?"

Skins shook his head. "Yeah, I know what'cho mean. Someone's been jivin' the Sister, man"

Lewandowski nodded. "All I've seen is, *You gimme money, I do for you...No have VD...No sweat, GI.* Hey, I know it ain't smart to go skinny dipping, but I know I ain't about take no celibacy vows when that perimeter of ours may not hold some night. I'm a heck of a lot less worried about the clap than I am a human wave assault."

The buckets were transferred to the planters in the mess tent under the skeptical supervision of mess sergeant Lugo.

"They look dead," Lugo complained to Lewandowski. "Why

you bringing me dead flowers?"

"Aw, Sarge, they ain't dead. All you gotta do is give'em some water and they'll come right back, good as new."

Lugo wasn't convinced. "I don't care if you say Hail Marys over these flowers, they ain't comin' back."

Lewandowski was in no mood to argue. "Take it to the IG, Sarge. We did our part. The rest is up to you. By the way, you seen Masters hanging around tent city? I thought he'd be here to give us a ration of shit when we pulled in."

"He headed for his hooch about an hour ago," Lugo said.

Lewandowski muttered to himself, disappointed that Masters hadn't waited around to hear his war stories.

"I got cold cuts and bread waitin' for you," Lugo offered.

"Thanks anyway, Sarge, but I was gonna break open some cold beer in the supply tent."

"Don't you wanna eat?" Lugo asked. "I got good salami and baloney."

"We can chow down on some cans of PX lasagne when we get the munchies," Lewandowski said. "Thanks anyway, Sarge."

"Eff Tee Yaye! Puck De Armay!" The poppasans shouted as the Originals exited the mess tent.

"FTA," the Originals answered.

"PX lasagna," Lugo said with a distainful snort. "I hope they get heartburn from it."

Chapter Seven

"So, what's the plan?" Skins asked.

It was 0730 hours, the morning after Lewandowski finished the shake'n'bake construction honcho course at the 62nd Combat Engineers. He had assembled the Dirty Dozen and Charlie Edwards in the supply tent for a de–briefing that opened with an unusually honest appraisal of the regulatory landmines they would be treading upon when throwing monkey wrenchs into the construction of the new company area and personnel center.

"Last night Louie went over the regulations we'll be mangling if we're gonna save tent city. And I don't mind telling you, it scared the hell out'a me when he started talking punishment. If they can prove we intentionally screwed–up the project, we'll be in a world of hurt."

Lewandowski allowed them to chew on the bad news a moment before continuing. GI's tend to look on the negative side, even with good news, and he wanted them to get all the negatives out of their system before he hit them with the good news. Even a bad meal can be fondly recalled when it is followed by a particularly delicious desert.

"The key words are prove and intent, "Lewandowski continued. "It's like Louie said, they have to prove we intended to screw–up the work if they're gonna court martial us. Now, that sort of thing is pretty hard to prove. They'd need witnesses who heard us brag about it, things like that, so we gotta keep our big mouths shut around the Lifers."

"Ain't no Original ever gonna testify against another Original," Skins boasted.

Lewandowski nodded, but he wasn't yet ready to serve the desert. They had to finish the vegetables remaining on their plates.

"But if they can prove intent, then they just might go for a more serious charge...like sabotage. For which, the maximum penalty is death before a firing squad."

"Aw, hey, that's rotten, man," Frenchie said. "They can't do that, can they?"

Lewandowski nodded. "Yup. They sure can."

"That's all I need to hear," Skins announced and rose from his pile of soiled bedding, ready to resign from the conspiracy. "Count me out'a this, man. You start talkin' gettin' shot and this muh'fuh' starts lookin' fo' the door."

"Si'down, si'down," Lewandowski said consolingly. He had expected such a reaction. "That's all the bad news. It gets easier to hear from now on."

"It better," Skins warned while resuming his seat.

Lewandowski opened the desert menu with a wide grin. "They won't know what hit'em. Check this out...it won't be **our** fault if the cement for the floors gets mixed wrong by someone else and started cracking like crazy after it was poured. Right?"

"Right," Skins agreed reluctantly. "Keep goin'...I'm listenin'. I ain't signed on no dotted line yet, neither."

"It ain't **our** fault if we don't get the building materials we need when we need them," Lewandowski added with exaggerated innocence. "You can't build somethin' with nothin', right?"

The frowns were beginning to turn into smiles.

"And nobody can give me **too** much trouble if I make you guys do some things that create problems later on. Like, hey, I don't know nothin' about construction. I'm just a dumb jock that was drafted into the Army and sent to some school for six days. Heck, I can't remember half the stuff I was taught. And that's the truth...it was coming at me too fast. I did my best, but you can't expect miracles. Ain't that right?"

"Right," several agreed, with all but one nodding their heads.

Only Frenchie remained skeptical. "Yeah, well, what happens if it don't work out that way? Mistakes happen, people talk. We could find our butts hangin' in the wind if we get caught messin' around like this."

"We won't be doing it alone," Lewandowski explained. "The guys down at the personnel center will be doing some horse trading with troops in other units to get most of it handled. Half the time I won't even know what kind of deals have been made until we start having problems...like with supplies being sent to other units by mistake, or going to Nhan Ai...and bad materials coming our way.

That sort of thing. Louie says we'll be doing it just like the Mafia. No one will know enough to get anyone else in a serious jam. Louie calls it Deniability, and we're gonna make sure we got enough of it to cover everyone."

Lewandowski paused, satisfied that the plan devised by the board of directors the night before was airtight and waterproof. All bases were covered. They even had their legal defense ready to be implemented, should it become necessary.

"All we gotta do is keep any hint of what's happening from Masters," Lewandowski added. "Watch what you say around him. Dummy up if you see him within a hundred yards. If we get past him, the brass won't know what's happening. And even if they do, they won't be able to prove anything."

"Masters is gonna hammer us no matter what you say," Frenchie warned. "He ain't gonna like it when we get behind schedule."

"Leave Masters to me," Lewandowski said. "That's the way the chain of command is supposed to work. I'm in charge of the crew. If he's got problems, he's supposed to come to me, not you guys."

"As long as I don't end up in Camp LBJ, I don't care how it's handled," Frenchie said.

Lewandowski looked from man to man, gauging their unity and resolve until he was satisfied they were ready to perform their duty in the mission to save tent city.

"I think we got it made in the shade," Lewandowski predicted confidently. "They ain't gonna touch us. Tent city will be Home Sweet Home for the rest of our tours. It'll be up to our replacements to finish the project."

The conference was interrupted when the phone rang. Hanley, the morning meport clerk, had a message for Lewandowski. "Masters wants to see you in the orderly tent on the double."

"Did he say what about?"

"Naw."

"He prob'ly wants to put a bee up my ass about the project," Lewandowski said with a wink at the others. "I'll be right up."

"Some of you give Charlie a hand counting the gas masks for

inventory. The rest start getting the tools together. Clean'em up and oil'em so they look nice and pretty. Masters might be in an inspection mood."

Lewandowski headed for the orderly tent, where he saw two jeeps parked outside the rear tent flap. One belonged to Masters, but the other carried the painted bumper tag for the 62nd Combat Engineers. Even so, no alarm bells were ringing in Lewandowski's cranium. He was riding the crest of a wave that had no end. Gone were the dark clouds promising slow death by conformity in the sterile suburbs. The future looked bright and clear for tent city.

Lewandowski entered the orderly tent through the front flap and paused to tap on the door to Masters' office. Once directed inside, he rendered a crisp salute Front and Center. It wasn't until he was put At Ease that he glanced at the other presence in the office, a Staff Sergeant he recognized as being one of the classroom instructors at the 62nd Combat Engineers. The Sergeant, who was sitting at stiff semi–Attention, nodded when recognized by Lewandowski.

"Have a seat," Masters offered pleasantly, indicating Lewandowski's place in a vacant chair. "Perhaps you remember Sergeant Slater from a course he taught at the 62nd."

Lewandowski nodded and shook Slater's hand before sitting down. Slater taught a short course Lewandowski daydreamed his way through...something to do with roof rafters. Lewandowski figured the work on the project would never get that far, so he tuned out to recollect moments of past glory on the gridiron.

Masters continued: "Sergeant Slater will be acting as an on–site advisor during the construction of the new company area and personnel center."

The announcement brought Lewandowski abruptly back to reality. "Advisor, Sir?"

"Yes, advisor," Masters confirmed. "Sergeant Slater has been attached to the 516th for duty purposes and will remain until our work is completed. I thought it would be wise to have someone with more extensive construction experience in overall charge of the project. From now on, you'll report to Sergeant Slater and Sergeant Slater will report to me. Of course, you'll remain in charge of the supply tent. That hasn't changed. Which is another reason why I need someone like Slater in charge. The supply function is critical to the success of this project, and it would be asking too much to ask one man to wear both hats."

Lewandowski eyed Slater more closely. The man had Lifer written all over him from the soles of his spitshined boots to the stubble of his white–sidewall regulation haircut.

Masters continued. "We have a lot of work to do over the next few months. I'll leave it up to you to introduce Sergeant Slater to the crewmembers."

Masters directed his next comment to Slater. "I assume I won't be hearing from you unless you encounter problems you cannot handle on your own."

The warning from Masters was implicit. 'Make sure you don't come to me with problems that complicate my life.'

"You gotta see this guy to believe him," Lewandowski confided to the other members of the board of directors that evening. They had gathered in the sand dunes behind tent city, well beyond the dim light reflecting from the whitewashed movie screen. Below them, the troops were watching yet another screening of THE GLASS BOTTOM BOAT, starring Doris Day and Rock Hudson. Charlie was handling the movie projector, assisted by Frenchie Beaumont.

"He's a Lifer's Lifer," Lewandowski continued, keeping his voice low. "A Sergeant Rock type. He's real gung ho, not just irritatingly gung ho. He keeps talking about the Baptism of Fire and crap like that. He keeps it up all day long. And Lord, does he love to give orders. He's got the Dirty Dozen so pissed that somebody's gonna bust him in the chops and end up going to Camp LBJ, if he don't back off. And you can bet yer boots, he won't back off. I tell ya, we gotta get rid of this guy. If we don't, I might bust him myself."

"Cool down," Louie said while accepting the opium–laced marijuana joint from Jackson. He took a small hit before passing it on to Peters.

The perimeter had been particularly active that night. The fireworks commenced shortly after nightfall, opening with a heavy rocket and mortar attack in the vicinity of the North perimeter gate, followed by what appeared to be a ground attack. It was unusually early for such a large attack to take place, and the defenders were taken by surprise. Five Huey gunships quickly came down, and more choppers were disabled when lifting off to defend the perimeter.

Louie Donnatelli watched the distant attack without saying much of anything, though he and his crew could expect to be busy processing personnel files for the KIAs and WIAs tomorrow. Usually he passed on the marijuana, but this evening he accepted the offer.

"Slater's full of it," Jackson said after he exhaled. "I looked at his 201 file after you called me. This is his first combat assignment in fifteen years in the Army."

Louie again accepted the marijuana when it came back around.

"He spent his last nine years at Ft. Sill Oklahoma," Jackson continued.

"So, Slater's a phony," Lewandowski grumbled.

"I called a guy I know in the 62nd to get the skinny on him," Jackson continued. "The word is, nobody has any use for him....even the other Lifers. He harasses the troops under him and sucks up to the brass. Since coming in–country he's been going to the Chaplain, bucking for a hardship transfer back to The World because his wife is splitting the sheets on him. The head docs laughed him off when he tried for a Section Eight transfer."

"Masters should'a kept his big mouth shut," Lewandowski said. "He asked for an advisor and they send us the company jerk."

"Masters didn't bring this down," Jackson said. "It came from Brigade. We got Slater dumped on us to get him out'a the 62nd. That's the story that I got, anyway. The best way to get along with Slater is to stay out of his way."

"Yeah, well that won't work for those of us who'll be working with him," Lewandowski said. He tossed a handful of sand into the darkness. "We're screwed...Slater changes everything. Tent city is history. We'll be lucky to get through this without someone doing bad time in LBJ."

Louie spoke from the darkness, his voice soft, almost feminine under the influence of the marijuana. He sounded distant, but completely at peace with himself.

"I don't agree," Louie said. "If Masters were really gung ho behind this guy, you'd be screwed. But he isn't...and that opens doors of opportunity for us."

"What'cha mean?" Lewandowski asked.

"You need to make Slater as irritating to Masters as he is to you," Louie suggested. "In the meantime, I can go to work finding opportunities for Sergeant Slater to experience the Baptism of Fire first hand."

Louie spoke to Jackson. "You saw his 201 file, Jackson. Is it flagged for re–assignment?"

"No, he's clear," Jackson said.

"Good, that'll make it easier," Louie said softly. "We'll put his name on every MOS levee we can find, starting tomorrow morning. If he's qualified in more than one MOS, it increases the odds in our favor."

"What's an MOS Levee?" Lewandowski asked.

"All the replacement requests from field units are combined into a master list," Jackson explained. "The list tells us they need so many Eleven Bravos or whatever, and we fill the open slots with names and service numbers. Within a couple of days, the orders are cut and they're gone. Sorry 'bout that, GI. You got a new home."

"How long will it take to get rid of Slater?" Lewandowski asked.

"It's hard to say," Louie answered. "It depends on what his primary and secondary MOSes are. If we're taking a lot of casualties in those MOSes, it won't take long. It could be just a matter of days, depending on how many levees we get and what MOSes they're looking for. In the meantime, you gotta keep your cool."

"I'm more worried about the Dirty Dozen than myself," Lewandowski said. "Even Charlie's talking knuckle sandwich. I tell ya, this guy really gets on your nerves."

"You can use that to your advantage," Louie suggested. "Masters doesn't suffer fools gladly. You need to create ways for him to get to know Slater as he really is. Allow familiarity to breed contempt. It's like allowing gravity to do the work for you."

"Okay, now you got me," Lewandowski said. "What are you

talking about?"

"Every manager has his own style," Louie said. "You have yours...Masters has his, I have mine. Masters likes to manage from a distance. He's not a hands–on type. He doesn't want to know the details...the chickenshit problems that pop up. He just wants it done. Am I right?"

"Yeah, you got'im nailed," Lewandowski answered.

"That's why he made you the honcho of the Dirty Dozen," Louie continued. "You make his job easier. With this guy Slater, you gotta turn that to your advantage. Figure out ways to make him go running to Masters with chickenshit problems. Make things happen. If you can do that, you got it handled. Before you know it, Masters will be doing everything he can to get Slater out'a his hair."

"You're a genius, Louie," Lewandowski said.

"Not really," Louie said. "I just stayed awake in Management 101 my freshman year at NYU. Talk to Charlie and the Dirty Dozen...bring them into it. I'm sure they'll help you come up with some creative solutions."

Sergeant Slater's problems with the Dirty Dozen began early the next morning, when a deuceload of plywood arrived at the construction site, and Slater ordered Lewandowski to order the crew to unload the plywood ASAP. As was his management style, Slater hovered in place, waiting for his orders to be carried out in a timely and expeditious fashion.

"It's really a better idea just to tell'em what you want done and leave'em to do it," Lewandowski suggested, knowing Slater was likely to do just the opposite. "They work better when they're not being watched."

"In a pig's eye," Slater growled. "When I give an order, I expect it to be followed. If they don't want me watching, they better learn they gotta jump right to it; not hang around with their thumbs up their butts, like these goofballs."

To make his point, Slater singled out Frenchie Beaumont for a tongue lashing.

"Get a move on there, soldier. I wanna see assholes and elbows out'a you."

Frenchie replied in Cajun heavily spiced with an attitude that couldn't be misinterpreted.

Slater turned to Lewandowski, his face livid. "Did you hear what he said to me?"

"I heard something," Lewandowski admitted. "But I got no idea what he said."

"Yeah, well, you don't hav'ta speak French to know he was showing disrespect," Slater countered.

"That wasn't French," Lewandowski explained. "That was Cajun. Frenchie's Cajun, not French."

"Then why do you call him Frenchie?" Slater demanded.

"Because it would sound really dumb to call him Cagey," Lewandowski answered. "That don't even make sense. Hey, Cagey! See? He don't answer to it."

"You're as bad as they are," Slater said.

Lewandowski shrugged. "I tried to tell you, they work best when they're not being watched.

"Look at'em," Slater demanded. "They're taking all day to do a job that can be done in fifteen minutes."

Lewandowski watched as the crew slowly and carefully unloaded the sheets of plywood from the deuce–and–a–half, taking care not to crowd each other as they moved slowly to the truck, then to the small but growing stack of unloaded plywood.

"Maybe Frenchie was just making a suggestion or something," Lewandowski said, trying to sound helpful. "Sometimes he forgets to use English. He's a back bayou boy. Y'know, some of those boys are still fighting the Civil War. We're lucky he's on our side. 'Specially 'cuz I got no idea what he's saying unless he wants me to know."

"Bullshit," Slater growled. "I wasn't born yesterday. He was cursing me, I know he was. Christ, how the hell can they expect me to get anything accomplished with a detail like this? I've never seen such a lazy, worthless bunch of hardcases in my life."

"Maybe I ought'a lend the guys a hand, if you're in a hurry to get that truck unloaded," Lewandowski offered.

"No–way," Slater said firmly. "I've been watching how you handle those troops and it's about time I gave you a little lesson in leadership."

"Alright," Lewandowski said, sounding like the very soul of reason. "Teach me how to do it, Sarge."

"You're trying to be a buddy to them," Slater begain. "Leaders lead...they don't pal around. That's the worst mistake an NCO can make."

"I'm not an NCO," Lewandowski said proudly. "The only one who's ever called me Sergeant is a nun who didn't know the difference. I'm an E–4. Heck, I couldn't get into the NCO Club if I wanted to. Which I don't."

"I can't believe this outfit," Slater muttered to himself. "How the hell do you expect to get anything accomplished with an attitude like that?"

Lewandowski said nothing, refusing to dignify a trick question with an answer. Even someone as dumb as Slater should have arrived at the obvious conclusion that Lewandowski and his crew were trying to accomplish little or nothing while appearing fully occupied.

Slater lowered his voice. "Don't do their work for them, Lewandowski. Tell them to do it. If necessary, order them, but don't ever do it yourself. Show'em you got a pair of balls."

The crew had stopped work to eavesdrop on Slater's training session.

"You troops get your butts in gear," Slater snapped. The detail remained frozen in place, awaiting confirmation from Lewandowski that the unscheduled break was over.

"You heard me," Slater growled. "Get back to work."

Still no movement.

Slater glared at Lewandowski. "Well?"

"Please get back to work," Lewandowski asked.

The crew resumed their prior, agonizingly slow pace.

"Please?" Slater gasped. "Please?! I can't believe what I'm hearing. Enough of the please–and–thank–you shit, Lewandowski. I'm ordering you to order them to go to work!"

"They're already working," Lewandowski countered.

"No they're not," Slater insisted. "They're faking it. You can't call what they're doing **work**. It's an insult to the word. Order them again, and this time sound like you mean it."

"Go back to work," Lewandowski said to the crew.

The crew stopped moving.

"Please go back to work," he said.

Slowly, they began to move again.

Lewandowski looked at Slater with an 'I told you so' shrug of his shoulders.

"Good grief, I just can't believe I'm seeing this," Slater grumbled. "I swear, if this happens again I'm going to put all of you on report. All of you."

"Get fucked," Frenchie said to Slater early the next day, not bothering with the Cajun this time.

"That's IT!" Slater shouted. "Now you went too far! I'm gonna burn your ass, Beaumont! I've had it with this lazy–assed detail! You're going to shape up or I'm gonna goddamned see that you get shipped out!"

"Why are you yelling at Frenchie?" Lewandowski asked as he strolled over to mediate the conflict.

"You heard what he said," Slater snapped. "I know you did. You weren't twenty feet away when he said it. I've had it! This is it! I'm through playing games with you jokers! I'm going to Masters with this!"

Lewandowski shrugged. "Okey doke. Do what'cho gotta do."

"I'm not kidding," Slater warned.

Frenchie snickered. "He's just blowing smoke, Lew. He ain't gonna do nothin'."

Slater turned to glare at Frenchie. "Do you realize what can happen to you if I go to Lt. Masters with this?"

"You can Kiss my ass, that's what'll happen," Frenchie answered.

Slater turned back to Lewandowski, his face several shades darker, his clenched fists shaking at his side.

"You heard **that**, didn't you?"

"Heard what?" Lewandowski asked.

Slater took a deep, calming breath. "Okay, so that's how its gonna be, huh? Alright, I can play that game as much as you like. I won't allow you to get by with this. You WILL be hearing from Lt.

Masters. I can promise you that."

A moment later, Slater was in his jeep, heading for tent city.

Lewandowski turned to Skins, who had walked over to join the mediation team. "Did you hear Frenchie say anything, Skins?"

"Ack–shu–ully," Skins answered with a stylishly English accent. "I heard Slater call Frenchie a dumb, lazy–assed Cajun."

"Did anyone else hear Slater say that?" Lewandowski asked the entire detail.

Everyone raised their hands.

"Well, okey doke then," Lewandowski said. "We can't allow that kind'a talk around here, can we?"

Agreement was immediate and unanimous.

"Very well done, gentlemen," Lewandowski said. "Now, let's get those bags of cement unloaded and wait around for Slater to tell us what to do next."

"Sergeant, I won't talk to them for you," Masters repeated. "If I did, I'd be hurting you, not helping you. I told you before, these are not the typical troops you can intimidate with threats of punishment. These guys probably know the regulations better than most career men. And they're definitely not dummies. They're smart. They know how to protect themselves."

"But, Sir," Slater argued. "He told me to get fucked. I heard him. I know I heard him, Sir."

"Do you have anyone else who would testify that he said it?"

"Just Lewandowski, Sir," Slater answered.

Masters maintained a blank expression, hiding his thoughts. He was wondering if Slater wasn't more than just a little flaky.

Slater corrected himself. "I don't have witnesses, Sir, but I would swear that Frenchie said it."

"But you have no corroborating witnesses," Masters suggested tonelessly.

"No, Sir," Slater admitted.

"You tried to order them around, didn't you?" Masters said accusingly.

"I did my job as I've been trained to do it, Sir."

"Aaah...you did your job," Masters repeated, followed by another sigh. "And tell me, Sergeant…since you started doing your job, how much have you been able to accomplish toward the mission of building a new company area and personnel center?"

Slater paused to consider his words before he spoke. "Sir, this is just my second day with the crew. I can honestly say I've done everything but say please, Sir, but they refuse to follow orders."

Masters sighed again. "You played it by the book, but you got nothing accomplished, right?"

Slater avoided direct eye contact, admitting nothing.

"They were one step ahead of you all the way," Masters said. "You never had them guessing, Sergeant. Didn't I tell you to keep them guessing what you were going to do next?"

Slater maintained his silence. He was coming to the conclusion that Masters was one of those New Action Army Lieutenants, a college boy who was afraid to get tough on the troops. Maybe even the lowest of the low…a West Pointer.

"Sergeant," Masters continued. "If I talk to them it would be the same as announcing to the whole company that Lewandowski is a better NCO than you are. You have to get them under control. You have to lead them. Not me."

"Sir, it shouldn't be like this," Slater protested. "If they don't follow orders they should be punished for it."

"It's my job to make those decisions, isn't it, Sergeant Slater?" Masters asked, sounding dangerously pleasant.

Slater nodded forlournly. "Yes, Sir."

Masters sighed again. He could understand why Lewandowski and his crew were giving Slater such a hard time. He really was a dumb sonofabitch.

"Sergeant, you apparently don't understand what we're dealing with here in the 516th AG. We have a critical mission to fulfill. To get it accomplished, we must maintain a high level of morale. And we won't be able to do that if we start busting the troops every time they step a little out of line. These troops stick together, Sergeant. It may not always be in ways you or I like, but it is a kind of Esprite de Corps that gets things done. We weren't sent over here to build barracks. We were sent here to make sure the troops in the field get the best damn support that is possible."

"Watch how Lewandowski operates," Masters advised. "He doesn't go by the book, but he gets things done. This is the same crew that built tent city, Sergeant Slater. When they want to, they do good work...and they work hard while they're doing it."

Slater was deeply insulted and hurt. After almost fifteen years in the Army, he was expected to learn leadership skills from someone like Lewandowski.

"Sir," Slater protested. "I could get the job done a lot faster if Lewandowski wasn't around. Let me have them by myself, Sir. I'll get them straightened out in two weeks."

Masters shook his head. "Within two weeks half of them would be up on charges and I'd be facing a company–wide morale problem. Serious stuff...not the chickenshit problems you brought me today. I'll bet Lewandowski has been told to get fucked at least fifty times in the past three months. And they like him...they work for him...they get the job done. From what you told me, they don't like you, Sarge. It doesn't surprise me if one of them told you to get fucked. I'm about ready to say it myself."

"I'm not paid to be liked...Sir," Slater countered.

"But you are paid to get the job done," Masters said with a smile that would have made Lewandowski shiver. "I'm through discussing this, Sergeant Slater. I'm going to make it simple. You have two weeks to get that crew working as well as they did under Lewandowski or I WILL send you back to the 62nd. Do you understand me, Sergeant?"

Slater rose to lock his heels and stand at Attention. "Yes, Sir."

"Good. You're dismissed."

The next morning Masters called Lewandowski into his office. "Lewandowski," he began...then paused quite deliberately, forcing Lewandowski to speak.

"Yes, Sir." Lewandowski was standing Front and Center, his heels locked in a position of rigid Attention.

"I'm recommending you for promotion to Speck Five."

"Sir?"

"You heard me!" Masters snapped, lifting his feet and to plant both boots on the desktop, a relaxed position that Lewandowski couldn't share.

Masters glared up at Lewandowski, his eyes set and hard.

Lewandowski looked confused and frightened, caught completely off guard, his world turned upside down.

"Your promotion isn't in the bag yet," Masters continued. "You'll have to go before the promotion board at Brigade."

He again paused.

Lewandowski filled the silence. "Yes, Sir."

"Fair warning," Masters continued. "You better pass that board. You better get E–5 or I'll find a **real** NCO to get that crew of yours humping. Do I make myself CLEAR, Lewandowski?"

"Yes, Sir."

"Stop picking on Slater," Masters said in a milder voice. "It's becoming a problem for me."

"Sir?"

"You heard me. And you know what I mean," Masters said as he picked a bit of lint from his fatigue pants. "Don't play dumb."

Masters glanced up and smiled.

Lewandowski swallowed hard. "Yes, Sir."

"Pass the word to the others," Masters added.

"Yes, Sir."

"This morning."

"Yes, Sir."

"Do you know why I'm recommending you for promotion to Speck Five, Lewandowski?"

"No, Sir."

"You don't think you deserve it, do you?"

"No, Sir. Actually, that's an affirmative, Sir."

"Thank you for your honesty."

"You're welcome, Sir."

"Would you like to know why I'm recommending you for promotion?"

"Yes, Sir," Lewandowski answered, though it wasn't really a question that went begging for an answer. Getting promoted again was just another example of faulty military logic that he would endure rather than ponder.

"You'll get quite a pay raise when you get Speck Five, won't you?" Masters asked.

"Yes, Sir."

"If I'm not mistaken, with your time in the service, it will almost double your pay."

"Yes, Sir," Lewandowski agreed.

"I want you to think about that the next time you face a choice between doing the right thing and the wrong thing," Masters explained. "I want you to think how much money you'll lose if you choose to do the wrong thing…such as picking on Sergeant Slater. Does that make sense to you, Lewandowski?"

"Yes, Sir."

"Good, because this is an experiment that will cost you dearly if you make the wrong decisions," Masters promised. "I won't bust you down to Speck Four if you screw up. I'll take you all the way down to Buck Private. And then I'll assign you to the mess tent to work with the poppasans for the rest of your tour. Now, is that the kind of thing you want me to do?"

"No, Sir."

"Good," Masters acknowledged. "Because I want you to really hate the idea of what will happen to you if you continue to lead the rebellion against Sergeant Slater."

Lewandowski glanced down at Masters. It would do him no good to lie. The man could read his mind. "Yes, Sir."

"I believe we understand each other," Masters said. "You're dismissed."

Lewandowski made a side trip to the personnel center before returning to the construction site. He went straight to Louie.

"We gotta get Slater out'a here," Lewandowski demanded. "He's driving us nuts. Now Masters is riding my tail because we're picking on him. He just told me he's gonna promote me to Speck Five just so's he can bust me down to Buck Private and put me on permanent KP if I don't get along with the Slater. That's the sickest thing I ever heard of."

"Slater's on his way to the First Infantry Division in Cu Chi," Louie said quietly. "We just got his orders this morning."

"Woo, that was quick," Lewandowski said. "Oh wow, that

takes a load off my mind. Thank you, Louie. Thank you, thank you, thank you. Happy days are here again. Man, I could see myself doing KP the next nine months with the poppasans."

Louie was unimpressed with the gushing gratitude. "You better concentrate on keeping Masters happy in the weeks ahead, or he'll start pulling strings of his own to get a replacement for Slater."

"Yeah, that's basically what he told me," Lewandowski admitted sourly.

"He's recommending you for Speck Five?" Louie asked.

Lewandowski shrugged, nodded.

"Good," Louie said. "Once Slater is gone we can start putting our plan into action."

"We could screw up building the command bunker first," Lewandowski suggested. "That'll get the ball rolling."

Louie nodded. "Yes, that would be a good starting point."

"How soon will Slater be out of here?" Lewandowski asked.

"He's to report to the Big Red One in three days," Louie answered. "The orders will be waiting for him when he returns to the 62nd this evening. I doubt you'll ever see him again."

"He'll try pulling strings to get out of it," Lewandowski predicted.

"He has no strings to pull," Louie said primly. "Everything was done quite correctly. Sergeant Slater will be receiving his Baptism of Fire as per USARV orders that cannot be altered by subordinate commands. He's history. Now it's up to you to control Masters."

"No suweat, GI," Lewandowski promised. "I'll have him eating out of my hand."

"I would have felt better if you hadn't put it that way," Louie said with a frown. "One should never underestimate the opposition."

Shots from Cam Ranh
An abbreviated photo album

Preface

I was not an Original, but came to the 518th AG as a replacement in July, 1967. Many of these photographs were taken on the day tent city was dismantled, and the unit was moved to the sterile suburbs of Cam Ranh.

My Cam Ranh Hilton Tentmates

I am terrible with names and cannot, for the life of me, remember a single name of my tentmates. I can, however, vouch for their character. They were all good guys, and no doubt entered the priesthood shortly after getting back to The World. Where am I in the photo? I was the guy taking the photograph.

I'm in the Middle

Yup, that's me, the goofy looking guy in the middle. I cannot remember the name of the guy to my right, but the guy to my left was Rodney DeCormier, from—as I recall—Baton Rouge, Louisiana. We are sitting with our backs to the rear porch of the Cam Ranh Hilton, showing off our Vill outfits. Note that the tent next to the Cam Ranh Hilton has an enclosed, screened porch; a nicety that was far too individualistic for the sterile suburbs of Cam Ranh.

Panorama of Tent City

This shot was taken when tent city was being dismantled. Note the poop houses along the crest of the sand dune.

Aligned below are the two rows of tents, some of which have been dismantled. It was a sad, sad day. We knew what was awaiting us in the sterile suburbs.

The 518ᵗʰ AG Orderly Tent

I was the replacement company clerk. Under me was a morning report clerk; over me, as always, was the Executive Officer, 1st LT. William R. Forney. Note Forney's jeep, parked behind his office door, ready for a quick exit at the end of the duty day. Parked in front of Forney's jeep in The Rat Patrol, a Korean War–vintage jeep that was of a far superior design than the contemporary jeeps, which were considered unsafe to drive over 36 miles per hour, which was just fast enough to get on shot while driving in the boonies. Forney and I received permanent reassignments to units near the Coastal City of Nha Trang during the Tet Offensive of 1968. That is a whole other story, which I may tell one of these days.

Trudging Back to Tent City
at the End of a Duty Day

I must have taken this shot during the monsoon season, judging by the overcast sky. Some referred to this barren patch of real estate between the personnel center and the distant outskirts of tent city as Death Valley. And you might well have referred to it as such, too, had you ever found yourself sludging through the clinging sand during the heat and humidity of summer.

Dental Hygiene in Tent City

We had no running water in tent city, so we would fill a canteen cup with potable water and brush, rinse and spit into the sand, covering the mess with a quick kick of the nearby sand. Perhaps you can make out the canteen cup that he has perched on the top of the white post at about mid–thigh level.

Republic of South Vietnam Twenty Dong Note

Hai Muoi means twenty (two, ten), and the Dong was the official name of the South Vietnamese currency in use at the time. It was referred to as 'p' in business dealings between the GI's and the locals. The official exchange rate was 118 'p' to the American dollar, but those who dabbled in the black market could get somewhat more favorable exchange rates, or they might also get six months hard labor in Camp LBJ, the stockade at Long Binh, near Saigon.

A Small Portion of the Cam Ranh Panorama

…as seen from the top of the sand dunes overlooking the personnel center and the bay of Cam Ranh, which was one of the largest deep water bays in the whole of East Asia. A full panoramic photo would require a folding page encompassing at least five or six normal pages of photographs. Cam Ranh was a massive installation. And it probably didn't help to win the hearts and minds of the Vietnamese people when the United States was granted a 99–year lease on Cam Ranh Bay. Later, the Russians would make use of Cam Ranh, though their GIs wouldn't have had nearly as much money to spend.

Poppasan: In Charge of the Barbecue During a Beach Party

I must have taken this shot shortly after my arrival, because the GIs surrounding poppasan, one of the two mess tent KPs, are all Originals. We had an abundance of food to waste, with cases of frozen beef steaks and chicken at our disposal. How impressive that must have been to the impoverished local Vietnamese.

Sterile Suburbs

This scene shows a portion of the new company area for the 518th AG and the 516th Finance, which were relocated as neighbors in the sterile suburbs. Everything looks very neat and tidy, very uniform. Note the tiered seats for the movie theatre, the neat and tidy projector hut, the flat terrain, the ordered rows of sandbags on the roofs, which otherwise might take flight during a monsoon storm. It was ghastly!

Tai, The Cam Ranh Hilton Housegirl

This is Tai, and I must apologize if I spelled her name incorrectly. She was a very sweet kid. I say 'kid' because the housegirls were protected, much like little sisters. If anyone had stepped out of line with a housegirl, he would have had to answer for it with the other guys. Hanky panky or any kind of abuse, physical or verbal, was strictly forbidden. Tai was paid 2,000 'p' per month from every tentmate in the Cam Ranh Hilton. As I recall, there were ten or twelve of us in the Hilton, which gave her a pretty good income by local standards. In return, she would wash our clothes, shine our boots, sweep out the tent, and socialize like crazy with the other housegirls, one of which was her sister. I hope she's had a good life.

A Small Corner of the Vill

I vaguely recall taking this shot because it was the only time I'd seen a civilian automobile in the Vill. I would have taken some shots of the seamy side of the Vill, but I was having my slides mailed back home for safe keeping, and I didn't want my dear sainted mother to get the wrong (right) idea about how I was spending my off–duty Sundays. A friend I served with in the 518th recently told me he sent home a film that he had taken while in the Vill, not thinking his father, bursting with pride, would show the flick to friends and family alike without taking a sneak peek to make sure nothing was X–rated. Unfortunately, John had filmed one of the fallen angels of the Vill, including a scene in which she flashed all of John's loved ones back home. Dad never again showed John's film epics of life in a war zone.

*Formation Dismissed, as
Seen From the Orderly Tent*

I took this shot from the front door of the orderly tent as the final unit formation in tent city was being dismissed. Note the white wheel rim hanging from the post to the right of the photo; that is the unit alert bell, which would be rung only during emergencies. Also note the shower hut, with the barrels standing on the roof, and the pooper huts along the dune crest.

Rodney DeCormier Struttin' His Vill Outfit

Rodney and I were tight buddies until I was promoted to Speck Five and took my place on the second floor of the three–story outhouse. After my promotion, he considered me a persona non grata Lifer.

Struttin' My Stuff in My Vill Clothes

Note the tasteful combination of white T–shirt, silk smoking jacket, and imported headgear. Very chic! Ah, yes, those were the bad old days.

Another Panoramic from the
Top of the Tent City Dunes

Four cargo ships are docked, with two more in the bay. Again, this is just a small portion of the actual Cam Ranh Bay panorama.

Movie Projector Booth, Pissoir Screen,
and Movie Screen in Tent City

The "vanity" screen for the pissoir was not installed for the sake of privacy, but rather as a windscreen, it being very unwise to stand downstream from the pissoir, which would have consisted of two steel drums buried neck deep in the sand. The drawback to the entertainment center for tent city was the nearness of the poophuts. The shit burning details would bury the residue of their work on the dune slope, which occasionally made movie viewing a risky business. Only a fool would sit on the sand. Folding chairs from the tents were S.O.P., and it was always best to prod the ground first with the legs of the chair, making sure there was solid sand below prior to placing one's full weight on the seat. Otherwise, one might find oneself sinking into a mucky situation.

Interior Shot of the Cam Ranh Hilton

The Hilton was a very cozy home. Note that some cots are of the canvas folding style, while others are regulation steel bunks with squeaky springs and thin mattresses. There were two kinds of poison to choose from.

View of Tent City and Shower Hut

Note the barrels perched atop the roof of the shower hut. One would think the water would be warmed to a comfortable temperature in the heat of Cam Ranh, but such was not the case. The water remained miserably cold, making the showers a matter of a quick splash from the water spigots, followed by a sudden soaping and a miserable thirty seconds or so of a bone chilling rinse. Perhaps that was why the steam baths in the Vill were so popular. But then again, perhaps that bit of consumerism was inspired by other considerations.

Close-up of Move Screen, Tent City and Sterile Suburbs in Distant Horizon

Need I say more? The beauty of tent city versus the beast of the sterile suburbs.

Moi in Penang, Malaysia, on R&R

I am in the Temple of the Reclining Buddha in Penang. This shot was taken my by a nearby Malaysian, using my camera, who kindly offered to take my picture while I am grasping the hand of the Buddha designated for the month of my birth. He told me it was great good luck to do so. I was doing a little sight seeing on the final day of my R&R, taking photographs that could be sent home to my saintly mother, thus proving to even the most cynical that I hadn't done anything to be ashamed of while visiting Penang, Malaysia. Note the startled look in my eyes, not unlike a deer caught in the headlights of an on–coming car. I had just realized the kind Malay expected to be paid handsomely for taking my photograph.

A shot of the Tent City Motor Pool

A 2 ½ ton (deuce–and–a–half) on the left, and a ¾ ton truck on the right. The grease rack ramp is between the trucks, with a conex storage container in front of the grease rack.

Saying Our Farewells to the Cam Ranh Hilton

My tentmates taking final photographs of the Cam Ranh Hilton, before we started taking her down.

Oprah Winfrey Show

In early 1987, as I recall, I was a guest on the Oprah Winfrey Show when the subject matter was Vietnamese Amerasians who were searching for their biological fathers. There were instances in which the name of the father was known, but that was unusual. The sad reality was that most children were not the result of relationships that lasted beyond a few minutes. I encountered only one long term relationship during my fifteen months in Vietnam, and that was my own. Which is a whole other story. Following the Oprah Winfrey Show, I returned to Sacramento, California, where I helped start a group that worked with young Amerasians who were then being brought from Vietnam to resettlement centers in America, and later was able to help in arranging the reunification of a Vietnam Veteran with his Vietnamese wife and two sons.

K. P. Duty in all its Glory

I snapped this shot of a Cam Ranh Hilton tentmate when he was on K.P. Note the immersible water heaters, powered by diesel fuel, the potable water tank sitting atop a conex storage hut, tent city in the background. The water was heated to near simmering temperatures, and the soap was strong enough to melt axle grease. I wish I had some panoramic shots of the mess tent. It was quite a creative mixture of wood, tin, and canvas. The Originals deserve to be proud of what they created in tent city.

*The New Home of the 518th AG in
the Sterile Suburbs of Cam Ranh*

Chapter Eight

The first storm of the monsoon season hit Cam Ranh just two days after Slater reported for duty at the Big Red One. The maelstrom began with innocent gusts of wind about halfway through the ninth showing of THE GREEN BERETS in tent city. Within brief minutes, the weather abruptly turned downright mean.

"I'm getting the hell out'a here," Hillbilly announced as he joined the others in beating a quick retreat to his tent. He was thinking of Mississipp, tropical storms, and hurricanes.

The 516th AG was in full retreat, and it was anything but orderly. Had it been daylight, the Originals would have seen a massive blue–black wall of clouds charging toward them from the South China Sea. The wind struck first, followed shortly thereafter by great, pelting globules of rain. Suddenly, everything in tent city went black when a distant utility pole was snapped by the wind.

Charlie Edwards stepped on Lewandowski's size thirteen–D combat boots on his way out of the projection booth.

"Dang it, Charlie, you're steppin' on my foot!"

"Well, get it out'a the way!"

"At EASE, soldier! I'm closest to the door. I get out first."

"At EASE, yourself! Get your big butt out'a the way!"

"Don't MAKE me pull rank on you, Charlie!"

The wind and rain gained force as the front transformed the calm waters of the bay into an angry sea. Moments later, when the worst of it arrived in tent city, there was reason to wonder if mom nature might be on the side of the Viet Cong. Half the movie screen came down, two shitters were toppled over, and a large portion of the mess tent roof skittered off on an adventure all its' own. The blasts of wind were so strong that the rain was being driven in horizontal sheets that obscured vision beyond a few feet. Outside tent city, telephone and power poles were slammed to the earth, corrugated roofing became airborne, flash floods filled dry ravines, aircraft were overturned and the main PX was awash in ten inches of crud that spoiled a small fortune in cigarettes, booze and beer.

Then the wind suddenly died down, leaving only the drenching rain as an after–effect. Tent city had survived the buffeting with only relatively minor damage.

It wasn't long before an Original came up with the idea of using the downpour for an impromptu warm–water shower. Soon every man in tent city was stripped and heading outside with a bar of soap for the first real showers they'd had since stepping aboard the USS Webster.

After a time, the power of the rain subsided to an impotent drizzle that would become the norm for the remainder of the monsoon season. The Originals would see many more monsoon storms, but none would be so memorable as the first.

The claps of manmade thunder recommenced shortly after the troops returned to their tents to dry off and change into clean clothes. The Cam Ranh Bay offensive and defensive systems found themselves besieged by frantic calls for artillery and close air support, anything that could be mustered to beat back the waves of bad guys who were taking advantage of the cloud cover to go for targets of opportunity. But the support would be spread among more targets, some of which would be impossible to see through the low cloud cover. It was the kind of weather that the Viet Cong could use to their advantage.

The war had suddenly become more dangerous for the cowboys wearing the white hats.

Four days later, Lt. Masters made a rare appearance at a dawn reveille formation. Usually the reveille formations were handled by Numbnuts Bolton, or one of the senior NCOs, so something big had to be up if Masters was showing signs of life at 0530 hours.

Masters didn't waste time getting around to explaining his objective. "It has been brought to my attention that the men of the 516th AG have not been gracious hosts for the Red Cross Donut Dollies during their weekly visits."

Masters was pacing back and forth in the gloomy half–light, his expression grim, perhaps angry, certainly humorless. A light rain was falling. The formation was gathered on the steel tarmac between the mess tent and the orderly tent. The uniform of the day now included rubberized rain ponchos.

The story behind the formation began the afternoon before when Masters found himself reporting Front and Center to Captain Ortega.

"The men WILL be assembled in the mess tent for chow at 1230 hours tomorrow," Ortega began. "Those who are missing in action WILL be filling sandbags for the next two weeks."

With the formalities over, Ortega could continue in the relaxed Bill–and–Manny style that he preferred to use with his executive officer. "I got a call from Brigade yesterday," Ortega explained with a sour expression.

"The Donut Dollies filed a report saying that attendance has been down for their weekly dog and pony shows in the mess tent."

Masters could appreciate Ortega's predicament. The job description of a company commander included a number of tasks that were far more political than military in nature. Career–ending black eyes could be earned for matters ranging from less than 100 percent participation in a United Way campaign to—in this case—poor attendance when the Donut Dollies came to town.

Ortega had his work cut out for him. It was common knowledge that only the social outcasts of the 516th AG chowed down in the mess tent during Donut Dolly Wednesdays. All the others—officers, NCOs and Originals alike—quietly disappeared, with the Originals and NCOs heading for their tents to open cans of PX chow, or skipping noon chow altogether…doing whatever was necessary and expedient to avoid the plague of Donut Dollies that descended on the mess tent every Wednesday.

Masters had attended the first Donut Dolly Wednesday with an eager crowd of Originals and NCOs ready to socialize with round–eyed girls from The World. But their expectations proved to be about ten stories too high. Socializing with the Donut Dollies turned out to be about as much fun as dancing with your sister. The powder blue searsucker uniforms gave them an ominous, asexual military air. And the girls didn't cuss, smoke or chew and—most telling of all—their uniforms showed no thigh or cleavage. To give the girls credit, they made heroic efforts to get the Originals and NCO's involved in Pin The Tail On The Donkey and Charades, and they were more than generous with the trays of donuts and cookies, but they didn't grab anyone by the gonads, so to speak. It was a show that could be missed with no regret.

Once was enough for nearly all of the Originals and NCOs. Soon the attendance for Donut Dolly Wednesdays was as low as whale poop. Even Lt. Masters and Captain Ortega would use the weekly visits as an excuse to drive to the Officer's Club for hamburgers and malteds. Nor was it a problem that was limited to the 516th AG. The Officer's Club lunch receipts were getting a big boost from company level officers who were avoiding the many Donut Dolly A–teams that were conducting cookies–and–koolaid missions every day but Sunday throughout the entire support command.

But the jig was up at the 516th AG. Brigade didn't want to be bothered by any more letters from the Red Cross. Ortega had to accept his fate; it was just another of those Army Ways of Doing Things. He had been passed over twice for Major and he couldn't take any chances. If he didn't get the brass maple leaves on the third try, he would be mustered out. It was Up or Out for Captains in the New Action Army. There would be no more career captains, just like there would be no more career corporals.

"The Red Cross reported that only six men were present for their last show in the 516th," Ortega continued, despising the pettiness of the subject. "And two of those were the KP Poppasans."

Masters didn't smile, though he was imagining the two Poppasans competing in Charades and Pin The Tail On The Donkey while delicately nibbling cookies and donuts, sipping Cool Aid from tiny paper cups, and later reporting the strange social rituals of the American GIs to Ho Chi Minh.

"I think we can put out this little grass fire by coming up with a good showing tomorrow," Ortega continued, basing his hopes on a strong reliance on style over substance. In a completely fair world, his positive attitude alone would have qualified him to be a West Point Graduate. "I don't care how you do it…I want the mess tent packed for tomorrow's performance. That ought'a get Brigade off our backs."

Masters nodded. "Consider it done."

"Every enlisted man WILL be in the mess tent today to greet

the Donut Dollies," Masters announced to the reveille formation in a manner that said all excuses would be considered inoperable. "And every one of you WILL look like he is having a wonderful time. Headcount will be taken, and if you turn up AWOL you WILL be filling sandbags for the next two weeks. Are there any questions?"

Of course, there were none.

"Very good," Masters said calmly, a clear indication that he WOULD explode if EVERYTHING didn't go his way. "You WILL form up here again at 1200 hours, at which time you WILL be marched into the mess tent where you WILL chow down. After that, I WILL turn over command of the company to the Donut Dollies, and you will NOT be dismissed until I dismiss you."

Masters turned to Bolton. "Dismiss the formation when you have completed your business, Sergeant."

Bolton added his own comments as Masters headed for the mess tent and a canteen cup of Sgt. Lugo's killer coffee.

"Make that double for me," Bolton warned. "If you screw this up, you gotta deal with me when the Lieutenant's done with you."

A loud fart answered his warning. Snickers rose from the formation like wild quail flushed from a bush, but Bolton ignored the fart and the laughter. Experience told him he would never find the guilty party, though he was almost sure it was Lewandowski or one of the Dirty Dozen who had cut the cheese. Bolton was longing for a stateside rotation not so much to leave Vietnam as to escape from the Originals.

Later that morning Charlie Edwards turned off the highway onto the new driveway leading into the Nhan Ai orphanage. Lewandowski asked Charlie to come along for the ride, hoping they could patch up some differences that had arisen the night before, when Charlie stopped talking to him.

Charlie was driving the 3/4 ton truck at a pace that wouldn't have been possible before the driveway had been graded and resurfaced by the 62nd Combat Engineers. No favors had been exchanged between the 516th and the 62nd for the work on the driveway. Labor and materials were gladly donated once the 62nd understood the nature of the project. GI's love to love kids. It is a tradition of sorts, and Nhan Ai soon found itself being adopted by several units when their plight became known. Masters and Ortega made pilgrimages to Nhan Ai, as had Numbnuts and most of the other NCOs, several of whom had approached their wives about adopting certain kids. One NCO had already started the mountain of paperwork that had to be completed before the adoption was approved by the many Army and Vietnamese and American government agencies that were involved.

Lewandowski was wearing his new Speck Five stripes. As an E–5 he was now fully qualified to do his boozing at the NCO Club on the second floor of the outhouse. His promotion, along with a number of Speck Fours from the 516th AG and other units, had been included on the Brigade promotion list that was published three days earlier, though it wasn't until yesterday that Masters gave Lewandowski a do–it–or–else deadline to have his E–5 stripes sewn on.

"Wear'em or lose'em, Lewandowski. Have those stripes sewn on the next time I see you, or I'll start you on the KP training course."

Lewandowski had been wondering why it had taken Masters so long to issue the face–saving ultimatum. He had been bragging far and wide that he wouldn't sew on the stripes until ordered to do so.

The days since the promotions had been miserable for all the new Speck Fives, except Lewandowski. Eventually, little Louie Donnatelli confronted Lewandowski in the chow line, doing it right out in front of God and everyone.

"You're a no–good lowlife scumbag, Lewandowski. I know what you're up to, and it won't work. I know how you think…I know you can't wait to wear those stripes. You just don't have the balls to sew'em on like the rest of us did."

Uneasy laughter rose from the ranks. It was anyone's guess how Lewandowski would react to such a direct challenge. But his only response was a hurt, confused expression, as if he couldn't understand why Louie would resort such libelous character assassination. Donnatelli snorted disdainfully and took his dinner tray and canteen cup to the simmering, sudsy water of the washtub.

"Eff tee yaye," Poppasan said consolingly as Jackson made room for Donnatelli. "Puck de armay."

"Right on, poppasan," Jackson agreed as he rinsed his canteen cup and tray. He gave Lewandowski a long, sullen look before heading back to his tent to crank up the sounds of Motown. Jackson had been on the same promotion list.

The next morning Masters called Lewandowski into his office to read the riot act about being out of uniform, which drew a smile from Lewandowski and made Masters wonder if perhaps his Supply Sergeant was setting the stage for a Section Eight psycho discharge or an early R&R.

"Get out of here, Lewandowski. Don't let me see you again without those Speck Five patches."

"Yes, Sir. Will do, Sir."

Lewandowski stitched on the patches that evening between sips of beer in the supply tent.

"So I said, 'Sir, if that's an order, then I guess I gotta do it.' And Masters said: 'Did I stutter, Lewandowski? You'll do it or else.' And I said...."

Charlie rose from his bunk, mumbling something about the bullcrap being so deep that he had to go somewhere else for a little fresh air.

"Huh?" Lewandowski asked.

"Shut up, Lew. Donnatelli was right. You are full of shit."

It would be the final words Lewandowski would hear from Charlie Edwards for a length of time that would become decidedly uncomfortable.

"Well, I like that. After all I've done for you...."

Before leaving, Charlie headed to the small refrigerator he and Lewandowski had purchased for the supply tent. Lewandowski paused in his stitching to watch as Charlie began removing cans of Pabst Blue Ribbon. When his arms were full, Charlie headed for the tent flap.

"Half of those cold ones are mine, y'know," Lewandowski warned.

Charlie didn't answer as he ducked through the tent flap into the lazy rainfall.

"Hey, where you goin'?" Lewandowski demanded. "You're a rude sonofabitch, Charlie Edwards!"

But Charlie's footsteps had already melded into the clamor that permeated tent city during the early evening hours, particularly now that the monsoon rains made the outdoor movies an experience that offended the body as well as the mind.

By midnight, Lewandowski had all the patches sewn on and had turned out the light. A few minutes later he heard Charlie stumbling into the tent, mumbling drunkenly to himself and banging around until he made it to his cot. Lewandowski had rolled back Charlie's sheet and blanket, telling himself he didn't want Charlie catching a fever and become an even bigger pain in the ass because he was sick. It could get downright cold during the long, wet nights of the monsoon season.

After Masters made his Donut Dolly speech for reveille that morning, Lewandowski took the crew to the construction site and left them with instructions to look busy if Masters came nosing around. Then he took Charlie with him to pick up a load of supplies they'd scrounged for Nhan Ai.

As a peace offering, Lewandowski allowed Charlie to drive the truck. He was prepared to accept whatever blame he had to accept in the interests of peace. Everyone had been a little on edge lately. So what if Charlie was on the rag; so what if he was acting like a jerk.

"Well, are you still pissed off at me?" Lewandowski asked as they turned into the supply depot on their way to the orphanage.

Charlie stared ahead, saying nothing.

Lewandowski let it pass.

Later, when they were nearing Nhan Ai, he made yet another attempt to bury the hatchet.

"Y'know, Charlie, Mother M–T is gonna figure out right away that you're pissed off at me, and before you know it we'll be getting a sermon about brotherly love. Now, you don't want to be responsible for all that happening, do you?"

Charlie didn't answer.

"Well, excuse me for living," Lewandowski grumped, and proceeded to ignore Charlie with a studied intensity that lasted about twenty seconds.

"You're acting downright childish, y'know. I hope you know that."

More silence.

When they entered the church grounds, Charlie parked near the new one–story Quonset that served as kitchen, dining hall, class-room, and girl's dormitory. A second Quonset was destined to become a boy's dormitory. The next dorm to be constructed would be for the girls.

As usual, the kids figured they had another unscheduled recess from school when they heard the racket made by the clattering diesel engine of the deuce. They came running out to greet their GI benefactors before the engine was shut down.

"We brought the chow we told you about," Lewandowski explained to Mother M–T as he led the sisters around to the back of the truck, where Charlie was ready to hand down the loot from the cargo bed. There were three three–gallon olive–drab tins of dehydrated potatoes, two 100–pound bags of flour, four 100–pound bags of rice and ten cases of canned fruits and vegetables.

"It's not the best tasting chow in the world but it gets the job done," Lewandowski said when the last of it was off the truck and being carried to the dining hall by the older children. Mother M–T was gushing with gratitude. "Oh, merci beau coup. Merci. You and your friends are so good to us."

"Thank Uncle Sam," Charlie said before he jumped down. "Stuff like this is easy to come by once they know it's for Nhan Ai, ma'am. All we're doing is drive it out here."

"We know better," Mother Marie–Teresa chided. "Everything was a struggle for us before God sent you that afternoon."

Charlie shrugged noncommittally, knowing he was much less a saint than a sinner.

"You must come this Sunday," Mother M–T said as she walked them back to the truck cab, her arms entwined with theirs, holding them hostage while she made yet another attempt to seduce them into avoiding the Vill on their day off. "The mass will be presented by Captain Hollingsworth, an Air Force chaplain. Have you attended mass with Captain Hollingsworth?"

"No, ma'am," Lewandowski answered politely.

"Ah, then you must come. He is a wonderful speaker."

"Well, we probably would, ma'am, but me'n Charlie gotta put

in some overtime, Sunday. Ain't that right, Charlie?"

"Yeah, that's right," Charlie agreed, adding a sigh that was intended to convey deep regret. "We gotta work all day."

Mother M–T allowed the lie to pass without comment. She wasn't one to shoo away the sinners she was trying to save.

"God Bless both of you," she said as Lewandowski and Edwards entered the cab. "I will light a candle and say a prayer for you tonight."

"Bye, ma'am," Charlie said.

"So long. See you in a few days," Lewandowski promised.

Lewandowski turned his attention back to Charlie when they were nearing the suburbs of Cam Ranh.

"Well, are you talking to me again?" Lewandowski asked gruffly, fully expecting another rejection.

"You can really be an asshole sometimes," Charlie said. "You're always bragging about something or other, and you never shut up for longer than five minutes. Never. I mean, even in your sleep. You snore, y'know."

"I know," Lewandowski admitted with no hesitation. "Now, are we buddies again, or are we gonna keep at each other's throats?"

Charlie glanced over and saw that Lewandowski was about as sincerely sorry as he would ever manage, short of judgement day. There was no use making life miserable for both of them any longer. He had made his point.

"Okay. You got it. Buddies again."

Lewandowski grinned. "You worthless piece of shit, you really had me going there. Goddamn, you got me that time."

"I know," Charlie said with a smile. "Those classes in child psychology are finally starting to pay off."

Lewandowski found Masters waiting for him in the suburbs, standing beside a wide deep hole that had been bulldozed into the sand a few yards from the site for the future orderly Quonset and supply Quonset. A large pile of filled sandbags was growing beside the hole. Half the Dirty Dozen were in the hole, filling sandbags from the litter at the bottom, while the others had formed a bucket brigade to get the filled bags from the hole to a waiting pile.

"When are you going to finish with this bunker?" Masters asked as Edwards stole away to disappear within the ranks of the Dirty Dozen.

"Well, Sir," Lewandowski began, appearing to give the question long and serious thought while he, too, gazed into the hole. "We would'a been done with it by now, but the roof caved in when we were stacking the sandbags on top. The rafters just gave way from out of nowhere, Sir. It was so messed–up, we hadda start over. We might'a been piling on too many sandbags, but I always say you can't really have too many sandbags when you're building a bunker. Who knows, maybe we'll get hit with artillery rounds some day."

"Do you want to know what I always say?" Masters asked serenely.

"Yes, Sir," Lewandowski lied.

"I say you have a week to finish this bunker," Masters continued. "After this is done, you can start on the floor slabs. I hope you don't get too far behind, Lewandowski. I would rather not enroll you in the KP–trainee course I mentioned before. You haven't forgotten about that, have you?"

"No, Sir. I sure haven't," Lewandowski answered truthfully. Finishing the bunker within a week would be a piece of cake. Masters must be getting soft in his old age.

Lewandowski watched Masters stroll to his jeep and drive away, unaware that Masters—like himself—had only been going through the motions of fulfilling his responsibilities as the Officer In Charge.

"I bet his dog don't even like him," Lewandowski muttered to the Dirty Dozen when the jeep was safely out of sight.

"Ah, don't let him get to you, man," Skins advised from where he was leaning on a shovel handle within the belly of the emerging bunker.

"No shit," Frenchie added. "He don't know nothin'. He's just a sorry–assed Lifer."

Lewandowski was about to agree when it dawned on him that all activity had ceased. At this pace, the bunker wouldn't be completed until the Dirty Dozen had a new honcho and Alfred G. Lewandowski was enrolled in the William R. Masters Career KP

Enrichment course.

"Man, I can't believe you guys," Lewandowski grumbled.

"What?" Skins asked.

"Yeah, what?" Frenchie added, expanding on the vacuous thoughts of Skins Williams.

"Hey, just look at you," Lewandowski continued. "ALL of you...just standing around or sitting on your keesters when you know what'll happen to me if we don't get this bunker built."

Skins and Frenchie exchanged confused shrugs.

"I mean—Jeese!—c'mon! What about me? Don't you care that Masters will saddle me with the crummiest, rottenest duties that he can think of if we don't get this bunker done this week? Doesn't that matter to you?"

Lewandowski had included too many random thoughts in his questions, which left the Dirty Dozen far more confused than chastised.

Frenchie spoke when the silence was beginning to turn embarrassing for everyone. "Well, hey man. You're an NCO...his Main Man. He wouldn't do that to you."

"Oh, he wouldn't, huh?" Lewandowski growled. "So, that's all I mean to you guys, huh? Do you know what you'd get done if I didn't act like a Lifer?"

Lewandowski didn't bother to wait for an answer. "Nothin', that's what. You'd hide out some place, doin' nothin' until you DEROS. Then you'd be bitchin' all the way back to The World on your Freedom Flight, pissin' and moaning about how hard you had it over here. If you ever wanna know why I come down on you, that's reason enough. I don't **wanna** act like a Lifer. You **make** me act like a lifer."

"Wow," Frenchie interjected. "Man, I never thought of it that way before. You got a good point there, Lewandowski. I think we ought'a sit down and talk it over. Chew on it awhile, as the cowboys say in the movies."

His suggestion was greeted warmly by the other members of the Dirty Dozen.

"I got a better idea," Lewandowski said with a sadistic grin not unlike that used by Masters. "I think all you guys ought'a start humping butt or I'm gonna hold the damn detail over an extra two hours tonight. Now, do you still wanna have that talk, Frenchie?"

"Man," Frenchie complained. "You ain't got no sense of humor no more."

Lewandowski ignored the pissing and moaning rising from the hole.

"Charlie, you take four bodies to start building roof beams from the pile of six–by–eights we got. I want this bunker up and functional in six days, even if we gotta work nights to do it."

The two Donut Dollies dined as guests in the NCO dining room situated behind the partition planter box ,which was now filled with bone dry dirt containing only the shriveled remains of local flora.

Noon chow was nearly complete and the Donut Dollies were about to take command. Both of the young Donut Dollies were built of solid Midwestern stock, with none of the fancy frills that sometimes come with girls who hail from Los Angeles, or New York City. They were made for the long haul and could handle a lot of punishment, much like the jeeps they drove from unit to unit with donuts, cookies and game paraphernalia. It wasn't their fault that they were condemned to such a thankless job...and it is sincerely hoped that they lived long, fruitful lives well into an era when they were remembered with great fondness by the very GI's who so assiduously avoided them in the Republic of South Vietnam.

After a menu of Sgt. Lugo's Shit–On–a–Shingle followed by chocolate cake, the Donut Dollies came out to socialize with the Originals. One was short and one was tall. Both were white, or nearly so. Charlie Edwards figured they were immersed deep into an extreme manic state, as evidenced by their unassailable good humor as they went from table to table to introduce themselves to the troops, exhilarated by the extraordinarily large turnout. Perched atop their heads were baby–blue sear sucker service hats of a style that GI's had been referring to as "cunt caps" since decades long past.

With the glad–handing over, they set to work.

"Hi, I'm Jane," the taller of the two announced from where she stood near the entrance. The other dolly, named Barbie, was passing around trays generously mounded with cookies and donuts. "Take all the treats you want. We have plenty for everyone."

The Originals were determined not to trade their bad attitudes for perky pleasantries and easy access to carbohydrates. Masters may have the power to order them to be here, but no one—not even Masters—could order them to have a good time. Even GI's got some rights.

Barbie joined Jane near the doorway, ready to do her part. She had to raise her voice to be heard over the undercurrent of resentful grumbling. "Hello, everyone. Hello, hello! I have an announcement to make."

"At Ease out there!" Numbnuts bellowed from the NCO dining room.

"I have an announcement to make," Barbie repeated over the mutinous mutterings that followed Bolton's command. "Please...just a brief announcement."

She paused, using silence to tame the beast. Within moments, the Originals had been shamed into shushing each other.

"The Red Cross canteen located at Tank Hill will be open until 2200 hours, starting tomorrow night," Barbie continued without shouting. "Come on down and enjoy yourselves. And don't forget...we have real homemade hamburgers and hotdogs for sale."

The grumbling was gaining new life...the patience of her audience was as limited as their ration of good manners.

Barbie raised her volume two notches.

"The canteen will be open until 2200 hours from Monday through Thursday, with Friday, Saturday and Sunday closing times continuing to be midnight."

New sounds intervened—filtered inside through the screened windows—the clanging and banging of pots and pans as the two Poppasans pressed on with their KP chores.

Barbie raised the volume another notch. "For those of you who haven't visited the Red Cross canteen, we have bumper pool, darts, shuffle board, checkers, chess...and now we have a color television set. Yesterday evening we watched the Ed Sullivan Show. It was almost like being back home. The shows are pre–recorded, but they're so much fun to watch that you don't care. Barbra Streisand was on last night's show!"

A groan arose from the ranks. Barbie had inadvertently managed to insult nearly everyone's taste in music.

Barbie gamely tried to continue with the announcements, but the banging of the pots and pans was so overpowering that Bolton rose from his seat to look through the window screen, suspicious that someone put the poppasans up to making even more racket than usual…probably Lewandowski. However, it wasn't a problem that couldn't be cured by a good set of lungs.

"Hey, Poppasan!" Bolton shouted over Barbie. "Knock it off out there!"

The banging stopped and Bolton nodded at Barbie. "Scuse me, ma'am. Go right ahead with what you were saying."

The banging resumed when Barbie continued.

Joan stepped in to relieve Barbie. Though somewhat the shorter of the two, she had a pair of lungs that could call cows from the north forty in the middle of a cyclone.

"We can help you compose letters home, or you can check out a book from our library!" Joan shouted. "Next month we'll be opening a pizza oven!"

The screen door suddenly swung open with a loud bang.

Poppasan entered with a precarious tower of clanging, dripping aluminum cooking pots, which he carefully sat on the chowline to await further storage. This time the racket was too much for even Joan to handle, so she paused for the interruption to play itself out.

"Hey, Poppasan…can't you do that later?" Bolton shouted from the NCO dining room.

"No bic," Poppasan yelled back at Bolton with a confused expression. Meaning 'I don't understand.'

Appreciative chuckles rose from the Originals. Poppasan could bic a heck of lot more than he would ever admit. Some wondered if he might be a communist spy, maybe even a cousin of Ho Chi Minh. There was a kind of family resemblance of sorts.

"Dee dee, Poppasan!" Bolton shouted. "Dee dee mow! Go away and doan come back!"

Bolton considered himself bilingual, having heard the phrase 'Get out of here' many a time while visiting the bars and steam baths with his Cheap–GI NCO buddies.

Poppasan grumbled back in unapologetic Vietnamese, then added a deep bow meant to flatter the village idiot. When in doubt, kiss ass. When completing his bow, he knocked one elbow into the tower of pots and pans, which brought them all tumbling down into a clattering pile.

"Dang it, somebody get him out'a here," Bolton shouted as Poppasan scrambled to reconstruct the tower. Just about then, Stoned Poppasan entered the mess tent with a second tower and stumbled into Poppasan, adding his pile of pots and pans to the mess already on the floor.

"Eff Tee Yaye," Poppasan explained to Bolton as he set about reconstructing his tower a third time. "Puck De Armay."

A chorus of Originals were quick to agree. "FTA, Poppasan."

"Eff Tee Yaye," Poppasan reiterated. "Puck De Armay."

The door opened and Hanley entered with a message he had received over the phone in the orderly tent. His expression was unusually bleak as he handed the note to Woody Woods, who read it, frowned, and rose from his seat to pass it along to Masters, who also frowned before handing the note to Bolton. Masters leaned over to confer with Bolton a moment before standing to address the troops.

A moment later, Bolton shouted for quiet. "At Ease! The Lieutenant's got something to announce."

"Cam Ranh village has been closed indefinitely, starting at 1200 hours today," Masters said without prelude. "The medics have found signs of plague."

Gasps, whispers and other sounds of dismay rose from his audience. Even the Donut Dollies seemed taken back by the news.

"The vill has been declared Off Limits to all personnel until further notice," Masters repeated.

"AT Ease out there!" Bolton shouted.

"What about the housegirls, Sir?" one of the Originals asked. "Will we be losing them, too?"

"It says nothing about the housegirls coming and going from the vill," Masters explained. "As of now, they're not restricted from entering Cam Ranh. But that could change at any time. We don't know much yet. We just know the Vill is closed until further notice because of plague."

Skins nudged Frenchie's elbow. He had it all figured out. "Plague, my mu'fuh' ass. There ain't no plague down there, man. What'choo think, they'd let the housegirls come and go as they please if it was really the plague they was worried about?"

Frenchie nodded. "No way, Jose. They're just giving us a hard time, that's all. Besides, we been indoctrinated against the plague, ain't we? Wasn't that one of the shots we got back in The World?"

"Yeah," Skins agreed. "They's just playin' with our heads, man. The vill's too much freedom."

"Yeah, and too much clap," Frenchie added.

The Donut Dollies began gathering their things. Even they had to admit the show was over, the magic was gone.

Charlie Edwards turned to Lewandowski. "Well, it looks like we can make it out to Nhan Ai next Sunday, afterall. This is gonna be one horny bunch of GI's before its over."

Lewandowski winked and scooted closer. "Charlie, I never realized what soft blue eyes you have. Man, you are one seductive sonofabitch."

"Hey, GI, no sweat," Frenchie said to Skins. "All we gotta do is get Lewandowski to take us on a little drive to that whorehouse on Highway One. Screw the Vill, man. We don't need it."

Skins shook his head. "No muh'fuh' way, man. The VC been raising too much hell out there. Not me, I'm not goin'. I'm staying alive right here in Cam Ranh. There ain't no ass worth dyin' for."

Frenchie nodded, deep in thought. "Yeah...I forgot about the monsoons, man. Dang, this is serious shit."

The awful truth was just beginning to sink in. Mother M–T's prayers were being answered with a vengeance. The Vill was history.

Chapter Nine

Masters opened with a simple question. "Can you explain this mess, Lewandowski?"

They were gazing upon the results of six weeks labor lost.

Lewandowski had rehearsed his explanation so often that Charlie Edwards said he sounded like a fifth grader reciting the Gettysburg Address.

"Well, Sir, everything was going just great until we poured the concrete. We worked our butts off prepping the ground, building the forms and putting in the re–bar. We had everything ready to go for the three barracks, the orderly Quonset and the supply Quonset, the messhall *and* the personnel center. We were ready to rock and roll, Sir. You saw it, Sir. We really did a good job this time."

Masters winced at the use of the phrase 'this time', but didn't pause to discuss Lewandowski's semantics as he might have done if a lesser tragedy were at hand. The problem was much bigger than a few words here and there. Heads have rolled for lesser offenses, and Masters had to come up with an explanation that would protect his and Ortega's collective butts with the Brigade brass. Questions were beginning to be raised about the lack of progress being shown at the new, improved home for the 516th AG.

"I know, Lewandowski. I know all about that. My question was, what made the cement crack like this? It was just a question…it wasn't an accusation."

Masters nudged the toe of one boot at a half–inch wide crack that led to more cracks that in turn led to still more cracks, until the entire surface of the messhall floor had a peculiar shattered appearance about it.

Lewandowski shook his head sadly. "Well, Sir, they must'a mixed the concrete wrong. That's the only thing I can figure, Sir. It looked great when it was being poured and finished, but went to hell during the cure stage."

"No kidding," Masters observed dryly. He hadn't expected this from Lewandowski. The man had outdone himself, creating a major setback for the construction schedule in a way that left him entirely blameless. It was a maneuver that contained such seeds of brilliance that he could only draw the conclusion that more and better minds than Lewandowski's had been involved.

"How long will it take to get this mess out of here so you can start over?" Masters asked.

"Well, Sir, it's all in there with re–bar. We did a real good job of reinforcing it, Sir."

"How long?" Masters repeated tonelessly.

"And it's hard as a rock, Sir. We'll need jackhammers and crowbars to break it up. Then we'll have cut the re–bar with torches and haul the pieces out, then level the sand again, build new forms, put in new re–bar. A good cement saw would help speed things up."

"For the last time, Lewandowski. How long?"

Lewandowski forced a quick summation.

"About eight to twelve weeks, Sir. Half of that will be clean–up time. I figure we'll be able to do the rest of it faster the second time around because we're more experienced...and more efficient."

"I'll give you six weeks," Masters said.

"Yes, Sir, six weeks it is," Lewandowski agreed. Humping butt, even with a little screw–off time, they could do it in four weeks.

"I don't want this happening again," Masters warned. And he truly did not want it to happen a second time. Brigade wouldn't accept the same excuse twice. Lewandowski would have to find new ways to delay the completion date. "If necessary, I want you down there watching when they mix the concrete. You'll be taking that KP course we talked about if this happens again."

"Yes, Sir."

Masters gave the area one more quick glance and headed for his jeep while Lewandowski joined Charlie and the Dirty Dozen.

"We got six weeks," Lewandowski announced.

"Alright," Skins said. "We ain't never gonna get this muh'fuh' built."

Lewandowski nodded, vaguely ill at ease with the outcome. He had expected Masters to blow his top when he saw the cracked floors, but he handled it rather well. Too well. What could he be up to?

It really wasn't all that much of a fight. The event was noteworthy primarily because it was the first time punches had been thrown between Originals, but there was enough of a fight that the evidence couldn't be hidden from the Lifers. Hillbilly was wearing a big shiner the next day, and Jackson's lip was swollen and split from a jab he bobbed into when he should have been weaving. Other than a random collection of body bruises and scrapes, that was the extent of the physical damage.

But the physical damage wasn't the real problem. Those injuries would heal quickly. The greater damage had been done to the host of intangibles that had been holding the Originals together despite their many differences. For months they had been able to avoid the internal conflicts—particularly racial conflicts—that had plagued other units. The "Us Against Them" philosophy of being an Original had bound them together, making the other racial, educational and rank differences seem unimportant. Now that era was over.

The outside pressures had begun to intrude, straining the unity like never before. Race riots back in The World were making the news. The World back home seemed to be as much a war zone as Vietnam, with the extremists placing the moderates squarely in the middle of their chosen battlegrounds. The Vill remained closed, making it impossible to escape the unending regimentation. The casualty figures were on the rise in the field units, as was the hollow thumping of incoming and outgoing rounds. The once beautiful colors of the distant explosions were becoming increasingly ugly. The Cam Ranh perimeter had been breeched twice during early morning attacks, putting everyone on edge. And the war was beginning to take on the rotting stink of futility. There had been no decisive battles, and the Viet Cong and NVA seemed to have an endless supply of expendable replacements, whereas every American casualty was not only counted, but deeply mourned.

The Originals had started thinking of tent city as a soggy prison camp deluged by nearly constant rainfall that kept them confined to their tents, where differing accents, race and tastes in music were amplified. They continued to trashmouth each other, but without the old good–natured give and take. Stereo volume controls were being turned up to drown out the competition. The blacks drew closer, as did the whites, playing out the worst expectations of both.

And to make matters much worse, the holiday season was approaching like a roaring convoy of trucks loaded to capacity with loneliness. The memories of past holidays served only to underscore that home wasn't just a different place, it was part of a different life that included simple joys that seemed totally alien to Vietnam.

"Hey, Jackson, turn down that goddamned stereo! We're not all fans of Motown, y'know."

Hillbilly was standing just inside the front breeze flap to Jackson's tent, wearing his vill smoking jacket over a t–shirt and cutoffs, at least half smacked on bourbon and water.

"I'll turn down my sounds when you turn off that hillbilly redneck shit you been playin', MAN," Jackson shot back at him. "And I'll thank you not to show yore ugly peckerwood face in here again, less'n yore invited."

Jackson had been drinking scotch and water, and was just as drunk as Hillbilly. He was grooving on Aretha Franklin with six other brothers, including Skins, who were drunk and angry.

Nobody was in any mood to take any shit off anyone.

While Jackson was telling Hillbilly to kiss off, several white Originals from Hillbilly's tent took it upon themselves to gather outside Jackson's tent to show support for the champion of their cause.

"You talk big when you got someone backing you up, but you ain't jack shit when you're alone," Hillbilly yelled over the sounds of Aretha demanding R–E–S, P–E–C–T.

"Say what?" Jackson said with sudden interest. His supporters snickered loudly. "Who you talkin' to, Redneck?"

"Wash the shit out'a your ears, nigger. Or are you too fucking ignorant to understand plain English without a fucking interpreter?"

Jackson rose and advanced toward Hillbilly, his supporters just a step behind. Several more whites joined Hillbilly's gathering of supporters, providing the confrontation with the makings of a genuine race riot.

"You'n'me, Jackson," Hillbilly said as he untied the waist belt of his smoking jacket. "Outside...on the dunes. I've had enough of your jiveass bullshit. It's time we had it out...IF you got the balls to do it on your own. Or maybe you gotta have help."

Hillbilly grinned and took off his jacket, handing it to an unseen second as he kept his eyes trained on Jackson.

Jackson did the same with his smoking jacket. "You're on, suckah. I'm gonna kick yo mu'fuckin' hunky ass, cocksuckah!"

Hillbilly laughed. "Yeah, right, Cassius."

The word spread quickly that Jackson and Hillbilly were about to go at it. Both fighters had sizable followings trailing them out to the dark, damp dunes. More than forty Originals tagged along to watch the fight, with the whites on one side, the blacks on the other.

Lewandowski wasn't among them.

"Let'em have at it," he said when Frenchie came by the supply tent with the news. "They're not gonna hurt each other much. It's better to let'em get it out'a their systems."

He proved to be partially right in that more punches were thrown than connected by either of the two pugilists. Style meant nothing in the match. They rolled around in the sand, sometimes standing semi–erect in exaggerated offensive crouches. Eventually Bolton, Lugo, and six other Lifers broke up the fight. By then, Jackson and Hillbilly were so winded, generally pooped, and bloodied that they wanted someone, anyone, to step in so they could retreat and lick their wounds with their pride intact.

The final score was one swollen eye and one split lip, with numerous bruises and abrasions and twin bloodied noses. The blacks escorted Jackson back to his tent while the whites showed equal support for Hillbilly, with Skins and Frenchie going separate ways. The small cracks that were just beginning to show in the solidarity of the Originals had suddenly turned into wide fissures that threatened to take everything down.

The Charge of Quarters got on the phone and informed Lieutenant Masters that a fight had broken out. Masters immediately drove to tent city and sent the CQ runner to tell Hillbilly and Jackson to report Front and Center ASAP, if not sooner. When the two pugilists reported to the orderly tent, they found Woody at his desk, already typing the Article 15 paperwork. Masters was going to come down hard and fast to stop the crap before it could spread further.

"Two weeks extra duty for both of you," Masters said after he heard their stories. "You'll be filling sandbags, working together, from 1800 hours to 2400 hours until the end of the month. On Sunday, you'll be filling sandbags from 0730 hours until 2400 hours. I'm also withholding $120 from your pay for the next three months. It is your right to refuse my terms of punishment. If either or both of you should choose to do so, I will have the Summary Courts Martial paperwork ready for you to sign in your cell at the Support Command stockade tomorrow morning. Do you understand everything I have said so far?"

Dejected, bruised, bloodied, hung over and now deeply ashamed of themselves, both answered with a murmured "Yes, Sir."

Masters nodded. "Do you accept the provisions of the Article 15's?"

Both took deep breaths. "Yes, Sir."

"Very well," Masters said. He raised his voice enough to be heard in the front office. "Woody, bring in the Article 15's to be signed."

The next morning Masters had more to say to the whole company.

"Fighting is and always will be totally unacceptable in the 516th AG. Our mission is too critical to allow a lack of discipline to place it in jeopardy. Teamwork is essential, and the kind of thing that happened last night will make teamwork impossible. It is my understanding that none of you tried to stop the fight, so I am holding all of you responsible for what happened. Consequently, there will be no alcohol of any kind allowed in the company area for the next two weeks."

There were no objections. They knew he was serious and no one wanted to provide an excuse to create even stiffer company–wide penalties.

"If that doesn't take care of the alcohol problems, I'll order the refrigerators out of the company area. In addition to the alcohol restrictions, the entire company will be building bunkers every night until six bunkers, each capable of holding thirty troops, have been constructed. If I don't like what I see when I inspect the completed bunkers, you'll start over from scratch and continue building bunkers until I'm happy or you've DEROSed, whichever comes first."

He paused. "AND IF I EVER, EVER HEAR OF ANOTHER FIGHT IN TENT CITY, I PROMISE I WILL MAKE THE GUILTY PARTIES WISH THEY HAD NEVER BEEN BORN. DO–YOU–UNDERSTAND?"

The formation was dismissed to begin the duty day.

Command Warrant Officer 4 Mobley had more to say to Jackson and Hillbilly when they arrived at the personnel center later that morning.

Mobley was the grand old man of the 516th AG. He began his career in the old segregated Army during World War Two, had seen it all and most likely had done it all, too. He had been busted back to buck private for cracking Redneck skulls in Alabama, back in the days when a black man was supposed to cross to the opposite side of the road when a white man walked his way. He had three Purple Hearts, two Bronze Stars and one Silver Star to his credit. When Mobley spoke, everyone listened, even the Captain.

Mobley stopped at Jackson's office first.

"Put your headgear on, soldier. You're coming with me." His next stop was Hillbilly's desk. "Put on your cap. Let's go."

"Where we goin'?" Hillbilly asked. His eyes were on Jackson, returning the hard look he was receiving.

Mobley leaned over Hillbilly's desk and spoke in a low, rumbling bassoon that could chill ice. "Move it or lose it, Burns. Now."

Hillbilly reached for his cap and rose from the chair. Jackson made the mistake of smiling ever so slightly, thinking Mobley was one blood the Honkies wouldn't mess with.

Mobley saw the smile and reacted instantly with a cold in–your–face eagerness that took Jackson totally by surprise. "Did I give you permission to smile, soldier?"

Jackson blinked, then snapped his mouth shut...his face frozen into an expression of complete, sober neutrality. "No, Sir. I'm sorry, Sir."

Mobley next glared at Hillbilly until he was satisfied there was no smile, then checked out Jackson again, finding not even the barest hint of a smile.

"Form up outside and await further orders."

"Yes, Sir."

"Yes, Sir."

Mobley was hovering over the Quonset hut like a dark cloud of doom. His two victims were eager to escape his presence, if only for a brief moment. He watched as they trooped outside and formed up side by side, Jackson on the left, Hillbilly on the right.

"Eyes RIGHT!" Mobley snapped when they didn't form up 'By The Numbers'.

Jackson and Hillbilly immediately snapped to Attention, turning their heads to the right. Hillbilly snapped his left hand to his hip, sticking his arm out at an oblique angle with the tip of his elbow presenting the point where Jackson's right elbow must be. Several shuffling movements brought them to precise positions in a two–man formation that required they hold a rigid Eyes Right until relieved by further orders.

"Eyes FRONT," Mobley snapped with a precisely enunciated bassoon that had at one time been heard by Basic Trainees in Camp Polk, Louisiana. "Puh–RADE REST!"

Mobley turned to face Conners and Bolton, who had stepped outside the command hut to watch the show. His look asked if they had any questions and dared them to say even one word.

It was clear this wasn't going to be another disciplinary dog–and–pony show. Mobley was taking care of the discipline, and it would be done as it should be done. The problems in tent city wouldn't carry over into the personnel center. Mobley would put an end to it.

"When I return these troops, it will be finished," Mobley rumbled menacingly to Conners and Bolton, placing them on notice that any further harassment would be deeply resented by the Old Man. This wasn't a time for chickenshit harassment. There was a job to be done and he was the man who would do it.

Mobley gave his marching order just outside the doorway. "TROOP, Uh–Ten–SHUN! For–WARD, HARCH!"

Hillbilly and Jackson began marching in lock–step toward the main boardwalk.

"Left Flank, HARCH," Mobley shouted just before they arrived at the main boardwalk, his command directing them into a crisp ninety–degree maneuver that set their bearings for the dunes behind the personnel center.

Originals and NCOs rushed to peer through the screens along the boardwalk, relaying reports to those who couldn't see what was happening.

Mobley looked like the military version of an angel of death, but inside he was smiling with a satisfaction he hadn't felt for years. THIS is the Army…THIS is discipline the way it is supposed to be done. No whining, no amateur psychology, none of the bogus bullshit that was coming down in The New, Action Army. A soldier was a soldier no matter what the hell his job was, and a soldier had to know how to do only five basic things:

A soldier had to know how to field strip, clean and fire his weapon

…he had to know and do his job

…he had to know how to follow orders

…he had to know how to do close order drill

…and he had to know how to be an infantryman when he was under attack, no matter what his damned MOS was supposed to be.

If a man in olive drab could fulfill those missions, he could say with pride that he was a soldier in the United States Army. If he couldn't, he wasn't worth shit and it didn't matter if he was a general or a buck private.

Mobley was carrying out the mission assigned to him by Captain Ortega. The officers had met for a working breakfast in the orderly tent early that morning. Ortega wanted to give the Originals a brief back–to–basics course in soldiering. Everybody had been getting too lax and it had to end now before it could get out of control. Masters would handle tent city and Mobley would get it handled in the personnel center. Nobody could claim Mobley was prejudiced, nobody could bullshit him, and nobody had damned well better try.

Mobley marched Jackson and Hillbilly beyond Cutler's piss tube until they reached an isolated spot.

"Trooooop, HALT!"

He left Burns and Jackson standing at Attention as he slowly circled the two–man formation, finally taking his place Front and Center. Mobley didn't dislike Hillbilly and Jackson personally, but he thoroughly detested what they had done the night before. Mobley didn't care about race, politics, or personality. Those were problems for civilians. Mobley was a soldier...he thought like a soldier, and at all times he acted like a soldier. Furthermore, he expected those under his command to do the same. Jackson and Hillbilly were here because they hadn't thought or acted like soldiers the night before. If they had, there wouldn't have been a fight, there wouldn't have been the name calling, and they wouldn't have allowed the booze do their thinking for them. What they did was civilian sloppy, and Mobley would have none of it.

"Both of you are a disgrace to the uniforms you wear and the ranks you have been awarded," he began as his hard eyes moved from man to man, dispensing his disgust equally. "You behaved like spoiled children who use their fists and call other people names."

He looked at Hillbilly. "Jackson called you a redneck and a peckerwood." He looked at Jackson. "Burns called you a nigger and said you were ignorant."

Mobley shoved his face into Jackson's. "Nigger...jungle bunny ...boy." He did the same with Hillbilly. "Peckerwood...honkey... white trash."

Then Mobley stood back. "Do you feel like less of a man because I called you those names?"

He didn't wait for a reply. "If you do, it is because you aren't the man you or I thought you were. You haven't yet learned that a man looks within himself for the respect he needs. He doesn't look to others because he dislikes flattery as much as he dislikes insults. He has learned to believe in himself, and once that is learned, the flattery and the insults mean nothing to him. I had thought this was a lesson I wouldn't be required to teach young men like you, but I was wrong. You have learned enough to graduate from college, but you never learned about PRIDE and SELF–RESPECT."

He paused, daring them to speak in defense of themselves, but they said nothing.

"Next, the loud music," Mobley continued. "Jackson, you say you turned your stereo up so you could hear your music over the music being played by Burns. Burns, you said the same."

He paused to take a deep breath. "DO THE TWO OF YOU

REALIZE HOW GOD–DAMNED CHILDISH THAT SOUNDS?"

He paused, allowing his anger to subside.

"Both of you were promoted because I recommended you for promotion," he reminded them coldly. "I thought I was dealing with mature young men who knew how to soldier. College graduates, no less," he snapped, allowing his tone to take on an even more cutting edge.

"I didn't know I was promoting college kids who can't control their emotions when they're drinking booze. I gave you a chance to prove you were up to the job and you shit on me. Fortunately for you, I wasn't around when Lieutenant Masters gave you a choice between an Article 15 and a Summary Court Martial. I wouldn't have given you a choice. You'd be doing hard time in the stockade right now, if it were up to me."

"Don't ever shit on me again," he warned, his eyes flashing. "Not ever. If either of you takes one step out of line—just ONE—I'll put your ass in a sling that it'll take you a year to get out of."

He glared at them, moving his eyes from face to face, keeping the heat turned on high while saying nothing.

"Yes, Sir," Jackson ventured to say.

Mobley looked at Hillbilly.

"Yes, Sir," Hillbilly said.

"Did I give you troops permission to speak?"

"No, Sir," they answered together.

"A FINAL subject," Mobley snapped. "You two used to be TIGHT and now you FIGHT. Lemme tell you a little fact of life you won't be hearing from your mommas. You need each other in this man's war. You may THINK you got it made here in Cam Ranh, but there's Viet Cong hiding out there that want a piece of your ass very bad. Maybe they can't take Cam Ranh and hold it, but that won't stop them from coming in here and making mincemeat out've all the smart–ass little college boys they can find. If that happens, you're gonna need every brother you have, and I don't care if his ass is black as night or pink as pussy. You're gonna need him and he's gonna need you. Can you two smart–assed college boys understand what I'm saying, or am I talking over your college–educated heads?"

Again, he looked from man to man.

Jackson nodded. "I understand, Sir."

"Me, too, Sir," Hillbilly agreed.

"Do you two feel as dumb as I know you are?"

"I'm starting to," Jackson admitted.

Mobley looked at Hillbilly.

"I'm feeling pretty stupid right now, Sir."

Mobley nodded, appraising their responses. "If you're lying, you're even dumber than I think you are."

"We're not lying, Sir," Jackson answered.

"Yes, Sir," Hillbilly agreed.

Mobley nodded again. He liked Jackson's answer. It wasn't 'I'm not lying' or 'He's not lying', it was 'We're not lying', and that's the way it's supposed to be. A good soldier with his head on straight says 'We' not 'I'. If they were telling the truth, the problem —for now, at least—was history. If they were shuckin', Mobley would make sure they paid a very high price. He wasn't looking for them to kiss his ass and shower him with outpourings of gratitude, but he demanded professionalism, even from draftees.

"Very well, you're both dismissed. I'm gonna leave you two alone for awhile. I think you got some things to talk over."

The Originals built the six bunkers in six days of back breaking extra duty that had them dropping into their bunks after midnight only to rise to the calls of the CQ five short hours later. There was no time for booze, so they didn't miss the liquor until the bunkers were completed, inspected and passed by Lieutenant Masters and Captain Ortega. By then they were too exhausted to care about booze or dope. All that mattered was catching up on their lost Z's and healing their aching bodies.

By Cam Ranh standards, the open pit bunkers were acceptable, but only because Cam Ranh was so large that the odds were slim that tent city would ever get hit by 122mm rockets, heavy artillery or a successful ground attack. The same bunkers would have been considered laughably inadequate for units beyond the Cam Ranh perimeter.

It is one of the great ironies of the military that strength breeds attitudes that create vulnerability. Adequate defense measures often aren't taken until lives have been sacrificed needlessly.

Hillbilly and Jackson didn't work off their Article 15's until a few days before Thanksgiving. By then the cause of the disciplinary measure was a bad memory they had largely put behind them. As often happens following fights between two friends, Jackson and Hillbilly came out of it tighter than they had been before the bloodletting.

Chapter Ten

Thanksgiving was a bit too early for the troops in the 516th AG to be taking their five–day, four–night, out–of–country R&R's, but Masters put out the word that he would forward to Brigade any requests that were submitted. He preferred they wait until January, the hump–month of their twelve–month tours, but for those who were particularly determined to get laid, every request for an early R&R would be given serious consideration.

"It'll make the time go faster those final months if you put it off until January," Masters advised during the reveille formation the day before Thanksgiving.

That said, he went on to the next item of business. "I have invited Nhan Ai orphanage to join us for Christmas this year, and Mother Marie–Teresa has graciously consented."

The response was universally enthusiastic, including hand slaps and other breeches of formation discipline that Masters saw as a sure sign that company morale was back on track. He had been working on obtaining approval for his Christmas plans for several weeks now, and Nhan Ai was only part of the Christmas day package. He had also requested Brigade approval for an allocation of twenty "nationals" for the purpose of "Cultural Exchange" activities.

"Cultural Exchange?" Woody repeated disdainfully, interrupting Masters as he dictated the contents of the 1049 request form.

"Continuing with the text," Masters said. If he told Woody what he was planning, he might as well tell the entire company, and this was one scheme he wanted to keep to himself until the last minute. "Say something about sharing the holiday spirit with the Vietnamese and close with the standard Respectfully Yours," Masters directed. "Get it to me for signature by 1500 hours today and I'll can hand–carry it to Brigade."

Masters continued to address the troops during the pre–Thanksgiving reveille formation:

"We need to buy gifts for the kids, so I've asked Sergeant Bolton and Specialist Lewandowski to take charge of the gift detail. We can use the company special service fund to buy some of the gifts, but we'll need cash donations if we're going to do this right. We want each kid to have at least one gift. And we should get some nice things for the Sisters, too. And I do mean *nice* things. I don't mean lingerie from the Vill."

His comment was greeted by universal chuckles, many nudges and more than a few faked expressions of disappointment. The boys were relaxed enough to be boys again. They were on a shared mission now. The three–story outhouse was far less important than the kids and nuns at Nhan Ai.

Masters continued. "We'll need more committees for food and decorations, and we'll need a Santa. Maybe some of you can get candy and cookies from home, and whatever else we can come up with that'll make it a day to remember."

Masters glanced around the formation, feeling a warmth for his men that would have been a dangerous luxury if they were preparing for a combat mission that some weren't likely to survive. "Are we together on this?"

The troops answered in unison. "YES, SIR!"

"Good. Let's make it happen. Sergeant Bolton, dismiss the formation."

"Yes, Sir," Bolton said with a sharp salute. "CumpunEEE, DisMISSED!"

Sometimes the Army ain't so bad.

The Originals weren't expecting fresh roast turkey with all the fixins' for Thanksgiving day, but that was what the Quartermaster Corps and the mess sergeants came up with for all the troops scattered throughout Vietnam. A holiday Cease Fire brought a temporary lull to the fighting until the early hours of the morning after, when the war started all over again.

The Vill was allowed to open for business again after Thanksgiving, but the gate was closed again two weeks later, after the Army medics conducted their usual inspection of the bar girls on Crotch Tuesday. The same rationale was used again, blaming the closure on the plague, but few believed it this time around. Too much had happened to make the plague story credible. The housegirls of Cam

Ranh came and went from their jobs as usual while the Vill was closed, with no evidence or testimony of sickness. If asked, they would just shrug their shoulders and say "No bic", "I don't understand."

The bar girls seemed equally healthy and unaffected during the two–week window of opportunity. They denied any sickness beyond the usual VD. Some of them couldn't be found when their regular customers returned, but the other girls explained away their absences by saying they had left Cam Ranh to find work elsewhere, or had returned to home villages to be with family until Cam Ranh re–opened.

The Vill rats needed no further evidence to come to the conclusion they were being flimflammed by the brass, who wanted to shut down the Vill because it had become too much of a safe haven for the professional short timers. Additional evidence was presented when newspapers, magazines, and letters from friends and family at home began to arrive. Phantom or real, the plague may have played only a minor role, if any, in the decision to make the Vill Off Limits. Stateside politics seemed to be the real culprit.

The feces began hitting the air facilitator back in The World when a major weekly news magazine ran a series of articles about the brothels and bars of Vietnam, offering readers new insights into the seamier side of the war, raising questions about how the American military men were spending their time, their money, and their lives. How could America expect to win a war in such a corrupt environment? Weren't the troops who won World War Two both brave and chaste? Even if the war could be won, was it worth all the tax dollars and human sacrifice that would be needed to defeat the communists?

The folks back home were beginning to wonder if America was losing its moral center along with the lives of sons, brothers, and husbands.

The major troop concentration centers were covered in the story, including Saigon, Danang, Nha Trang, Hue, and Cam Ranh. The Army camp in Pleiku received particular coverage because of an Army sponsored, health inspected brothel that had been built to lure the troops away from the commie–and–clap–infested bars and massage parlors in the nearby shanty towns. In terms of practical solutions to an age–old problem, the official brothel had its advantages, but in terms of political realities, it was a public relations disaster.

After the magazine hit the news stands, the big three television networks jumped on the story, bringing the discotheques of Saigon to the living rooms of America, juxtaposing body bags in the boonies with Saigon cyclo girls in tight mini skirts. Cam Ranh was only briefly covered in a segment that showed a line of GIs waiting for their clap shots at a dispensary. Prostitution had always been a part of war, but never had it been shown so graphically to the folks back home, and at such an inopportune time.

The death toll of the war was rising along with the unfavorable coverage. Outrage was pouring in from the moral guardians of the left and the right. The emerging Feminist movement jumped on the bargirl bandwagon, condemning the degradation and economic slavery of the women of Vietnam, while the Bible thumpers tended to blame the moral degradation of the American military on the prostitutes and commies. Regardless of the source of the criticism, it meant big trouble for the military politcians and civilian politicians who were selling the idea that the war in Vietnam was both moral and winnable.

Perhaps there had been a plague in Cam Ranh village, perhaps the news stories and the closures were only coincidental, but most of the GI's in Cam Ranh didn't buy it. The official explanations seemed to be loaded with holes. It was a perception that would grow and spread from the troops in Vietnam back to the voters in the World, eventually becoming a plague of doubt that was called a Credibility Gap.

Lewandowski figured Masters had been in a mean–tempered funk lately because he needed to get his tubes cleaned, just like everyone else in Cam Ranh. But his problems with Masters were only part of his misery. The Dirty Dozen and Charlie had been giving him a particularly hard time lately.

"We know what you're up to," Frenchie said accusingly on Christmas Eve. "You're just making us hump butt so Masters will approve your R&R request."

Lewandowski was again experiencing the loneliness of leadership, being the bad guy they looked up to whenever they wanted someone to blame for their misery. He felt less a leader than a punching bag. It would have been far wiser if he had kept it to himself when Masters turned down his R&R request.

"You'll be eligible for an R&R when I get my cement floor slabs," Masters told him after tearing up the typed request form. "I gave you six weeks, and from what I've seen so far you won't make it. If I let you go on R&R now, I *know* you won't. Edwards can't handle those guys like you can. We're way behind schedule. We should be framing the walls to the barracks, but we're still stuck on the floor slabs."

"Sir, I think it would do the Dirty Dozen good to get a break from me for awhile," Lewandowski said. He had a second R&R form typed and ready to go, should he be able to talk Masters into signing it. "What with the Vill being closed, and me giving them orders all the time, I think I've got a morale problem on my hands, Sir. They keep goofing off, Sir. Even when *I* give'em orders. Its almost as bad as it was with Slater, Sir."

"We all have a morale problem," Masters answered, unmoved by the logic. "Get those slabs finished and you'll get your R&R. Until then, don't bother me with another request. You're dismissed."

Frenchie was glad to provide the first kicks when Lewandowski was down. "Y'know, if I was you I'd start being *real* nice to the guys doing the dirty work. Without us, nothin'll ever get done. And you won't ever get your R&R if the work ain't done."

Lewandowski was as astounded by Frenchie's mercenary attitude as by his latent perceptivity. "Oh, man, that's cold. That's really cold. What happened to the old Originals spirit, huh? What happened to All For One And One For All, huh? Will you listen to what he said, guys? I mean, is that any attitude to have? What happened to the brotherhood we had when we first came in–country? We used to share everything. Now I might as well be talking to the Lifers. I'd get about as much sympathy."

"You don't share your pay with us," Skins said accusingly.

"You don't do guard duty with us," Frenchie added. "And you

sure as hell don't burn shit."

"Hey, I do CQ duty," Lewandowski said defensively.

"Oooo, I'm impressed," Frenchie countered. "Big deal, man. You get to play honcho when you inspect the guard detail. You like doing that, man. You get off on the power trip of it."

"I resent that."

Even Edwards had to laugh at Lewandowski's denial. They knew Lew better than he cared to know himself.

Lewandowski changed the subject. "Hey, it's Christmas Eve, guys. This is no time to be arguing. Lets get the tools put away and call it a day. I'll buy the first round at the EM club."

"What if Masters comes poking around here while we're gone?" Skins asked.

"He won't. Not on Christmas Eve. Even Masters ain't that much of a prick."

Charlie stood, feeling sluggish and lazy. Christmas Eve was no time to be humping butt. "What time are we picking up the kids tomorrow?"

"Nine," Lewandowski said as he started gathering the tools for the equipment shed.

"What time we taking them back?" Frenchie asked.

"Oh, four, four–thirty," Lewandowski said as he unlocked the door to the shed and held it open for the others. "Masters said he'd let me know once we see how the party is going. We just gotta make sure they get back home before sunset. I don't know what Masters has planned after that, but Woody told me he's got something up his sleeve."

"He'll prob'ly have us singing Christmas carols in muh'fuh' cadence," Skins grumbled as he tossed a shovel into the shed.

Moments later they climbed into the deuce and headed for the distant EM Club, where they would join the many others who had no better place to go on Christmas Eve.

Mess Sergeant Lugo was volunteered to play Santa because he didn't need extra padding to fill out the suit. Lugo was as much a victim of his MOS as any Eleven Bravo infantryman. His greatest failing as a Santa came when his Bronx/Puerto Rican accent was combined with a voice that made him sound like a cheap hood who would gladly break the legs of any kid or nun who dared not be joyful.

Every man assigned to the 516th was there, including all the officers. Hillbilly and Jackson made a point of approaching Mobley together to wish him a merry Christmas and happy New Year. Mobley returned the favor along with the handshakes. They didn't thank him for setting them straight, but the gratitude was there and Mobley could see it.

Captain Ortega approached him next.

"You've got them on the right track now, Mr. Mobley. Good job."

"We did it together, Sir," Mobley said, not out of false modesty but because it was true.

Lewandowski and the crew rolled in with the kids and the sisters shortly before 1000 hours. The nuns were almost as startled as the kids when they found themselves confronted by a looming, booming American–style Santa Claus wearing a costume made from bedsheets dyed red with food coloring. Lugo was shouting "Ho, Ho, Ho! Merrrr–ry Christmas!" with so much gusto that the smaller children began to cry and wouldn't stop until Lugo disappeared into the NCO tent to change uniforms, returning a few minutes later in fatigues, minus the "Ho, Ho, Ho".

So much for the export of great American traditions.

Lugo took up residence in the mess tent with all the presents and packets of candy. The children from the toddlers on up were brought to him in a ragged line that led from the mess tent out to the water tank, where the housegirls did the laundry. Each one of the kids were held or accompanied by GIs of all ranks.

After receiving their presents, the children were handed a bag of rock candy and taken to a section of the mess tent that had been cleared of tables and chairs to create a space where the presents could be opened. The first of the kids had to be taught what to do with their presents, but they proved to be fast studies. Some of the kids seemed confused by all the excitement and joy of the big people surrounding them, but there were no more tears to contend with, except perhaps from several of the GI hosts. There wasn't a man in the 516th AG who didn't know he was getting more out it than the kids. Without the kids, it would have been a dreary day filled with thoughts of home, friends and family.

A lot of work was invested in the preparations, and not all of it had been accomplished in the 516th AG. The troops couldn't drive down to the nearest suburban shopping center and dash through the stores with shopping lists. The PX had no call for children's toys and the Vill wasn't designed for kiddy clientele, so the shopping lists were sent to friends and family back in The World. Lewandowski and Bolton put aside their differences long enough to get everyone organized. Letters were written and it wasn't long before the presents began to arrive by priority mail. The outlay for gifts and postal charges were to be reimbursed from the company fund, but the volunteers back in The World didn't ask to be paid back. It seemed like an impossibly limited time frame, but the gifts arrived with time to spare. The first sure sign of impending success cropped up when Bolton and Lewandowski re–commenced hostilities.

Christmas dinner was served buffet style at 1300 hours, with the two Poppasans sitting down with everyone else, wearing their new fatigue caps with shiny Captain's bars. Once again Lugo and his crew came up with a stateside–quality holiday dinner of turkey with all the traditional side dishes and three kinds of pie. The big meal just about finished off the little ones after the earlier excitement, so they were taken to the tents for naps, accompanied by the nuns and plenty of volunteer sitters dressed in faded jungle fatigues.

Masters pulled Lewandowski aside when the kids were sleeping. "It's about time to take them back to Nhan Ai," he said as he led Lewandowski toward the orderly tent.

"Yes, Sir. It'll be tough to see them go."

"Yes, it will," Masters agreed. "I'm glad you told us about Nhan Ai. They've been good for the men."

Lewandowski nodded. "Yeah, they have."

"I have a little job for you to do on the way back from Nhan Ai," Masters said as he opened the rear breeze flap of the orderly tent. "The paperwork is on my desk. Just show it to the MPs at the gate to the Vill. It's all been arranged. Everything is proper. You have nothing to worry about."

"Exactly what has been arranged, Sir?"

Lieutenants normally do not explain their actions to Specialist Fives, but Masters made an exception in this case. He needed a willing accomplice. His explanation was brief and to the point.

"I'm going to get the men laid for Christmas."

"Choi oi!" Lewandowski exclaimed. Roughly translated, 'Choi oi' meant 'Oh, my god' in Vietnamese. "How'd you pull that off, Sir?"

Masters paused at the door to his office. "I yanked a few strings," he answered with a slight smile. "You aren't the only one in this company who knows how to wheel and deal."

Lewandowski wondered how much Masters knew about the deals that had been made to save tent city.

"Yes, Sir."

Masters led the way into his office, where he handed Lewandowski a thick packet of forms that were generated during the approval process. The topmost form was the original1049 form that had been typed by Woody five weeks earlier, followed by endorsements from the various levels of the chain of command in Brigade, finally landing on the desk of the Deputy Commander, USASUP-COMCRB, the United States Army Support Command Cam Ranh Bay.

Lewandowski scanned the packet of forms and whistled appreciatively. "This is alright, Sir. I guarantee you, it'll be one Christmas present that'll be remembered for a long, long time."

"They have it coming," Masters said. "They're good soldiers, even if they don't want to admit it. They've accomplished a lot during the past six months. They deserve a break."

Lewandowski nodded. "They're lucky to have an XO like you," he said, surprising himself with the compliment even more than he surprised Masters. "I'm gonna make sure the guys know who to thank for this."

"Forget about the thanks," Masters said. "Just don't let it get out of hand tonight. Keep an eye peeled so the troops don't get too rowdy. We can't have any fights. And the girls have to be treated nice and gentle. Those are the ground rules and I'll burn anyone who breaks them. Get whoever you can to help you and I'll have Bolton do the same. None of the officers will be here, so you'll be on your own. We'll be having a party of our own over at the Captain's hooch."

Lewandowski nodded. "Sure thing, Sir."

"I'm sticking my neck out a mile with this," Masters added. "I'm counting on your support to pull it off."

"You've got it, Sir," Lewandowski promised. He held out his hand. "Merry Christmas, Sir."

"Merry Christmas, Lewandowski. You better get your crew ready to take the kids to Nhan Ai. I want everyone back here before dark. There's no telling how long this truce will hold."

It was just turning dusk when the three deuces rolled onto the tarmac at tent city, with gallant members of the Dirty Dozen jumping down from the cargo beds to help down the giggling cargo, all of whom had eagerly volunteered to participate in the Christmas "Cultural Exchange" program. None of them came from the Saigon Club, no doubt because Masters and his officer pals had hangouts frequented primarily by officers. All were wearing mini–skirts and automatically formed themselves into a tight group of twenty as soon as they hit the tarmac. Once having inspected tent city, they seemed not altogether impressed by what they saw.

The feminine voices and industrial strength perfumes quickly carried beyond the tarmac to the surrounding tents, drawing the troops like moths to a light. The word spread quickly—usually shouted from one tent to the next—so it wasn't long before the giggling guests were surrounded by Originals and NCOs who couldn't quite believe what they were seeing. Almost to a man, the troops milled around, hesitating to do anything until they received further orders.

Lewandowski and Bolton climbed to the bed of the deuce to set the rules for the night.

"Woh! Hold it!" Lewandowski shouted. "AT EASE OUT THERE! AT EASE! Okay, this is Lieutenant Masters' gift to the troops for Christmas...BUT YOU GOTTA BE COOL ABOUT IT, OKAY? NO FIGHTING, NO ROUGH STUFF AT ALL. YOU GOTTA BE NICE TO EACH OTHER AND, OF COURSE, TO

THESE BEAUTIFUL GIRLS."

Lewandowski tipped his fatigue cap to the "girls", a couple of whom would never see forty again. The deal had been arranged sight unseen with a bar mommasan who cared far less about quality than quantity.

"THE SARGE AND I NEED VOLUNTEERS TO KEEP THE LID ON TONIGHT. MAYBE SOME OF YOU GUYS WHO DON'T WANNA PARTAKE CAN GIVE US A HAND. AND THE NEXT TIME YOU SEE LIEUTENANT MASTERS, TELL HIM THANKS FOR THIS, OKAY? You got anything to say to'em, Sarge?"

"JUST, MERRY CHRISTMAS," Bolton shouted. "I'M REAL PROUD OF WHAT YOU MEN DID FOR THE KIDS TODAY. GOD BLESS YOU. And I mean that."

Bolton moved back a step, returning the formation to Lewandowski.

"OKAY!" Lewandowski shouted. "REMEMBER....TAKE YOUR TURN. AND DON'T BUTT IN LINE. IT'S UP TO YOU TO MAKE THE DEALS WITH THE GIRLS. BE NICE TO'EM. IF YOU DON'T, YOU'LL FIND YOURSELF NECK DEEP IN SERIOUS SHIT. YOU GOT ALL NIGHT TO ENJOY YOURSELVES, SO THERE'S NO NEED TO BE IN A RUSH. PEACE, BROTHERS! AND MERRY CHRISTMAS!! NEXT CHRISTMAS WE'LL ALL BE BACK HOME!! SHORT!!"

Later that night, a group of Originals and NCO's joined together in a chorus of Silent Night, their voices drifting down from a spot high in the dunes. Shenanigans ceased as others joined in. Eventually, the whole of tent city was transformed into an unlikely cathedral, with a decidely imperfect choir.

When it was over, everyone went back to what they were doing.

The truce ended at Midnight. The moment was celebrated by the sodden thumps of incoming and outgoing rounds.

It proved to be a Christmas to remember.

Feliz Navidad.

Chapter Eleven

Specialist Four Charles R. Cutler, he of the dedicated pisser fame, was getting very Short.

"How Short are ya, Charlie?"

"I left yesterday."

"How Short are ya, Charlie?"

"I'm so Short, when I look up, all I see are Lifer assholes."

"How Short are ya, Charlie?"

"My Freedom Flight just landed."

"How Short are ya, Charlie?"

"Kiss my ass, Lewandowski." Charlie Edwards snapped.

"Oops, wrong Charlie."

"Yeah, very funny."

Charlie Cutler's impending DEROS was sufficient cause to justify a company–wide going away party. January was just a feeble survivor, barely holding on with two days remaining. They had passed the hump month. It was all down hill from here.

Cutler's short timer party would be the practice run for that wonderful time when every Original and Lifer in the 516th AG would be short enough to ask that supremely delightful leading question:

How short are YOU...this day...this hour...this minute?

A Board of Director's meeting was called to plan the short timer's party for Charlie Cutler. Lewandowski offered to scrounge, concoct or arrange for enough beer, booze, bread, barbecue sauce, chicken, steaks and potato salad to make it a bon voyage worthy of the first 516th AG short timer.

His supply list did not need to include any girls from the vill, which was wide open for business once again. The stateside protests had died down, the political heat was off and the gate to the vill swung open shortly after 1966 became 1967. The sex lives of the Vill rats had become fishwrap for the gossip–starved minions of the news media back home in "TheWorld", where the newsies continued to flit from hot story to hot story like butterflies confused by a cornucopia of blossoms in a field of spring clover. Of course, the re–

opening of the vill made the subjects of the gentle Nhan Ai sermon-ettes business as usual, as well. Mother M–T wasn't yet ready to concede defeat.

Louie Donnatelli was stoned when they met to plan the short timer's party. It was becoming unusual to see Donnatelli when he wasn't at least partially stoned. He said he preferred life in–country with the edge blunted by whatever he could get. Of late, his poison of choice was a particularly potent combination of marijuana laced with opium. Some had tried to tell Louie he was getting hooked, but the well–intended talk didn't do any good, particularly when he tended to listen best to those who were as strung–out as he was. There was no telling how long his tail could be covered.

"I can count the dead and wounded just as easily stoned as straight," Donnatelli was heard to say when the O.J.'s made him a little too numb for his condition to be overlooked at the personnel center. "Wake me up when it's over, man. I want my ass straight when I fly out'a here."

An acceptably sluggish level of progress had been achieved at the site for the new and improved 516th AG. Masters had been mollified…the recent progress allowed him to placate his tormen-tors, the Brigade master planners. Everyone had reason to be happy for the time being. The floor slabs were down, with only minor cracks this time, and the walls and roofs were going up.

Lewandowski decided to wait on his R&R request. He figured the Vill would close again, so he was saving R&R for more desper-ate times.

Frenchie was driving the deuce today, while Lewandowski rode shotgun with the target of opportunity being the supply depot, where they would scrounge the supplies for Cutler's party. Charlie Edwards was left in charge of the monthly inventory count back in tent city.

"Pull in there," Lewandowski said as the deuce lumbered past a row of warehouses that eventually opened onto a square half–mile of 105mm Howitzers awaiting assignments to field units.

Lewandowski's destination was one of four gargantuan ware-houses that held long rows of refrigerated reefers powered by platoons of V–16 Detroit Diesel generators stationed just outside the warehouse. Between the reefers and the generators, the racket in and around the warehouses was deafening in a literal sense. Construction was underway in a nearby field for what would be a dairy plant specializing in converting powdered milk into enough ice cream and liquid milk to raise the cholesterol level of every American within a twenty mile radius of Cam Ranh. It was just one of many projects in progress. There was no end in sight to the growth phase of the US Army Support Command, Cam Ranh Bay.

The GI population of Cam Ranh had nearly doubled since the 516th arrived in–country. The troop replacement depot once could be confined to thirty acres. Now the repple depple covered more than three hundred acres, with dozens of two–story barracks and six sprawling administrative buildings accommodating the hundreds of clerks who processed the thousands of incoming and outgoing troops being transported by hundreds of commercial jet airliners and military cargo planes. The commercial airliners, known as Freedom Flights, had become so commonplace in the skies of Cam Ranh that the glistening aircraft rarely drew more than mild notice from the troops on the ground.

Frenchie allowed the deuce to idle to a stop at the entrance to the warehouse.

"Park just inside the doorway," Lewandowski said. "Leave the motor running, in case someone needs to move it while we're running down Barlow."

Lewandowski climbed down from the passenger seat while Frenchie put the transmission in neutral and engaged the parking brake, allowing the clacking diesel to chatter to itself while they went searching for the man in charge. Master Sergeant Barlow controlled the receipt, storage and shipment of dozens of tons of frozen beef, including prime sirloin steak, pork and chicken. Master Sergeant E–8 Adolphus P. Barlow was the man. Lewandowski wasn't searching for Second Lieutenant Earl C. Kofsky, also known as The Captain's Kid, or Captain Willard M. Mogull, the CO of the 523rd Logistical Supply Company, and he certainly had no interest in locating Colonel Wyatt N. Longstaff, the Commanding Officer of the Combined Logistical Supply Support Command, Cam Ranh Bay. Lewandowski needed to get things done in a hurry, and Adolphus P.

Barlow—formerly of Sims, Alabama—was the man who could get it handled.

Lewandowski paused to organize the Search and Scrounge mission. Barlow was nowhere in sight and a quick glance told Lewandowski the small administrative office to their right was deserted.

"WE'LL HAVE TO HUNT HIM DOWN," Lewandowski shouted over the incessant roar of more than four hundred freezer compressor motors.

Frenchie nodded, not bothering to shout a response to the obvious.

The warehouse was divided into four double rows of olive drab reefers, separated by three aisles wide enough to easily accommodate a deuce–and–a–half for loading and unloading, with the middle two rows piggybacked to provide additional storage space. Each reefer was packed with several hundred cases of frozen meat products. Plans were underway to build at least two more warehouses of the same size and design.

"HE MUST BE OUT IN THE REEFERS," Lewandowski shouted over the compressors.

"NO WONDER BARLOW WANTS AN EARLY DEROS," Frenchie shouted back. "EVEN I'D RE–UP TO GET OUT'A THIS PLACE."

"YOU TAKE THE LEFT ROWS AND I'LL TAKE THE MIDDLE," Lewandowski shouted. "WE'LL MEET IN THE BACK AND COME UP THE MIDDLE ISLE TOGETHER, IF WE AIN'T FOUND HIM YET! LOOK FOR A BLUE AND RED RAG TIED TO A REEFER DOOR HANDLE! THAT'S BARLOW! HE'LL BE INSIDE! IF YOU FIND HIM FIRST, STAY WHERE YOU ARE AND I'LL FIND MY WAY BACK TO YOU!"

"CHECK!! LET'S DO IT!!"

Frenchie headed for the far left aisle while Lewandowski strolled to the isle on the far right. Both were ambling along with the same lack of urgency. Every minute spent at the supply depot was time lost to the same Army that took two years off their lives as civilians. Turn around was fair play.

Lewandowski busied his mind by considering where he would

one day go for R&R. Charlie Edwards and Skins had already been to Hong Kong and were undergoing daily penicillin treatments at the dispensary to get the symptoms in full remission. Frenchie had been approved for five days and four nights in Bangkok in another nine days, a popular R&R destination despite its reputation for being a world–class breeding ground for the clap. One of the married members of the Dirty Dozen had put in for Hawaii, where he would meet his wife and try to patch up their marriage. She wrote that she had become "confused" by his long absence, but he suspected she wasn't as confused as she claimed to be. One of her old boyfriends was 4–F, which made him ineligible for the draft and left him conveniently available while the Old Man was stuck in the middle of Cam Ranh Bay. Others had put in for Australia, where it was said a guy didn't need hookers to get laid. Lewandowski liked the idea of Australia, but wondered if he might strike out with the local girls. He preferred the more direct and sure approach found in Hong Kong and Bangkok: Forty dollars Hong Kong a day would guarantee 24–hour companionship.

Lewandowski reached the end of his isle of reefers with no sign of Barlow. Frenchie wasn't in sight, so he headed for the middle isle of reefers on his own. Within moments, he had spotted a yellow rag conspicuously draped from a distant door handle. Yellow rags were used by the troops who worked for Barlow. Barlow alone had blue and red. Barlow explained the need for the colored rags during one of Lewandowski's prior visits.

"It's a safety thing," Barlow explained with his slow, southern drawl at it's slowest. "It gets mighty cold in there. If the cold don't get'cha, the suffercation will, if you stays in there too long."

Lewandowski liked Barlow. He was a regular guy, friendly to everyone, not the typical Lifer with a lot of stripes.

Skins had a different opinion. "He's a muh'fuh' Tom, man. He uses backwoods Nigger Shuck'n'Jive', the kind'a shit the Massah like to hear' because he don't havta worry about his niggers being smarter than he is."

Lewandowski didn't argue with Skins, but he didn't agree with him either. He thought it was more likely that Skins didn't like Barlow because he was friendly with everyone, whites included, and he definitely wasn't made from the Black Power mold that defined so many of the younger black troops in–country. But it was an opinion Lewandowski kept to himself, figuring it would only make matters worse if he came to Barlow's defense...the "massah" defending the "good nigger".

Lewandowski opened the door to the reefer with the yellow rag and poked his head inside. "Yo, I'm looking for Barlow," he said as his breath misted, mixing with the frigid fog that formed when the hot and humid exterior air met the teeth–chattering environment within the reefers. "Know where he is?"

"Last I heard, he was running inventory in 189," came the slightly muffled reply. The supply clerk was wearing arctic survival gear, his mouth covered by a scarf.

Lewandowski closed the door, shivering from a delayed chill as he read the reefer numbers around him. He was at reefer 302 with 303 on his right and 301 to his left, so left it would be. He began walking toward the front of the warehouse, singing scattered patches of refrain from I FOUGHT THE LAW while he continued his search for Barlow's reefer.

Breakin' rocks in the hot sun,
I fought the law and the law won,
I fought the law and the law won.
Makin' somethin'–or–other with a six gun,
I fought the law and the law won,
I fought the law and dum–de–dum

He switched to another oft–requested favorite for the Armed Forces Radio Network.

"There's somethin' hap'nen' 'round here,
What it is ain't exactly clear,
There's a man with a gun over there,
Telling me I got to beware.
You gotta stop now, what's that sound?
Everybody knows what's comin' down,
UmmummUmmmmm—UmmmmmUmmmmm
Par–uh–noy–uh strikes DEEP
In–to your mind it will creep.
It starts when you're always afraid.

Step out'a line, the man come and take you a–way.

Lewandowski turned right at the end of the isle, following the path previously taken by Frenchie. Moments later he spotted Frenchie leaning against a reefer door with a blue and red rag tied to its handle.

"SO, WHAT TOOK YOU SO LONG?!" Frenchie shouted as Lewandowski reached his side.

"BARLOW'S IN THERE?" Lewandowski shouted.

"NO, HE'S IN BUMFUCK, EGYPT! OF COURSE HE'S IN THERE! I TOLD HIM YOU'RE ON THE WAY!"

"WANNA COME IN?"

"NAW, I'LL LET YOU FREEZE YOUR BALLS OFF BY YOURSELF!"

Lewandowski opened the reefer door and stepped inside, his arms folded tightly against his chest, providing himself with feeble protection against the cold.

"YO, IT'S LEW!"

"Yo y'sef," Barlow answered back. "No need to shout in here."

Lewandowski shut the door, closing out the roar of the compressor motors along with the hot air. When fans began to clear the fog, he saw Barlow was at the far end of the reefer, dressed in arctic survival gear, making notes on a clipboard.

Barlow grinned at Lewandowski. "Does this cold remind you of anything, Lew? Like maybe freezing your ass off playing football in December? Sometimes I can almost ferget I'm in Vee–et–nam when I'm in one'a'these reefers. It's nice'n'quiet in here. A man can do some thinkin'. And the cold ain't so bad once you gets used to it. I don't think I'd mind if I never saw no hot places again. I just may move up to Alaska when I retires next year."

Barlow chuckled and set his clipboard on a cardboard box containing 233 prime–grade beef steaks, the best that Uncle Sam could buy for prices that weren't always competitive, as would be revealed by a purchasing scandal that would erupt three years later. It wouldn't be the first such scandal involving food supplies for soldiers in the field. Hundreds of Union troops died in the Civil War from eating canned beef that had been cured with formaldehyde.

"What's up, Lew? What can I do for you today?"

"I need two cases of steaks and two of chicken," Lewandowski said. "We got a short timer's party coming up this Sunday. One of our guys is DEROSing early, the lucky sonofabitch."

"I was gonna say, it seems a might early for you folks to be having short timer parties," Barlow said. "When you want the steaks and chicken?"

"Now, if its okay," Lewandowski answered. "We can let'em thaw out slow in the mess tent refrigerator."

"You got'em," Barlow said. "Just wait a minute and I'll finish up in here. Maybe you oughta drive down your truck in the meantime. We'll have you on the road in a jiffy."

"You got it, Sarge. Like always, if you want a favor from us, just let me know and I'll get it handled."

"Don't worry, I won't be shy," Barlow promised. "You better get out'a here before you catch pneuMOnia, my man."

"Got'cha," Lewandowski agreed. "Of course, you're invited to the party. All the booze, beer and chow you want, and it's all on the house."

"Well, I might just do that, Lew. Le's wait'n'see, jus' wait'n'see. Where's it gonna be?"

"At China Beach, if it's a sunny day, and in tent city if it ain't."

"Okay, I'll be thinkin' on it. You better get out'a here, man. You gonna catch yo'self a chill stannin' in here dressed like that."

Lewandowski waved adios. "Me'n Frenchie'll be back in a minute with the deuce. We got more runnin' around to do after we leave here."

"I'll be waitin' fo'ya right here," Barlow promised.

The ceaseless nature of the monsoon rains was slowly reverting back to the dry season. Whole days of bright sunshine were beginning to lure the troops outside for impromptu games of baseball and touch football. One of the more popular gathering places in Cam Ranh was China Beach. During the dry season, China Beach was always crowded on Sundays, the day when most units maintained only skeleton staffing to allow the troops a day off.

The 516th started their invasion of China Beach at 0800 hours and immediately secured a perimeter that included four (4) stationary oil drum barbecues, two (2) double–tube pissers, one (1) four–hole shitter, four (4) cabanas with palm frond roofs, and one hundred (100) feet of uncontested surf along the southern edge of the half–mile beachhead. Their armaments included barbecue briquettes, five (5) gallons of Mess Sergeant Lugo's Bombshell barbecue sauce, two (2) jeep trailers loaded with ice scrounged from the supply depot, 250 six–packs of Miller 'Highlife' beer, one hundred (100) six–packs of Coke, two (2) cases of Jim Beam Select, two (2) cases of Johnny Walker Red Label, thirty (30) gallons of Lugo's Momma's Secret Recipe potato salad, 300 pounds of Choice–grade beef steaks, 300 pounds of chicken and enough battery–powered radios to fill the air with a bedlam of conflicting musical styles.

A one–day undeclared peace treaty had been declared between the ranks, with the R.H.I.P. barriers being temporarily lowered out of respect for Cutler's short–short–short timer status. Beer, booze, bathing suits, beach towels, barbecue and beach bum athletic competitions would rule the day. The word was out. Anyone who pulled rank would be in danger of an immediate dunking in the rolling surf of the South China Sea.

The day began with teams being formed for baseball, football and volleyball, with intramural matchups designed by Lewandowski, who promised that first, second and third place championship teams would eventually emerge. The less competitive in nature could head for the water or gather for bull sessions, or just knock off Z's on the warm sand, catching up on hours lost to the previous night's poker games.

The beer started foaming and flowing shortly before 1000 hours, when timeouts were called between the intramural games. The normal niceties of proper timing for the consumption of alcoholic beverages were a luxury they could not afford. They had a lot of partying to do in a limited time frame.

"We gotta get Cutler drunk," Lewandowski suggested to Hill-billy as he passed the church key to Jackson. They were on the same team, which had lost 21–to–18 to a volleyball team that included Numbnuts and Connors. Wagers would follow when the Lifers were filled with confidence.

"Yeah, drunk enough to miss his Freedom Flight," Hillbilly

agreed with an evil glint in his eye.

"Shame on you," Lewandowski said with an evil glint of his own.

Popular support for Cutler was dwindling away, along with the number of days hours and minutes Cutler had to endure before reporting to the repple depple for his Freedom Flight. Charlie Edwards came up with a name for the phenomenon, calling it Cutler Envy. He said the short timer's party was an exercise in group envy, if not fullblown masochism that, no doubt, was the result of bottle feeding and the teachings of Dr. Spock.

"We got too much behavioral modification and too little tit," Charlie explained to whoever would listen. "We feel compelled to satisfy others with our actions, while leaving our own needs unsatisfied."

"You're crazy, Charlie," Lewandowski said the night before the party, after lights out in the supply tent. "Just plain dingydow."

"And you're living proof that it's true," Charlie countered. "You can't help yourself, Lewandowski. You try to satisfy everyone."

"Dingydow," Lewandowski repeated.

"You know I'm right," Charlie continued, unwilling to call a halt to the argument until Lewandowski conceded defeat. "You bust your butt to satisfy the Originals by being anti–Lifer, then you try to satisfy Masters by asking how high when he tells you to jump. When you played ball, you tried to satisfy the coach. Before the coach, you tried to satisfy your mother. It's all in the books, Lewandowski. It's all documented. You're suffering from a combination of classic symptoms relating to social manipulation and breast deprivation."

"Yer sick, Charlie. Yer the one always thinking about tits all the time, not me. I got better things to think about."

"We're all sick, Lewandowski. Our whole generation is heading for hard times."

"Oh, go suck a tit—fer godsakes—and shut–up so I can get some sleep."

"We're doomed to be followers, not leaders," Charlie added, getting in the last word.

Cutler had taken to wearing a shit–eating grin that acted as salt being poured into the open wounds of those around him.

"Ask me how short I am," Cutler would urge, apparently un–
aware of or unconcerned about the growing resentment that sur–
rounded his world of rapidly dwindling days, hours and minutes in–
country.

"You ain't Short enough, in my opinion," Hillbilly told Cutler
the day before. "I'll be glad when you're out'a here so's I don't
have'ta hear your big mouth no more."

Even such a direct rebuff was unable to stop Cutler, who was
infused with daydreams of his future as a free man, a civilian who
could walk by an officer without saluting, who could leave his bed
unmade if he so selected, a young man who would never again have
to do KP, Shit Burning or Guard Duty.

Jackson was a ringer on Lewandowski's volleyball team. "It
might not be a bad idea," Jackson pondered from where he lay on the
sand.

"What idea?" Lewandowski asked.

"What Hillbilly was saying about Cutler," Jackson explained.
"Maybe we could get him so drunk that he misses his Freedom
Flight tomorrow morning."

That'd be a mean thing to do," Lewandowski said with ingrati-
ating insincerity.

"I mean, it won't mess him up that much if we can pull it off,"
Jackson continued. "He can always get on a later flight."

Hillbilly yawned, half asleep from a long night of poker. He
had walked away from a poker game with forty yards of green that
once belonged to others, having prospered particularly well in the
games of Chi–Town, a variation of 7–card Stud wherein the high
poker hand and the high ace in the hole would split the pot.

"I think it would be a nice farewell present from us to Cutler,"
Hillbilly said.

"Aw, it ain't likely to happen," Lewandowski said sourly.
"Cutler's been so clean lately that he squeaks when he walks. He
ain't even been going to the Vill for more'n a month now. He's
convinced he'll get the clap and the medics will flag his records for
six weeks. I should'a kept my mouth shut about that."

"Maybe we can get one of the guys who have the clap to take

the test in his name," Hillbilly suggested with a dry chuckle. "Skins would do it for the right price."

Jackson rose to his elbows to drink from his can of tepid beer. "Skins is still drippin', huh?"

"Like a leaky faucet," Lewandowski said. "Him'n'Charlie, both." He took another sip of beer. "We gotta go to work on Cutler."

"Should we get Louie in on this?" Jackson asked.

Lewandowski shook his head. "I saw him head over to the Off Limits area with some others to get stoned. He's gone for the day."

"He's turning into a junkie," Jackson opined.

"It don't do any good to try to talk to him," Lewandowski said. "He just bites your head off for it."

"It would be a dirty trick if we did something to screw over Cutler this late in the game," Jackson said.

"Yup, it sure would," Lewandowski agreed. "But it wouldn't be any fun if it wasn't a dirty trick."

"Right on," Hillbilly echoed.

"So, it's agreed," Lewandowski said. "We do a job on him."

"Agreed," the others said.

"Okay, what'll we do?" Lewandowski asked.

"Cutler's Freedom Flight is scheduled for 1730 hours tomorrow, right?" Jackson said.

"Hey, don't we all know it?" Hillbilly answered. "I'm surprised he don't have it tattooed on his forehead, the way he's been throwing it around."

"That don't give us much time to come up with a plan," Hillbilly said.

"It is a challenge," Lewandowski agreed. "But we owe it to Cutler to do our best."

"How's that?" Hillbilly asked, intrigued by the idea that screwing over Cutler might be a moral imperative.

"Look at it this way," Lewandowski said. "The way it is, Cutler's going back to the world without even one good war story to tell his kids and grandkids. *'What'd you do in the war, daddy? Aw, shucks, son, I don't like to brag, but I was one of the best personnel clerks in Cam Ranh Bay.'* Cutler deserves better than that. We'd be doing him a big favor if we screw up his DEROS. And the bigger the screw, the better. He won't like it at first, but years later he'll wanna thank us for giving him a good story to tell his grandkids. It's the kind of thing buddies should do for each other, but most of'em are just too darned selfish to do it."

Hillbilly was chuckling, but it wasn't Lewandowski that was inspiring his good humor. He was coming up with an idea of his own.

Lewandowski glanced over to where Cutler was sipping a Coke with several other Originals on break between volleyball games. "We can get it handled if we put our minds to it."

"You're right, Lew," Hillbilly agreed. "This is the kind of thing good buddies do for each other. And I think I've got an idea that'll work."

Lewandowski was ready for anything. "Alright, let's hear it."

Hillbilly rolled over on his belly. "Okay, here goes. Tomorrow afternoon, we'll get the Cap'n to lend us his jeep to take Cutler out to the airbase. Just the three of us, seeing him off. He won't suspect a thing. Then we take a back road as a short cut way out in the boonies and...."

The barbecues were fired up at 1100 hours. Both mess tent Poppasans were brought along to take charge of cooking the steaks and chicken. They were being paid double overtime for the day, plus all the leftovers they could carry back to Cam Ranh village with them.

Buffet–style picnic tables were set up so the troops could come and go, grazing on the chow as they wished, gorging themselves on the cornucopia of food. The Poppasans had long ago ceased being astonished by what they saw being wasted by the GIs. It was just one of the oddities that they came to expect from the Americans, who seemed to generate more problems caused by an overabundance of supplies than by shortages. Whatever was on hand had to be used quickly and often wastefully in order to make room for that which had already arrived, which had to be moved out of the way for that which was on its way by ship or plane.

But if they were put off by the conspicuous consumption they saw at Cutler's short timer party, they didn't show it.

DEROS day for Charles R. Cutler finally arrived. Jackson and Hillbilly drove Cutler to the supply tent in Ortega's jeep to pick up Lewandowski. Cutler had insisted on a full hour to cover the ten miles to the replacement depot.

Lewandowski climbed into the back seat to join Cutler and his duffle bag.

"We told Cutler you insisted on seeing him off," Jackson explained.

"Yeah, I sure did," Lewandowski said with a hearty slap on Cutler's shoulder. "Damn! I'm gonna miss you, Charlie Cutler. I really am."

Cutler smiled, flattered by the attention he was receiving. "Thanks, Lew." He grinned and added: "Short."

Lewandowski smiled graciously. "Hey, you got us all on that one, Charlie. Just think about it. In an hour, you'll be on your way back to The World. No more Vietnam, no more Army. Man, I wish I could trade places with you."

"Short," Cutler repeated with a wider grin.

Lewandowski was glowing with the heat of revenge. *'This is gonna be sooo sweet.'*

Jackson was driving, so it was up to Hillbilly to lay the groundwork for the plan.

"What'cha say we take a short cut to the repple depple?" Hillbilly suggested. "We can save enough time to have a beer at the EM club before you report for your Freedom Flight."

Cutler was easy to get along with. "Sounds okay to me."

"Count me in," Lewandowski agreed.

"Sounds like a plan," Jackson said. "I'll buy the first round when we get to the club."

About three miles from tent city, Jackson turned off the asphalt road to enter the rolling sea of sand dunes, forging onward via a path that promised to halve the remaining seven miles to the repple depple. They had been driving about ten minutes when the engine began to hesitate, aided by some fancy footwork by Jackson.

"Oh, man! What's wrong?" Lewandowski shouted from the back seat.

Cutler's grin had disappeared...his face was ashen.

Jackson pumped the gas pedal. "I don't know. It's acting like it's out of gas."

"What?!" Cutler screeched.

The engine died, bringing the jeep to a standstill.

"Heck, Jackson," Lewandowski grumbled. "Didn't you fill the tank before you took off?"

"Hey, man. At Ease back there. The Cap'n didn't say nothin' about being low on gas. How was I to know?"

"Well, you could'a looked at the gas gauge," Lewandowski said sarcastically, playing his role to the hilt.

Cutler was beyond mere sarcasm. He was in the midst of a panic attack. "Are you telling me we're stuck out here in the middle of nowhere?"

"Yeah," Lewandowski grumbled. "You really should'a looked at the gas gauge, Jackson. Dang, if this don't beat all."

"The gas gauge don't work," Jackson said defensively. "Look at it...it's showing half full."

"It ain't Jackson's fault," Hillbilly intervened. "If we gotta blame anyone, it's the Captain. Or the guys in the motor pool. But it ain't Jackson's fault."

"Try it again," Cutler pleaded. "It can't be out'a gas. It just can't be. I can't believe this happening to me!"

"Lemme look under the hood," Lewandowski offered, nudging Hillbilly's seat forward. "I know a little about these things. Maybe it's not out'a gas at all. Maybe the carburetor's just clogged with sand or something. Lemme out'a here, Hillbilly. I'll get us moving again."

Lewandowski climbed out and noisily checked under the hood. "Yup, it's out'a gas, alright. Looks like we're stuck."

"Maybe we're close enough to walk the rest of the way," Jackson suggested. "Lew, why don't you check from the top of that dune over there. Maybe we can see the repple depple from here."

"Oh, God," Cutler moaned. "I'm screwed. I'll never get there in time."

Chuckling to himself, Lewandowski waded through the sand to the distant dune crest. On his way he heard the hood of the jeep being dropped back down, but he paid no heed as he climbed to the crest and surveyed the miles of desolation that lay beyond. If Jackson did his job right, they were close to eight miles from the repple depple and eight miles from tent city.

"Good grief, we must be lost!" Lewandowski shouted. "You must'a taken a wrong turn back there, Jackson. I can't even see the repple depple from here. Lord knows where we are. Heck, this is disappointing. I can't tell ya how bad I feel about it, Cutler. Dang!"

Suddenly, the jeep engine roared to life. Lewandowski glanced over his shoulder and saw Cutler, Jackson and Hillbilly waving at him.

"Hey, Lew," Cutler shouted. "Have a nice walk back to tent city. And remember, we did this because you're our buddy. We wanted you to have a real war story to tell your grandkids. Short! Sayonara, GI!"

Without further adieu, Jackson let out the clutch and the jeep roared away, leaving Lewandowski shaking his head in bewilderment.

"Well, I'll be. Wow, that was good. Very well done, gentlemen. I owe you one. I might even owe you three or four for that one. Dang, I never would'a guessed."

Lewandowski took a moment to scout his surroundings, assuring himself that nothing civilized was in sight. Having no natural sense of direction, he decided to follow the jeep tracks, hoping he was walking back to the main road by the fastest possible route. From there, he could hitch a ride to tent city.

"Looks like I got some walking to do."

"Somethin's hap'nen 'round here,
What it is ain't exactly clear.
There's a man with a gun over there,
Tellin' me I got to beware.
Dum–dum–dum.
Young people speakin' their mind,
Gettin' so much re–sis–tence from behind.
Dum–dee–dum."

With barely a pause, he switched to another personal favorite.

"We gotta get out'a this place

If it's the last thing we ev–ver do.
We gotta get out'a this place.
Girl, there's a better land for me'n'you."

Chapter Twelve

Captain Ortega and Lieutenant Masters parked in one of the few open spaces remaining in the Brigade parking lot, ready to report for the You WILL Attend briefing that was being conducted in the air–conditioned general assembly hall. Once inside the hall, they located vacant seats near the back of the room, far removed from the West Point alumni gathered in the foremost rows, where they could see and be seen by those who could mentor them into wearing stars of their own.

It was the first command–wide briefing to be ordered by Major General Walter L. Sims, the new CO of the support command. The word filtering down through the grapevine was that Sims was foaming at the mouth over several articles that appeared in one of the weekly news magazines back in The World. The headline for the articles, which were collaborative pieces with in–country as well as stateside coverage, was titled "**Drug Abuse In Vietnam: The Hidden Casualties Start Coming Home**". The entire series consisted of four articles written by seven reporters. The critical overview written by the brigade information officer summarized the articles as being highly critical of the military leadership in Vietnam, concentrating much of their criticism on largely undocumented rumors and innuendo of widespread drug abuse among the lower enlisted ranks, particularly within the Army. The reporters quoted a variety of sources who laid the blame squarely on the back of the military leadership, who seemed proud to display a stubborn unwillingness to admit that a drug problem even existed. One general said his command was as drug free as comparable units he served with in World War Two and Korea..." a few troops may be using drugs, but it isn't a widespread problem."

Back in The World, the reporters had no difficulty finding drug abuse counselors who testified they were treating an ever increasing number of Vietnam veterans who were hooked on one or more drugs when they returned from the war. Sources in Veterans Administration clinics were quoted as saying they weren't prepared to treat widespread drug addictions. By comparison, the civilian drug clinics, particularly those that were springing up to treat the growing hippy peacenik movement, seemed to have a better handle on the problem. Several Vietnam veterans, now civilians and admitted drug addicts, were quoted as saying that getting stoned in 'Nam' was an everyday thing in some units, and went on to say they didn't seek help for their habits when they were in the military because they would have been court–martialled for doing drugs in the first place. It was a no–win situation, they said. Two of them also called for the U.S. to get out of Vietnam.

Drug addiction was a subject of debate that was new to the American military experience. The credo that had sustained the military leadership since the Boxer rebellion in China and the native revolts in the Phillipine Islands had been easy to understand: American soldiers and sailors do not use illicit drugs. Beer, okay…booze, okay…but not drugs. Drug use was the kind of thing that occurred in nations like The Peoples Republic of China and North Korea and North Vietnam, where soldiers were forced to fight and die for causes they didn't support. It happened within Armies where soldiers used drugs to escape the futility of their missions and the low value that had been placed on their lives. Communist soldiers used drugs to sustain them, whereas American soldiers used courage, purpose, superior training, superior tactics and superior armaments to sustain themselves.

The other media outlets, both print and televised, were already jumping on the bandwagon. And bad news being big news, it wasn't likely the drug story would disappear as conveniently and quickly as the brothel expose. When Johnny came marching home again from this war, he might be a dope addict.

Pandora's box had been opened and the brass had to slam the lid shut and keep it shut with heavy–duty combination locks. Perhaps, just perhaps, there really was a bit of a problem with drugs, but it could—no doubt—easily be corrected with large doses of good old fashioned military discipline. Come down on the guilty parties like a ton of bricks, make examples of them and send a message to the Hippy peacenik dopeheads. Do it hard, do it fast, count your casualties, and then get on with the business of winning this god-damned war.

There were no smiling faces awaiting the arrival of General Sims, not even among the West Point sycophants. Everyone knew that Sims hadn't called them together to say they were doing a great job.

Brigade deputy commander, Colonel Harvey B. Tuttle, stepped to the podium microphone to announce the arrival of General Sims.

"UH–TENN–SHUN!"

As one, the assembled officers rose from their seats and stood at rigid Attention, awaiting the command that would put them At Ease.

Sims entered through a backstage curtain and strode to the podium, where he paused to glare at the assembled officers for what seemed an eternity before he placed them "At Ease".

Sims held up a copy of the offending news rag, displaying the prominent headline for the lead story:

Drug Abuse in Vietnam:
The Hidden Casualties Start Coming Home

"I'll be brief," Sims began. "If there is the slightest bit of truth to this story, if any soldiers under my command are using drugs, I will hold their unit commanders directly responsible. In short, if you cannot handle your command duties in Cam Ranh, I will either request your immediate resignation or I will send you to a field unit where drug abuse is not a problem."

Later that afternoon, Captain Ortega convened a staff meeting for the officers and senior NCOs in his office at the personnel center. His message was simple: He would not allow a few dopeheads to place his career in jeopardy.

The surprise inspection of tent city began at precisely 0200 hours.

At least one NCO had been assigned to every tent, with commissioned officers nearby to issue direct orders, should it become necessary. They converged on the tents like a platoon of angry, shouting prison guards, switching on the overhead lightbulbs as they stepped through the tent flaps.

The shock effect was immediate and totally unexpected.

"EVERYBODY UP! OUTTA YOUR COTS, ON YOUR FEET! STAND AT PARADE REST BESIDE YOUR FOOT LOCKERS! EVERYBODY! MOVE IT, MOVE IT! EVERYBODY UP! PARADE REST! BESIDE YOUR FOOTLOCKERS! MOVE IT, MOVE I!"

Those Originals who reacted with anger found themselves standing in the center of a furious tornado.

"STAND AT PARADE REST, SOLDIER! THAT'S A DIRECT ORDER! DO IT NOW OR FACE CHARGES!"

There were ominous nose–to–nose confrontations.

"Do it NOW or lose your stripes and spend the next six weeks filling sandbags. Which will it be, Soldier?"

And sullen retreats from positions that couldn't be defended.

"That's better. NOW, EVERYBODY UNLOCK YOUR FOOTLOCKERS AND WALL LOCKERS AND STAND ASIDE AT THE POSITION OF PARADE REST."

Some Originals refused to back down despite the warnings.

"What the hell's going on around here? You can't pull shit like this! We got our rights, even if we are in the goddamned Army!"

"Unlock your wall locker and foot locker, Soldier, or we'll use the bar cutter. Then we'll bust you for refusing to follow orders. It's up to you, Soldier. You just better hope I don't find any dope in your personal gear. If I do, you're gonna find out more about military law than you care to know."

"This ain't nothin' but harassment."

"This is the Army soldier, and the Army don't like hippy dope-heads any more than I do. One more word out'a you and I'll have you placed under arrest. Do you understand?"

When the pandemonium began to settle, the NCO's and officers began rummaging through wall lockers and footlockers, bedding, soiled laundry bags, boots, shoes, shaving kits, cigarette packs that wern't sealed, anything and everything that might conceivably hold a diminutive bag of marijuana. When marijuana was found, the message was roughly the same for each offender.

"WHAT IS THIS, SOLDIER? HUH? FUNNY–FUCKING CIGARETTES? HOW COULD YOU BE SO FUCKING STUPID? CAN YOU GIVE ME ONE GOOD REASON WHY YOU GOTTA

USE THIS SHIT? CAN'T YOU HANDLE CAM RANH? YOU
DISGUST ME! YOU FUCKING DISGUST ME! GET YOUR ASS
OUT'A THIS TENT! LINE UP ON THE TARMAC WITH THE
OTHER DOPEHEADS WAITING TO SIGN THEIR COURT
MARTIAL PAPERS! GET OUT'A MY SIGHT, LOSER!"

Those sent to the tarmac displayed similar emotions: shame,
terror, regret and a numb inability to think straight. It had happened
so fast and they all were so obviously guilty that they complied with
perfect obedience when they saw Bolton and Mr. Mobley waiting for
their arrival on the tarmac, placing them at Attention, demanding
silence, offering no pity. Two of the Originals standing at Attention
couldn't control their shaking hands, and one was weeping.

They were just beginning to realize the impact this would have
not only on them, but the lives of everyone they cared about....their
parents and siblings, the wives and sweethearts who had been
counting the days. The disappointment would be terrible thing for
them to bear. And the shame; God, the shame it would bring. There
was time to be considered...the months and perhaps even years that
would be lost to a hellhole stockade or federal prison, followed by
combat duty or a dishonorable discharge.

An NCO carried a message to Masters. "Sir, Lewandowski
won't open his footlocker and wall locker to be searched."

Masters nodded, not surprised. "Okay, let's go."

The NCO and Masters entered the supply tent, where Lewandowski was standing at Parade Rest beside his footlocker. Edwards
was standing at Parade Rest beside his opened wall locker and
footlocker, his eyes staring straight ahead. The worst of it was over
for Charlie. His belongings had already been inspected and found
clean.

Masters suddenly felt very old, very tired. He had been afraid
Lewandowski was one of the dopers, but there was nothing to be
done about it now. There could be no exceptions.

Masters placed himself directly in front of Lewandowski, who
spoke first. "Sir, he can't give me a direct order, like he tried to do.
Only a commissioned officer can give a direct order, Sir."

"Very well," Masters said quietly. "I am giving you a direct
order, Specialist Lewandowski. Open your wall locker and foot-

locker for inspection."

Masters saw something change in Lewandowski's expression. It wasn't fear, nor did Lewandowski appear angry. Rather, it looked more like disappointment, as if Masters had violated some unspoken agreement that had evolved between them over the months. Masters found himself recalling the night the bar girls came to tent city, when Lewandowski made sure his butt was protected. Without Lewandowski being there to take charge of the Originals, Masters never would have taken the chance with such a risky scheme. Too many things could have gone wrong that night, all with career–ending consequences. But Lewandowski had made sure everything went as smooth as silk.

Now, Masters found himself repaying the debt by ordering Lewandowski to do something that might well cost him very dearly. For the first time in his career, William R. Masters hated what he was doing. From the outside, he showed no hesitation, but from deep inside he was working all too hard at reminding himself that his feelings didn't matter, that it was all a matter of honor and duty. No exceptions could be made.

Without hesitation, Lewandowski kneeled down to open the combination lock for his footlocker, then moved to do the same for the lock to his wall locker. With both locks open, he stepped aside and resumed the position of Parade Rest with his eyes focused directly ahead.

Masters spoke to the NCO. "Inspect his gear, Sergeant,"

The NCO kneeled down to rummage through the footlocker first, taking great care to check every possible hiding place. Several long moments passed before he moved to the wall locker. Eventually he stepped away from the wall locker as well.

"Nothing, Sir. He's clean."

Masters nodded, his eyes on Lewandowski. He wanted a reaction, but Lewandowski's blank expression didn't falter.

"Good," Masters said. "You may stand At Ease. Both of you. What will I find if I order an inspection of the whole tent, Specialist Lewandowski?"

"You'll find nothing that shouldn't be here," Lewandowski answered with no hesitation.

Masters nodded, not doubting it was true.

"Sir, may I speak?" Lewandowski asked.

"You may."

"This is wrong, Sir. We weren't given a chance to take care of the problem ourselves."

"Everyone knows the regulations," Masters said tonelessly. "The Captain and I are responsible for your actions, Specialist Lewandowski. Every man in this unit is aware of that, yet some of the men have decided to use marijuana. We won't allow it and we'll punish those who use it. No matter who they are."

"You could have warned us, Sir. You could have told us that you were coming down hard on the dopers."

"Did you warn us that some of the men were using dope?" Masters asked.

Lewandowski took a deep breath before answering. "I see your point, Sir."

"You're soldiers," Masters said. "That says it all. I have troops waiting for me on the tarmac. I'll be speaking to the entire company during reveille formation this morning."

Masters led the NCO from the supply tent.

Lewandowski and Edwards sat on their cots. Charlie threw one of his boots to the back of the tent. "Damn."

Lewandowski looked at him with a hollow expression, saying nothing.

Thirteen Originals were waiting on the tarmac, where charges were formally read to them as a group. Then they were marched to the mess tent, where they would do KP for Sergeant Lugo while the court martial documents were being typed. The thirteen included Louie Donnatelli, Frenchie, Peters the file clerk, Skins, and Hanley the Morning Report clerk.

The casualty list would have been higher, but some dopers had hidden their bags of marijuana out in the dunes and others just happened to be out at the time of the search. Nearly ten percent of the Originals could forget about their DEROS dates; they wouldn't be going home with the others. Most likely, they would still be doing bad time at Camp LBJ when the Freedom Flights were transporting the other Originals back to The World. It was as if the company had suffered heavy combat casualties, except that losses of this type made even less sense than combat casualties.

Captain Ortega and Masters were present at the reveille formation that morning. When Ortega spoke, he was even more brief and to the point than General Sims.

"Everyone in this unit knows that the possession or use of marijuana is a court martil offense. Now you know how we intend to handle the problem in the future. No excuses will be accepted. If you get caught with marijuana or any other unauthorized drug, you will be court martialled."

When Ortega was finished, Masters took command of the formation to announce that the paperwork for thirteen General Court–martials would be initiated that morning.

After reveille, Ortega and Masters retired to the orderly tent for a confidential conversation.

"It's up to them now," Ortega said as he plopped down on a vacant chair. Like Masters, he had been up all night with the preparations and aftermath of the pot raid. "We've done our part."

"If it works, we should know by late today or early tomorrow," Masters said as he started a fresh pot of coffee. "If it takes any longer than that, I miscalculated."

"No, Bill. We miscalculated. We're in this together."

Masters forced a smile. "Thanks, Manny."

Only Masters and Ortega were aware of the plan of attack they had devised over noon chow the day before. Between themselves, they had nursed to life an experiment that might either work like a charm or fail utterly and miserably. If it worked, the 516th would have survived a very bad situation relatively unscathed. If it failed, the lives of thirteen Originals would be permanently scarred. Ortega and Masters will have earned their next promotions the hard way. The outcome was solely dependent upon their ability to predict the reactions of the men in their unit.

Later, when Ortega climbed into his jeep to head for the personnel center, he tried to reassure his subordinate. "It'll turn out alright," he said over the roar of the engine. "You worry too much, Bill."

Masters saluted, forcing a weak smile. "Yes, Sir. I'll call if I hear anything, but they'll probably go to you."

"Check," Ortega said as he returned the salute. "I'll get you on the horn, if I hear anything."

Masters had Woody begin the paperwork for the court–martials when he arrived for his duty day in the orderly tent. With Hanley confined to quarters, Woody had to get out the Morning Report as well, which alone was enough to make him generally pissed off at the world. Nothing else happened that day. There were no contacts from the Originals. Breakfast and noon chow in the mess tent were filled with uncomfortable silence. Few Originals had any idea what to say to the doomed thirteen, so they avoided eye contact and said nothing. The NCOs and officers avoided the mess tent by chowing down at the NCO and officer clubs. It was a difficult time for everyone, but particularly so for Masters and Ortega, who were beginning to feel very pregnant and alone as they second–guessed the wisdom of their plan.

By breakfast the next morning, Masters and Ortega were pre-pared to go through with the Court–martials. Later that morning, Ortega called Masters.

Ortgega sounded cautiously optimistic. "Bill, I just had a visit from a delegation of ten Originals. They said they have some ideas they want to share with us. I told them we could meet at 1300 hours today in my office."

"I'll be there," Masters said.

The ten Originals were waiting outside Ortega's office when Masters strode into the command hut. Among those in attendance were Jackson, Hillbilly, and Lewandowski. The Originals avoided eye contact as Masters passed them to knock on Ortega's door.

"Come in," Ortega said.

Masters entered and closed the door. "Well, this is it," he said quietly.

Ortega pointed Masters to a chair. He kept his volume low as well. "Do you have anything to discuss before I bring them in?"

"No, there's no use putting it off," Masters answered. "Either we get a solution out of this, or we don't. There's no middle ground."

Ortega nodded and lifted his phone. "Sergeant Bolton, send in the men. Lieutenant Masters and I will see them now."

"All of them, Sir?"

"All of them. And yourself, as the senior enlisted man."

"Yes, Sir. Will do."

Bolton entered first, followed by Lewandowski and the others until the small office was crowded with perspiring bodies. The enlisted men reported, rendered very disciplined salutes, and remained standing at Attention.

"At Ease," Ortega ordered. His expression was blank.

Lewandowski was holding a thick manila envelope from which he extracted a sheaf of soiled notebook papers displaying hand printed names, followed by longhand signatures. He handed the papers to Masters, who found himself gazing at the signatures with emotions struggling between doubt and hope.

"And what is the meaning of that?" Ortega asked.

Lewandowski spoke quickly. "Sir, we'd like to give this to you."

"Why?" Ortega asked.

Lewandowski took a deep breath. "Sir, it's signed confessions, Sir. Every man who signed this is saying he smoked marijuana at one time or another while he was in–country and figures he should be punished, just like the others from the inspection."

Masters allowed himself to relax ever so slightly. The approach wasn't exactly what he had hoped for, but it had possibilities.

Ortega's expression remained blank. "Really," he said. "I'd like to see those documents."

Masters handed the petitions to Ortega, who perused the contents before returning the packet to Masters. "How many men signed the confession, Specialist Lewandowski?"

"Just about everyone under the rank of E–6, Sir," Lewandowski answered.

"Do you realize what the consequences of such a confession could be?" Ortega asked. "Let me rephrase that to be clearer: Do you realize that everyone who signed that document could be court martialled?"

Lewandowski didn't check with his fellow Originals before answering.

"Yes, Sir. We all know you can do that, if that's what you want to do, Sir. It wouldn't be fair, but you have the power to do it, Sir."

Ortega was unmoved. "Are you suggesting an alternative, Specialist? Or are you just stating an opinion on what is or is not fair, as you put it?"

"We have an alternative, Sir."

Masters allowed himself to relax a bit more in his chair.

"I am ready to hear solutions," Ortega warned, "But I won't waste my time listening to what you think is fair or not fair. I want the drug and discipline problems eliminated. Period. In that context, I'm ready to hear what you have to say, Specialist."

Lewandowski paused to gather his thoughts before continuing.

"Well, Sir, we'll do everything we can to take care of the dope problem, if you agree not to Court Martial the guys who have been busted."

Ortega shook his head. "Not good enough."

Lewandowski's face fell, along with the others with him. "Sir, could I ask why not?"

"Under the circumstances, yes," Ortega said. "I want guarantees, not promises that you'll do your best. I also have problems with you thinking you can wheel and deal with me about the punishment. That'll never happen, GI. I don't make deals."

Lewandowkski wasn't yet ready to retreat. "What if we offer some kind of guarantee, Sir?"

"What kind of guarantee?" Ortega asked.

"Sir, I can personally guarantee I will never again use marijuana while assigned to the 516th AG."

He looked to the Originals with him. "Are you guys willing to do the same?"

All nodded.

Hillbilly spoke. "We'll guarantee it, Sir, if you'll drop the Court Martials against the others."

"Still not good enough," Ortega said, shaking his head. "I want all the Originals on the wagon from now on. Right now, that means only dope, but it'll include booze and beer if there are any trouble with those substances."

Lewandowski checked with the others before answering. They all nodded and Lewandowski turned to Ortega. "We'll make it happen, Sir, if we've got a deal."

"Officers don't make deals," Ortega said.

"Yes, Sir. I apologize."

"We make decisions based on what is best for our mission and our troops."

"Yessir," Lewandowski repeated, and stood a bit straighter to emphasize his sincerity.

Ortega looked at Masters, who placed the signed confessions on Ortega's desk.

"We'll just hold on to these," Ortega said. He didn't doubt that more than a few of the confessions were false. Several Originals were known to be teetotalers who didn't smoke, drink alcohol or even cuss, but he suspected he might find their names on the list. At first glance, the group confession seemed foolhardy, but only at first glance. The reality was somewhat more complex. It would have been impossible to prosecute all of the Originals without destroying the effectiveness of the unit mission. Devious minds had been at work here, just as Masters predicted would happen

We might have the beginning of a solution to our problems here," Ortega mused openly. "But just a beginning."

He turned to Masters. "How do you feel about this, Lt. Masters?"

I have a problem with it," Masters said, and turned to the Originals. "I hope you're not proposing that we forget the whole thing and go on our merry way. There has been a very serious violation of regulations here, not to mention the rules of common sense. Punishment is called for. Not necessarily Court–Martials, but certainly stiff punishment with Article 15's attached. Meaning major losses of rank, major loss of pay, and at least thirty days of hard–labor extra duty…penalties somewhat more harsh than those handed down for the amateur boxing match we experienced before."

Lewandowski glanced at his fellow Originals, taking a silent survey of opinion. They all nodded.

"Yes, Sir," Lewandowski said. "We think that would be fair."

Masters glared at the Orginals while speaking to Captain Ortega. "I suggest we call off this meeting the next time the word 'fair' is used, Captain Ortega. Apparently we're having a failure to communicate here, Sir."

"I agree," Ortega said. "Continue, Lieutenant."

"The Captain has already demonstrated his willingness to work with you in eliminating this drug problem in the 516th," Masters said. "Will this be the end of the drug problem, or will we be hearing more of this crap about your ideas on fairness?"

"Consider it ended, Sir."

"Do you know what will happen if we find any more evidence of drug use?" Masters asked.

"Court Martials, Sir," Lewandowski answered.

Masters nodded. "And we WILL be having more surprise inspections, and Brigade WILL be conducting similar inspections, as well. I want to be sure that everyone knows that. Anyone found with drugs WILL be given the most severe punishment allowable under the UCMJ."

The Originals answered in near unison "Yes, Sir."

Masters looked at them a long moment before turning to Ortega. "It's up to you, Sir. If this doesn't work, we can always send the hardheads to LBJ."

Ortega turned to Bolton for his opinion.

"Anything you say, Sir," Bolton agreed, though it was obvious he did so reluctantly. What he had witnessed was enough to leave an old soldier shaking his head.

Ortega spoke to the Originals. "I will reduce the penalties from General Court Martial to Article 15's with loss of rank, loss of pay and 45–days extra duty for the thirteen men who were found with marijuana during the inspection. In return, I expect active cooperation from all of you to end this problem once and for all."

Ortega's next words were enunciated slowly for extra emphasis. "Now, listen–up: I swear if I ever again find evidence of drug use in my company, I will personally see to it that the guilty ones spend at least the next twelve months in Camp LBJ. Is that understood?"

"Yessir," the Originals said.

"Get the word out," Ortega growled. "You're dismissed."

After rendering salutes, the Originals filed out, all of them mumbling "Thank you, Sir," to Ortega.

Bolton paused at the door. "I hope that takes care of it, Sir," he said, sounding less than convinced that the 'deal' would have a lasting impact.

Ortega had a warning for Bolton. "I expect you to make it work, Sergeant Bolton."

"Yessir," Bolton said and closed the door after him.

Ortega turned to Masters when they were alone. "Think it will work?"

Masters shrugged. "If it doesn't, we can always do it the hard way."

Ortega sighed, relaxing into his chair. "That's about the size of it. This is going to generate a very unusual report to Brigade."

"Who knows, they might give you a letter of commendation for coming up with such a creative solution," Masters suggested with a cynical grin.

Ortega shook his head. "More likely, they'll send me to the Section Eight shrinks for an evaluation."

Lewandowski said nothing to the others, but he could see the fingerprints of William R. Masters scattered throughout the agreement that had been reached with Ortega. Afterall, he reminded himself, Masters was the man who had manipulated him into manipulating the Dirty Dozen and Charlie into risking their necks to get flowers for the mess tent. Nothing was beyond him. Masters and Ortega probably didn't even want to Court Martial anyone in the first place, and in return for not doing what they didn't want to do anyway, they got the whole blasted company to climb on the wagon.

"Aw, the heck with it," Lewandowski grumbled to himself. "I only got 135 days to DEROS. I'm gettin' too Short to sweat the small stuff."

Chapter Thirteen

"This is **IT!**" Lewandowski bellowed when returning to the Dirty Dozen after a making a courier trip to Brigade for Masters.

The Dirty Dozen had been gearing down for lunch for the past half–hour. The first floor of four barracks had been erected, with exterior walls now in place. The exterior walls of the barracks were a labor of love for the Dirty Dozen after they discovered the enclosed barracks could hide them from prying eyes during their frequent breaks. They had spent the last half–hour chewing the fat or playing quick hands of poker, waiting patiently for Lewandowski to return with the deuce so he could haul them back to tent city for noon chow.

"What's he talking about?" Frenchie asked everyone but Lewandowski.

"This," Lewandowski announced, waving a sheaf of Brigade orders in the air, "...is a gold plated guarantee that we won't be moving out'a tent city before we DEROS."

"He's dingydow, right?" Frenchie asked the others.

"Crazy like a fox," Lewandowski said as he waved the papers in Frenchie's face. "Allow me to read the following."

Lewandowski brought his eyes to bear on the mimeographed sheets. "From the commanding officer, United States Army Support Command duh–duh–duh, to the following unit commanders duh–duh–duh, duh–duh, including the 516th AG. Attached, find revised regulations concerning the construction of type A diagram personnel living quarters in compliance with USARV Regulation 1410–16 (a thru n), dated 4 May 65, as revised 16 Jan 67."

Frenchie pointed a finger at his right temple and twirled it around meaningfully. "Dingydow. He finally slipped over the edge."

"Nuts, man," Skins agreed.

Charlie nodded. "It's time to call the men in white jackets."

"To WIT," Lewandowski continued, "The placement of wall studs in said living quarters constructed in the Type A diagram will be revised from a standard of twenty–four (24) inch centers to a standard of eighteen (18) inch centers. In compliance with said directives and USARV regulations and at the direction of the commanding officer—duh–duh—all completed and occupied structures in the duh–duh Cam Ranh Bay, will be altered to be in compliance with the aforementioned directives and USARV regulations."

Lewandowski raised the volume two notches. "This is the good stuff. Type A diagram personnel living quarters not yet completed and occupied will be either modified or demolished and reconstructed to comply with the aforementioned directives and USARV regulations, at the discretion of appropriate personnel within the 302nd Combat Engineers, United States Army Support Command, duh–duh."

When concluded, Lewandowski carefully folded the papers. "Now, are there any questions, gentlemen?"

"Yeah," Frenchie said. "In plain English, what'd you just say?"

"Ah, YES!" Lewandowski exclaimed joyfully. "Once again I find myself being called upon to serve as translator for the unwashed masses."

Frenchie raised his right index finger. "Translate this."

"Right," Lewandowski said sourly. "Okay, short and sweet. What you see around you is both incomplete and unoccupied. In other words, the walls gotta come tumbling down so's they can be rebuilt with the wall studs on eighteen–inch centers. Everything here, even the new personnel center and messhall is a Type–A diagram structure. In other words, there's no way we can tear all that stuff down, start over and finish the job in the next three and a half months. It's impossible and even Masters will have to admit it can't be done. And—to top it all off—NONE of it is our fault. In a nutshell, the Army made me do it, momma."

Charlie raised his hand, waving it with a puzzled–skeptical expression. "Wait a second. Go back to that part about the 302nd Combat Engineers. Doesn't all that discretion business add up to a big Maybe instead of a For Sure? I mean, if they tell us we just gotta add more wall studs instead of starting over, it won't take nearly as long, right? It'll be a one–week job instead of a two–month job."

Lewandowski shrugged. "Yeah, right, but it's no big deal. We've faced bigger challenges than this, Charlie. We can get it handled, no sweat. All we gotta do is grease a few palms in the 302nd."

"I don't know," Charlie said. "There's so many new faces. Most of the guys we knew are already DEROSed back to The World."

"With muh'fuh' early DEROSes *we* made happen," Skins added, pointing out the ironies inherent in trading favors with troops who shared the same goal of returning home early and safely.

"Maybe we should just hope for the best and not try to make any more deals," Charlie suggested. "Our collective asses will be grass if Masters gets wind that we're dealing early DEROSes to stay in tent city. I have the feeling we better not push him too far."

Everyone knew what he meant. Masters had proven he could be a real horse's ass during the dope busts and the extra–duty details that followed. The word was out, and the word was much like the lyrics of an early 60's MoTown hit: *Don't Mess With Bill.*

"If we get caught playing around we could find ourselves in deep, serious shit," Charlie concluded.

Lewandowski could see the group consensus swinging to the side of taking the safe way out. Even the Dirty Dozen were starting to play it safe now that genuine short timer status was just around the bend.

Lewandowski wanted to remind them that no war was ever won by the fainthearted, or something like that, but he would have been laughed out of Cam Ranh with such an approach. Instead, he turned on his considerable salesmanship skills.

"Hey, guys, this is a golden opportunity to guarantee we stay in tent city. We'll end up kicking ourselves if we don't give it a shot. I mean, wouldn't it be a bummer—a big GIANT bummer—if we found ourselves spending the last month or six weeks in stateside wooden barracks with stateside wall–locker/foot–locker and full–field inspections coming down on us? Just think how rotten that would be. If that don't inspire you, then you're not the men I thought you were."

The reaction was limited to feeble shrugs, so he plunged on-ward with his onerous premonitions of what lay ahead for the fainthearted.

"Look around you…if we really humped butt, we could be moving out'a tent city in fifty, sixty days. Now, who wants that to happen, huh? I say we got no choice. If we quit now, everything we did in the past will mean nothing."

Still no reaction.

"Not to mention the fact that we're doing this for the future generations who get assigned to the 516th. We owe them Type–A structures that are as strong as we can make'em. It's our responsibil-ity, guys. Heck, what if a mutha of a storm comes along and blows all this down and kills everyone inside. How could you live with yourselves knowing you could have prevented it from happening by taking a few extra precautions right now? I think it would be downright selfish of us if we didn't do everything we could to make sure we give our replacements a safe living environment."

Edwards stood. "I've gotta stand to keep my head above the bullshit around here."

"But how we gonna do any big time horse tradin' without get-ting caught?" Frenchie asked. "That's the million dollar question."

"I'll start nosing around," Lewandowski said. "I think I have some good prospects in mind at the 302nd. One of the NCO's who trained me is still there. I heard he's willing to listen to reason."

"Oops," Skins said after glancing around for a little change of scenery. "Eyes left," he warned. "V.I.P. Alert. Coming from the bay, a convoy of tourists. It looks like Sims, followed by enough brass to start a new war."

"Let's get outside and look busy," Lewandowski ordered.

As the Originals exited the barracks, they saw a long line of shining vehicles—all the color of spitshined green olives—that were coming toward them at a leisurely pace. The lead vehicle was a gleaming four–door Chevrolet sedan with small flags perched on both front fenders. Each flag possessed two white stars advertising the presence of General Sims, who had earned the accolade 'The Ball Crusher of Cam Ranh'. Every man–jack GI on the sands of Cam Ranh WOULD salute the generalmobile whenever and wherever it drove by, even if the General was relaxing at home in his air–conditioned doublewide trailer, and the lone occupant of the Chevy was his Master Sergeant driver.

The General also had his own steel–reinforced, air–conditioned, hardened concrete bunker within easy walking distance of his air–conditioned doublewide trailer. Never let it be said that the top brass didn't suffer in Vietnam.

In total, there were six Chevy sedans and four highly polished jeeps in today's V.I.P. convoy.

"He must'a brought his whole staff with him today," Charlie murmured warily as the convoy continued to crawl toward them.

"He's probably rolling out the red carpet for some bigwigs from The World," Lewandowski observed.

"And lots of reporters," Frenchie added.

"And maybe a muh'fuh' congressman or two," Skins said disgustedly.

"Okay, it looks like they're gonna pay us a visit. We gotta look sharp and salute," Lewandowski grumbled. "And hold the salute, whatever you do. Maybe they'll just do a drive–by if we don't encourage them."

But the spitshined Chevy rolled to a halt a short distance from the battered, dusty deuce, with the Originals holding their salutes, maintaining the most rigid positions of Attention they had achieved since the initial terrors of Boot Camp.

The heavily tinted front passenger window of the lead Chevy began to roll down.

"You're it, Lewandowski," Skins said through clenched teeth. "You duh man. You do the talking."

Events began to unfold at a doubletime pace. The head and shoulders of a spitshined young Captain appeared as the dark window slowly disappeared into the lower part of his door.

"Are there any officers in the area?" the Captain asked Lewandowski, who happened to be wearing his fatigue shirt with Speck Five stripes at the moment. Usually he wore only a faded olive drab T–shirt, like Charlie and the Dirty Dozen, making it impossible for an outsider to know who was the ranking soldier was

"No, Sir," Lewandowski answered, sounding much sharper than he looked or felt.

"Ah," the Captain said, sounding disappointed to find Himself communing directly with a Speck Five. "The General wanted to ask a few questions. And we have some guests with us who may have questions of their own."

"Oh, jeese, Sir, I...."

The Captain interrupted. "You'll handle it just fine, Specialist Lewandowski. I did pronounce that right, didn't I? It is Lew–an–dow–ski, isn't it?"

"Yes, Sir. You pronounced it right. I was just about to say...."

But Lewandowski was already too late. The right rear window rolled down to reveal the greying visage of Major General John J. Sims.

"At Ease, Specialist," the General ordered.

Technically, Lewandowski and the other members of the crew could drop their salutes, but it was taking a big risk to be genuinely At Ease when in the rarified presence of a Major General. So Lewandowski and the crew assumed postures that were a cross between Attention and At Ease.

The general seemed pleased at their display of subservience.

"You have nothing to worry about," the General advised the lowly masses with a wave of the hand that was displaying his West Point Ring, class of '42. "Just be yourself...stand At Ease. This isn't an inspection. I'm just showing some visitors around Cam Ranh."

Sims was sharing the back seat with a civilian wearing khakis made of the finest polished cotten, definitely not the kind that could be bought at the Monkey Ward sporting goods department.

The Captain in the front seat was inspecting the Originals with an unmistakable You Better Look Sharp expression.

A gust of chilled air drifted towards the Originals from the interior of the Chevy.

The windows of the following Chevies remained rolled up out of respect for the heat and humidity of Cam Ranh. The four jeeps behind the Chevies were loaded with cameramen and reporters, with each jeepload of civilians being accompanied by a Brigade Information Officer. The cameramen and reporters climbed from the jeeps, surging toward the Originals with their 35 mm cameras clicking, tape recorders switched on and film cameras rolling. The cameramen scanned the Originals and whatever else could be seen, recording mundane vignettes that might someday be considered worthy of presentation over the six o'clock evening news, with mom/dad and the kids sitting around the dinner table. The Information Officers, attached to the reporters by invisible umbilical cords, were speaking in low undertones as they guided their charges around the site. The media circus was in town, with the Originals gazing out at the world through the sides of their fish bowl, fascinated by the wonders that were unfolding around them.

So, this is Big Time TV News. Oh yeah.

"Are you in charge of this detail, Specialist?" the General asked as he, too, glanced around.

"Yessir," Lewandowski answered, all the while wishing he had set the crew to policing the area for stray trash and cigarette butts so it would have looked a little—actually, a lot—neater.

"Good work, men," the General said as he continued to inspect the area from the climate controlled luxury of his Chevy. "I imagine you're looking forward to moving into the new barracks, aren't you?"

"Yes, Sir," Lewandowski lied. "We can hardly wait."

"That's what I like to hear," Sims said, offering another stiff smile punctuated by a quick nod that looked a lot like a nervous tic.

The civilian in luxury khakis leaned over Sims to speak through the window.

"Senator Frank Dellman from Missouri," he said warmly. "Do we have any Show Me staters out there, by chance?"

"No, Sir, not a one," Lewandowski answered.

Frenchie nudged Skins. "Show me what–ers?"

Skins shrugged and shook his head.

The senator's smile faded some. "Oh well, if you know anybody from Missouri, pass on the word that I'm paying a little visit to Cam Rahn. Two congressmen are in the car behind us. One is from California and the other from Michigan. Are any of you from California or Michigan?"

Lewandowski shook his head, figuring he had much to lose and nothing to gain by revealing his home State. It was much safer hiding in anonymity when stray congressmen, reporters, and very high ranking Lifers were sniffing around. He glanced at the crew knowing there was at least one more Californian and a MoTowner, but both were wisely denying their heritage.

The pressure was easing…the Dirty Dozen were beginning to feel relaxed enough to follow the General's order to be themselves. Frenchie and Skins were waving at the camera crews, trying to attract attention, hoping their smiling faces would make it to the tube back home, with them mouthing the words 'Hi, Mom! Hi, Dad!'.

"No, Sir. No one from California or Michigan," Lewandowski lied. He was doing so well that he decided to pile even more poop on the bigwigs. "We'll tell our buddies, though, Sir. They'll be real glad to know you stopped by."

"We would appreciate it, Sergeant," the senator said. "We're all real proud of you boys back home. Don't pay no attention to those sign–carrying, long–haired, hippy dopeheads and their draft dodging and demonstrations. They don't know shit from Shinola."

Frenchie nudged Skins and giggled when he heard the Senator mention dopeheads.

Senator Pellman offered a sloppy salute to the crew before leaning back into the comfort of the rear seat, having done did his duty for the fighting men in Vietnam.

"Carry on," General Sims said to Lewandowski.

"Yessir, will do," Lewandowski said agreeably.

The general stared at Lewandowski and Lewandowski stared back, not knowing what else Sims might have on his mind.

"Salute!" the Captain hissed at Lewandowski.

"Oh, yessir!" Lewandowski said. He turned to Charlie and the Dirty Dozen. "Troop, Preseeeeeent Harms!"

The Captain was rolling his eyes as he disappeared behind the tinted window.

The crew held their farewell salutes as the cameras clicked and whirred, creating images that would completely mislead the masses back in America.

A moment later the entourage was moving to the next highlight of their tour. The crew waited until the last jeep had disappeared before unloading on Lewandowski.

"Oooh, Yessir, we can hardly wait to move in," Skins mimicked.

The taunts continued until Lewandowski started to show signs of terminal irritation.

"Oooh, it's up to you, Lewandowski, you duh man," Lewandowski retaliated.

"Hey, man, we was just raggin' on ya," Skins said defensively. "Don't get bent out'a shape. You right. All our assholes was suckin' wind when that Chevy pulled in."

"Well, I'm glad to hear someone admit it," Lewandowski grunted. "Let's go get some chow before Lugo starts giving it away. There's too much brass running around out here for my taste. Frenchie and Skins: hang back a sec'. I wanna talk to you."

Frenchie and Skins stayed behind as the others headed for the deuce.

Lewandowski lowered his voice. "I just want you guys to know that we can expect a Brigade dope inspection in the next few days. That's all I got to say, okay?

"We're hip, man," Frenchie said, sounding totally unconcerned. "We got the same sources you got."

Lewandowski glared at him. "Hey, I'm sorry for caring about you guys, okay? I just wanted to make sure you're covered. Excuse me if I wasted your time."

Skins intervened. "That ain't it, man. Look...we know you're trying to help, but it don't help if you ride us about it, okay? Can you understand?"

"We won't get busted again," Frenchie vowed. "You can't be our mother, man. We don't need you or anyone else telling us what we can smoke. We're not gonna get busted again, and that's all you gotta worry about."

Lewandowski nodded. "Okay, if that's the way you want it, I'll mind my own business. Just know, you'll be on your own if you do get busted."

"That's the way we want it," Frenchie said. He spoke with a more conciliatory tone when Lewandowski turned to leave. "Look, we know where you're coming from, Lew. We know you wanna help, and that's good, but it's up to us, man. Y'see what I'm saying?"

Lewandowski nodded. "Okay. I just don't wanna see you guys get busted this late in the game. We're too short for that."

Frenchie offered a chest–high clenched fist for Frenchie and Lew to tap with fists of their own. "Hey, man, Short."

"Short," they all agreed before heading for the deuce.

Every man was awake, alert and moving within seconds of the sound of incoming rounds, followed by automatic weapons fire that sounded much too close to tent city. The men of tent city had grown accustomed to the thump of outgoing rounds and the roar of Phantoms passing overhead toward targets beyond the perimeter during the night, but never had they heard incoming high explosive rounds and small arms fire. The message was simple. This time the battle wasn't Out There—beyond the perimeter—it was happening within the Cam Ranh perimeter, and it sounded like it was heading their way.

No shouting was necessary, no orders were necessary. Every man knew what he had to do during a Red Alert, and it was being done at a triple–time pace. They had ceased being support personnel; they were Eleven Bravo infantrymen with two immediate objectives: First, to arm themselves…Second, to establish an effective defensive perimeter.

The troops dashed through the dimly lit supply tent to receive their M–14's from Lewandowski and full ammo clips from Charlie Edwards. The NCO's were waiting outside the supply tent, ready to form the troops into squads and platoons that would be taken to pre–designated positions in the sand dunes. The Red Alert procedures were being carried out with a smooth precision that had never been achieved during the many practice alerts. Within minutes, the 516th was as ready to defend itself as it ever would be. About that time, the officers roared into tent city in their jeeps.

The automatic weapons fire was increasing in intensity, becoming an undulating roar punctuated by explosions, colored by the streaking flash of tracer rounds. From the dunes, the troops could see the battle line as a colorful, undulating shape—not terribly unlike that of a sparkling amoebae—as the battle flowed toward the airbase.

The bad guys seemed to be winning…the battle was moving the wrong direction. The frontier dunes near the airbase were alive with the colors and sounds of ground troops locked in combat.

"At least it's headin' away from us," Lewandowski said to Charlie as they observed the action from their positions along the peak of a dune, after they transported nearly 3,000 rounds of 7.62 mm ball ammo, establishing a supply base nearer the reactionary platoons. There would be a price to be paid if the Viet Cong wanted to come through tent city.

"God, I hope so," Charlie answered, continuing his non–stop prayers that the battle would continue going toward the air base.

The VC sappers leading the attack came equipped with assault rifles, machineguns, satchel charges and rocket propelled grenades, but no heavy weapons. They were relying on surprise and momentum to carry the attack far deeper into Cam Ranh than they had ever probed before. The defenders had air power and heavy artillery, but such weapons can destroy defenders as well as aggressors when combat is being engaged in such close quarters. The battle had quickly evolved into a classic contest of tactics.

Charlie nudged Lewandowski's elbow. "Look over there at the mountains…gunships are coming."

Lewandowski had seen them, too…a large formation of blinking lights coming toward Cam Ranh after cresting the low mountains, rushing headlong toward the battleground. The field units were coming to the aid of Cam Ranh; favors were being returned. A cheer rose from the sand dunes as others spotted the formation.

The gunships formed a wide front as they neared the battle zone. Once over the battle, they scattered to attack targets of opportunity with their roaring mini–guns streaking yellow–red lines of fire onto the Main Force Viet Cong below, while other gunships ripped the darkness with rounds from rocket pods and grenade launchers. The roar of the battle had become an overpowering cataclysimic symphony.

A second formation of gunships soon appeared over the coastal mountain range, racing to join the battle. One gunship went down to a rocket propelled grenade, then two more to other groundfire, but the number of active gunships would soon prove to be overpowering.

The weapons fire from the Viet Cong began to dwindle, but the number of gunships and friendly ground assaults continued to swell. Those GI's who survived the battle would have good reason to wonder what would have happened if the Viet Cong had possessed airpower of their own.

Parachute flares were being dropped, giving the battleground an eery, satanic glow. Many of those in tent city would later swear they could hear shouts and screams.

The American ground troops were clearly on the offensive. The surviving Viet Cong were being forced into small pockets of resistance that had to quickly choose between surrender and annihilation. A major two–pronged flanking counter–attack by the Americans soon succeeded in closing off the only escape route for the Viet Cong, most of whom continued to fight as though they believed they could pull out a victory of some kind.

The battlefield wasn't completely calm until three hours later, when dawn was beginning to appear on the Eastern horizon. The few prisoners taken had immediately been secregated and removed to safe areas, where interrogations would take place. The VC would be asked if they would like to join the winning side, becoming Chieu Hoi's, commonly known as Kit Carson scouts, but most would be turned over to the South Vietnamese ARVN's for further interrogation sessions that many would not survive.

Shortly after dawn, Captain Ortega received a call from Brigade on the field phone and announced that the Red Alert status had been downgraded to Yellow. The men were put At Ease and told to unload their weapons with the muzzles pointing skyward.

Ortega addressed the troops from the dune crest. "You reacted well tonight. I'm proud of all of you. Do you have anything to add, Lieutenant Masters?"

"No, Sir. They did a great job."

Ortega turned to Bolton. "Have the men clean their weapons and return them to the supply tent."

Ortega raised his voice to be heard by everyone. "We have a long day ahead of us, but hang in there the best you can. Give your buddy a hand if he's overloaded. Some of our units were hit pretty hard by this, but don't let it get under your skin. It's war…it's what happens. Just be thankful we weren't closer to the perimeter tonight. We were very lucky."

After morning chow, Lewandowski, Charlie and the Dirty

Dozen took the deuce to see what could be seen at the battleground. It was still early, barely 0700 hours when they joined the other sightseers, many of whom were carrying cameras. The ground was littered with spent shell casings, discarded AK–47 assault rifles and too many black–clad bodies to count. Two HU1B gunships were grounded nearby, ready to lift the heavy nets that were being loaded with the bodies of dead Viet Cong who had been searched and deemed ready to be placed in mass grave trenches that were being bulldozed further inland.

Television news crews were on the scene, accompanied by brass from the Information Office. Lewandowski learned from a cameraman than General Sims and the other bigwigs had been there and gone after photo–ops and interviews.

Frenchie and Skins were again waving at cameramen panning the crew. This time they shouted the words "Hi, mom—Hi, dad!" with broad, silly grins, entertaining the cameramen and reporters while avoiding looking directly at the bodies.

A reporter approached the Dirty Dozen for interviews, drawn first to Lewandowski by virtue of his size and rank.

A film camera was pointed at Lewandowski as the reporter posed his question. "What are you thinking when you look at this?"

Lewandowski glanced down at the microphone near his chin, resenting the intrusion. His thoughts belonged to himself. No one had the right to take them from him.

"I don't know," Lewandowski told the reporter. "I'm not thinking much of anything right now."

"Were you in the battle?" the reporter persisted.

Lewandowski shook his head. "We watched from our perimeter futher inland. That's all. We're not heroes."

"What were you thinking at the time?" the reporter persisted.

"Not a whole lot," Lewandowski said. "We just watched and waited to see if it would come our way. I can't remember thinking much of anything. I was scared. I remember that. We were all scared."

"It was a suicide attack from the outset."

The opinion was offered by the information officer standing beside the reporter. He was wearing Captain's bars on the lapels of his starched and pressed jungle fatigues.

"It was an act of desperation, with no realistic military goals in mind. They know they're losing the war, so they use terror tactics and human wave assaults like this. We're seeing a lot more of it lately. They don't care about human life the way we do. You'd never find an American commander using tactics like this."

Lewandowski watched as a gunship dusted off with a netload of VC. He found himself wondering how many lives had been lost/wasted the night before. He wondered how many GIs had been killed, or would live the rest of their lives screwed–up because of what happened last night.

The reporter turned to Frenchie. "What are you thinking when you look at this?"

Frenchie shrugged. "I really don't care that much either way. I mean, hey, I got just over a hundred days to go before I'm out'a here, man, and that's all I really care about. It ain't my war. I didn't start it. I'm just puttin' in my time, man."

The Captain frowned at Frenchie and took the reporter by the arm, escorting him to a more favorable news source. "I see a Lieutenant over there that was in the battle. I'm sure he'd be glad to talk about it from a more professional perspective."

"Sure," the reporter agreed, though he continued to eye Frenchie.

"Hi, mom," Skins said, grinning broadly, waving for attention as yet another camera pointed his way.

"Hi, mom," Frenchie agreed, waving as well, drawing the attention of the camera to his own silly grin. "Hi, dad. I'm gettin' SHOOORT! Leave the light on for me!"

The reporter followed the Captain to the Infantry Lieutenant as another gunship lifted off with a netload of the dead.

Charlie took Lewandowski by the arm. "We better get out'a here before we get our butts in a sling."

"What for, man?" Frenchie asked. "We ain't done nothin'. Hell, I just told the guy what was on my mind. I got a right to do that, don't I?"

"Not in the Army, you don't," Charlie warned. "When you get back to the World, you can say anything you want. Until then, you can bet they got regulations covering that sort of thing. And that Captain looks like the type who'd use'em. Be cool, man. Don't get your tit in a wringer over something like this."

Charlie was making sense for once, so the crew began meandering toward the deuce.

Lewandowski paused to give the scene a final once over before following the others."Y'know somethin', Charlie?"

Edwards stopped and turned around, waiting for Lewandowski to catch up.

"What?"

"I'm not so sure we can win this war."

Charlie shrugged. "Maybe, maybe not. I'm just glad I'm getting short."

"Yeah," Lewandowski said. "Me too, I guess. It's time we make like a hockey player and get the puck out'a here."

"Well said, Shakespeare."

Chapter Fourteen

"So, I said to him: 'Sir, it ain't my fault. How could I know they were gonna change the wall studs? The Army don't consult me before they make changes like that.'"

Lewandowski was on one of his monologue story–telling gigs that obliterated the customs and ettiquette of normal dialogue. Hillbilly was pretending to listen more as a matter of courtesy rather than genuine interest, having heard a similar version of the same story a couple of days before. A kind–hearted critic might say Lewandowski had thoroughly mastered the art of exaggeration, while others less kind might simply say that Lewandowski was full of it.

"So," Lewandowski continued as they plodded through the littered sand on their way to the Saigon Club, "…then Masters gives me this odd little grin. *I've approved your R&R request for Hong Kong, Lewandowski. You'll be leaving next Wednesday.* Then he got into his jeep and drove away. You could'a knocked me over with a feather. I expected him to ream my tail for what I just told him, but all he did was smile."

"Maybe he's getting a Short–timer attitude, like the rest of us," Hillbilly suggested.

"Naw, it's gotta be more than that," Lewandowski argued. "He's got something going. That's the way his head works. He's always got an exterior motive."

"Ulterior motive," Hillbilly corrected. "Maybe it could be he's had an attitude adjustment since we got hit the other night. That's enough to make anyone stand back and take a look at what is really important. It did me. Now I don't let the little stuff bother me as much as it did."

Lewandowski shook his head. "He's got something up his sleeve. He's gonna play with my mind in some way."

Hillbilly laughed. "Well, if that's his objective, then I'd say it's working. You've been stewing about this for the past three days."

Lewandowski wasn't listening. "Nah, he's too happy. He's got something up his sleeve."

Jackson joined the conversation. "Maybe he's just glad to get you out'a his hair for five days and four nights."

"Yeah," Charlie agreed. "I know I'm looking forward to it."

"Thanks for the support," Lewandowski grumbled. "I swear, I'm half of a mind to turn down the R&R just so's I can make everyone else miserable."

"You're always half of a mind," Charlie countered when they reached the Saigon Club.

Familiar faces greeted them on the porch landing, but Sally wasn't among them. Lewandowski figured she was with another customer. Even so, he didn't make an alternative selection, nor did any of the girls throw passes his way. A certain proprietary mutuality had evolved between himself and Sally over the months they had known each other. Inexplicable elements had been added that made Lewandowski more than just another customer; one the most important elements being that Sally and Lewandowski found they could talk about things that really mattered, unloading some of the burdens of everyday life. Lewandowski hadn't put that much thought into it, and Sally didn't talk about it directly, but there was a reliability to their relationship that both had learned to count on. Ironically, some of their better moments had happened not long after Sally had finished with another customer and Lewandowski was in no mood for fooling around. It was a phenomenon that Lewandowski couldn't explain, and it was far too close to home to be taken to Charlie Edwards for analysis, so it remained an unexplored/ unexplained phenomenon.

Lewandowski was the last of his group to enter the club. When Suzie saw him, she excused herself from a customer to pull Lewandowski aside for whispered conversation.

"Sally doan feel so good today. She doan see nobody," Suzie explained as Lewandowski bent over to seek her level. She looked very concerned for her friend. Suzie and Sally had been raised in the same village, just southwest of Saigon. "Maybe you go see her, huh? I t'ink she like that."

"Sure," Lewandowski said. "She's in her room?"

Suzie nodded, her expression sad...not at all flirtatious. Her personality would be altogether different when she returned to her customers, where she would resume being a perfectly immodest seductress.

Lewandowski headed for Sally's tiny cubicle, off the back hallway. He paused at the curtain. "Yo, Sally. Are you in there?"

He heard a soft rustling sound, then Sally's voice.

"Lew, is that you?"

"Yeah, it's me. Suzie told me you're not feeling so good today."

"Yes, is true, mon oi," she answered in a small voice, adding the Vietnamese endearment that could be roughly translated as 'sweetheart'. She had been using the term more often of late, but Lewandowski didn't mind. It felt good to know she thought of him that way.

"Do you wan' to see me?" Sally asked.

The question was posed as if she expected a negative reply. That was something else he'd noticed about her lately. She didn't have the same confidence she had before. She wasn't the Girl In Charge, like she'd been when they first met.

"That's why I'm here," Lewandowski answered, sounding much more gentle than he would have allowed himself to sound in GI company. He instinctively glanced down the hallway to see if any GI's, particularly Originals, were within hearing distance. He figured it was nobody's damned business the way he talked to Sally, especially when she wasn't feeling too hot, but on the other hand, there was no reason to leave himself open to cheapshots. Sally was just another cyclo girl to those guys, but there was more to her than that…a whole helluva lot more. She was a good kid who'd had some tough breaks in life, and he wasn't about to take any crap because he was treating her with the kind of respect she deserved, by God.

"Look, I can come back later if you want." He figured she might have some kind of girl thing that needed to get handled before she was ready for his company.

"Cam ung…thank you," Sally answered. "Yes, I wan' to see you, but I t'ink it be better if you come back maybe five more minute."

"Okay, you got it. Is there anything I can get for you?"

"No, I doan t'ink so, mon oi. If you want beer, I souvenir (buy it) for you."

Sally had long since ceased working Lewandowski for five dollar Saigon Teas, though she continued to be a merciless gold digger when dealing with the walk–in trade.

Lewandowski smiled. "Hey, I ain't gonna let no girl of mine buy me no drinks."

He said it with a huffy indignation that he knew would bring a smile to her face. He smiled himself when he heard a soft laugh on the other side of the curtain. He always got a kick out of making her laugh; though it was something she hadn't been doing very often lately. "I'll be back in five minutes, mon oi."

"You bettah or I cockadow you, Lew–WAN–dow–ski," she promised.

Lewandowski returned to the bar. The stereo system was playing SERGEANT PEPPER'S LONELY HEARTS CLUB BAND, to be followed by two FOUR TOPS hits, the DOORS doing LIGHT MY FIRE and the ANIMALS doing THE HOUSE OF THE RISING SUN. The girls were particularly fond of THE HOUSE OF THE RISING SUN, it being a sad song about a whorehouse in New Orleans. It was like a lot of Vietnamese songs in that it was a sad, romantic memorial to lost loves and tragic lives battered by the fickle forces of Kharma. Whenever HOUSE would play, the girls would abruptly put aside their bar personas and radiate sadness while adding their own soft whispery voices to to the harsh rendition by Eric Burton, transforming HOUSE into something quite special. As always when the song was concluded, they would abruptly revert to being seductive, carefree cyclo girls.

Hillbilly and the others were still waiting for their beers to be delivered when Lewandowski rejoined them.

"How's Sally feeling today?" Hillbilly asked.

Lewandowski shrugged. "She sounds okay. Just down in the dumps a bit. Who'd blame her, working in a place like this in her condition."

Hillbilly nodded as Suzie handed him a cold Schlitz and took her place on his lap. He nuzzled her hair. "My, my you smell nice today, sugarplum."

Suzie accepted the compliment with a flirtatious giggle, using various body parts to let Hillbilly know he had her full and undivided attention as long as the MPC kept coming her way.

Frenchie was a self–proclaimed anti–romantic, with both feet planted firmly on the ground. "You're pussywhipped, man," he said to Lewandowski. "That girl's got you eating out'a her hand."

"Screw you," Lewandowski muttered, using a tone that couldn't be mistaken as friendly. They'd been down this road before, and he wasn't about to travel it again. He finished his beer in glowering silence before returning to Sally's doorway.

"It's Lew again. You okay in there?"

Her voice was soft and sweet when she answered. "You can come in now, mon oi."

Lewandowski pushed aside the curtain to step inside the dimly lighted cubicle, where he saw Sally sitting on the edge of her bed, which was a regulation Army steel–framed cot that had been squeezed into the right corner. Colorful woven grass mats covered the plank floor, with more mats camouflaging the wallstuds to give the room a personalized, cozy appearance rather like the tents in tent city. An upended wooden crate was nestled into the left exterior corner, with the interior of the crate holding an incense burner, a small bronze statue of Buddha and several photographs, including one of Sally posing in a white ao dai dress, with the overall effect being one of virginal purity. There were also several snapshots of what must have been her family, along with a photograph of a bargirl who died the year before. She once told Lewandowski she was the oldest of six children, but she didn't talk about her family very much. The few times she did share bits and pieces of that part of her life, the gems of knowledge were offered with quiet sadness.

While Lewandowski was waiting, Sally had brushed her black hair into a warm, glistening fall that surrounded her pretty face like a halo. Her throat was adorned with a simple gold necklace, flattering the slim beauty of her neck. She was wearing white–on–white silk pajamas that replicated the virginal aura of her photographs, as if she were a young bride awaiting the appearance of her new husband. One hand was resting on the blanket, the other placed near her enlarged waistline.

Lewandowski had no idea how far along she was. He didn't

ask and she didn't say. Six months, seven months, he had no experience in such matters, and the varying estimates of the Originals only made the issue more uncertain. He only knew she was just about as pregnant as any one girl could be.

Lewandowski allowed the curtain to close behind him.

"Oh, my," he sighed. "Aren't you pretty today. Dep, mon oi. Very pretty. Dep lum," he added, showing off a little of the Vietnamese she had tried to get through his thick skull when they had shared private moments after lovemaking sessions.

Sally blushed and turned her head to one side, hiding the smile his compliments inspired. Underneath her brazen exterior, she was a very shy and modest girl, but she kept that side of herself hidden from all the GI's, except Lewandowski.

"You sow (lie)," she chided him. "I doan t'ink I look so good no more."

She spread her hand over her belly and looked at him with a smile that begged for more compliments. "I get beau ceau mop. Very fat, mon oi."

Lewandowski shook his head. "Naw, that ain't true, mon oi. You're dep. Dep lum."

She giggled. "I t'ink you sow, but I like what you say, Lew–WAN–dow–ski."

"Hey, you're the prettiest girl I've ever seen," Lewandowski insisted as he stepped closer, feeling overly large and clumsy in her presence. Lying down, the differences were less noticeable.

Sally stood and stepped toward him. "Hold me," she said.

Lewandowski wrapped his big arms around her and she closed her eyes, doing her utmost to block out the sounds and sights that surrounded them.

"Hows about we take a walk somewhere," Lewandowski suggested after a moment. "Maybe we can go to a cafe and get something to eat."

Lewandowski had been sampling food in the Vill for several months now, which was extraordinarily adventurous for even the most ardent of Vill Rats. In the opinion of most Originals, Lewandowski was dingydow for eating anthing that could be found in the Vill.

"No, I doan wan' to. I doan feel so good for walking, I t'ink."

"Okay, what'cha wanna do then?" Lewandowski asked. In the not so distant past, there would have been no discussion, they would have already been well into lovemaking, but it just wasn't the same now that Sally was a momma. Lewandowski's upbringing had more or less taught him that mommas should be protected rather lusted after, even if it was difficult to do from time to time. Once he knew Sally was pregnant, Lewandowski started thinking of himself more as her protector than as her customer/lover.

Sally began to gently rock from side to side, leading Lewandowski with powers far beyond her size. "I t'ink I wan' to make love today," she whispered.

"Oh?"

"Yes, mon oi. Thas' why I buy new clothes. For you to see me in...to make me dep so you wan' to make love to me."

She reached her hand to touch him.

"Oooooh my," Lewandowski said. "I don't know, mon oi. I don't wanna hurt you or the babysan. Oh, jeeze. Don't do that."

She giggled and stood back. "You say no, but you doan do the same as no. Come, mon oi. You won't hurt me or babysan. I have new Vietnamee words to teach you."

She took his hand to lead him to the cot, and Lewandowski followed without argument. Sally stayed his hand when he started to remove his smoking jacket.

"Let me do for you, mon oi. You doan do notting. Let me do for you dis time."

Next door, Suzie was ushering Hillbilly into her own cubicle.

"Hey, sugarbun. When you gonna souvenir me with a free boom–boom?" Hillbilly asked. "Just one time for free, okay?"

"You be dingydow," Suziee giggled. "Ah–ah, no–no. You pay furst...six hun'red 'p', okay?"

"Six hundred?" Hillbilly complained. "Heck, it was only five hundred last week."

"Mommasan wan' more money now," Suziee explained. "In Saigon, you pay maybe two tous'an' 'p' for same."

"The heck I would," Hillbilly vowed as he counted out a 500 piaster bill, followed by a 100 'P' bill.

"Let me fini clothes for you now," Lewandowski whispered when Sally had finished with him.

"I am too fat now, mon oi," Sally whispered as Lewandowski's hands lifted the top of her white silk pajamas.

"No, you're not," Lewandowski insisted. "You're more beautiful than ever."

"Alright, dang it all," Hillbilly grumbled as he handed over the cash. "It's a damned shame, if you ask me. The price of everything's going up around here like there's no tomorrow. It won't be the Viet Cong that drives us out of Vietnam. It'll be the high price of pussy."

Suzie giggled and stepped from the room to give the money to the mommasan standing guard over the cashbox up front.

Lewandowski leaned over to whisper in Sally's ear as he touched her breasts. "You feel so good, mon oi." He moved to her thighs and buttocks, gently probing as she returned his touch.

Sally sat Lewandowski on the bed, then moved to sit facing him on his lap. "We do this way now, mon oi. Let me do for you this time. Mommasan say it doan hurt notting dis way."

Suzie returned to her cubicle and immediately began to undress.

"Alright, ready to rock'n'roll," Hillbilly announced, being one step ahead of her. "Oh, baby. I DO like the way that looks."

Suzie giggled obligingly.

Sally concentrated on Lewandowski's face as she made love to him, etching his features into her memory. He was a good man. He would be a good husband and father. All the other GIs were easily forgotten, but not Lewandowski. He would always be a part of her, a part of her babysan. Between the two of them the lovemaking after the first time had always been better than it was with the others; something good and clean, not like the short–time boom–boom of a cyclo girl with a GI. It was the kind of comfortable and clean love that could be passed on with great pride to a son or daughter.

The bedsprings of Suzie's army–issue steel cot began to screech rhythmically, protesting the weight of an extra body.

Sally didn't close her eyes until she saw Lewandowski reach his moment of joy, afterwhich she allowed herself to share the moment.

The bedsprings abruptly ceased screeching in Suzie's room.

"Anh neu em eu lum," Sally whispered as she slowly came down. 'I love you very much.'

"Anh neu em eu lum," Lewandowski answered.

"Wooooh, baby! Now, that was one FINE boom–boom," Hillbilly crowed. "You sure do know how to use that thang, little Suzie." Suzie again giggled obligingly.

Lewandowski picked up a cold beer at the bar before sitting on a chair between Charlie Edwards and Skins.

Charlie nudged his elbow. "Hey, Lew. Check out that kid over there at the table by himself. He's been doing that since before we got in here. Up and down, up and down. Lift the short timer stick, drop it. Lift it, drop it. Man, talk about your compulsive obsessive behavior. He's either bonkers or he's bucking for a Section Eight."

Lew glanced over at 'the kid', a Speck Four about eighteen or nineteen–years–old wearing faded, wrinkled fatigues with a 173rd Airborne Brigade patch on his left shoulder. The lived–in look of the fatigues spoke of months of use in the field, well away from showers and housegirls. If his behavior drew the initial attention, it was his expression that held it. He was staring at his hands with an almost painfully unfocused intensity while lifting and dropping a carved short timer stick, never altering the slow rhythm he had established. Up–thunk, up–thunk, up–thunk, up–thunk.

Lewandowski noticed a further piece of evidence that might explain the strange behavior. The kid was wearing a right shoulder patch containing the letters L.R.R.P., for Long Range Reconnaissance Patrol. He was a Lurp, one of those who specialized in recon patrols deep into the boonies, sometimes spending weeks probing the defenses of the NVA and Viet Cong. The Lurps worked in small teams. If they made it to a predesignated retrieval point, they would be extracted by a chopper. If not, they would be presumed dead.

Lewandowski felt drawn to the kid for reasons that he didn't fully understand. Some of it was easy; even Charlie could figure it out. If the kid was for real, he had likely seen and done things far beyond Lewandowski's experience, which meant he might have answers for questions that had been bugging Lewandowski for a long time.

The kid was sitting alone. Even the bargirls were steering clear of his strange presence. A warm can of beer was sitting on the table in front of him.

"I'll buy him a beer. Maybe it'll break the ice a little," Lewandowski said to the others as he rose.

"Why?" Charlie asked.

Lewandowski shrugged. "Just curious about what makes him tick, I guess."

"Leave him alone," Charlie urged. "He's not hurtin' anyone. So what if he's psycho. It ain't our problem."

Lewandowski ignored Charlie and went to the bar for a can of Schlitz that he placed on the table in front of the kid.

"Thought you might want a cold one," Lewandowski said when he sat down.

The kid answered with a strained smile, accepting the beer.

"It can get mighty lonely in here without a little conversation," Lewandowski explained.

The kid nodded but seemed not to care either way. The I.D. tag over his left breast pocket said his name was Carlisle; his sleeve patches said he was a Speck Four. Up close, Lewandowski wondered if he might be even less than eighteen–years–old, the youngest age for enlistment without parental or guardian permission. The fuzzy stubble of beard suggested that Carlisle might have to wait more than three years before being old enough to vote.

Lewandowski's basic training company had contained several fuzzy–cheeks. It was strange, but all of them volunteered for airborne, as if they were trying to prove something. One of them was even a bedwetter. Lewandowski sometimes wondered what happened to those kids after Basic. How many of them had made it through A.I.T.? How many had made it through jump school? How many were sent to Nam, and how many of those were still alive? If they were still alive, were they like the kid he was with now? Was that kid from basic training still wetting his bed?

Lewandowski broke the ice. "That's a 173rd patch you're wearing, ain't it?"

The kid nodded, giving Lewandowski only a brief glance before returning his eyes to his hands and the short timer stick.

Up–thunk, up–thunk.

Charlie Edwards caught Lewandowski's eye and shook his head in disapproval. *'Leave the kid alone.'*

Skins rose from his chair and headed toward Lewandowski and the kid, his own curiosity getting the best of him.

"Man, you're a long way from the 173rd around here," Lewandowski said as Skins invited himself to join the conversation. "This is Skins Williams," Lewandowski added. "We work together."

"Hey, whuzhappenin'," Skins said, extending his right hand palm side up to get some skin from the young white brother.

Carlisle was slowly gaining some semblance of life… "Wut–iz…" he answered as he slapped Skins' palm.

"Itbewutiz," Skins said as he took a seat. "Whutchoo doin' down this way, man? You a long muh'fuh' way from home."

"We were on our way back from R&R in Hong Kong when we had engine trouble and ended up here," Carlisle said. "We're flying to Long Binh tomorrow. In the meantime, they gave us passes to the Vill."

Lewandowski nodded. The kid and his fellow passengers weren't likely to go AWOL in–county, so they could be trusted with passes. Even if they missed a flight or two, it wasn't a problem for the R&R center at the Replacement Depot. Punishments for AWOL R&R's were handled at the local unit level once they were caught.

Lewandowski figured it was as good a time as ever to open the subject that brought him to the kid in the first place.

"I read in Stars and Stripes how the 173rd took some hill a couple of weeks ago," he began.

The kid nodded.

"Hill 364, or something like that…." Lewandowski continued.

Carlisle shrugged. "Close enough. It was 367."

"Were you in on that?" Lewandowski asked.

Charlie Edwards and Frenchie decided to join them, making further introductions necessary before Carlisle could continue. He was emerging from his shell now, even managing to smile when he shook hands with the new arrivals.

"I was just asking him about that hill they took a couple of weeks ago," Lewandowski explained to the Originals. He turned to Carlisle. "I read the Stars and Stripes version, but it's a government newspaper, if you know what I mean."

"Yeah," Frenchie quipped. "They could be feeding us a line of bull and we wouldn't know the difference."

Carlisle nodded. "Yeah. I don't know what they wrote about 367, but they put out crap about other actions. What'd they say this time?"

"This ain't word for word," Lewandowski said, "...but it's pretty close. It was about how you guys took the hill from NVA that were holed up inside bunkers. They said the battle lasted, like, three days and you took light to moderate casualties before the hill was taken. That was the gist of it."

Carlisle shook his head and tapped the short timer stick on the tabletop. "Nah, that's bull. We had our asses handed to us. It was bad news. Bad, bad news, man."

"What happened?" Lewandowski asked.

Carlisle shook his head, saying nothing.

"You don't havta talk about it if you don't wanna," Charlie said. "Just let it drop."

Carlisle shook his head. "Nah, it's okay."

"Whatever," Lewandowski said. "I was just curious, that's all. I don't wanna pry if its stuff you don't wanna talk about."

"It took us five days to take that hill," Carlisle began with no introduction. The first few words said, he then started speaking more quickly, with a vacant expression, his eyes focused briefly on a distant, unseen object, then dropping down to avoid contact.

"There were four LZs around the hill when we went in, and all of 'em were hot. That's when we knew were were gonna get some heavy shit, that this was one hill Chuck wanted to keep. We took heavy in–coming before we hit the ground. The hill had been hit with artillery and air strikes for three days before we went in. We were hoping we'd have a walk–in, but they must've been just waitin' it out. They were in concrete bunkers, reinforced stuff. Real heavy, the walls eight and ten–feet thick. The Air Force used some big stuff on it, but nothin' could penetrate. We didn't know about that until after it was over. I don't know if we'd gone in, if we'd known what those bunkers were like. And the NVA, too. Man, don't let anybody ever tell you the NVA ain't tough motherfuckin' soldiers. I mean to tell ya, they sure got my respect."

"We took three casualties on the slick I was in before we touched down. We were able to set up a base, but we were getting hit hard with incoming. We called in more air strikes and artillery, but the in–coming never let up. We kept hitting that hill with everything we had, and when we were ordered to saddle up three days later, the NVA just popped out'a their holes and opened up on us. We were taking heavy fire from three sides as soon as we got maybe a hundred feet up the hillside. They were nailing us with crossfire like…god, I don't know. It was like hell. It really was like something from hell."

Carlisle lowered his voice. "We ran up that hill shouting Airborne, Airborne, Airborne. For four days we did that. Charge and retreat with the dead and wounded we could carry down the hill, then charge and retreat again, with everybody screaming like we were fuckin' nuts. There was crap flying all over the place. The NVA had us dead on, firing from caves and anywhere else they could hide. It was like a big fort built into the hill, with tunnels connecting everything. It seemed like they were everywhere around us, firing from holes then disappearing when we returned fire. We didn't have cover, but they had all the cover they needed and they were holding the high ground. They had us no matter what we did. We had incoming if we held, or went forward, or tried to fall back. They'd shoot down the slicks that were brought in to medivac our wounded. They had us by the balls."

"We took so many casualties we were running out of replacements. Finally, we held enough ground to spend the night on the hill. Man, that was something I'll never forget. Everything was stinking, like we were all dying of jungle rot."

"We took the hill the next day, about noon," Carlisle concluded. "There was nothin' fancy about it. Just plain old frontal assaults. There was hand–to–hand in the bunker, once we got in. That was the only way to get the job done. By that time, we were down to about half our operational strength, even with the replacements. When it was all over, I was the only guy from my original platoon to make it out'a that hill without getting hit. About half were killed, the rest of them medivacked out. Most of them won't be back."

Carlisle paused to drink from a fresh can of beer. Several of the bargirls had joined the audience.

"What were you thinking while all this was going on?" Lewandowski asked.

"Thinking?" Carlisle asked. "I wasn't thinking much of anything. I felt high as a kite, really. When when it was over, all I wanted to do was fall dead asleep. It didn't matter where I was. I could have slept on a pile of bodies without even thinking about it."

"I do remember thinking I was gonna die," Carlisle added. "Several times, I knew I was gonna die, but it didn't scare me. It scares me now, but it didn't scare me then. Weird shit like that happens."

"Have the NVA tried to take it back? Lewandowski asked.

"They don't havta try," Carlisle answered with a humorless smirk. "We screwed it up with H.E. as much as we could and destroyed their weapons, rice and ammo, then we dee–dee'd out'a there after and went back to base camp to regroup. All the NVA havta do is walk back in, do a little housecleaning and they're back in business. That's what Search and Destroy is all about. We find'em, we kill'em, we mess with whatever they got for supplies, then we go somewhere else and do the same thing all over again."

Carlisle shrugged. "That's it. That's the way it's done. I'll just be glad when I DEROS out'a here. I've had it. This is the stupidest goddamned way to fight a war that I ever hear of. We're playing their game by their rules. We should'a never tried to take that fucking hill. We could'a surrounded it and kept hitting it from the sky and forced them to come to us, but we hadda do it the hard-headed way. Yelling Airborne, Airborne, Airborne. And then what'd we do after we took the hill? We walked away from it." He took a long chug of beer. "Any you guys know where I could score some dope?"

Skins nodded. "Sure, I got it handled, man."

Carlisle reached for his wallet, but Skins shook his head. "Don't sweat it, man. It's on the house."

Lewandowski roused himself and looked around. "We gotta get you lined up with a honey," he said. "I'll talk to a girl I know and get it handled."

"Heck, you don't havta do that," Carlisle protested.

"Yeah, we do," Charlie answered. "It's an old family tradition with us. Whenever we get company from the boonies, we get him laid for free."

"Just keep your hand off your wallet for the rest of the day," Lewandowski said. "We're footing the bill. Hey, if you go AWOL and miss a flight or two, what're they gonna do? Send you to Vietnam?"

Frenchie held up his beer can to propose a toast. "F.T.A...All The Way."

None of the Originals said Short. It wouldn't have been the right thing to say. Even dumb GIs can have good manners.

Chapter Fifteen

The entire 516th AG was finally getting Short.

How Short were they?

Even Numbnuts Bolton had been heard to mutter an occasional "Short" as he went about his nefarious duties as Top Shirt.

The Standard Operating Procedure signs of short timer status were on display throughout tent city and the personnel center. The proliferation of short timer calendars had been suitably rampant, displaying crude drawings of badaciously buxom bimbos with their bountiful body parts suggestively sectioned into 365 numbered segments, with the final day—DEROS—invariably being centrally located.

PFC Donnatelli—formerly SP5 Donnatelli—was the first to put up a short timer calendar beside his desk, with another inside his wall locker. Utilizing a multi–colored frenzy of crayon strokes, he created short–timer sweeties who could have been victims of a disfiguring skin ailment that might have been contracted in one of the sleazier bars in the vill.

short timer swagger sticks were becoming so fashionable that Masters found it necessary to issue a company–wide directive forbidding them in company formations, using typically blunt language in the typed notice that appeared on company bulletin boards in tent city and the personnel center.

"…Anyone seen in company formations with ANY kind of un-authorized short timer paraphernalia WILL be assigned to KP until they reach DEROS."

William R. Masters
CAPTAIN, Infantry
Executive Officer,
516th AG Pers Svc Co
USASUPCOM, CRB
As endorsed by
Manuel S. Ortega
MAJOR, Infantry
Commanding Officer,

516th AG Pers Svc Co

USASUPCOM, CRB

"Well, I'll be darned," Lewandowski said as he and Charlie observed buck private Hanley—formerly SP4 Hanley—posting the directive on the orderly tent bulletin board.

"Are they trying to tell us something, Charlie, or are they trying to tell us something?"

Lewandowski tapped Hanley's shoulder as he stapled the final corner of the onion skin copy. "Is this for real? Is Masters really a Captain now?"

"He's wearing Captain's bars" Hanley answered. "And he's hung over from boozing it up at the officers club last night. You tell me, Lewandowski. Is he a Captain, or ain't he?"

"Sounds like the real thing," Lewandowski had to admit, grinning obscenely as brilliant ideas began to invade his conscious mind. "Maybe I can talk them into throwing a promotion party for the troops who got'em promoted. I'll tell Masters how proud we are of him...how we'd like to celebrate their promotions. He'll buy into it."

"Not if it comes from you," Charlie predicted. "But it might work if someone else does the brown nosing."

"He knows nobody likes him. I'm the closest thing to a friend that he's got," Lewandowski said.

"What about Woody?" Charlie suggested to Hanley. "He could drop hints over a couple or three days. It won't be so obvious that way."

Hanley shook his head. "I'll bring it up, but Woody pretty much stopped kissing ass after he got Speck Five."

"Don't they all?" Charlie asked.

"Some of us never started," Lewandowski said defensively before turning his attention back to Hanley. "Tell Woody not to press too hard. Manipulating Masters is an art."

Charlie laughed. "The expert speaks. Everyone listen."

"Hey, be nice, GI," Lewandowski said. "I've handled him pretty well so far, haven't I? He let me go on R&R didn't he?"

"Yeah, and you were sweating it out the whole time," Charlie said as they started meandering toward the three–quarter–ton truck they'd be using that day to re–rout corrugated roofing sheets from the suburbs to Nhan Ai. "Not to mention that you came back with a dose of the clap. It's lucky for you that Sally's so knocked up. She'd cockadow your family jewels if she knew you butterflied her on R&R."

Hanley watched them go, longing for the freedom they took for granted. Lewandowski and Edwards didn't have Masters sitting a few feet away within the stifling confines of a troop tent, separated by only a thin plywood partition. They could say what they wanted and do what they wanted, dealing with Masters only during his increasingly infrequent visits to the construction area. Lewandowski and Edwards had it made in the shade.

Hanley's loathing for the Morning Report had been increasing as his days–to–DEROS dwindled in number. Everyone else had been looking forward to the arrival of the first replacements, but the invasion of replacements meant only more work for Hanley. It was Hanley who would have to rise well before dawn every morning to create flawless typed morning report entries transferring the re-placements from USA REPLDPT, USARSUPCOMCRB APO SF 96824 to 516TH AG, USARSUPCOMCRB. APO SF 95824. His escape from the drudgery of the Morning Reports would come only when his own replacement arrived and he could train the unlucky sap to perform the odious task. Until such time, Hanley could not consider himself a genuine short timer.

Hanley was feeling very sorry for himself as he entered the orderly tent.

"Yo, Hanley," Woody called out. "I got some Hot Stuff...the Cap'n wants it done yesterday."

Woody held up a handwritten rough–draft letter that needed to be typed before it could be consigned to the bureaucratic chain of command. The handwriting was the classic illegible scrawl of William R. Masters, now Captain Masters.

"So, what else is new?" Hanley asked.

"I heard that," Masters called out from his office. "Are we having a morale problem I need to be aware of?"

Woody lifted a finger to his lips to signal silence from Hanley. "No, Sir. No problem at all, Sir. Hanley's getting started on it right now."

"I don't hear typing," Masters said.

Woody pointed at Hanley's typewriter, mouthing the words 'Do It Now'. Masters was being particularly grouchy today, a side–effect of his promotion hangover.

"I'm starting on it, Sir," Hanley promised while pointing an index finger at the divider wall. "Sixty–two more days and I'm out'a here," he mumbled while enroute to his desk.

"I heard that too," Masters called out from his office.

The first 516th AG replacement arrived three days later, on day fifty–nine to DEROS. His name was Taylor and he presented as a rumpled, wrinkled Speck Four who had been living out of his duffle bag the past five days while intransit from Fort Lewis, Washington to the Repple Depple, finally arriving at the personnel center with orders assigning him to the 516th AG.

The news spread through the personnel center like warm butter on hot toast: "WHAT'S HIS RANK…HIS MOS? I WANT HIM …HE'S MINE!"

Taylor was sent from the command shack to SP4 Bagley, who handled the personnel records for the 516th.

Bagley couldn't have been more gracious. "Ah, my replacement, my good man, you dear–sweet–wonderful guy. Have a seat right here, my good man! Rest your feet, make yourself at home and tell me all about yourself!"

Bagley's phone rang. It was Jackson calling from Ortega's office with the message that the replacement would be going to the orderly tent.

"Taylor's gonna be Woody's replacement," Jackson explained.

"Oooh Maaaan," Bagley whined. "If that don't beat all! Woody don't need no replacement. He don't know what to do with his time the way it is, man!"

"No matter," Jackson said. "Masters gets first pick. Process him in and send him on his way to tent city, with orders to report to Masters on the double."

Bagley hung up the phone and glared at Taylor as if he were responsible for all the injustices done to Bagley and all his ancestors going back to the last ice age.

"Gimme your 201 file, man. I got work to do. I can't be messin' 'round with this all day."

When Bagley opened the 201 file, he abruptly turned joyful again, having seen the prefix to Taylor's service number.

"Choi Oi!!" Bagley exclaimed loud enough for everyone around him to hear. "OHMYGOD," he repeated to make sure he had the attention of the other clerks.

Taylor settled back in his chair, knowing what would be coming next. The RA prefix to his service number had done it to him again. As a three–year enlistee, he had spent the past one year, five months and fourteen days being harassed by two–year draftees. Taylor had learned from experience that he had no choice but to ride out the harassment until the US's around him had gotten it out of their systems. It only made it worse when he tried to defend his decision to join the Army for three years instead of waiting for the two–year draft notice. The recruiting sergeant had all but guaranteed Taylor he would get a tour of duty in Germany, if he would only sign on the dotted line.

"He's an R.A.," Bagley announced for everyone to hear. "Let's take a look at that ETS date. Choi Oi! February 27, 1969. Man...they ain't even close to printin' that calendar yet! Nine–teen Sixty–nine! Maaa–an, that's a loooong time from now!"

Bagley counted the months with his fingers, "That's NINE-TEEN months from now!" He turned to Taylor. "How do you live with it, man? I'd shoot myself if I had that much time to do!"

Taylor squirmed, surrounded by laughter at his expense. The harassment was unusually brutal this time, but he would live through it. He had to. He was a three–year RA with nineteen months to go.

"Wanna know how many days I got to my ETS?" Bagley asked.

Taylor didn't bother answering, knowing he would hear it whether he wanted to or not.

Bagley tapped the short timer calendar that was taped to his file cabinet. "Fifty–nine days," he announced with a serene smile. "Count'em, if you want. Five nine days. Fifty–nine...and tomorrow its gonna be Fifty–eight."

Taylor glanced at Bagley's multi–colored mistress of short

timer status long enough to note that the section for day "1" had received particularly creative attention. He had seen more than his share of short timer calendars while being processed through the replacement depot, but Bagley's was more graphic than most. Whoever was waiting for him back in The World, be it wife or girlfriend, should be forewarned.

"Oh man, it must be awful," Bagley continued with concern that couldn't be mistaken for anything genuine. "Dang, how'd they get you to sign on the dotted line? Did they get you in Basic with that old line about sending you to the Infantry if you didn't give'em another year? They tried that with me...they tried it with all of us. But we told'em to shove it."

Taylor remained cool and detached. "Where do I go after I leave here?"

"You'll be hoofin' it to tent city," Bagley answered.

"Tent city? What's that?" Taylor was anxious to pursue any subject other than his being a three–year R.A..

"It's where we live, man. You'll see for yourself soon enough. It ain't so bad as it sounds. We got it pretty good compared to the guys living in barracks. You'll find out about that, too," Bagley promised as he handed Taylor documents that needed his signature. "Sign on the X, man. Just like you did when you went RA."

Taylor concentrated on the documents, ignoring Bagley's taunts.

"Oh, yeah, there's one more thing I gotta tell you," Bagley added, appearing quite serious now.

"What's that?" Taylor asked, thinking it might be a critical bit of information.

"Short," Bagley said with a wide smile.

Taylor cleared his throat. There was no reason to get angry; he had walked into that with his eyes open. Do it once, shame on you; do it twice, shame on me. "Thanks. I needed that."

"Oh, you'll be hearing it again," Bagley promised, chuckling to himself. "I can guarantee you'll be hearing a lot of it. That's all you need from me. Now you gotta report to the orderly tent. Tent city ain't far...maybe a half mile inland. There's a trail we use out back, past the shitters. You can't miss it. Just follow your nose heading west. A little advice before you go, and this is no shit, man."

Tylor was wary, but listened anyway.

Watch out for Captain Masters," Bagley said confidentially. "He's twisted...you know what I mean? He's gone psycho on us several times over here, man. We don't know what he'll do next. He can flip out over nothin'. He's busted troops for just lookin' at him the wrong way. Talk to Lewandowski in the supply tent about Masters. He'll set you straight."

"Thanks for the warning," Taylor said as he rose and shouldered his duffle bag.

Bagley spoke again before Taylor reached the exit. "One more thing," he added.

"Yeah, I know. Short."

A chorus of "Short" rose from most of the other clerks, who were making absolutely sure that Taylor fully realized he was completely surrounded by short timers.

When Taylor was gone, Bagley got on the phone to Lewandowski, asking for support in his Mad Dog Masters scenario.

"Hey, I can't do that," Lewandowski protested. "We're trying to work him for a promotion party with the 'We're so proud of you' crap. We can't get our messages mixed, or we'll come out of it with a big zero."

"Aw, c'mon," Bagley begged. "He's our first replacement, man. We gotta freak him out. Otherwise, we're giving up half the fun of being Short."

Lwandowski paused to consider the argument. "Yeah, you're right, Bagley. I wasn't thinking straight there for a minute. Maybe I got an idea comin'. Yeah, it's comin'...yeah, I'm on to somethin' good. Leave it up to Charlie'n'me. We'll take care of this guy."

"Show no mercy," Bagley urged.

"No suweat, GI," Lewandowski promised. "I don't think you'll havta worry about that."

Woody was waiting for Taylor to arrive at the orderly tent.

"Ah, my replacement," Woody said when Taylor lurched in from out of the hot sun with the heavy duffle bag slung over his shoulder. "Have a seat. Make yourself right at home."

"No," Masters said from his rear office hideaway. "He's MY replacement, Specialist Woods. Captains decide what to do with replacements, not Specialists. Just tell him to report to me."

"Yes, Sir," Woody said with fatalistic shrug. He nodded his head toward the open doorway into Masters' office. "Report Front and Center. The Cap'n is waiting."

Taylor dropped his duffle bag to the floor and started walking toward the open doorway in the plywood room divider.

"U.S.," Woody quipped to his back. "Short."

"U.S.," Hanley added as Taylor passed his desk. "Short."

Hanley now had reason to smile thanks to Taylor, who would ETS long after Hanley was back on the streets in civilian clothes.

Taylor halted at the open doorway. Masters was sitting at his desk, his eyes cast down as he scanned paperwork. Taylor stood at the door, waiting for an invitation to enter.

"You gotta knock," Woody said.

Taylor tapped the doorframe.

Masters glanced up with a mildly surprised expression. "Yes?"

"Announce yourself," Woody directed.

"Specialist Taylor reporting, Sir," Taylor said, watchful for signs of the madness that Bagley had described.

"Ah, Specialist Taylor," Masters said with a brief smile. "You may report for duty."

Taylor walked through the doorway and placed himself Front and Center to render a salute intended to satisfy even the most twisted military mind. Masters took his time inspecting Taylor's wrinkled fatigues, the unshined boots and unpolished brass before rendering a semi–snappy return salute that allowed Taylor to drop his arm to his side.

"At Ease," Masters said, remaining watchful as Taylor assumed the position of Parade Rest, nodding his approval at the conclusion of the maneuver. It was a pleasure to see a young soldier who cared about such things. "Welcome to the 516th AG," Masters said.

"Thank you, Sir."

Taylor couldn't help but notice that Masters had been perusing a PLAYBOY centerfold. Other than the magazine, his desktop was as clean as a hound's tooth.

"I've been told you're a Regular Army man," Masters began as he leaned back in his officer's–grade padded chair.

"Yessir," Taylor said, but none too loudly, hoping the clerks in the front office wouldn't be listening. But distant snickers dashed even that modest hope.

"Will you be making a career of the Army?" Masters asked with a warm smile.

More low snickers drifted from the front office. Not loud enough to draw Masters' wrath, but loud enough to get the point across to Taylor.

Taylor was thinking about Bagley's warning, but just couldn't bring himself to say he would Re–up. "Not really, Sir. I, uh..I was thinking of going back to college on the GI Bill, Sir."

The smile faded....Masters changed the subject. "I've been told you were a company clerk back in the States."

"Yessir," Taylor answered, glad to be able to provide some information that might please the Captain. "Fort Rucker, Alabama, Sir. Third Enlisted Student Company."

"Ah," Masters said with a brief, uncaring nod. "How many words can you type per minute?"

"Twenty–five, Sir," Taylor lied, adding ten WPM to his actual score. Typing had never been his strong suit.

"Twenty–five?" Masters asked, openly disappointed.

"Thirty–five, Sir," Taylor corrected.

"Oh," Masters said with a nod, wondering if Taylor might be another Lewandowski in disguise. "Well, you can do the job, right?"

"Yessir."

"Very good. The supply sergeant and his clerk are waiting to issue your field gear in the supply tent. Report there after I dismiss you."

"Yessir."

"You're dismissed," Masters said with a wave of his hand.

Taylor saluted, did an About Face and stepped quickly from the office, anxious to escape from Masters.

"The Do Not Disturb The Captain Unless There's A Real Emergency sign is up again," Masters announced through the doorway.

"Roger, Sir," Woody shouted back.

Taylor exited the orderly tent with a puzzled expression.

Masters returned his attention the airbrushed perfection of Miss July. His own short timer calendar was kept tucked away in a desk drawer, just in case a superior officer from Brigade dropped in. Officers don't have short timer calendars. Officers are volunteers …officers don't count their days to DEROS. Even so, Masters was fully aware he had just sixty–two days remaining before he would take delivery on the Corvette Stingray 427 he had ordered through the Cam Ranh PX at a sizable discount. It would be a bright red coupe with detachable roof, four speed, red leather seats, eight–track stereo, power steering and brakes, and air–conditioning.

Masters already knew what his new duty assignment would be. In roughly one hundred days, he would be the commander of a freshly formed Infantry OCS company in the 5th Officer Candidate School Battalion at Fort Benning School For Boys.

Mommas and poppas, hide your daughters. The kid would be coming home in style.

Taylor entered the supply tent with his duffle bag, where he found Lewandowski and Charlie Edwards waiting behind the countertop that separated the small entry area from the supplies and weapons racks. Behind Lewandowski and Edwards, he saw two rows of weapons racks filled to capacity with well oiled, sparkling M–14 elephant guns. Taylor dropped his duffle bag to the plank floor.

Charlie was sporting a vacuous smile. "Short. U.S."

"Aw, doggonit," Lewandowski growled, looking and sounding like a big friendly bear. "Don't rub it in, Charlie. Taylor don't need to be hearing shit like that. He's one of us now. A member of the Fightin' 516th. A brother."

Lewandowski held out his big paw, inviting Taylor to shake. "Al Lewandowski. You can call me Lew. And this here's Charlie Edwards."

"Roger Taylor," Taylor said as he returned the handshakes. He liked Lewandowski immediately. Lewandowski hadn't ragged on his RA status…Lewandowski had a heart…Lewandowski could be trusted.

"Sorry 'bout that, GI," Charlie apologized. "...but I had to say it. You'll understand when you're getting Short. It ain't no fun if you can't brag about it."

Taylor shrugged and forced a smile. "Aw, it's okay. I understand."

"Of course, you won't be short for a looooong, looong time yet," Charlie added with a chuckle. "February Sixty–nine. Man, that's a bummer."

"Now, Charlie," Lewandowski cautioned again. "Be Nice, GI. We gotta get this young troop checked into the combat zone."

Lewandowski reached for one of the clipboards hanging from the tent pole behind him and scanned the topmost form on the clipboard. "Okay, let's get this show on the road for Specialist Taylor here. Lemme see now. I'm gonna assign you to tent eight, Taylor. They got a couple'a open spaces from some casualties we took last week. You ought'a be able to squeeze in there real good."

Taylor tensed at the mention of casualties, but said nothing, remaining outwardly calm and collected. One year, five months and fourteen days of harassment from U.S.'s had taught him how keep his cool under pressure.

"Okay, Charlie, let's get his gear issued," Lewandowski said with abrupt and copious enthusiasm. "We need one...."

"One!" Charlie repeated.

"One–each wood–frame folding canvas cot!" Lewandowski barked.

Charlie took off for the back of the tent, repeating the nomenclature as he dashed to the supply of canvas cots. A moment later, he returned to place the folded cot on the countertop.

"One–each wood–frame folding canvas cot," Charlie said breathlessly. "Next."

"Two–each cotton sheets, one–each pillow, one–each pillow case and one each O.D. wool cot blanket," Lewandowski rattled off in a staccato voice not unlike the dry rattle of machinegun fire. "You get the sheets and blanket, I'll get the rest of it."

Taylor watched as Lewandowski and Edwards dashed for separate destinations, returning a moment later to add their designated items to the pile of gear that was growing on the countertop.

"One–each footlocker!" Lewandowski shouted.

"One–each footlocker not in inventory!" Charlie answered, and turned to Taylor. "Make sure you don't sign for that item. You can keep your gear in your duffle bag until we can scrounge more footlockers…or take more casualties."

"One–each flak vest!" Lewandowski continued. "One–each steel pot, one–each webbed ammo belt, one–each helmet liner, one–each bayonet, one–each canteen with O.D. canvas canteen cover, plus one–each aluminum canteen cup! One–each stainless steel dinner tray with knife, fork and spoon!"

Lewandowski and Charlie hustled to gather the aforementioned, eventually adding them to the pile.

"Now for the war clothes," Lewandowski continued as Taylor stared at the equipment he would be signing for on his supply paperwork. "Four–each O.D. jungle fatigues. What size do you wear, Taylor?"

"Uh, thirty–three waist, thirty–one length on the pants. Forty–two jacket."

"Thirty–three, thirty–one, forty–two!" Lewandowski shouted to Edwards, who was already dashing to the rear of the tent .

"How 'bout thirty–four, thirty, forty–one?" Charlie shouted back.

"Close enough!" Lewandowski shouted over his shoulder as he made marks and remarks on Taylor's standardized supply forms. Charlie returned a moment later with an armload of jungle fatigue jackets and pants.

"Boot size?" Lewandowski asked Taylor.

"Eleven and a half 'D'," Taylor answered as he accepted the fatigues from Charlie.

"YO! 'Lev'a'half 'D!" Lewandowski repeated, sending Charlie toward a section of shelves loaded with jungle boots.

Charlie searched. " YO! 'Lev'a'half 'D'!" he repeated, and tossed two pair of canvas–top boots to Taylor.

"Whew," Lewandowski said, sounding out of breath. "I'm glad that's over. Now, sign right here and initial where I made the checkmarks. We'll be all set."

Taylor did as directed while Lewandowski double–checked his work on a different form.

"YO! Taylor! You signed here for the footlocker you ain't got. Here," Lewandowski added with sudden gentleness. "Just mark through that and put your initials beside it. Ole Lew'll take care of ya so's ya don't havta worry 'bout a thing."

Lewandowski watched to make sure it was done right before returning the clipboard to the tent pole and gathering a new clipboard.

"Okay, now the next bit of business," Lewandowski continued with a grim and foreboding look that could inspire chills.

"We issue the best friend you're gonna have over here, Taylor. Your weapon...the M–14 elephant gun. We don't get issued M–16's in Cam Ranh. Nope. We need longer range stuff, so's we can open fire before the dirty bastards make it all the way in here to tent city."

Taylor nodded and swallowed hard.

"Unfortunately," Lewandowski continued grimly. "We've been kinda low on ammo since the last time the 516th had Night Patrol, so you won't be able to practice–fire your weapon. You have fired yer basic M–14 back in the World, haven't you, Taylor?"

Taylor nodded, his eyes wide with growing anxiety. "But not since Basic Training," he added quickly.

Lewandowski waved it off, suddenly chipper. "Aw, that's okay. The Viet Cong don't know that. They'll think you know what yer doing when you return fire on'em. Believe me, I know. As long as you know how to lock–and–load and know where the safety is, that's all that really matters around here. Safety First...that's the word here in tent city. We don't wanna be shooting each other by mistake. We can't let that sorta thing happen again. Right, Charlie?"

Charlie shook his head while staring at Taylor with a disturbingly intense expression.

"Okay, just sign right here for your Elephant Gun," Lewandowski directed as he laid the clipboard on the countertop in front of Taylor. "Just look for space 168 in the weapons rack when we come under attack. Now, remember that: Space 168. Don't forget. The guys around here can get downright mean if someone grabs their weapon when the Vee–et Cong are coming in all drugged–up and crazy, with that strange look they get in their eyes....as if they got something personal against you."

"They get half crazy on drugs before they attack," Charlie amplified for Taylor's edification.

"Charlie here is almost a doctor," Lewandowski explained brightly.

"If you see me taking notes, don't worry about it," Charlie said. "I'm working on my Doctoral thesis."

Taylor stared at Charlie a long moment while Charlie stared back, making mental notes.

"Ah–hem," Lewandowski said as he reached for another clipboard. A series of explosions destroyed the peace somewhere beyond the perimeter, and Taylor jumped reflexively, his eyes wide.

Lewandowski chuckled. "You'll never hear the one that gets ya, Taylor. That's a little joke we tell around here to cheer each other up."

Charlie wasn't smiling. "It really is true, y'know. It's one'a the things a guy's gotta think about over here."

"But not too much," Lewandowski advised. "You'll go crazy if you think about it too much. You can ask ole Charlie here about that. He knows all about what it takes to go nutso–freako."

Taylor jumped again as Lewandowski slapped the final clipboard onto the countertop. "Okay, my friend...now we gotta find a slot for you on Night Patrol."

Taylor was beginning to assume the behavior of a puppy that had been yelled at one too many times for peeing on the carpet. "Night Patrol? I thought this was a personnel company."

"Yup, sure is," Lewandowski agreed. "But we gotta do our part to protect Cam Ranh, right along with ever'body else. You know the old saying: Every soldier's Basic MOS is Eleven Bravo, Light Weapons Infantryman. Well, that's the way it is here in Cam Ranh. If we don't protect our perimeter, no one else will. Tell him what our motto is here in the Fighting 516th Charlie."

Edwards nodded. "Clerks By Day...Killers By Night."

Taylor's jaw dropped open in dismay.

"What it boils down to is this," Lewandowski continued. "We got slots open in several Night Patrol squads, so you'll get your choice of which one you want. You're lucky that way. It won't be long before we'll have all the slots filled. Then we'll hav'ta start stickin' fresh bodies in the most convenient place we can find. Unless, of course, we take some new casualties that open a few more slots."

Lewandowski scanned the clipboard. "Okay, here it goes. Mortar Crew," he said and looked up for Taylor's response.

"I...I don't know anything about mortars," Taylor stuttered.

"That's alright. We ain't exactly what you'd call experts either. All these positions are On The Job Training, y'know. If it weren't for OJT's we wouldn't have nobody at all. Then we'd really be in trouble. Right, Charlie?"

Taylor glanced at Charlie, who whistled appreciatively, arching his eyebrows, nodding affirmatively.

"Next," Lewandowski announced. "The Fifty–caliber machine gun crew. Now that's a fun crew, if I do say so myself. There's nothing more exciting than watching your tracers take out a whole damn platoon of Viet Cong in the dead of the night. Hot Damn! Bodies flying all over the place! You can see'em flying up in the air and coming back down again, dead as a doornail. That'd be my choice if I was you. In fact, I'm the squad leader of that crew."

Lewandowski winked. "I can guarantee you some hot times if you're on the Fifty crew. We specialize in barbecues, beer busts and blood. Want me to go on with the other crews, or have you heard enough already?"

"Go on," Taylor said in a faraway voice, entranced by Lewandowski's enthusiasm.

"Oh–kay, lemme see now...duh–duh–duh–duh–duh...duh–duh–duh. Hey, YEAH, there's a slot open on the Claymore Mine crew until Emerson gets back from the field hospital."

"I don't think he's coming back," Charlie interrupted. "I heard he's being medivacked back to The World. They're having troubles with the gangrene again."

Lewandowski made a sour face. "Damn, those belly wounds can be bastards." He turned to Taylor with a wide grin. "Well, that's about it. Which crew is it gonna be?"

"We don't have to rush him," Charlie suggested. "We won't be on Night Patrol again until next month, so he's got some time to think about it. Maybe he'd like to talk to some Originals before he decides which crew he wants."

"Well, I'm throwing a beer bust for my crew next week," Lewandowski explained. "I was kinda hopin' I'd have a body count early on so's I'd know how much beer to buy. But I guess it's no big deal, if you wanna put a little more thought into it."

Taylor took a deep breath, shaking his head, not wanting to believe what he was hearing, while not doubting it was true, his personal propensity for bad luck being what it was.

"Exactly, what is this Night Patrol thing?" Taylor asked cautiously.

"Tell him, Charlie."

"We do Night Patrol one month out'a every three," Charlie explained. "The units in Cam Ranh take turns holding sections of the perimeter, but it really isn't as bad as it sounds. Usually it's a piece of cake, a nice break in the routine."

"Unless that section of perimeter gets hit while you're on Night Patrol," Lewandowski added with a telling shiver. "Then it's no fun. No fun a'tall."

"Nope," Charlie agreed.

The telephone rang and was promptly answered by Lewandowski. "516th supply, Sir. Lewandowski speaking."

Pause.

"Yessir, he's right here, Sir. No problem, Sir. Yessir, I'll tell him."

Pause.

"You bet, Sir. Oh, nooo, Sir. Nosir, I wouldn't do anything like that, Sir. Nosir, I sure wouldn't. Yessir, I sure will, Sir. And thank you for calling, Sir. Yessir, I will do that, Sir. And may I say, Sir, we're all really proud of you and the Major for your well deserved promotions."

Pause

"Yessir. Good–bye, Sir."

Lewandowski returned the phone back to its cradle and spoke to Taylor.

"Cap'n Masters wanted me to tell you to report for duty at

0700 hours—sharp—tomorrow morning. You're a lucky guy," he added with a wink. "Cap'n Masters is a wonderful officer. I swear, I'd follow him to hell and back, and you can tell him I said that, too. And you can remind him how proud were are of him for being promoted to Captain."

Lewandowski peered closely at Taylor. "Remember to tell him all that, okay? It's best to stay on his good side, if you know what I mean."

"Mad Dog," Edwards added. "Need I say more?"

Taylor nodded, though he was hearing Lewandowski and Edwards through a dark fog of gloomy thoughts about an insane Captain and the impending terrors of Night Patrol.

"Can you get this stuff to your tent on your own?" Lewandowski asked.

Taylor nodded with a vacuous expression and reached for a portion of his mound of field gear.

"It's the last tent on the left as you turn to your military left from here," Charlie explained while piling the jungle boots on top of the bedding and jungle fatigues that were already in Taylor's arms. He added the pillow last. "You can't miss it."

"I'll find it," Taylor said from behind the pillow, his voice muffled and melancholy.

"I'll get the door for ya," Lewandowski offered as he moved around the countertop to hold the door open so Charlie could guide Taylor out onto the boardwalk.

They waited for Taylor's footsteps to recede into the distance before breaking up.

"Did you see his face?" Charlie wheezed.

"He swallowed it hook, line and sinker," Lewandowski giggled. "We gotta get the word to the guys down at the personnel center. Nobody better wise this guy up. We gotta play him for all it's worth."

"What did Masters want?" Charlie asked.

"It was a weird conversation," Lewandowski answered with a puzzled expression.

"How weird?" Charlie asked.

Lewandowski shrugged. "He told me to stop picking on the replacement."

Footsteps approached on the boardwalk.

"Shh, it's Taylor," Charlie said.

The door opened and Taylor entered.

"As I was saying," Lewandowski continued loudly, "We gotta get more M–14 ammo or we'll be in a world of hurt come next month on Night Patrol. Here, let us help you, Taylor. Hold out you arms so's we can load you up. I'll get that door for you again."

Taylor received what was to become the standardized in–county orientation for the flood of 516th AG replacements that were to arrive over the next six weeks. Eventually he would joyfully join in on the theatrics that were necessary to make such a wonderful thing happen over and over again.

During the weeks ahead, Taylor would be particularly watchful for those few troopers who had an ETS date later than February 27, 1969. For those so honored, his first word would always be "Short".

But that was all in the future.

For now, Taylor was the lone replacement and would remain so for the next three days, during which time he found himself surrounded by Originals who gladly offered helpful suggestions on how to survive the horrors of Night Patrol, while avoiding the bite of Mad Dog Masters.

During his first evening in tent city, after the lights were out and the sounds of distant battles were chilling his soul, Specialist Four Roger K. Taylor found himself lying on his bunk with his eyes wide open, wondering if he would make it through the next year alive. Before dozing off, he said a little prayer, thanking the good Lord for the kindness, wisdom and protection of the Supply Sergeant.

What was his name? Ah, yes. Lewandowski.

Chapter Sixteen

The heavy tailgate was slammed shut and secured when the last of the hold baggage crates had been manhandled onto the cargo bed of the deuce. Lewandowski was ready to make his morning run to the docks to deliver another load of hold baggage for the departing Originals, NCOs and Officers. For the most part, the wooden crates held PX duty–free stereos, tape recorders and other gear that had been purchased with MPC that somehow managed to escape the clutches of the bargirls in the vill. There were rumors that a reckless few had hidden enough dope to keep them stoned or wealthy for years to come. Dope sniffing dogs weren't yet included in the inventory of tools that being used by the military to combat drug use, and nobody was aware of any hold baggage inspections being conducted, so it was a crime begging to happen.

The crates would be tucked away in the cargo holds of ships destined to return to one of several U.S. ports of call, with the hold baggage later being trucked to the scattered addresses of those returning home, finally reaching the owners six to eight weeks later. If the hold baggage didn't arrive within eight to twelve weeks, the addressee could reasonably assume it had been stolen somewhere between here and there.

Lewandowski had six replacements helping him that morning. Most of the replacements were at the personnel center, learning the ropes from the Originals and departing NCO's who had started calling themselves Originals in a belated show of comraderie with the lower ranks.

Replacements were everywhere. Even poor Hanley finally had been allocated a replacement to train. New faces, new voices and new personalities had been flowing into the 516th for the past six weeks, effectively doubling the assignment numbers. Ortega had a Captain to train and Masters was allocated a First Lieutenant. Alter–ego trainees were as common as mice in a wheat field. Lewandowski was being replaced by a Staff Sergeant who didn't take well to the idea of being trained by a draftee short timer, which was just fine with Lewandowski. Leaving the Lifer alone meant he had more time to get his act together during his rapidly dwindling days in–county.

Even the Dirty Dozen had replacements to train, though as yet only eight replacements had performed so poorly at the personnel center that they found themselves being assigned to the construction detail. Regardless, the Dirty Dozen were taking their training responsibilities seriously, doing their best to teach the green peas how to be first–rate gold bricks and general malcontents, so the traditions of the Dirty Dozen would be carried forward.

But the old ways seemed be doomed to disappear. The replacements weren't bound by the brotherhood that made the Originals a unit within a unit within the impersonal enormity of the United States Army. The replacements had arrived in commercial aircraft as individuals from dozens of different stateside assignments, not as a unit. They were strangers who just happened to get thrown together and were forced to rely on the usual bonding agents of race, region and rank…the prototypical three Rs that virtually guaranteed there would be conflict in the months ahead.

Tent city was packed to overflowing with bodies. Meals were being served in two shifts, with Lugo and his crew handling one shift and their replacements taking the next shift. The tents were packed so tight that there was barely enough room to squeeze between the cots.

Masters was having a hard time creating enough busy work to keep all his clerks out of trouble. He was able to create some time consuming projects, with his finest creative moment coming when he assigned Woody the task of writing a history of the 516th AG. Woody complied with a somewhat profane but truthful presentation that made entertaining reading, but would never make it into any official archives. Ortega would get the original copy, with Masters and Woody each getting an onion skin copy.

The Vietnam experience was about to become a historical footnote in the lives of the Originals, or so they thought. They had no way of knowing that the adventures, emotions, and experiences would follow them to their graves, becoming something that couldn't be forgotten.

Most of the Originals had already received their DEROS orders. They knew when and where they were to report for Freedom

Flight processing. They would sign out of the 516th AG log book and sign in at the Repple Depple, where they would be expected to attend morning, noon and evening formations while names were called out when flight orders were ready to be issued. Temporary platoons would be formed. Hurry up and wait. Form up in squads of eight. March to the airfield tarmac. File up the stairs into the aircraft; usually a Boeing 707. Don't touch the stewardesses, watch your language, be a gentleman, do not disgrace the uniform you are wearing. You'll be arriving at a stateside Air Force Base in about 27 hours. You'll then be transported to an Army processing center where you will be given orders for a new assignment, or you will be discharged from active duty. Thank you for visiting Vietnam. We hope you enjoyed your stay.

The Originals with the most distant DEROS dates could look forward to no more than six additional days in–country. Though they arrived as a unit, they would be going home in random Freedom Flights, becoming mere numbers again, products to be moved back to The World by the most efficient means possible.

Lewandowski re–checked the hooks securing the tailgate of the deuce. "Good work," he said to the replacements, and climbed up to the cab.

Lewandowski and Charlie were taking turns driving the hold baggage to the port of Cam Ranh, each taking an entire morning or afternoon to do what could easily be done in two hours. They possessed more time than they wanted. Time would have passed faster if they had something other than busy work to keep them occupied. Better yet, it would have been nice to take a nap and wake up with DEROS orders in hand. *Voila! Get dressed and climb aboard your Freedom Flight.* But that wasn't going to happen. Every minute of every hour of every remaining day had to be endured.

"Woody's waiting in the orderly tent to give you a ride back out to the worksite," Lewandowski said. "The Cap'n may be stopping by, so try to look busy without busting your butts too much."

Lewandowski was considered one of the good guys by the re-placements. He didn't grind it in once he'd done his best to shake them up with outrageous war stories. And he always did it with good humor, so even his dupes could get a laugh out of it once they wised up.

Not all the Originals were as kindly as Lewandowski. Some were angry, embittered by the experience. Louie Donnatelli was one of the angry ones. He'd changed during his tour. Most of the Originals attributed his bad humor to being burned out on dope, but those who knew him best said Louie was convinced that the war was a waste of lives and money, all forever lost, sacrificed for nothing. From Louie's perspective, it was a matter of simple accounting. The bills were piling up and there was no income to show for it. Some day the auditors would show up, and the game would be over.

Lewandowski's thoughts weren't on hold baggage or his short timer status as he drove to the port of Cam Ranh. He was only vaguely aware of the MP's as they waved him through the gate, allowing the deuce to join the flow of jeeps and trucks heading for the piers. He was thinking about something that happened late the afternoon before, when he had gone to the vill to visit Sally at the Saigon Club. Lately, his thoughts had become muddled with emotions he couldn't understand. He had questions with no answers, and answers he didn't want to believe were true. Life was becoming very complicated for Alfred G. Lewandowski.

He joined a line of trucks that were crawling at a snail's pace along a pier walled in on both sides by the rusting hulls of aging freighters. Eventually the line halted, with the truck drivers waiting their turn to be unloaded or loaded by the dozens of sailors and longshoremen working with nets, cranes and winches. Most of the drivers dismounted from their trucks, seeking the shade provided by the looming cargo ships. Several were reading the latest issue of STARS AND STRIPES, but most were chewing the fat, exchanging gossip with drivers from units stationed far beyond the confines of Cam Ranh Bay.

Lewandowski climbed down to join them.

"Do you guys mind if I crowd in line ahead of you today? I got some things I gotta get humpin' on right away."

"Have at it," one of the loungers said. "All you guys can go ahead of me, if you want."

No one other than Lewandowski took him up on the generous

offer. The drivers felt no urgent need to return to their home units. The responses would have been different if sunset were near. The Viet Cong had staged several bloody ambushes on Highway One just outside Cam Ranh the past several weeks, so it was best not to be out when the sun was going down.

Lewandowski asked around. None objected, so he returned to the deuce and drove to the head of the line, where the cargo handlers motioned him forward. Twenty minutes later he was heading for the perimeter gate, where an MP had no trouble recognizing him.

"Nhan Ai again?" the MP asked.

Lewandowski nodded. He was far too tense to engage in the usual small talk, so he kept it short and sweet. "Yeah. Out to Nhan Ai."

"You sure do spend a lot of time out there."

Lewandowski nodded. "Yup, sure do."

"Keep your head down," the MP advised. "Chuck has been taking potshots at traffic lately."

"Check."

Lewandowski was waved onto the tail of a departing convoy. A few minutes later, he turned onto the driveway leading into Nhan Ai with his heart beating faster, his palms greasy with sweat.

Sally wasn't at the Saigon Club when Lewandowski dropped by yesterday. When he asked where she was, he was kissed off by Suzie.

"Sally not here," Suzie said, but offered no additional information.

"Where's she at?" Lewandowski asked. He figured she couldn't be far away, maybe at one of the cafes along the beach. Sally was so big now that she was having trouble walking.

Suzie shrugged, avoiding Lewandowski's eyes. "I doan know where she go."

A thought occurred to him, left him so staggered that he found himself sitting down on the nearest chair. "Did she have the baby, Suzie?"

Suzie looked away. "I doan know notting."

He could feel the anger rising. "What do you mean, you doan know notting?" he demanded. "You know a helluva lot more than you're telling me now, Suzie. Is she sick? Where is she?"

Suziee flinched, but wouldn't back down. She knew how to handle GI's in all their many moods. She looked at him with fire in her eyes, returning anger with anger.

"Sally doan wan' me to say notting to nobody. She go'way, doan wan' no one to know where she go."

"Not even me?" Lewandowski asked.

"Not you, not nobody," Suzie answered.

Several other girls had been looking from Lewandowski to Suzie with sympathetic expressions. One of them spoke to Suzie in Vietnamese, and a brief argument followed. Suzie seemed to be losing when more girls began to join in, with none of them appearing to take Suzie's side. The sharp edge was gone when Suzie spoke to Lewandowski again.

"Sally go'way from Cam Ranh to have babysan," she explained, continuing to avoid eye contact. "She nevah come back, I t'ink."

Suzie continued as tears welled up in her eyes. "She doan wanna t'ink 'bou' Cam Ranh no more. She say she go home to be with mommasan and poppasan for her."

Lewandowski said nothing for several moments. When he did speak, it was to cuss under his breath. It hurt…it really did hurt that she didn't say good–bye and was trying to exclude him from something so important. She should have at least let him know she would be leaving; she owed him that much. Then he remembered a time when she told him that her parents lived down south, near Saigon in a fishing Village, a distance that would have been impossible for her to travel in her condition.

Lewandowski turned to one of the more sympathetic girls with his question. "Did Sally go to Nhan Ai?"

The girl looked confused, glanced at Suzie, then shook her head with her eyes turned downward, as though shamed by her answer.

Lewandowski turned to Suzie for confirmation. "She went to Nhan Ai, didn't she?"

Suzie looked away. "I doan know notting. Sally go 'way. I doan tell you notting more."

Lewandowski rose from the chair. It was too late to get out to Nhan Ai that afternoon. It would have to wait until tomorrow morning, when he made the baggage run.

He spoke to Suzie on his way out. "If Sally asks me, I'll tell her you doan tell me notting."

Suzie nodded. "Okay. Cam ung (thank you)."

Lewandowski left the Saigon Club with a heavy weight of nagging, unanswered questions. Not only about Sally, but about himself, what kind of man he was.

Now within minutes of arriving at Nhan Ai, his mind was filled to overflowing with the unanswered questions. First: Was Sally alright? Next: Would Mother Marie–Teresa let him see her? Did she have the baby? Who does the baby look like? Does it look like me? What will I do if it does look like me? What will I do if it doesn't? What if it is black?

He allowed the deuce to idle into the churchyard and parked a few yards from the front steps of the chapel. He was climbing down from the cab when Mother Marie–Teresa and another nun came out to greet him with their usual chaste embraces. Mother M–T looked deep into his troubled face and immediately adjusted to the needs of the moment.

"Sergeant Lewandowski, is something wrong? You look very unhappy. What can we do to help you?"

Lewandowski tried to speak, but his voice wavered. He cleared his throat, waited a moment, and began again.

"Ma'am, yesterday I was told that a girl from the Vill came here to have her baby. Her name is Sally, ma'am. That's how I know her, anyway. If she's here, I just wanna make sure she's alright. And the baby, too, if she's had the baby."

She touched his arm, her expression filled with concern. "We had a visiting mother, but I cannot say if it was this girl you call Sally. They do not use their American names when they come here."

Lewandowski was at a loss. Sally never told him her Vietnamese name. She was always just Sally...good ole Sally.

"Is she kinda thin, with a real pretty face?" he asked.

She hesitated. "I have never had this happen before, Sergeant. I do not know what to say to you. We are here to protect the privacy as well as the health of the mothers and the children."

"Could you ask her if she is the girl I know as Sally?" He was on the verge of pleading, if necessary. "If she is, then I'd like to talk to her, if she'll see me."

"Tell me, Sergeant...was she your lover?"

Lewandowski nodded, feeling shame he hadn't expected. He could have defended himself by saying he was one of many customer, but that would have been so disrespectful of Sally. Defending himself would have only cheapened the truth, which was that he had been Sally's only true lover. He didn't fully understand the why's of it, but Sally had managed to become very important to him. He didn't know if it was love or not, but it was so powerful that love likely would have been fatal if it was any stronger than this. Without Sally, he might have become as bitter as Louie Donnatelli, searching for solace from drugs rather than a young woman who made him feel good about himself. Without Sally, Lewandowski realized he might well be as strung–out as Louie.

He couldn't shake the feeling that she needed him now, even if she didn't want to see him. And he knew he needed her, even if he didn't understand why. Logic was telling him that she was just another Cam Ranh bargirl, but that voice was infinitely weaker than the emotions that were saying she was much more than that.

Mother M–T patted his arm. "Wait here. We will return very soon."

He nodded. "Yes, ma'am."

Lewandowski watched as the two nuns crossed the churchyard to a single–story clapboard structure of type 'B' Cam Ranh design. Nothing fancy, but certainly strong and highly functional. It had been christened for use as the Nhan Ai medical dispensary, serving the civilian population for miles around. Army and Air Force medical personnel had started making regular day trips out to Nhan Ai, offering free inoculations and outpatient services. Sally had chosen wisely if this was where she decided to have her babysan.

The churchyard had been vacant when Lewandowski arrived, but that changed when the nuns allowed the children to leave the classrooms for a recess. Shrieks of glee suddenly filled the churchyard and Lewandowski found himself smiling when the children ran his way, eager to be among the first to touch him. The kids were like troops on R&R, with only limited time to enjoy themselves. Every moment of freedom would be used to the max.

The older kids held out their hands palms up to be slapped by Lewandowski, with the small ones hovering around his meaty thighs. The more outgoing of the older kids used the moment to practice their American slang.

"What's happening, man?"

"How you doing, man?"

"What's up?"

"Right on, gimme five, man."

While others preferred to use the formal English they were being taught in the classroom.

"It is very good to see you," a girl said, offering her hand as she spoke. "How have you been, Sergeant?"

And some who were not yet so adept at the language.

"You are happy to see me today."

Lewandowski didn't have the heart to correct the grammatical errors. He left that sort of thing up to the nuns and the GI's who were better teachers than himself. Besides, his own lame attempts at Vietnamese were so pitifully inadequate that he felt he had no business telling any kid that he had screwed–up when giving English the old college try.

A short while later Mother Marie–Teresa stepped out of the dispensary and returned to Lewandowski, scattering the children with gentle words as she neared his side. When they were alone, she took his arm in hers and began guiding him toward the dispensary.

"You must know some things before I take you inside," she began with a gentle but sensible manner. "The girl you know as Sally is known to us as Nguyen Minh Kien. She had heard from others that we could help her. When she arrived, she wasn't feeling very well. We cannot always have a doctor here to help us, but in Miss Kien's case we were able to do that. We sent word to Cam Ranh and an Army doctor came out on his own time to deliver the baby. Without him, we might have lost both the mother and the child. It was a very difficult delivery for both of them."

She paused midway to the dispensary. "Miss Tien is not a large person, as you know, but the baby was unusually large." She noted Lewandowski's sudden intake of breath, but continued as though nothing had happened. "Early this morning she gave birth to a baby girl that she has since named Nguyen Mai Chi."

"Is she alright?" Lewandowski asked.

"Both are doing very well," she answered. She observed Lewandowski's reaction with a sideward glance, recognizing relief among the many other emotions.

She plunged forward with a question of her own. "Pardon me, Sergeant, but I must know. Do you believe you are the father of this child?"

Lewandowski paused to take a deep breath before answering. It was one of the questions he feared, but was relieved that it was coming out into the open.

"I don't know," he answered. Emotions he wasn't prepared to handle were beginning to surface. His voice was thick as he continued. "Maybe...I don't know. I came out here hoping I'd find out one way or the other. I thought maybe I could talk to Sally or look at the baby and know, but it won't be that easy, will it?"

She touched his hand and Lewandowski began to cry. He paused to turn away, shamed by the tears, and she acted instinctively, wrapping her arms around him, offering what comfort she could until he regained control.

She stepped back to say what she believed had to be said. "You are right, Sergeant. You will not leave here knowing anything for certain. I am sorry. I wish it were that simple, but newborn infants look more like each other than they do their mothers or fathers. They are all small, they are all wrinkled, and they all have tiny faces. You would have difficulty recognizing her as your own even if you knew the child was yours."

"And if you did know the child was yours, what would you do?" she asked. When Lewandowski didn't answer, she continued. "Would you marry the mother for the sake of the child? Would you take Miss Tien to America and be a good husband and father, knowing as you do that you were one of many? If you did take her home, would she be happy in America? She would have no one there; no family and no friends. And there is religion to think of, too.

She is Buddhist, and you are Christian. The differences are greater than you think. She thinks like a Vietnamese Buddhist, and you think like an American Christian. It would be a marriage that requires difficult adjustments under the best of circumstances, and it would be very unlikely to succeed if you and she haven't thought everything through and discussed it very thoroughly. Have you done all that, Sergeant?"

Lewandowski shook his head.

She patted his arm. "You are an intelligent man, Sergeant. You would be marrying her for the wrong reasons. Sometimes it is better to leave things as they are. Fewer people will be hurt. I think she knows that is true. Otherwise, why did she not want you to know she is here at Nhan Ai."

She resumed leading him to the dispensary. "I have always told you I thought you were a good man, and today you have shown me that I did not misjudge you. You are a very good man, Sergeant Lewandowski. You have a good heart. And now you must use it to make Miss Tien feel good about herself and her baby. Are you ready to do that?"

Lewandowski cleared his eyes with his sleeve. "Yeah, I guess so, ma'am."

"Good. I want you to show her the love that is within you, Sergeant Lewandowski. Show her that you are proud of her, that you think she is beautiful and the baby looks just like her. If you can do that, it will help her more than any medicine I could give. She is a very sad and lonely young woman right now, and that worries me more than all else. Try to make her happy, but do not lie to make it happen. Underneath her sadness and loneliness, she is strong."

She led Lewandowski inside. "Miss Kien is our only patient at the moment. "You can speak to her alone."

She left him standing just inside the doorway.

Lewandowski took another step inside the dimly lit interior and paused to look around, allowing his eyes to adjust. There was a long line of Army cots on either side of a central isle, with an overhead framework holding mosquito netting for each cot. The netting was folded up and out of the way over all but one of the cots, where the netting created a semi–private niche for the patient. He looked closer and could make out the vague form of Sally sitting upright on her mattress, her back and neck supported by a mound of Army–issue pillows. She was holding the baby in her arms, the face of the child hidden by nursery blankets.

"Hi," Lewandowski said.

Sally smiled and lifted the edge of the mosquito netting. "Come, mon oi, and put dis up for me, please, so we can see each other."

He walked to her bedside and lifted the mosquito netting, securing it to the overhead framework. He reached out and gently touched her cheek. Sally looked very pretty, very feminine in a white nightgown that was far too expensive and frilly to have been supplied by the nuns.

"Hi," she said.

"How are you?" he asked.

"Very good," she said quietly. "Sit here so I can see you bettah, mon oi. See, there is chair for you."

Lewandowski sat on the chair, his eyes on Sally. She seemed flawless, beautiful. "Why didn't you want to see me?"

She glanced down at the baby, hiding her eyes. "I doan know. I was dingydow, I t'ink. Very sick. I doan wanna see nobody when I say it before to Suzie."

Suddenly, she brightened. "Look at the baby, mon oi. She is very beautiful, I t'ink." She uncovered the face, allowing Lewandowski his first glimpse.

"She is beautiful," he said and found himself wondering if the tiny pug nose might be a copy of his own. He hoped it wasn't. He wouldn't want to wish his looks on any girl.

She had light brown hair that wasn't at all Vietnamese, and her skin tone was a touch lighter than Sally's. She was sleeping with her eyes squinted shut against the intruding light.

Lewandowski looked at Sally, confused by his emotions. "Dep lum," he said. "You're very beautiful too, mon oi."

"Cam ung," she whispered with a slight smile. "I am happy you come to see me, mon oi. Before, I t'ink it bettah not to see you. Ever'time I t'ink of saying good–bye to you, I cry too much. Alla time I cry. I tell girls at Saigon Club to doan tell you notting, but now I t'ink it is very good you come see me."

She smiled a moment longer and turned away, weeping silently while Lewandowski felt helpless. He didn't know what to say, so he said nothing. When the tears were over, she wiped her eyes with a corner of the baby blanket.

"She sleep alla time," Sally announced, straining out a smile. "Would you like to hold her, mon oi?"

Lewandowski nodded. "Yeah, that would be nice."

Sally lifted the baby to his arms with a smile that was now warm and contented. She was collecting a mountain of memories.

Lewandowski chuckled as he gazed down upon the tiny face. "Choi oi! This is something else...incredible, amazing. Jeeze, I can hardly feel her. She's so small, mon oi."

Sally smiled indulgently. "Not for me, mon oi. She is very big for Vietnamee baby." She felt very contented. Everything was good for her at this moment in time.

Lewandowski slowly rocked the baby, captivated by the wrinkled face. When he glanced at Sally, he found her watching him.

"You look very happy, mon oi," he said.

She nodded. "I am happy."

Silence followed. Eventually Lewandowski found the courage to seek the answer to one of his questions. "What are you going to do now, Sally?"

The baby started to fuss.

Sally reached for the bundle, "She is hungry, I t'ink." And opened the bodice of her gown to offer her left breast.

Lewandowski looked away, embarrassed by the private–personal, mother–stuff of the feeding. The Sally from the Saigon Club was nothing like this girl.

"I name her Mai Chi," Sally explained as the baby suckled. "It is name for very pretty flower."

When the baby stopped feeding, Sally replaced the blanket over her face.

"She will sleep now," Sally explained as she returned her full attention to Lewandowski with a smile that was perhaps a tad too brave.

Lewandowski nodded that he understood.

Sally began straightening the blanket covering her lap. "Very soon I will go home to see my family," she announced. "It will be very good for them to see the baby, I t'ink."

Her voice faltered and she turned away, reaching for the baby blanket to cover her tears. She wept for several moments, then abruptly called on the brave smile for a return engagement.

"Tea time," Mother Marie–Teresa announced as she entered with a tray of tea service and pastries.

Lewandowski was thinking she couldn't have picked a better time to interrupt. He couldn't handle Sally's tears, and there was nothing he could truthfully say that would make them disappear. It was one of those crummy moments in life when the truth was painful and lies would only increase the pain in the long run. Mother M–T was right.

Sally assumed the role of hostess, making sure Lewandowski had plenty of tea and pastries while Mother M–T showered Mai Chi with attention at the far end of the dispensary. It was an uncomfortable time for Lewandowski. He would have preferred having other Originals with him to remove himself from the center of attention. He felt like a fool for not getting to know the real Sally. He thought he had her figured out, but he was about as wrong as a guy could be. She was in her element now, a natural born mother.

"I'll take the baby with me and leave you alone," Mother M–T announced when another nun retrieved the tea service. "You need to get some sleep, Miss Tien."

She turned to Lewandowski. "Don't keep her much longer, Sergeant. She needs her sleep."

Lewandowski nodded. "Yes, ma'am. I'll be leaving real soon. I won't be much longer."

Sally looked like she was about to cry again, so he reached for her hand. "Have the girls from the Saigon Club been here to see you?"

Sally smiled, relieved to have something neutral to talk about. "They come tomorrow, I t'ink. It will be good to see them. I miss them very much. They are very good frien's for me."

Silence followed, finally broken by Sally. "Charlie and other frien's for you, are they okay, too?"

"Oh, yeah. They're doing great. No suweat. They're very happy about being Short."

She nodded, knowing the meaning of the word all too well. She could have cried again, but she laughed instead. "You doan have no fun wid'out me at Saigon Club, huh?"

Lewandowski laughed with her. "You got it. Without you, there's no fun at the Saigon Club."

Another silence followed as Lewandowski tried to put together words that needed to be said. Finally he took her hand. "I'll be going home to America very soon, mon oi."

She immediately started to cry. "I know, but I doan wan' you to talk about same, you unnerstan'? I doan wanna hear that ki'na talk," she pleaded.

"I wish we could have known each other some other place," Lewandowski said. "Maybe it would'a worked out alright then."

She reached to touch his face. "I know what you say is true, mon oi. I t'ink you love me the same I love you, but ever'ting no good for us now."

"Everything about this war sucks," he said bitterly.

"Doan talk bad, mon oi. It not good for you." She touched his face again. "There is very old Vietnamee story about a boy and a girl who love each other very much. Can I tell you now? It doan take so long."

"Yeah, sure. Go ahead."

"Okay, dis boy an dis girl, they love each other very much, but mother for boy and mother for girl say they cannot be togedder. They must marry other people."

Lewandowski reached to hold her hand.

"So the girl marry a dif'rent boy and the boy marry a dif'rent girl. And they live to be very old, but they nevah forget each other. They always love each other."

"When they get very old, the girl pray to Buddha. She say...'I always be very good, I nevah try to hurt nobody. Now maybe when I die, you let me be with boy I love.' An Buddha listen and he t'ink it is true, so he say to her...'You will be with boy you love when you come back after you die.' "

Sally paused. "I don't know how to say in English, but after she die she will come back. Do you unnerstand' what I say, mon oi?"

Lewandowski nodded. "Yes, I do."

She nodded. "So, the boy, he die furst and Buddha make him a very pretty flower, all by himself. He is very beautiful. He doan hurt nobody and nobody hurt him. He is very happy now. He doan feel sad no more. Then the girl, she die and Buddha make her a flower just the same as the boy, so they can be togedder just like this."

Sally reached for Lewandowski's hand, placing the small first finger of her hand against the much larger first finger of Lewandowski's hand. "They be like that. Two flower togedder forevah. Very happy, very beautiful."

Lewandowski smiled. "I like that story."

Sally nodded. "Me, too, mon oi. I t'ink maybe you and me are like boy and girl in the story. I love you and you love me just the same, but I doan t'ink we can evah be togedder."

Lewsandowski pondered the thought and nodded. "You're a helluva gal, Sally."

"Is that how you say I love you? You nevah say to me in English before, mon oi."

Lewandowski smiled. "Yeah, I guess it is my way of saying it. I do love you, Sally." He leaned over to kiss both her cheeks, her forehead, her chin, then her lips.

"I love you, Lewandowski. I love you very much. Anh neu em eu lum."

"And I love you, Miss Tien."

She brightened. "You know my Vietnamee name now, huh?"

"Yup, sure do."

She continued to smile. "Will you come back to see me again before you go?"

He nodded. "For sure. Every day I'm here, I'll be back. I promise."

"You better come see me and babysan, or I cockadow you," she warned, drawing one finger across her throat with an exaggerated scowl.

"Don't worry, I'll be here. You better get some sleep now. I want you feeling better when I come back."

"Kiss me one more time before you go," she begged. "Please. I doan ask you for no more kisses if you kiss me now."

When he leaned over to kiss her, she whispered…"I wan' to make love to you very much, but I canno' do now. You unnerstan', doan you?"

He winked. "You're making me horney, mon oi."

She giggled. "Mmmm, me too, I t'ink."

Lewandowski kissed her forehead. "Anh neu em."

"Anh neu em," she said in return.

Lewandowski stood. "I'll be back as soon as I can."

"You bettah," she teased.

Chapter Seventeen

The exodus was about to begin. Fifty–nine Originals and three NCOs were scheduled to report to the Repple Depple at 0900 hours the next morning, with another 25 Originals and two NCOs scheduled to report at 1300 hours, and 18 more Originals reporting at 1700 hours. The following days would see the evacuation of the remaining members of the original 516th Adjutant General Personnel Services Company, with the officers being among the last to go. Day one could finally be colored in for the 189 short timer calendars that had been maintained throughout tent city and the personnel center.

If there were to be a final, final short timers party, it had to be a party to remember, and it had to be now, before the exodus began.

And so it would be. There would be no separate parties for the officers or the NCOs. They would party out as they as they came in; as a unit. All prior short timer's parties were mere practice runs for this, the Big Kahuna of parties.

Vows to party all night had been made, though few were likely to be kept. The Army didn't take kindly to troops showing up half stewed for final processing at the Repple Depple. Lewandowski, Numbnuts Bolton, Hillbilly, and Skins would be in the first wave of Freedom Flights. Charlie Edwards, Frenchie, and Louie Donnatelli would be leaving later that day, followed by Jackson, Peters, Mr. Mobley and CW2 Conners, who would remain a sycophant pain in the patootie until he was six feet under. Major Ortega and Captain Masters would be leaving in the final wave.

All the Originals were openly counting the hours now. Even the officers. Those who were particularly inclined toward mathematics, including Donnatelli, could recite the minutes remaining to their reporting time. Most would be flown to Travis Air Force Base in California and later bused to the Oakland Army Terminal, where they would encounter their first protestors carrying signs that called them baby killers. It was all very legal because the words were protected by the same Constitution the returning troops had vowed to protect.

"Hey, Hey, GI Joe, how many babies did you kill today?"

More than a few returning veterans would wish they could arrange for the protestors to do a tour in 'Nam, but it was just a passing thought, an idea that wasn't workable. Soldiers must be able to rely on each other, and the dudes and dudettes with the hand–lettered signs were so totally self–possessed that they couldn't be trusted with the lives of others.

With so little time remaining to their two–year obligations, the Originals would be discharged at the Oakland Army Terminal, exit the gates, and hail cabs to the airport as bonafide civilians.

The homecoming for many Viet vets would prove disappointing. Most of them would feel alienated from The World to which they had longed to return. They would miss the comradeship and excitement, forgetting the guys that got under their skin, and the boredom that ruled between the short bursts of adrenaline. Life back in the World would seem tame, boring, and predictable, and they would find themselves surrounded by people who couldn't possibly understand. So, they would keep their stories to themselves, hiding the horrors in dark closets at the back of their minds, allowing the monsters to grow larger and stronger, until they couldn't be controlled any more. The "experts" would eventually create a name for the condition, which would be called Post Traumatic Stress Disorder.

Masters and Ortega reached deep to buy a hundred cases of beer and four cases of whiskey for the party. Lewandowski scrounged the steaks and chicken as his final act as a larcenous, wheeling–dealing Supply Sergeant. His list of contacts would be departing with him, with the various elements of the vast Cam Ranh underground economy being guaranteed anonymity. It would have been tantamount to self–incrimination if he had passed along his knowledge to the Staff Sergeant who was inheriting the supply tent.

The personal farewells had already been said. Most found it surprisingly difficult to find the words to express themselves. There was the predictable euphoria connected to being within hours of going home, but they were being blindsided by a sadness they hadn't expected. But cowboys don't cry, so no one—not even Charlie Edwards—spoke of the sadness that was residing just under the joy. Addresses and phone numbers were exchanged, along with promises to stay in touch, but it would never be the same again. No reunion would be real without the thump of incoming and outgoing rounds, the screech of F–4 Phantoms, gunships, shithouses, pisstubes, reveille formations and Sgt Lugo's Shit On a Shingle.

"They're calling us baby–killers now, y'know" Charlie said a couple of evenings before in the supply tent, just after lights out.

Lewandowski had been about to doze off. "Huh? What'd you say?"

"They're calling us baby killers now," Charlie repeated. "The war protestors, I mean. My brother told me about it in the letter I got today. He wanted me to know about it so I could be prepared when I got home."

Lewandowski laughed humorlessly. "Baby killers, huh? I'd say they got their facts a little backassedwards. We're making a helluva lot more babies than we're killing."

Charlie had been out to Nhan Ai to visit Sally with Lewandowski that day. She was full of life, able to move about some now that her strength was coming back. She asked about Charlie's plans for the future.

"Oh, I'll go back to school, I guess," he said.

"School?" she asked. "What ki'na school?"

"I'm gonna be a psychologist," Charlie said.

"Si–what? No bic, Sharly."

"A doctor for dingydow people," Charlie explained.

Sally was very impressed. "Oh, maybe you come back Vietnam some day. We have beau ceau dingydow people here."

"I was thinking of California or New York City," Charlie said. "They have lots of dingydows with lots of money."

"Oh, very good," Sally said. "You get very rich, huh?"

"He'll be spending all that money on head doctors for himself," Lewandowski predicted with a dry chuckle. "Ole Charlie here is as dingydow as they come."

Lewandowski made his final visit by himself the morning of the Final–Final–Final short timer's party. There wasn't much conversation during the short visit. Nor were there any tears. He had given Mother M–T three hundred dollars MPC that she was to give to Sally after he had gone. It was all the cash he could flash after twelve months in Vietnam.

"Do you want me to write letters to you?" he asked.

Sally shook her head. "No, I doan t'ink so. VC everywhere, mon oi. They see letter from you, I t'ink maybe they try to hurt me and Mai Chi. Is bettah for you to go away and forget about me."

He shook his head. "I can't do that, mon oi. I'll never be able to forget you."

She smiled, pleased with his answer.

"I nevah forget you," Sally promised as she reached for his hand.

They held hands for several minutes without talking.

"When are you going home?" he asked to break the silence.

"When do you go?" she asked.

"Tomorrow morning."

"Then I go tomorrow, too. I pray to Buddha to make you happy."

"I don't do much praying, but I'll say some words for you," Lewandowski promised.

Sally nodded, starting to tear–up. "We will miss you, Mai Chi and me."

Lewandowski didn't want to endure the tears, and Charlie was waiting outside in the deuce, so he stood, letting her know it was time to be on his way.

"You take care of yourself," he said. "Do me one favor. Don't ever go back to the Saigon Club. It's no good for you, mon oi."

She smiled, but made no promises. Lewandowski was a good man, but he didn't understand. She had sent most of her money to her mother and father when she worked at the Saigon Club. Now she had baby Mai Chi to think about, and she wanted Mai Chi to have good food, and good clothes, and someday go to a good school, and all of that takes beau ceau money. She would have to return to the Saigon Club, or maybe go to Saigon itself and join the thousands of other pretty girls who needed money. But it wasn't all bad. She was certain the suffering she experienced now would make her future lives better. It wasn't a matter of choice, so much as karma. If she must suffer, she would suffer well.

"Kiss me before you go," she said.

Lewandowski leaned over to kiss her cheek, then reached for

Mai Chi to give her chubby cheek a quick kiss. He didn't want to say good–bye, so he didn't. He just turned and walked away without looking back.

"What'll you do if they call you a baby killer?" Charlie asked Lewandowski the night before the Final–Final–Final party.

"Prob'ly nothing," Lewandowski answered. "They wouldn't listen to me, anyway. They think they got everything figured out. They think we're the bad guys, Charlie, and we ain't gonna change their minds. You see, they're running scared and you can't reason with people that are scared. I tell ya what pisses me off the most. It's that they think I'm for the war when it ain't true. I never met one guy in–country that was really for the war."

"Slater," Charlie suggested.

"Ah, Slater. He was full of it. You can't count him. But I'll tell you what, bad as Slater was, he's a one helluva lot better man than those bastards heading for Canada and Europe to get out'a the draft. They don't fool me for a second with their talk of peace and love, and shit like that. They're just afraid of getting their asses shot off over here. They're just looking out for Number One."

"My brother is one of them now," Charlie said. "That's why he wrote...he said he didn't want me to take it personal, he knows I'm not a baby killer, but he's heading for Canada."

"How the hell else are you gonna take it except personal?" Lewandowski asked.

"Would you do it over, knowing what you do now?" Charlie asked.

"If nothing changed, yeah I'd do most of it over," Lewandowski said. "I don't know what I'd do if I figured I'd get my ass blown away, like that kid we met in the Saigon Club. I wonder if he's still alive."

"Do you remember when he talked about what he wanted to do when he got back to The World?" Charlie asked. "He said he was gonna drive big rigs, like his dad."

"Yeah, what of it?"

"He was making plans," Charlie said. "He hadn't given up hope yet."

"Okay, so what's your point?"

"Think back, months ago, when we first came in–country, when we talked about whether or not we could handle it…getting hit every night, or the rice paddies and jungle, knowing you could buy the farm at any time?"

"Yeah?"

"I think I got it figured out. If we'd gotten a shitty assignment, we would've adjusted to it, just like that kid. I mean, who wants to be the only one who chickens out? It's easier to go with the flow and charge up that hill, hold that line. Its what we're trained to do from childhood. Girls have babies and boys go to war."

"If yer saying we got no way out, that they got us coming and going no matter what we do, then you got my vote," Lewandowski said. "There's no way out. Even so, I'd rather be here than in Canada. I couldn't live with myself if I did that."

"We do what we gotta do, and we hope for the best," Charlie said. "We adjust. I figure the guys who lose hope already have body bags with their names on them. The kid was keeping his hopes alive by talking about driving the big rigs. He was adjusting, he was giving himself a reason to believe he'd make it out alive, no matter what happened to everyone around him."

"Except for that battle, when he figured he was gonna die for sure," Lewandowski said.

"I don't know about that," Charlie said. "Maybe we have a part of our minds that takes over in situations like that and shuts down the emotions that could get us killed, so we can think better, protect ourselves better. Maybe the adrenaline does it. We're only just beginning to understand the human mind. That's the last frontier, Lew. It's between our ears, not out in space."

"God, I wish I could remember his name," Lewandowski said.

"Me, too."

"Oh well, that's life," Lewandowski said.

"FTA and Short," Charlie answered.

"Right on. FTA and Short."

"Goodnight, Lew."

"Goodnight, Charlie."

"I never thought I'd say it, but I'm gonna miss you."

"Aw, shuddup."

The Final–Final–Final short timer's party started early in the afternoon with three jeep trailers of iced beer, four barbecues and enough booze to flow like water. There was plenty of rowdy talk about hitting the streets back in the World, and some of the farewells started getting melancholy and unbearably mushy as the afternoon evolved into early evening. Good times were being recalled, with the bad times taking on a sepia tint that made even those moments seem good. The party was threatening to become an Irish wake until the rowdy ones took control and started an off–key medley of songs that had special meaning to those who had done their time in Vietnam.

The first tune was a natural for short timers:
GIMME A TICKET ON AN AERO–PLANE,
AIN'T GOT TIME FOR A FAST TRAIN.
LONELY DAYS ARE GONE,
I'M'A'GOIN' HOME.
MY BABY, SHE WROTE ME A LETTER.
Followed by a bit of Peter, Paul and Mary:
OH, I'M LEAVIN' ON A JET PLANE,
DON'T KNOW WHEN I'LL BE BACK AGAIN.
"NEVER!"
"NO WAY!"
"YOU GOTTA CATCH ME NEXT TIME!"
"F.T.A.!"

Which naturally led into yet another appropriate song.
WE GOTTA GET OUT'A THIS PLACE,
IF IT'S THE LAST THING WE EV–VER DO.
WE GOTTA GET OUT'A THIS PLACE.
GIRL, THERE'S A BETTER LAND FOR ME'N'YOU.
Once more, with feeling:
WE GOTTA GET OUT'A THIS PLACE
IF IT'S THE LAST THING WE EV–VER DO.
WE GOTTA GET OUT'A THIS PLACE.
GIRL, THERE'S A BETTER LAND FOR ME'N'YOU.
"RIGHT ON, RIGHT ON!"

"LEMME OUT'A THIS PLACE!"

"WATCH MY DUST, MAN!"

"I AM GONE!"

"HEY, YOU SHITHEADS," Lewandowski shouted. "WE GOTTA SING SOMETHING FOR THE ARMY!"

"GO TO HELL, LEWANDOWSKI!"

"LIFER!"

"LIFER!"

Ignoring his critics, Lewandowski commenced shouting his lyrics of choice, with the others joining in when they caught his drift:

WHO'S THE LEADER OF THE CLUB THAT'S MADE FOR YOU AND ME?

M–I–C, K–E–Y, M–O–U–S–E!!

COME ALONG AND SING OUR SONG AND JOIN OUR JAMBOREE

M–I–C, K–E–Y, M–O–U–S–E!!

The singing began dying off the second time around the ensemble of in–country hits. On to something new, keep the party moving, folks! About that time, Lewandowski sought the solitude of the sand dune for the final time in his tour, the final time in his life.

But the moments of solitude were to be short lived. Masters approached from below with two cans of beer, handing one to Lewandowski. "Lemme buy you a beer," he said.

In silence, they inspected tent city from afar.

Finally Lewandowski spoke. "It's been quite a year, hasn't it, Sir."

"Yes, Sir, it has," Masters answered.

Lewandowksi caught the 'Sir', but figured it was just a slip of the tongue.

Masters pointed with his can to the night sky. "Freedom Flight over there…just lifting off from the airbase."

Lewandowski nodded. "Yup. But for once, I don't envy those guys. Tonight is theirs, tomorrow is mine. There's no need to get pushy at the front of the line."

Another pause followed.

Masters spoke first this time. "Y'know, you were a pretty damned good soldier, Lewandowski. I mean that as a compliment."

"Hmm...I didn't expect that," Lewandowski said. "I suppose I owe you one now."

"That would be nice," Masters admitted dryly.

"Oh, well, I guess it won't hurt now that I'm leaving," Lewandowski said. "You were a pretty damned good officer, Sir. In fact, you were awful damned good. It couldn't have been a piece of cake putting up with us all year. You took a lot of crap...."

"And handed out some of my own," Masters added with a dry laugh.

"Boy, you got that right," Lewandowski admitted. "But taking everything into consideration, I'd say you handled the situation about as good as anyone could."

"I take that as high praise, coming from you," Masters said. "Thanks, Lew. It means more than you know. Sometimes even officers wanna chuck it all. Not often, but sometimes. I'm just glad I didn't have to court martial anyone. Especially you, with the way you were fracturing regulations to keep us in tent city."

Lewandowski chuckled. "You figured that out, huh?"

"I would've done the same thing in your boots," Masters said without hesitation. "The fact is, the Major and I were pulling for you all along. We wanted to keep the unit in tent city, but we couldn't let on. Orders are orders."

"Most other officers would have busted me a long time ago," Lewandowski said. "I owe you one for letting me skate by."

"Naw, you don't. Not for that," Masters said. "You did your job. I wanted to keep you just where you were, doing what you were doing. You made my life a lot easier than it would have been with someone who played by the book. God, do you remember Slater?"

Lewandowski chuckled. "I wonder what happened to him in the Big Red One."

Masters sighed. "Who knows, maybe he learned his lesson." He paused. "I just wanted to be sure I touched bases with you before we headed our separate ways, Lew."

"Thanks. I'm glad you did."

"No suweat, GI."

"The guys're really hanging one on tonight, Sir."

"Call me Bill," Masters said. "That is, if you promise not to re–

enlist and show up in some future command of mine. If that's in your plans, it's back to 'yes, Sir' and 'no, Sir'."

"In that case it's Bill," Lewandowski said. "Next time they'll have to come after me with a gun and a net."

They watched the perimeter light show in silence for several moments.

"I heard about the baby," Masters said without prologue.

"GI's are worse'n gossipy old women," Lewandowski said sourly. "What'd you hear, that it is mine?"

"That...and I heard that you had no way of knowing, which I took to be the most likely case. Either way, I thought it might help if you knew I went through something similar six years ago, when I was stationed in Korea. It isn't easy. At least it wasn't for me, and I figure you're the kind of guy who can't just kiss it off, either. I wanted you to know I think you did the right thing by being there."

"Thanks," Lewandowski said, genuinely touched. "I appreciate it. I've been feeling pretty down lately."

"You did the right thing," Masters assured him.

"I don't know about that. Maybe there's no really right thing I could do."

"Probably not," Masters agreed. "On a brighter note, you did manage to make this a year to remember."

Masters held out his hand.

Lewandowski reciprocated. "Someday I'd like to tell you a few stories. But not until I'm out'a uniform."

They began walking down the hill together.

"That sounds like a plan," Masters agreed. "Maybe I can come up with a few stories of my own."

"I'll bet you could."

"I was on to you the whole time," Masters said.

Lewandowski chuckled. "Something tells me you were one crazy sonofabitch before you got your commission."

"You would've eaten me alive if I hadn't earned a few notches on my own," Masters confided.

"Lemme buy you the next one," Lewandowski offered as he tossed his empty beer can toward a growing pile of litter that WOULD be policed up after reveille formation tomorrow morning, regardless of hangovers.

"Sounds good," Masters agreed, adding his own can to the pile.

Together, they headed for the nearest jeep trailer for refills of iced beer.

Frenchie and Skins were observing from afar.

"Hey, man," Frenchie said. "Look at that. I never would'a be-lieved it. They look like they're asshole buddies or somethin', man."

"No mu'fuh' schit," Skins agreed drunkenly.

"Hey, y'know what?" Frenchie said. "I bet Lewandowski re-upped and he's scared we'll find out and give him a hard time."

"Yeah," Skins said. "I always figgered him for a muh'fuh' Lifer."

"What say we get ole Lew over here later on and give him a ration of shit."

Skins belched. "Muh'fuh right, man."

Beyond the perimeter, an F–4 Phantom dropped canisters of napalm on a Viet Cong position, then veered away to where a mountaintop radio relay unit was being hit by incoming mortar fire. Further inland, a 17th Aviation Group medivac chopper was being lost to groundfire, with all seven aboard Killed In Action.

In the not so distant future, Major Ortega would receive a medical discharge from battle wounds suffered during Operation Kennedy in 1969. After discharge, he would return to his childhood home in New Mexico and buy a small ranchero to breed quarter horses.

Lewandowski would return to college and football, but it wouldn't be the same. He had learned not to be so trusting of authority figures, including football coaches and the wind sprints they demanded. His experiences in the college classroom on the GI Bill would reflect his newfound cynicism. He would dare argue with the anti–war professors, which only convinced them he was just another reactionary baby killer, a Vietnam Vet suffering from flashbacks, probably a drug addict. He changed his major from Phys Ed to Education and eventually became a high school history teacher in inner–city LA.

Hillbilly would eventually earn a professorship in the Anthropology department at Old Miss. Charlie Edwards would expand the pool of knowledge for humankind by writing his Doctoral thesis on breast deprivation induced psycho–trauma. Woody Woods would become a best–selling romance author under a feminine pseudonym. Hanley opened a biker bar in a St. Louis suburb. Conners was loathed by one and all until he retired in 1978. Numbnuts Bolton retired June, 1967. Mr. Mobley would retire and devote his remaining years to fishing for trophy trout and bass in Arkansas.

Louie Donnatelli remained disillusioned and angry until he was killed during a heroin deal that went sour.

Skins Williams would use the GI Bill to go to college and become a Social Worker. Frenchie Beaumont would get busted and do hard time for dealing drugs back home in Louisianna.

Nhan Ai would be closed by the communists after the fall of Saigon in 1975. The children would be scattered to the streets and private orphanages, several of which were founded by former American GIs. The Vietnamese nuns would be sent to re–education camps, and Mother Marie–Teresa would return to France. Sally would leave Mai Chi with her parents and go to the bars in Saigon where she would meet a kindly older American construction worker who would adopt Mai Chi and take them both to America. She would never forget Lewandowski, nor would she allow Mai Chi to forget.

"Your father was a good man, with a good heart. He was very brave and died a hero fighting the communists. You must always be like him so you do not bring dishonor on his memory."

William R. Masters would return to Vietnam as the commander of a 101st Airborne Division field unit in late 1969. He would later be killed in action while taking a hill designated by a number that no one would remember.

And life goes on.

Printed in the United States
25604LVS00002B/182